THREE FIRES
VOLCA...

TORKYN
FALL

GW01018114

WORLD
MOUNTAIN

Ethengar camp
✶

Lake
Talkai

LAND OF
BLACK SAND

SEA OF FLOWERS

...eel River

Krandai River

Styrdai
River

Hrap River

EPPES

OF THE

ETHENGAR

Fort Denwarf
●

ARFGATE
NTAINS

Stahl
●

Dengar
●

ROCKHOME

Lake
Stahl

●Evemur

...aven

Shadowdown

ALTAN TEPES

●Silvermist

MOUNTAINS

DAROKIN
TUNNEL

T OF

Lakes

EIM

of Selinar

The attack came in the deepest part of the night, and it came completely without warning. Ships standing at the piers or at anchor suddenly burst into flames, some catching fire so quickly and violently that they literally exploded. Indeed, since there was no immediate sign of any enemy, the first assumption of many was that a perfectly normal if disastrous fire was sweeping over the piers, spread by bits of burning canvas carried on the brisk sea breeze. But the fires seemed too selective, striking mostly at the swift war galleys and other naval vessels in the harbor, as well as the forts that stood guard over the port.

Defenders hurried to their stations, but there still was no enemy to be seen. No foreign warships stood out at sea, nor were any invading warriors in the streets of the city. The attack itself was swift and over in a matter of minutes. Only afterward did a few of the defenders speak of seeing vast, dark shapes passing below the stars in the moonless night sky. . . .

THE DRAGONLORD CHRONICLES

Thorarinn Gunnarsson

Dragonlord of Mystara

Dragonking of Mystara

Dragonmage of Mystara

Mystara®
BOOKS

BOOK THREE:
THE DRAGONLORD
CHRONICLES

Dragonmage
of Mystara

Thorarinn Gunnarsson

DRAGONMAGE OF MYSTARA
© 1996 TSR, Inc.
All rights reserved.

Cover art by Paul Jaquays. Map by David C. Sutherland III.

First Printing: April 1996
Printed in the United States of America.
Library of Congress Catalog Card Number: 95-62202

2508XXX1501

9 8 7 6 5 4 3 2 1

ISBN: 0-7869-0488-7

TSR, Inc.   TSR Ltd.
201 Sheridan Springs Rd.   120 Church End, Cherry Hinton
Lake Geneva, WI 53147   Cambridge CB1 3LB
United States of America   United Kingdom

PROLOGUE

Night seemed to gather like standing water from a gentle rain, slowly filling the narrow streets and alleys of the city and the low places where the walls met the cobbled streets. The gray stone of the buildings and the dull bluish tiles of the roofs deepened and gradually seemed to disappear into the shadows. The bitterness of the long winter had given way to a mild and pleasant spring, but night still came early to the Highlands, and the cold still seemed to gather with the darkness.

Alessa Vyledaar stood at the window of her private chamber, watching the deepening shadows of the approaching night. The wide window was one of the principal reasons why she had made this chamber her own, even if it was yet another flight of stairs higher in the Wizards' Residence of the Academy. She had never been comfortable in Byen Kalestraan's old chambers, which had seemed to her like a windowless cavern, dark and remote. But there had also been a rather disquieting presence to those chambers, almost as if they were haunted. She had never been one to worry much about ghosts, but she did not trust anything that might have involved

Kalestraan and the traitor wizards.

She had always felt a vague awareness in that place, almost as if something were calling out to her, or perhaps seeking something. The presence was so vague, in fact, that she had never been certain it was real and not just her own passive antipathy for Byen Kalestraan, a man she had never liked or trusted even before he had proven himself a traitor and assassin. She had simply preferred not to live with that constant distraction. But lately, even in her new chambers, a distant voice had been calling to her from far away.

This evening the mysterious voice was especially persistent, and less distant than it had ever seemed before. Alessa did her best to ignore it as she waited in her chamber for the carriage that was to take her to dinner that night with Solveig White-Gold. She had tried to pass the time with her spellbook, but she had soon realized the distraction was too great. The effort to ignore the voice disturbed her concentration, so that she had learned nothing. She gave it up at last, closing the book and hiding it away. But that left her alone with the voice and her own thoughts. On the nights when the voice was especially persistent, it would invade even her dreams with dim visions of dragons and strange monsters and endless, unexplained toil in the dreary desolation of some cold, dry wasteland.

Slowly Alessa began to realize that there was indeed a difference in the quality of the voice tonight. Always before, no matter how loud or determined it had been, it had simply been some unintelligible voice echoing in her mind, without any sense of direction except that it was always stronger and clearer in the chambers that had been left empty with the death of the traitor Byen Kalestraan. But this evening she sensed beyond all doubt that it was calling to her, even if she did not understand the words. She felt certain that if she followed the voice, it would lead her to its source.

That thought gave her a moment's hesitation—indeed, more than a moment. Whatever else the voice might be, she believed with all her heart that it was evil. Something about the voice and the dreams it conjured awakened a vague memory of fear, so distant that she had no clue of what she feared. All she knew was that her deepest instinct told her to run from that voice, to avoid it at all costs, even to destroy it if she could. And yet she had to know what it was. She could not simply ignore a thing of that nature, leaving it free to work its evil. If Kalestraan had brought a being or force of unknown magic into the Academy, it had to be found and the building made safe.

It also occurred to her that the voice might somehow be a clue to the location of the Collar of the Dragons. She had never been entirely sure just what the collar was, but she knew that it was an heirloom of tremendous value and importance to the dragons. Finding the collar had become Alessa's responsibility when she had replaced Byen Kalestraan as the senior wizard of her order, and she had never been able to discover even the smallest clue about where the traitorous wizards might have hidden it. Finding the collar was becoming more critical than ever. The dragons would be returning to the Highlands any time now, and they expected their treasure to be returned to them.

Having weighed her choices, Alessa decided to act while the mysterious call still seemed strong enough to lead her to its source. Caution told her not to do this alone, that she needed the support of at least one other senior wizard to help her if it proved to be a trap. And yet she preferred to keep this secret to herself until she knew what was involved. She slipped quietly out of her chamber, pausing a moment at the door to make certain no one was about. Since the lamps had not yet been lit, the passages of the Wizards' Residence were dark and gloomy in the gathering dusk.

She descended the stairs slowly and cautiously, then paused and smiled with amusement at her own fancies. She was the mistress of this place, not a thief in the night. All the same, she paused for a moment when she came to Kalestraan's door, reviewing in her mind all the magical traps that he might have employed to guard his most hidden secrets. He had been a Fire Wizard, and his traps would have somehow involved fire, possibly sudden jets of flame shot into the face of the curious or brilliant flashes of light to blind probing eyes. Her greatest advantage was that she knew the same fire magic, and her level of experience was nearly equal to what Kalestraan's had been.

Again Alessa reminded herself nervously that she was not stealing into the domain of a deadly enemy. She had been within these chambers time and again, seeking clues to the location of the stolen Collar of the Dragons. Sir George Kirbey had also helped her search this place, and his knowledge of magical traps and hiding places was even greater than her own. She had little reason to be concerned until she actually found the source of that mysterious voice, but then she would have to be very careful indeed.

Forcing back her fears, she opened the door of Kalestraan's former chambers and stepped into the darkness, quietly speaking a word of command to bring the magical lamps to life. The first room had been Kalestraan's office, the place where he had worked or received visitors in private. A door at the back of the room led into a small storage chamber. She knew that same door also led to the only hiding place that they had ever been able to find, but she had known about this secret place since Kalestraan's death and she also knew that the thing calling to her was not there. That lay beyond the third door, in the shadows deep in a narrow opening between two groups of bookcases, which led to the senior wizard's personal suite.

Alessa opened the door and spoke the word commanding the lights as she stepped inside, pausing for a moment to look about. The room looked just as it always had; she had ordered that nothing was to be removed or changed in any way, so that any possible clues to Kalestraan's conspiracies would not be lost. Now she moved more slowly and cautiously than ever as she began to trace the source of the mysterious call. If any traps remained, this was the most likely place for them. She hoped that any protective magic would have been designed in such a way that it recognized her as Kalestraan's successor, in a sense the heir to his secrets. The fact that the mysterious voice had been calling to her, and to her alone, certainly suggested that such a distinction had been made.

The voice was now louder than ever, so close that it no longer drew her in any specific direction. For a moment, she wondered if her search would be in vain. Then, as she remained standing just inside the door, she closed her eyes to permit the lure of the mysterious voice to guide her, without the distraction of searching for its source by sight. All her attention was given to her mind's ear, as it were, letting the silent voice guide her. The source of the call seemed a little more certain to her now, and she took slow, cautious steps in that direction, fighting the urge to open her eyes. The knowledge that she could be walking blindly into a trap kept her nerves on edge.

Alessa almost jumped back in fright when something touched her, although she realized in the next instant that she had bumped into the side of Kalestraan's bed. She opened her eyes in her moment of fright and she saw, almost to her surprise, that she had located the origin of that mysterious call. Kalestraan's cape with its high, stiff collar hung on a hook beside the bed; he had not been wearing it on the night of his death. Set above the right breast was a broach bearing the small stone indicating his rank, in his case the brilliant red signifying a senior wizard of fire magic. In the distant past of their race, the stone would have been a large, brilliant ruby, but since the Flaem had begun their journey from world to world, times had become more lean and the stone was nothing more than common colored glass.

Or perhaps this piece of glass was not so common. She saw immediately that a faint glow of red light emanated from deep within the stone, and it was not a reflection from the lamps. She was amused to realize that Kalestraan had not hidden this magical artifact in some safe place guarded with traps, but had worn it in plain sight nearly everywhere he had gone. She had a stone just like it in appearance, although hers really was nothing more than ordinary glass. She hesitated a moment longer, still fearful of traps and also mindful that any strange artifact of magic that Byen Kalestraan had found valuable might well be a thing of evil.

By her right as Kalestraan's successor, the stone now belonged to her. The object seemed to recognize that. Moving quickly, she reached out and released the pin, slipping the broach from the cape into her hand. The stone reacted to her touch, the distant light pulsing. The voice fell silent at that same instant, almost as if she had startled it. Then, as she stood staring into the stone, fearful of magically probing its secrets with her mind, the mysterious voice resumed, but now it sounded different. It seemed to be demanding to know who she was sharply, impatiently, as if the strange will behind the voice was annoyed at finding itself in an unfamiliar hand. Then, even before she could consider her reply, the voice fell silent and the pale light faded.

That seemed to put an end to the matter, and Alessa realized that the time had come for her to stop asking for trouble. If the enchanted jewel wasn't willing to talk to her now, then she needed to choose her own time to probe its secrets. That was something she was not prepared to attempt until she had prepared the necessary spells and wards to protect herself from every possible danger. For now, she thought it best to keep the jewel with her, which seemed the best way to prevent it from attempting to lure anyone else. She pinned it to the front of her jacket, amused to think that Kalestraan had kept an object of such value in plain sight, as if it were nothing more than a bauble of little value.

Alessa left the room and locked the door, then hurried back upstairs to her own rooms. As she walked through the darkening corridors of the Wizards' Residence, she was already considering the mysteries of Kalestraan's enchanted jewel. The fact that it had the ability to call attention to itself was less important to her than the question of why it had chosen to do so at that time. Did it possess a will of its own, or was it simply responding to the will of another, perhaps someone who was becoming curious about why Kalestraan had been away for so long? Of course, she had to admit that she could well be over-estimating the power or the potential of the thing. It might be nothing more than a ward, a means Kalestraan had devised to warn him if someone was poking about in his secrets.

Whatever its true nature, it had been trying to get her attention for some reason, perhaps to warn her of something. She still hoped that it might lead her to the Collar of the Dragons, but she was fearful that she might not have much time. She needed to learn its mysteries as quickly as she could.

For better or worse, her fascination with the jewel would have to be set aside for tonight. She selected a shawl to wear over her wizard's robe, knowing that it would be cold later on.

Then she left her chambers and hurried downstairs, certain that the carriage must be waiting by that time. A griffon rider had arrived from Thyatis late that afternoon, which likely meant that Darius Glantri had come for a visit. If so, this evening could be a pleasant one indeed, although Alessa reminded herself that she should excuse herself early and leave the rest of the night to her friends.

As she settled herself into the carriage for the short ride to Solveig's house, Alessa reflected upon the unexpected turns of her recent life. In the summer of the previous year, in the time of just a few short weeks, she had gone from being an unimportant sorceress at the Academy to the head of her order and an advisor to Thelvyn Fox-Eyes, the Dragonlord and for a time the last King of the Flaem. She had to admit that she had come into her new duties as scheming and self-centered as the old villain she was replacing. And like her predecessor, she had found that her schemes never worked nearly as well as she had expected.

Alessa had come to regret the part she had played in forcing the Dragonlord to abdicate as the last king of the Flaemish realm. Her only comfort was knowing that Thelvyn had always intended to surrender the throne as soon as the war with the dragons had been settled. Since that time, she had become a devoted member of the council that had been established to replace the king, and she had done much to turn the Fire Wizards of the Flaem from the suspicious, self-serving lot they had been to a genuinely wise and benevolent order. She had been a strong supporter of the leadership of Solveig White-Gold as the head of the council as well as a close friend, even though Solveig had been one of the original companions of the Dragonlord and Alessa's rival.

The carriage rattled over the cobblestones, the sound echoing dully through the narrow streets. Alessa stared out the window, watching the warm, soft lights that shone behind curtains or through cracks in the shutters of the houses she passed. She thought at times about Thelvyn, having finally come to understand the very last bit of wisdom he had tried to teach her. She had believed, with the conclusion of the war of the dragons, that he had lost everything; she had been sur-

prised and at first disdainful of his claim that he had actually
won. Perhaps he had won more than even he had anticipated
at the time. She envied him his freedom as a dragon, riding the
winds, living and hunting in the wild in the company of his
wise and devoted mate. Her own life seemed shallow and
demanding by comparison.

The carriage slowed and then turned to pass through the
gate into the yard of Solveig's large house in the wealthy quarter of Braejr, the house that had belonged to the Dragonlord
for several years before that. Even as she was stepping down
from the carriage, Alessa could hear the impatient calls of the
griffon stabled in the warehouse on the west side of the yard.
Alessa was often amused to consider what Kharendaen would
think if the proud gold dragon cleric knew that her home of
five years was now the abode of griffons. She wondered idly if
the neighbors believed that the dragon had been better company than the fierce and often noisy creatures now often in
residence.

The young valet, Taeryn, met her at the door, having heard
the sounds of her carriage. As far as Alessa knew, Taeryn had
been a child of lesser aristocracy who had been sent to Braejr
at an early age to work at the palace, where he had served as
valet to both King Jherridan and Thelvyn. He was a bit
simple, and his duties were the limit of his abilities, but he was
always cheerful and eager to please. Since there was no longer
any need for him at the palace, he had come here to work for
Solveig.

"Good evening, Alessa," he began. Seeing Solveig coming
up behind him, he seemed at a loss to know whether or not his
service was still required. After a brief moment, he withdrew
quietly. Alessa tried not to smile.

"Just in time for dinner," Solveig said. Solveig was the
tallest woman Alessa had ever seen, taller even than most
men. Her long hair, which she usually wore in a single loose
braid, was a pale gold in color, so pale that it was almost white
in sunlight.

"I hope I'm not intruding," Alessa said. "I couldn't help
noticing that there's a griffon in the old warehouse, so I wondered if Captain Glantri was here for a visit."

"No," Solveig said, standing back so that the sorceress could enter. "A messenger arrived this afternoon bearing a report from Emperor Cornelius."

"I hope he didn't bring bad news," Alessa commented with some apprehension, pausing to give Taeryn her shawl before she followed Solveig into the dining room.

"Good news, actually," Solveig explained. "Everything appears to be generally peaceful in the east. There's been no evidence that the Alphatians and the dragons are still in conflict, so it seems that they've finally made their peace."

Alessa frowned. "Meaning that the Alphatians have finally learned that they are not to trespass in lands the dragons claim as their own. I've heard that they lost at least a third of their fleet."

"I'm still amazed that they were so determined to take on the dragons."

"I'm not," Alessa commented sourly. "The Alphatians are related to my people. In taking on the Nation of Dragons, they displayed much the same hardheaded self-righteousness that leads the Flaem to believe that we can defeat the Alphatians."

They took their places at the table, and Alessa waited silently while Taeryn served dinner. She was thinking, as she always did, of her first night in that house, seated at that same table with Thelvyn and the others. She was embarrassed now to think how she had confidently weaved her schemes in what she had assumed to be a wizardly manner, immediately betraying Byen Kalestraan when the old villain had sent her into that house as his spy. The place always reminded her very much of Thelvyn, especially since Solveig had changed nothing in the few months that he had been gone.

"Have you heard anything from Thelvyn or Sir George?" she asked.

"Not since the last time you asked," Solveig replied, with no hint in her expression about whether she was amused. She paused a moment while Taeryn set her plate before her. "You don't miss Thelvyn, do you?"

"I just recall that he did not have much cause to think well of me the last time we spoke," Alessa admitted. "I've come to think that I would like to amend that. Do you ever regret that you didn't go with them?"

"From time to time," Solveig answered. "But mostly as a matter of curiosity. Then I remind myself where they were going, and that cures me. I'm not ready for the company of dragons, especially dragons who don't yet think much of Thelvyn and even less of his friends. I wonder if he's already found a way to break the spell that has always prevented him from assuming his true dragon form, or if that still is years away. I wonder what he looks like as a dragon, and if he's happier that way."

"Do you suppose that we'll ever see him again, or does his fate now entirely rest with the dragons?"

Solveig made a small helpless gesture. "I can't say for certain, but I suspect that we'll see him soon enough. Somehow I feel that all this business with the dragons is not yet finished, that there are still matters remaining unsettled."

They waited while Taeryn brought in glasses and a bottle of wine, then took out a corkscrew to pull the cork. Taeryn took a special delight in this particular task, and they were not about to interrupt. He extracted the cork deftly, and it slipped out with a satisfying *pop*.

"I would very much like to see Kharendaen again," he commented as he poured the wine. "She was a very nice dragon. Very polite."

"I wonder how polite she would be if she knew that you've been stabling griffons in her lair," Alessa observed. "And speaking of griffons, I was thinking that it must be about time for Darius Glantri to visit again. That's why I wondered if he were here tonight. It's been a while."

"Perhaps it has," Solveig agreed vaguely.

"So what about Darius?" Alessa continued. "How can the two of you have any meaningful relationship if weeks and weeks go by between visits from halfway across a continent? I know Darius visits every chance he gets, on the pretext of delivering important messages, but usually he's here only one night before he has to go home. You've never told me much about the relationship between the two of you, but if he's willing to go through that much trouble to visit you, something serious must be happening. You grew up in Thyatis, didn't you? Have you ever thought about going back? Might he consider coming here?"

"You're inquisitive tonight," Solveig remarked evasively.

"Are you going to avoid the question?"

"I don't know," she was forced to admit. "I've always thought that I would go back to Thyatis someday, but I can't abandon my responsibilities here in the Highlands any time soon. Darius and I both have important duties in our own lands, duties that we can't forsake at a time when all the known world is in such an unsettled state."

"What drove you away in the first place?" Alessa asked, then hastened to interrupt Solveig before she could answer. "I know the story people tell about how your barbarian heart just longed to be free, and also how you were sold into slavery by the northlanders and bought by one of the first families of Thyatis so that they would have a daughter to present to society. But I've always had the feeling that you left Thyatis for someone's peace of mind, and I'm not certain it was your own."

Solveig frowned. "Actually, that's the exact reason. As I was growing up, I realized that everything I was being taught was to prepare me to be the type of person my adopted parents expected me to be. And being naturally rebellious and contrary, I of course wanted to do exactly the opposite. Since I was supposed to be gentile, I wanted to be a warrior. Since I was supposed to be dignified and respectable, I wanted to be an unsavory adventurer. When I found out that my father was already planning my marriage to someone who would be an advantage to the family, I decided to get out of Thyatis until I was too old to be married away."

"And then Darius Glantri came along," Alessa observed.

"Yes, that's the irony of it. In the course of being everything I wasn't supposed to be, I actually found a Thyatian who is a far more prestigious match than my father could have ever arranged for me. But what about you? Let's discuss your personal life for a while."

"I don't have one," Alessa said with a hint of honest regret. "That's the problem with my profession. I only have my spellbook to keep me company at night."

"If you don't have anything else to distract you, I was wondering if you've discovered anything new about the Collar of the Dragons," Solveig said, pouring herself another glass of wine. "I keep thinking, now that winter has passed, the dragons could be coming back here at any time wanting to know what we've done about finding their collar. The last I heard, you were certain that Kalestraan must have had some part in stealing it."

"Not only that, but I'm also fairly sure that he was the one who hid it," Alessa said, then smiled in almost comic self-satisfaction. "In fact, I've run across one of Kalestraan's secrets just tonight. I don't know if it will help us find the collar, but it's the only possible clue I've managed to find in a long while. I'll need a little time to probe the secrets of this thing safely."

"If the dragons come back, I don't know how understanding they'll be about our excuses."

"Do you think Thelvyn would intercede on our behalf?" Alessa asked.

"I don't have much hope that he would be able to. He's never been very popular with the dragons, and I don't even know if he's found the way to become one himself by now. Even if he has, he'll need some time to assert his authority among his own kind."

The end of the war with the dragons had left things rather unsettled. Once Marthaen, the leader of the dragons, had revealed Thelvyn's hidden heritage as a gold dragon and destroyed his trust and support among his allies, the dragons had simply withdrawn. Whether or not they considered their complaint with the Flaem resolved was uncertain, but they would probably be willing to defer their other complaints if the Collar of the Dragons was returned. At least Alessa now had some hope of finding the collar, if only she could force the jewel to reveal its secrets.

Alessa was still considering that very question later that night when she rode home in her carriage. But once she was walking slowly through the dark and silent corridors of the Academy, another matter began to intrude upon her thoughts. The strange, soft voice returned, speaking in words too distant for her to hear, forcing itself slowly yet relentlessly upon her.

She ignored it at first, as she had often done in the past weeks. After changing into a robe, she tried again to spend some time with her spellbook. She had to spend several hours each day learning and relearning her spells, since the price of working magic was the memorization of spells. She had trained herself years ago to be religious about spending daily time with her spellbook.

But the voice of the jewel continued to call to her. Alessa did her best to ignore it, having left the stone on the table by her bed, but once again she found the distraction was too great. The effort it took to ignore the voice was disturbing her concentration, and she realized after some time that she had learned nothing. She gave it up at last, closing the book and returning it to its hiding place. Picking up the jewel from the table by her bed, she brought it over to the light of the lamp at her reading desk.

This was the first chance she had to inspect the jewel closely, since her original intention had been to leave it alone until she had the chance to research the matter and prepare protections. She still didn't dare to probe its secrets magically, but she thought that there could be little danger in simply looking. She laid it down on the desk just the same, careful not to touch it at the same time that she was staring at it intently. Only then did she see that, while the stone had little more beauty than a piece of colored glass, it was indeed a cut jewel of some unknown type. But it was definitely not a ruby.

A moment later, she felt the pull of the jewel, like a slight touch at the edge of her awareness. She drew back in sudden terror of the thing, almost more by instinct than by conscious choice. But in the same moment, she knew that the stone, or the will behind it, had not been trying to trap her but was merely exploring with a delicate touch. All it wanted, at least for now, was to know who she was. Just the same, Alessa was not about to take any chances. As a sorceress of some experience, she knew a great deal about magical traps designed to ensnare not the body but the mind or even the soul of the unwary.

Just to be certain that the jewel would remain harmless, she took it into the adjoining room, which served as her office, and

hid it inside the top drawer of a cabinet. She was determined
not to look at it again until she had researched the matter to
determine what type of magical artifact the jewel was and how
she could most safely approach it. Then she returned to her
own room and prepared for bed, leaving such mysteries for the
next day.

The dreams came again that night, as they often had since
the mysterious voice had first begun calling to her. Once again
she found herself in that strange, cold desert land, where an
icy wind drove sheets of gray, dusty sand. She could feel neither the cold nor the sting of the wind-whipped sand in her
dream, but odd, distant memories told her that the feel of
such things had once been very familiar to her. The sun was
dim and pale, obscured by the gray dust passing like thin, dark
clouds high above. There was something very old and familiar
about this raw, dying world, but its familiarity was hardly
comforting. She felt rather that this could be some forgotten
nightmare world that she hadn't visited in a very long time,
and she dreaded her return with a deep, cold fear.

Visions passed before her, or perhaps it was more accurate
to say that she passed before the visions, since she had the
impression she was looking down on them from a great height,
as if she were flying. She saw mountains so broken and desolate that only a few small, twisted trees managed to push their
way between broken stones. Lakes and seas of sand passed
below her, and plains of crushed stone. Then she saw, through
a momentary parting of the haze of dust, great fortresses as
large as cities. In a few sheltered places between the ridges and
peaks, armies of slaves fought to maintain fields of green. In
the fields, she saw people of races she did not know and beasts
the likes of which she had never seen.

Once again the clouds of gray dust closed about her, and
the next thing she knew, she was standing alone in some
strange place. It might have been a chamber of vast size, made
of cut stone like the floor beneath her. But the dust had
become a cold, dark mist that drifted and swirled slowly,
obscuring everything. She could neither see nor hear anyone,
but she could sense the menacing presence of many strange,
powerful beings gathered about her. In growing fear, she

would have run, but she sensed that there was nowhere she could run that she would not encounter the powerful beings who surrounded her.

With her heart pounding, Alessa waited, not daring to move from the small pocket of open space in the center of the chamber. After some time, she began to see the glimmer of large eyes peering at her from out of the mist. Then faces began to emerge from the darkness, long, narrow faces, like those of dragons. And yet they were unlike dragons, for they seemed not to be living creatures but carved or cut from precious stones. She could not recall ever seeing anything like these creatures, whether in half-remembered dreams or in obscure tomes of magic. They did not seem to be evil, but she had the distinct impression that they considered her so far beneath themselves that they would use her to serve their own purposes without regard for her welfare. Certainly this had not been a part of any of her previous dreams, and yet even these creatures seemed vaguely familiar.

After a short time, the alien dragons drew back into the dark obscurity of the mist. As great and powerful as they were, she sensed that even they were afraid, and now she began to feel even more frightened. She looked up, and for an instant, she beheld a glimpse of another face, never emerging completely from the mist before it withdrew slowly into the darkness. That face was also vaguely like that of a dragon but considerably different from the others. It was much wider, with a short, powerful snout, and it was of such massive size that the body it belonged to would have to be three or four times larger than any dragon she had ever seen. While the face of a dragon was often lean and noble, even wise, this face was brutish and hideous, filling her with terror. Even after it had drawn back into the mist, the great, menacing eyes continued to glitter like sparks of red light from the darkness, holding her in their fierce, calculating gaze.

The surroundings faded into complete darkness, although the glare of those terrible eyes lingered for a long moment after everything else had faded into blackness. She felt an odd awareness, as if her mind and will were now awake, even though her body continued to sleep. And while she seemed to be alone, she knew that she was not. That mysterious, almost godlike being maintained its contact with her mind, although she was now aware of just how distant it really was, as if it were not even a part of her own world. Then it spoke, and with a shock, she recognized it as the voice that had been calling to her.

Sleep now, and in your dreams tell me who you are.

Alessa's response seemed to form itself out of her own memories, without any need on her own part to consciously form a response. She was Alessa Vyledaar, now one of the most experienced Fire Wizards in all the Highlands and the leader of her order since the death of Byen Kalestraan and many other traitor wizards the previous summer. She was quite young for a sorceress of such high rank, the daughter of a family of lesser nobility. She had traveled outside the Highlands in the past, and she had been considering going out into the rest of the world again, admittedly to serve her own ambition, when events had brought her to her present state.

Sleep, and in your dreams tell me what became of Byen Kalestraan.

The memories of those desperate days of the previous summer seemed almost to be wrenched from her mind. Even as the Highlands had been preparing for war with the dragons, Kalestraan had sent her to assist the Dragonlord, but her true purpose had been to serve as a spy within his own house. She had known that Kalestraan was planning to seize control of the Highlands in some bold scheme; she had betrayed the mage to the Dragonlord, although her motive had been to further her personal schemes.

But it had been too late, for Kalestraan struck that very night. Assuming the form of a dragon, he had invaded the palace and had slain King Jherridan. And there he had waited, preparing a trap by which he intended to destroy the Dragonlord, removing his last rival to command of the Highlands. But he had either overestimated his own power or underestimated the power of the Dragonlord. The trap had failed. Kalestraan had been defeated and destroyed, and in the process revealed as a traitor and murderer.

Sleep, and dream of what became of the Dragonlord and the war with the dragons after the death of Kalestraan.

Thelvyn Fox-Eyes had reluctantly agreed to become King of the Highlands, but only for the duration of the war that threatened. But the dragons had mistaken his actions as ambition, and so they had feared him all the more. They had laid siege to the city of Braejr in incredible numbers, thousands in all, and gave every appearance of preparing for a final confrontation with the Dragonlord. But that battle never happened.

Why not?

Marthaen, the leader of the dragons, was too clever. He knew that the dragons could never hope to defeat the Dragonlord in battle, so he had sought to defeat the Dragonlord by other means. In the end, he had revealed secrets previously known only to the dragons themselves. Thelvyn Fox-Eyes, who had been chosen by the Immortals themselves to be the new Dragonlord, was himself a gold dragon in enchanted form and a cleric of the Great One, the Immortal patron of the dragons. And so the dragons achieved a form of victory. Mistakenly fearing that the Dragonlord sought power and conquest, they had made certain that all the other races and nations of the world would never trust the Dragonlord again.

Dream, and in your dreams recall what became of the Dragonlord.

Alessa honestly did not know. He had abdicated the throne of the Flaemish realm after only a short time, recommending that the rule of the king be replaced by the leadership of a council of representatives. In that way, he had broken forever the old struggle for power between the king, the dukes, and the Fire Wizards that had always been so detrimental to their land. Then Thelvyn had simply disappeared into the night, on a quest to break the spell that prevented him from becoming a dragon, eventually to fulfill his destiny among his own kind. Only the old, one-handed knight, Sir George Kirbey, his companion and mentor, had gone with him.

The mysterious voice remained silent for a long moment, as if considering all that it had learned and formulating new plans accordingly. Alessa waited in the darkness and silence. Now that she no longer had the distraction of the questions, she had a brief time to think for herself. She was beginning to feel

frightened once again, knowing that she was held by a will far
stronger than her own. Even her mind was no longer her own,
if her very memories could be so easily summoned forth for
review. And now that she had been ensnared, she knew that
she would not easily escape.

Sleep, and do not fear, the voice told her. *This was not a trap
but the only means we had of speaking across the vast distances of
time and space that separate us.*

"Who are you?" she dared to ask in return, only partly
reassured.

That was not for the moment important, she was told. All
she needed to know at that time was that the mysterious
speaker had ancient ties to her own people, having helped
them in the past. The voice then proceeded to relate aspects of
the history of the Flaem even she had never known, of events
that occurred during their long age of wandering and of the
enemies and the friends they had encountered along the way.
It spoke to her of matters that touched her own heart, of the
great antiquity of her people, of the power and authority and
the deep pride they had once possessed. Would she not wish
to recapture the power and the pride that the Flaem had once
known? Such a question hardly needed to be asked; the Flaem
thought of little else.

The Flaem are like a great tree, rooted in glory, the voice said,
soothing her with wise and gentle words. *They must not be
permitted to wither from neglect. They were never meant to be the
slaves of dragons; nor mere tools of the Dragonlord, serving the
base whims of the Immortals; nor a small, impoverished, and forgotten folk among the barbaric nations of the alien world in which
they found themselves. The Fire Wizards are the guardians of
their race, and you are now their leader. Do you not have a great
and noble responsibility? Who would be the champion of your
people if not you?*

As she listened, Alessa began to see the truth and wisdom of
what she heard. Why indeed should the rule of the Flaem have
rested in the hands of a misfit youth who had not even known
he was a dragon? Why should the leadership of the Flaemish
council belong to a barbarian war maiden, when it rightfully
belonged to her? Once, before she had been deluded by the

Dragonlord and his companions, she had understood the truth. But now the power and authority to command even her own fate seemed hopelessly lost. She had no idea how to claim the leadership of the council from Solveig, who was looked upon as a beloved defender of the kingdom, while the Fire Wizards were regarded as power-hungry traitors. Nor did she know how she could deal with the enemies of her people, enemies like the proud Thyatians and the evil Alphatians, and especially the dragons.

I can promise help in the form of secret knowledge and wise counsel, the voice continued in a low, soothing tone. *More assistance, in the form of the magic and the forces needed to take war directly to the enemies of the Flaem, will be forthcoming later. But for now, you must remain patient. Byen Kalestraan was an impatient fool and refused to heed my advice. He acted too soon. You would not make the same mistakes, for you understand well the subtle games of politics rather than the brute strength of magic.*

As the voice spoke to her, Alessa began to trust in her ability to do anything. Yet distant and unheard in the deepest part of her mind, the last shreds of her true will screamed in fury and frustration.

CHAPTER ONE

Thelvyn Fox-Eyes stood atop a rounded boulder amid towering pines on the steep mountainside, looking out across the dark, still expanse of forest that lay to the west. It was already nearly midmorning, although the sun was only now rising above the mountains behind him. It was cold for so late in the morning, so that he could still see the white mists of his breath when he stood with the sun at his back. But even the harsh cold of the northland winter had been of little consequence to him in the months since he had assumed his true form as a dragon. The bite of the icy air did not penetrate his thick armor.

As he watched and waited, the lean, graceful form of a gold dragon suddenly passed directly above him, hurtling down just above the treetops from the heights before rising and making a wide circle above the forest. Kharendaen was not hunting; she flew nearly every morning or evening for the joy of flight. Thelvyn was reminded of how they had flown together so many times in the past. Of course, on those flights, he had ridden in a saddle strapped to the base of her neck rather than actually flying with her. That had changed considerably in the past few months.

Thelvyn stepped to the front of the large boulder and then leapt out into the morning sky, with only a brief glance at the steep, wooded slope that fell quickly away below him. Even after all this time, he could not leap out into the open air without a moment of apprehension. He felt his broad wings snapped out, and he tucked up his legs against his belly as he began to rise with long, powerful strokes of his wings, gathering speed slowly. Flying was hardly as effortless as it looked, but getting airborne was the most difficult part. Once he gained speed and caught the cold mountain winds beneath his wings, it became much easier.

Kharendaen began to circle back slowly to join him. He appreciated her beauty as a dragon would, seeing her as a creature of remarkable grace, even delicacy, with a narrow head and tapered muzzle, deep chest, and long, narrow waist, with powerful haunches and legs for leaping into the sky. As far as he was concerned, this was and always would be the true Kharendaen, although he had by now become used to having her about in her Eldar form as well. The Eldar were the ancestors of the elves, taller than men and powerfully built, copperskinned, with black hair and large, black eyes, the same form that Thelvyn had been forced to assume by enchantment all his prior life. In the past, Kharendaen had also taken the form of the elf Sellianda, although the small, fragile elf maiden had always seemed like another person entirely to him.

The smaller female dragon came up slowly behind him, as if she intended to match his speed and remain close beside him. Instead, she rushed forward at the last moment with quick, powerful sweeps of her wings, darting past his nose so close that he was forced to draw back his head in alarm. The gesture was intended as a playful one, an invitation to match his skill in flight against hers, and she was no longer very forgiving of his inexperience. He turned and followed her as swiftly as he could, using his greater size and weight to overtake her while she remained in a shallow dive. She didn't allow him to draw too close, rising again to place him at a disadvantage, then making a tight turn that he was unable to duplicate.

Thelvyn had been frustrated with such games at first until

Marthaen, Kharendaen's older brother, had informed him privately that female dragons were almost always swifter than the males of the same breed, since they were leaner and lighter. And no dragon in the world was swifter in flight than a female gold. Thelvyn had to push himself to the limit just to hold his own, struggling not only with his inexperience but also with his large size. Still, he realized as he followed her twists and turns, maneuvers that had once taken a conscious effort were now beginning to feel natural.

He was beginning to feel comfortable using the small sails just behind and below his wings, attached to the base of his tail, to take all the effort of steering himself, folding and spreading the sails at need. Dropping his tail with the sails unfurled also helped to slow him quickly by cupping the wind. He was also beginning to acquire a feel for the air currents about him, knowing without deliberately searching where he would find rising or falling pockets of air, whether there was a strong wind or none at all. Learning to fly had been especially difficult for him, since he had to learn as a full-size adult, while most dragons learned to fly at a relatively young age. He still had dreams at night about falling.

Kharendaen suddenly broke off her playful antics and drifted on the morning breeze, as if she were listening to some distant voice. Thelvyn also spread his wings and glided, careful to keep his distance so he would not disturb her. After a moment she glanced over at him, then drifted as close as she dared to his side.

"I have been called," she said plainly. "The Great One wishes to give me new instructions."

"He wishes to speak with you?" Thelvyn asked, surprised. For whatever unknown reason, the Great One had had very little communication, even with his most trusted clerics, for the past twenty years.

"I half expected him to speak to me in a dream last night," she remarked. "But that is not important. We must return to Shadowmere at once."

She turned and headed northward, away from the mountains where they had been playing and out over the broad forests. Kharendaen set a brisk pace, although that was not a matter of concern to Thelvyn. He might not be the most agile of dragons in the air, but he had grown swift and tireless in long, straight flights over open land. Shadowmere lay somewhere in the center of the great pocket of woods that lay encircled within the mountains of the great Wendarian Range. Known to both the dragons and to the elves of Wendar as the Foxwoods, this was an ancient, enchanted land blanketed in a deep, dark forest of the tallest trees in the entire world.

Shadowmere had at one time been the largest and most important sanctuary of the Great One. Thelvyn's own mother, Arbendael, had been the senior cleric and mistress of this place, before the attack of the rogue dragons had forced her to flee into the wild. Shadowmere had been abandoned since that time, until late the previous summer when the Great One had Kharendaen bring Thelvyn here so that the spell preventing him from becoming a dragon could be removed. They had remained here ever since, together with Sir George and nearly a score of dragon clerics who had come to serve them and restore the sanctuary to life. Elvish clerics later emerged from the forests of Wendar to join them; the half-wild northern elves looked to both Terra and the Great One as their protectors, and many had become clerics of the dragon Immortal. They had served at Shadowmere in the past, and they had been eager to return.

The sanctuary was difficult to locate from above, hidden as it was by the great trees of the Foxwoods. Fortunately, dragons were guided in flight by an unerring instinct for direction far more accurate than sight, a magical instinct that guided them even to places they knew only by description. Thelvyn's own sense of direction was still developing, so he depended upon Kharendaen to guide him. Soon she began to descend slowly in a wide circle above a deep well of darkness in the forest that was the small clearing in the center of the sanctuary.

Thelvyn followed her down with some misgivings. The steep, rapid descent into the clearing had always been tricky for him, and he had injured himself slightly on a couple of occasions. He preferred to go in first, so that he would not collide with Kharendaen if he lost control while landing.

He began his landing by dropping his tail and spreading his

sails to slow himself until he felt he was just about to drop, cupping his vast wings to catch as much air as they could as he descended through the trees. The clearing still lay in morning shadow, so that even the night vision of a dragon could not show him the ground clearly until he was almost down. Only then was he able to select the exact place where he would land. He lowered himself with long, sharp thrusts of his wings until he struck the earth heavily on his braced legs. Kharendaen joined him a moment later, slowing herself and then landing lightly with long, graceful sweeps of her wings in the clearing several yards to his right.

She folded away her wings and walked over to join him, dipping her head to rub her nose gently against his chest, a draconic gesture of affection. Kharendaen had always been boundless in her affection, even in their first five years together when he would have never guessed that she loved him. He would have never thought that dragons, with their reputation as fierce, solitary creatures, were also capable of being deeply passionate. He had been surprised to find that dragons even kissed, although they were more fond of rubbing their faces and necks together. Their sense of touch through their leathery plates was rather different from what he had been used to as a human. Touch was more vague, yet dragons craved it all the more, apparently for that very reason.

Side by side, they walked across the clearing to a ring of rocky hills that formed the sanctuary itself. The face of the hills was lined by a great structure of stone and wood.

Thelvyn wondered about this sudden willingness of the Great One to speak. He had been expecting something like this ever since he had become a dragon, when the Great One had told him that he could be given only until the coming spring to learn the ways of his new life before his services would be needed. He and Kharendaen both had thought it best for him to remain in hiding while he became accustomed to life as a dragon. Since it hardly seemed likely that the dragons would be ready to accept him yet, he was inclined to dread the task of trying to convince them to accede to his leadership.

A couple of the younger dragons and several of the elves were busy in the inner yard of the sanctuary, attending their morning chores. Kharendaen led the way through the open doors into the main hall of the sanctuary, where she paused a moment to look about. A few dragon clerics, Sir George among them, were reclining on the massive couches, reading from large books set on stands before them. Sir George saw that his companions were staring at him and left his own chair near the fire and hurried over to join them.

"We must leave," Kharendaen explained simply. "The Great One has summoned us."

"I have no idea that what he wants," Thelvyn said, making a vague gesture when Sir George glanced up at him. "The Great One never talks to me, which is probably just as well. I dread what he might have to say."

"You may stay or go with us as you prefer," Kharendaen told the old knight. "But I warn you that we may not return here any time soon."

"Some things are easy enough to guess," Sir George said. "If the Great One thinks that the time has come for action, it will most likely involve finding the Collar of the Dragons. And you'll need me for that. Would it be fair of me to ask where we're going?"

"To Silvermist, of course," Kharendaen explained simply.

Sir George hurried away to prepare for their journey, while the two dragons went to their own chamber to collect the few things they would need. Thelvyn had a harness that he had never before needed to wear, since he had never traveled as a dragon. Although he did not carry any weapons, such as the dragon-sized sword that Marthaen usually sported, he did need the pouches for a few things such as his spellbook. One of the more difficult and unexpected adjustments he had had to make since he assumed dragon form was being naked all the time. While he had never thought of dragons as being naked, he had certainly felt that way. He was rather surprised when he saw Kharendaen pulling on the straps of her saddle, the same saddle in which he had ridden for five years as the Dragonlord.

"I can carry Sir George," he offered.

"I do not doubt that you can," she said agreeably. "But I doubt that the straps of the saddle are large enough to fit around your neck. This saddle was made specifically for me.

Do you feel ready to make such a long flight?"

"Yes, I believe so," he answered. "At least, I had better be. I seem to be running out of the time I was given to learn to be a dragon."

Kharendaen seemed very calm and businesslike about the upcoming journey and the purpose behind it, as if she considered it a matter of no great importance. Thelvyn was grateful that she took such an easygoing attitude, since it helped to calm his own apprehensions. Soon he might discover the answers to many of the mysteries that had surrounded him since he had learned that he was a dragon, particularly the remaining secrets of his origin and the part he was expected to play in the destiny of his race. He could only hope that those secrets were something that he would be pleased to discover.

The matter of his assuming the role of the Dragonking remained the greatest enigma to him. The dragons had awaited the coming of the Dragonking since the time of the first Dragonlord, when, according to prophecy, he would take up the Collar of the Dragons and become the first true king of their race. But the prophecy did not explain why the Dragonking was needed, or what he would do for the benefit of his people. As far as Thelvyn could tell, the troubles that the dragons had faced for the past three decades were more or less at an end. Their war with Alphatia had concluded in their favor, and their uncertain relationship with the Dragonlord was resolved. Everything should return to normal once the Collar of the Dragons was found, and the Great One had already told him that the recovery of the collar would be Thelvyn's task.

Thelvyn found dragons much more daunting, rather than less so, since he had become one himself. Perhaps, he thought, that was because both his own role and the methods he could use to carry out his policies had changed. Being the Dragonlord had been a relatively simple matter; if a dragon was a problem, he had the power and the invulnerability as the Dragonlord to enforce his will. As the Dragonking, he was hardly any more powerful than other dragons; in fact, he was disadvantaged by his own inexperience and possessed no special invulnerabilities. He suspected that, as the king of the dragons, he would be expected to enforce his will not by force or threat of violence but by more subtle and complex means.

The two dragons needed only a few minutes to prepare themselves for their journey, so they returned to the yard to wait for Sir George. Kharendaen spoke briefly with the senior clerics who would remain at Shadowmere, agreeing that the sanctuary should remain occupied unless the clerics were called away to serve elsewhere. Thelvyn was reminded again that it was probably his place to be making the decisions, if he was truly worthy of being the Dragonking, but he was reluctant to because he knew so little of the affairs of dragons. While he was most likely a cleric of the Great One himself, he preferred to stay out the business of the true clerics.

Sir George came out a short time later, tying his own travel bags to the straps before climbing up into Kharendaen's saddle. The two dragons crouched low and then leapt into the air as their broad wings snapped out, calling upon all the strength they commanded to lift themselves upward in a tight spiral through the narrow opening in the trees. Thelvyn felt better once they had risen above the forest and settled into their long flight. Their plan was to remain in the remote and uninhabited lands of the mountains for nearly the entire journey, traveling eastward along the Wendarian Range, southward over the Colossus Mountains, over the Broken Lands and then eastward again over the Altan Tepes between Rockhome and Alfheim.

Sir George had flown in Kharendaen's saddle before, and thus he took the long journey in stride. Of course, he had also known dragon flight from a more intimate perspective than that of a mere passenger, but not for some years now. Sir George was secretly a mandrake, one of the smaller dragonkin, and his inclusion in the greater Nation of Dragons had allowed him to claim the right to remain in Thelvyn's company. Unfortunately, Sir George had lost his left hand in combat years earlier, and his wing was damaged correspondingly when he took mandrake form, leaving him incapable of flight.

It was an advantage for the dragons to remain in the mountains as much as possible on such long journeys, since they could conserve their strength by riding the winds. Thelvyn wondered how long this flight would take. In the past,

Kharendaen had always made the trip from Braejr to Thyatis, as far apart as any two cities in the civilized eastern region of the continent, in a single day. The distance from Shadowmere to the sanctuary of Silvermist in Alfheim was considerably less. Kharendaen could easily reach their destination that same day. The only real question, he realized, was whether or not he could remain in flight for that long.

He was almost surprised when they passed southward from the Wendarian Range over the deep pass of the Northern Reach later that morning. He had traveled the Flaemish Frontier in the saddle of a horse often in the past, when a similar journey would have taken three days or more. He was surprised to find that he was holding up well, although Kharendaen insisted that they stop for a brief rest shortly after midday, when they were approaching the southern end of the rugged Colossus Mountains. Thelvyn felt he could have kept going, but he was glad for the rest. Sir George seemed to be having the hardest time of them all. He was no longer quite so used to long hours in the saddle, especially a rather wide dragon saddle.

"I can make it all the way to Silvermist today, I'm certain," Thelvyn assured his mate. "We should be nearly halfway there by now anyway."

"That is just as well," she responded. "The Great One wants us to be there by tonight."

They were on their way again soon, although they had only just returned to the sky when Kharendaen suddenly dropped back close to Thelvyn's side, slowing quickly. He looked around sharply, quickly spying a small band of six dragons approaching them from the west, hurtling forward with long, quick strokes of their wings on a course to intercept them. Since they were coming closer in a hurry, Thelvyn was soon able to see that they were all young red dragons, and he was immediately reminded of the rogue dragons from the time when he had first become the Dragonlord.

"Will they recognize me?" Thelvyn asked.

"I suspect they will," Kharendaen replied. "A dragon always knows another dragon by sight, even a dragon who has changed form. Some of them might have been in the Foxwoods on that night when you first took your true form. And, remember, you have rather remarkable features, so they might recognize you by appearance alone."

Thelvyn realized it was unlikely that these dragons would not know him. And Kharendaen was right about his features being remarkable; his muzzle was long and slender, and his large eyes were set somewhat more forward than usual even for a gold, giving him a distinctly feral appearance. Even in dragon form, he deserved the name 'Fox-Eyes' more than ever.

"They are all young red dragons," Kharendaen continued. "I suspect that one of the red leaders such as Jherdar has sent this band to watch the Highlands secretly from here in the mountains."

"Perhaps I should handle this," Thelvyn said. "I am an authority they have to respect, as both the Dragonlord and the Dragonking, whether they like it or not. And you have to watch out for Sir George."

"It's good not to be completely forgotten," the old knight remarked.

They turned and circled around toward the face of the mountain they had been skirting, preparing to land on the highest of a cluster of jagged boulders standing out from the steep, barren mountainside. This was one of the most difficult tricks that Thelvyn had yet attempted, landing atop a massive stone hardly large enough for him to stand with the cliff face blocking his approach from behind. He knew he needed to do it well, so that he would not appear awkward and inexperienced before the red dragons. He chose the highest of the rocky perches and landed without incident, and Kharendaen settled on a boulder close beside him, so that the young dragons were forced to land farther below them.

"Greetings, former Dragonlord," the leader of the reds called up to him in a mocking tone.

Thelvyn glared, aware that he was being subtly challenged. His best bet was to bluff his way through this confrontation, since he still was an unknown factor to these dragons. They could not ignore the fact that he was the chosen of the Great One, destined to become the Dragonking.

"Whoever told you that was mistaken," Thelvyn answered

coolly. "I am still the Dragonlord."

That gave them something to think about, and a few of them began to mutter softly among themselves. They were now more uncertain than ever about daring to confront him.

"But that is not an issue," Thelvyn continued, not wanting to lose the initiative. "I see that you are standing guard over the Highlands. Did Jherdar put you to this task, or are you here by the order of Marthaen and the parliament?"

"We are red dragons. We answer to Jherdar," their leader responded proudly. "But Jherdar has made it known that he still defers to the leadership of the gold dragon Marthaen, and we are here by his order. But I do not recognize your authority to command us."

"I have not given you any command," Thelvyn replied. "We are traveling to the sanctuary of Silvermist, and our business does not concern you. By the will of the Great One, you will allow us to pass."

The leader of the red dragons lifted his head sharply, responding to the challenge, then dropped his neck slowly as he began to hackle in rising fury. His companions rose to stand with their wings half-furled, ready to leap into battle. Thelvyn stood slowly, a gesture that was quietly menacing in its confidence, and he arched his long neck and back so that his crest lifted. He was bluffing, only too aware that his inexperience left him overmatched if there were a fight, but dragons settled most of their differences with posturing and bluff. His advantage was not only in his size as a gold dragon, but also in the formidable weight of his reputation.

The red dragon did not back down at once, but the fact that neither did he spring proved that he was hesitant to take on the Dragonking. After another tense moment, Thelvyn crouched forward toward his enemy, arching his back and lifting his half-furled wings. If he pushed his opponent too hard, the red dragon's fury would be stirred past the point of no return. But the red dragon relaxed slowly, careful that he did not look frightened or ashamed for backing down.

"Then I can only wish you well," he remarked darkly.

That seemed to be the end of the matter as far as the leader of the band was concerned. Without another word, he leapt outward from the large boulder on which he had been sitting, spreading his wings to head west, back toward the border of the Highlands. The other dragons followed him quickly. Thelvyn waited until they were well away before he relaxed, lowering his head and laying back his ears.

"That went rather well," Sir George commented. "It was perhaps the first time I've seen you impress a dragon without too much threat of force. Except for Kharendaen, who had her own reasons for being impressed with you."

"I have to agree," Kharendaen said, bending her long neck to glance briefly at the old knight. "The great, almost mindless fear that the dragons have held for the Dragonlord seems to be fading, replaced with the seeds of respect. Of course, so far that respect is due mostly to the fact that the Great One has endorsed you, and they are tremendously relieved that the Great One has returned. They also will not forget that you did not kill dragons during their conflict with the Highlands."

"Which is not to say that simply wearing the Collar of the Dragons will be enough to make me accepted as the true Dragonking," Thelvyn said. "I recognize that I must earn their respect, and I know that older dragons like Jherdar will be difficult to impress."

They continued on, passing swiftly over the rugged, desolate wastelands of the northeastern fringe of the Broken Lands. They did not dare to land or even fly too low, since there was no guarantee the orcs or other evil folk who dwelled there would have the sense not to attack a pair of dragons. Renegade dragons often made alliances with orcs or goblins, buying their loyalty with plunder, or simply capturing and enslaving all the warriors they required to serve them. But gold dragons were never renegades, so Thelvyn and Kharendaen would be recognized as enemies.

Night was falling swiftly by the time they began to descend over the dark woodlands of the Canolbarth Forest on the far northern border of Alfheim. Already it was too dark to spot the clearing of the sanctuary of Silvermist, so Thelvyn was forced to follow his mate and trust to her instinct to find her way. Kharendaen had been here often and had even lived here for several years in the guise of the elf maiden Sellianda, so she found it relatively easy to know where she was going.

The dragons descended into darkness, and Thelvyn braced his legs to catch himself when he landed. Suddenly warm lights appeared out of the deep shadows beneath the forest, and a moment later he landed in the wide yard before the large, rustic house that was the sanctuary of Silvermist. The main door burst open, and several elves hurried out to greet their visitors, keeping a discreet distance while the dragons folded away their wings. Sir George had already dropped down from his saddle, and Kharendaen crouched so he could remove his bags.

Silvermist was just as Thelvyn remembered it from nearly six years earlier. This place had always been special to him, although he had been here only once before. This was where he had first met Kharendaen, even if he had not known that it was her until recently. He was now aware that Silvermist was not a sanctuary of the Immortal Terra, as most outsiders believed, but of the Great One himself. For the first time, he was able to see that several of the elves were actually dragons in enchanted form. Previously, his natural ability to detect dragon-kin had been suppressed as a part of the spell that had prevented him from assuming his true form.

The only member of the gathering Thelvyn recognized was Derrion, a true elf. He approached Kharendaen eagerly, as if they were old friends. The tall female elf in his company, an enchanted dragon, was clearly the senior cleric of this sanctuary. Thelvyn suspected that this dragon cleric in enchanted form had come here to replace Kharendaen when she had left here five years earlier to serve the Dragonlord in her true form.

"Ferial," Kharendaen said, greeting the dragon cleric. "The last I had heard, you were at a sanctuary in the south of Alfheim."

"I have been here since you departed," Ferial replied. Then, to Thelvyn's surprise, she led the others in turning and bowing to him in respect. "Hail, Dragonking."

"That remains to be seen, but I thank you anyway," he answered awkwardly.

"How may we serve you?" Ferial asked.

"We have been directed here to speak with the Great One

tonight at his sacred place," Kharendaen explained. "We must be going there soon."

"We can at least offer you a quick meal," Ferial suggested.

Kharendaen removed her saddle and changed form, since the bulk of a gold dragon was awkward and inconvenient indoors. She did not return to the shape of the elf maiden Sellianda but took her Eldar form, taller and darker than modern elves, as she had when Thelvyn had last seen her. Thelvyn also removed his harness, but then he hesitated. He hadn't changed form since the night when the Great One had broken the spell that had held him in Eldar form. For a moment, standing on two legs was as difficult for him as walking on four had been at first.

"There are perhaps fewer of us here than you might recall," Ferial said as they walked slowly toward the house. "Several of the dragons flew back to the north last autumn when the northern sanctuaries were opened once again."

"Did many clerics of the Great One stay here in Alfheim during the last few years?" Thelvyn asked.

"That is so. Although we were not exactly in disgrace during the time of the Great One's absence, disappearing for a time helped us avoid difficult questions we were not permitted to answer."

They were given food and drink, then talked with the clerics of Silvermist for a time. Later Sir George was shown to his room, while Kharendaen and Thelvyn returned to dragon form and followed the forest path to the Great One's sacred place. The small, quiet pool below the waterfall was just as Thelvyn remembered it, and he was more sensitive than ever to the sense of ancient magic and a strange, mystical presence. This place was much smaller and more intimate than the sanctuary at Shadowmere. Even clerics did not often enter the sacred places unless they were invited.

The dragons did not sit together on the narrow bank at the near end of the pool as they had before. Instead, Kharendaen led them to the wide bank at the far end, where the cool water drained into a small forest stream. This bank was clad in deep, thick grass, not easily damaged by the armored bulk of dragons. Kharendaen settled herself on the bank to wait, and

Thelvyn sat close beside her.

"I do not believe that our wait will be a long one," she offered. "The Great One is no longer so restricted in his ability to act."

"And so it begins," Thelvyn remarked softly, almost to himself.

Kharendaen turned her head to regard him curiously. "Are you concerned?"

"I'm not frightened, if that's what you mean," he explained. "I've come to trust that I will always be granted the powers and even the guidance I need to do any task required of me. However, I am worried about making mistakes, especially because of my inexperience as a dragon. And more than anything else, I find myself regretting that we never had any real time together, to lead a common, uneventful life."

"I fear you ask the one thing that I cannot give you," a voice said, speaking out of the darkness.

They looked up sharply to see that the Great One had quietly manifested himself before them. He had not assumed the fierce and intimidating form of the great three-headed dragon as he sometimes did. Instead, he appeared in what may have been his true form, that of an old, wise dragon of some ancient breed, perhaps the ancestors of the golds. His ghostly form, radiating a soft light, seated itself on the mossy bank to their left.

"I know that you both must have many questions," he went on. "I fear that even now I cannot tell you everything that you might wish to know, but my powers are still returning, as you will soon understand. It is best that you proceed only a step at a time. The dragons face a new and unexpected danger. Only by acting together will they survive and prosper, and only you can bring them that unity."

"I recall being told, when I first became the Dragonlord, that a part of my task was to bring unity to the dragons in their time of conflict," Thelvyn said. "It is my impression that their conflicts have been largely resolved."

"Only their conflicts with themselves," the Great One answered. "The future of your people begins with you, and you must begin by understanding your past. All that you have been told is true. You are indeed Thelvaenir, a gold dragon and the child of the dragon cleric Arbendael. Have you given any thought about who your father might be?"

"That matter has eluded us," Kharendaen answered for him. "We know that none of the senior gold dragons such as Gheradaen or Lhorandyn could be his father, which leaves us with no hint of just who it might be."

"That is because his father is not a gold dragon," the Great One said. "I thought the full extent of my involvement in this matter would have been more obvious. You see, I am his father."

The Great One's statement was so unexpected that Thelvyn did not even appreciate its implications at first. He had to know more, and he needed time to consider what he was hearing before he could make sense of it. Kharendaen was so surprised that she had to sit down, and her unusual reaction distracted him from his thoughts.

"I always thought that was impossible," she said after a moment. "The Immortals have great powers, but their ability to interact directly with our world and the people in it is rather limited. Some of these restrictions they have placed upon themselves and each other to prevent insensitive or ambitious Immortals from using our world as their own. But it was my understanding that there were some things an Immortal simply did not have the power to do, such as having a child."

"That is true," the Great One said. "But my need for a special champion was great, so great that many other Immortals aided me or at least promised not to interfere in my quest to bring forth a champion to lead the dragons and save their world. But I will speak more of that in the near future. I confided the details of the danger and my secret need only to the gold dragon Arbendael, and she agreed to bear my child. But to accomplish that, I had to surrender for a time the greatest part of my own Immortality, so that I again became little more than a mortal dragon cleric."

"And that was why you removed yourself from the affairs of the dragons?" Kharendaen asked, lifting her head. "For more than two decades now, we have not known if you were forced to abandon us or if you had done so by choice."

"It was a dangerous time for the dragons, and I knew that it would be," he continued. "That was why I could give only limited help when Thelvyn's mother was pursued by the rogue dragons. At the time, I realized that Thelvyn would be best protected if he was brought up apart from dragons, and safer still if the dragons had no knowledge of his birth. I was required to spend many years since then in my own plane, regaining my former strength. I have not yet recovered fully, and I admit that Thelvyn is not as ready as he could be, but we are running out of time."

Thelvyn looked rather bemused. "At least now I have the answer to one question that has always bothered me. Why me? Now I know."

"That is so," the Great One agreed. "You were created for a specific purpose, to lead the dragons through their time of greatest danger and to set them on the path that will guide them toward a higher stage in their development. Needless to say, you are more than just a dragon, and more than just one of my clerics. Because of your heritage, you are inherently wiser and more powerful than other dragons and therefore suited to your task. But the dragons, especially the lesser, more violent breeds, already upset because I had removed myself from their affairs, did not understand the prophecy and assumed that you were being sent to subjugate them."

Thelvyn sighed. "Then what choice do I have? If I am needed, I must serve."

"You have always had a choice," the Great One insisted. "You are not my tool or my slave. You are my son, and that means no less to me than it would to any other dragon. But you serve best if you do so by choice, as your own master. And for now, we both have much to do. Do you accept this responsibility?"

"Of course I do," Thelvyn said without hesitation.

"Then this is the task I set before you, if you will accept it. The war of the dragons is not over. Mighty forces are allied against them, and the dragons face defeat if you do not rally them. To this end, you must find the lost Collar of the Dragons."

"I understand," Thelvyn said as the vision of the Great One faded into the night.

CHAPTER TWO

Early the next morning, Thelvyn and Kharendaen met with
Sir George on the porch behind the house to discuss a plan to
locate the missing Collar of the Dragons. Thelvyn was surprised to discover that he already disliked returning to his
Eldar form. The previous night had been the first one he had
ever spent with his mate in human form in a real bed, and it
had been a remarkably unromantic event. He was in a rather
foul mood that morning, although the old knight seemed to
find it all quietly amusing. Kharendaen told him of Thelvyn's
secret parentage, and he sat back in his chair wearing a curiously satisfied grin.

"Does Thelvyn look like his father?" he asked at last.

"He actually looks very much like his mother," Kharendaen
explained, showing her own amusement for the first time. "His
father came from a breed of dragons that no longer exists."

"Well, let's hope that he has inherited other talents from his
father," Sir George said. "That brings us to the problem of finding the Collar of the Dragons. The trouble is, I'm not sure that
we know anything more than we did when we left Braejr last

year. I don't suppose that the Great One had any suggestions."

"No, he didn't," Thelvyn said with annoyance. "I don't know whether that means that he cannot or will not help us, but at any rate, we have to assume that we are supposed to figure this out for ourselves."

"Well, he is your father," the old knight insisted.

"You don't wheedle the god of the dragons, even if he is your father. And I think it best that secret should remain known only to us three for now. I don't suppose that the dragons ever found out anything more about the theft of the collar."

"No. We can only infer that a dragon must have been involved," Kharendaen replied. "I've always been troubled by the fact that the location and even the existence of Windreach is supposed to be a secret. For that reason, I suspect that renegade dragons helped in the theft, considering its size and location. Only a dragon would have known of its existence and where to find it. Only a dragon could have made off with the better part of a ton of jewels and gold right from under the snouts of the parliament itself."

"But we do know that Byen Kalestraan was involved in the theft," Sir George added. "He was working with a band of renegade black dragons when they attacked you and Solveig. We can easily assume that those same black dragons took the collar. I've always wondered if the dragons might be able to identify who those renegades were."

"Not without more clues than we have," Kharendaen said. "The dragons distance themselves from the renegades. We don't have a very clear idea just who all the renegade bands are and where they might be. And while they almost certainly stole the collar for Kalestraan, they might not know where he hid it."

"Still, it's the best lead we have," Thelvyn commented. "If the dragons still have no idea who those renegades might have been, then perhaps the time has come for us to return to Braejr. Solveig and Alessa Vyledaar have had over half a year now to search for clues, and we have no way of knowing if they found anything yet. That seems the best place to begin."

Kharendaen looked rather uncertain. "How can we return to Braejr? After all, we are not entirely welcome there."

Sir George shrugged. "I don't expect that to be any real

problem if we go directly to Solveig's home at a time when she is most likely to be there."

Since Braejr was only a few hours away if they flew, they had to wait until that afternoon to depart so that they would arrive well after nightfall. Thelvyn hadn't expected to return to his old home so soon, if ever. But he thought that Sir George was right; he had not actually been run out of Braejr but had left by his own free will. As far as he knew, there was no formal decree exiling him from the Highlands. He knew it would be wise to be discreet. He was certain that Alessa Vyledaar and the Fire Wizards wouldn't be pleased with his return. But if they wanted him to save them from the wrath of the dragons, they would have to cooperate with him.

Although he often had to remind himself of the fact, Thelvyn had been the king of this land, even if only for a few short weeks. The circumstances had been so desperate that he had never felt so much like a king as a general, a leader of an army rather than a nation, and his leadership of the Highlands had been merely an extension of his duties as the Dragonlord. That seemed like a very long time ago to him, almost as if it had been in another life. In a way, it had been, since it was before he had become a dragon.

As the dragons approached Braejr, they saw that spring had definitely returned to the southern Highlands. The fields surrounding the city were carpeted in short grass that rippled in the night breezes, although even their keen eyes could not clearly discern the rich green in the darkness of night. Much of the destruction waged by the dragons during the previous summer was no longer visible, the ruined fences repaired and most of the burned homesteads and barns replaced. The city itself had actually suffered very little, since the dragons had not attacked Braejr except for one night of terror when they had unleashed a rain of fire upon the tiled roofs.

Once more Thelvyn had to trust to Kharendaen's lead, since the city at night from above looked like a maze of dark shapes to him. The dragons moved in over Braejr as quickly and quietly as they could, hoping to land before they were seen. Thelvyn disliked these nearly blind approaches. Just as he was beginning to feel completely lost, he recognized the distinctive forms of his old home with the warehouse standing, dark and massive, across the paved court. Kharendaen lowered herself deftly into the narrow front part of the court, just inside the closed gate. Thelvyn landed heavily just beyond her, beside the old warehouse.

They had only just settled to the ground and were folding away their wings when sounds began to emerge from the warehouse, like those of some wild, restless animal. It began with a loud and curiously high-pitched growl, rising in fury until a sound like the hoarse call of a hunting bird pierced the night. Kharendaen paused only long enough to allow Sir George to drop down from the saddle, then arched her back and lifted her neck to glare at the massive door of the warehouse. Obviously annoyed, she moved away from the warehouse into the wooded yard before the house. Thelvyn followed her, hoping that putting some distance between them might help calm the beast stabled within the warehouse.

The front door of the house opened, and warm light poured down the steps. The young valet, Taeryn, stepped outside but remained standing by the door. Solveig hurried out a moment later. True to her old habits, she was wearing her favorite white robe, which was barely long enough for her long legs. She recognized Kharendaen at once and hurried to help Sir George retrieve his travel bag, which was tied to the straps of the saddle. Solveig kept her distance from Thelvyn, staring at him in a way that suggested she did not know who he was. He was struggling to remove his harness so that he could change form, the most certain way to pacify the beast still voicing its complaints and challenges from within the warehouse.

"Why is there a griffon in my lair?" Kharendaen demanded, hardly containing her annoyance long enough to remove her saddle.

"It's not your lair anymore," Solveig insisted, undaunted. "Thyatian messengers come and go constantly, and I use the warehouse to board their griffons."

Thelvyn finished removing his harness and changed form.

"I wondered if that was you," Solveig remarked, watching cautiously. "So you've finally learned how to become a dragon."

"I've been a dragon for some time now," he told her. "But we should talk about that inside. I don't know if we were seen flying in, and I don't want anyone coming around to discover dragons in your yard—or the Dragonlord, for that matter."

Kharendaen finally managed to release the straps and slip out of her saddle, setting it aside before changing form. She assumed her Eldar form rather than becoming the elf maiden Sellianda. Solveig brought her visitors inside and led them to the den, where they had sat together often in the past. Then she had Taeryn find them something to eat from the kitchen while she hurried upstairs to dress. Thelvyn noticed that her habits were becoming steadily less barbaric, perhaps influenced by her new responsibilities.

"I suppose you must be here about the collar," she said when she joined the others in the den a few minutes later. "Are the dragons getting restless to have it back?"

"They probably are," Thelvyn explained simply. "We're here now because the Great One told me that the time has come that I need to find the collar. The Dragonking needs to wear it when he goes among the dragons for the first time."

"Then the Dragonking has already arrived?" Solveig asked, recalling the legends she had heard the previous summer. Then she paused and settled back in her chair, frowning as she stared at the drink Sir George had slipped into her hand. "You're the Dragonking yourself, aren't you? I should have figured that out for myself long ago."

"I know now why I was chosen as the object of all these prophecies," Thelvyn said. "I still don't know what the Great One expects of me, but it sounds very dire indeed."

Solveig shrugged. "I anticipated we were due for more trouble sooner or later."

"Then you probably guessed why we're here," Sir George added. "If you can't tell us where to search for the collar, I'm not sure what we can do but strangle every renegade dragon in the world looking for the ones who were in league with the Fire Wizards."

"Things might not be as desperate as all that," Solveig said, taking a quick sip from her glass. "I was having dinner with Alessa Vyledaar a few nights ago when she said something about finding a new clue to uncovering Byen Kalestraan's secrets. I never did find out what, but I can have her over here first thing in the morning to talk to you."

"Alessa?" Thelvyn said rather dubiously. "The last time I talked to her, I was trying to prevent her from seizing control of the Highlands once I was gone."

"Well, whatever you did certainly worked," Solveig insisted. "She really has changed. In fact, she's been my strongest supporter since the end of the war. I know she's wanted to see you again for some time now, to make amends for her part in driving you from the Highlands. Besides, you don't have very much choice, do you? It's the only possible clue I know that might lead you to the collar."

Thelvyn considered that briefly, frowning. "Very well. But there are a few secrets she doesn't need to know. For one thing, I don't want her to know that I'm the Dragonking."

"If you insist," Solveig agreed, sounding dubious. "But I'm not certain why."

He smiled wickedly. "There are a few things even you don't know about yet."

*   *   *   *   *

Early the next morning, Solveig set to work on the problem. First she hurried to the palace. Following Alessa's lead, she had established her own spies and supporters among the wizards. Although she felt some regret for treating her friend so suspiciously, she had every reason to question Alessa's motives and loyalties in the early days after she had become the first Prime Minister of the Parliament of the Realm. Solveig had been concerned that Alessa might try to use the power of the Radiance in an attempt to seize control of the Highlands. She had also worried that Alessa might locate the Collar of the Dragons but keep it hidden, hoping to use it in her own schemes.

As it happened, Solveig's spies had discovered nothing of any particular importance. As Alessa had said from the first, the connection between the wizards and the dragons had been limited strictly to Byen Kalestraan and his closest associates and a small band of renegade dragons who were trying to profit from the war by playing both sides. Of course, her spies were also able to confirm Alessa's new loyalty. One of the greatest troubles with politics in the Highlands in the past had been that no one dared to trust his own allies and advisors.

Solveig returned home late that afternoon with Alessa. Thelvyn still felt ambivalent about this meeting, remembering only too well his past difficulties with Alessa and how she had attempted to seduce, deceive, and finally discredit him. Alessa was surprised, since Solveig hadn't told her beforehand whom she was to meet. When she saw first Thelvyn and his companions seated about the den, she hesitated in the doorway for a long moment. She seemed uncertain what to do or say, and she nervously clutched the curious broach she wore on the breast of her wizard's robes.

"Dragonlord!" she breathed at last, coming into the room to take a seat across from him. "I didn't know if I would ever see you again."

"Solveig tells me that you've turned over a new leaf," he said. "If that's so, then you can prove it by helping me now. I have to find the Collar of the Dragons, and I have to find it soon. Solveig said that you may have found some clue."

"Finding the collar would divert the wrath of the dragons from the Highlands, which is in my best interests any way you look at it," she said, beginning to sound more certain. "But you must understand that I haven't found the collar itself, only what may be a hint."

"Even a hint would be welcome," Thelvyn told her. "Without any lead to follow, I'm not certain what I can do."

"Except to seek out and interrogate every renegade dragon in this part of the world," Sir George said, taking a small taste from his glass of cherry liqueur. "My word, I can't say how much I've missed this stuff!"

"I hope it won't come to that," Alessa commented, staring aimlessly at the wall as she appeared to consider, or perhaps to debate the matter with herself a moment longer. At last she frowned. "Unfortunately, the collar isn't in Braejr and apparently isn't even in the Highlands. The wizards, fearful of the wrath of the dragons, had sent it directly into hiding and were afraid to bring it home for experimentation."

"And, of course, the wizards who knew about the collar are either dead or they disappeared when their bid for power failed," Thelvyn said. "As for the dragon conspirators, I killed one in the assassination attempt. That's just the point. I need to find at least one of the surviving conspirators, either one of the wizards who disappeared or one of the renegade dragons."

"I have not been able to discover where the surviving wizards went," Alessa said. "They fled the Highlands when Kalestraan was defeated. But I might be able to tell you which renegade dragon to seek. All that is known is that they were all black dragons, that their leader was a renegade king, and that he wore a gold ring in one ear."

Kharendaen glanced up when she heard that, startled and obviously excited beneath her typically calm demeanor. "A gold ring? That might be all the clue we need. Dragons are not in the habit of wearing earrings. That would be remarkable enough that other dragons would remember it."

"If you can ask a dragon," Alessa said, staring at her.

Kharendaen had been sitting alone in the most dark and remote corner. Alessa had never met Kharendaen as a dragon, only in her secret form as the elf cleric Sellianda. As far as Alessa was concerned, she saw only a tall, dark-haired woman with the same racial features as Thelvyn, perhaps enough for her to surmise that this was another dragon in enchanted form. Alessa may have even deduced who it must be, but Thelvyn deliberately offered no introduction.

"Asking a dragon is the easy part," he said. "Is there anything else you might know?"

"I've discovered nothing else at this time," Alessa said. "But I'm still working at digging up Kalestraan's secrets. If you can't learn anything useful from this renegade dragon, I might have something more for you soon."

"We might need your help," Sir George remarked. "I keep thinking that this renegade would only know where Kalestraan hid the collar if he was the one who actually put it there. Which is not unlikely, considering the size and weight of the collar."

Soon after that, Solveig saw Alessa to the door to return to the Academy. The others were still discussing what they knew of renegade dragons when Solveig returned to the den a few minutes later. Their plan now was to leave as soon as it was fully dark and seek out dragons who might be able to tell them where to find a renegade black dragon who wore a ring in one ear.

"I'll have Taeryn get you something to eat before you go," Solveig said. "At least now you have a lead."

"Yes . . . apparently Alessa came through for us," Thelvyn said with some reservation. "Still, I'll have to take your word that she's come over completely to our side now. She didn't seem particularly happy to see me again."

"You probably frightened her," Solveig insisted. "I suspect that seeing you again unnerved her. You have to keep in mind that the old Alessa did a few things that the new one finds embarrassing."

Thelvyn and Kharendaen shared dinner with the others as a matter of courtesy. They would be returning to dragon form soon, and they would need a dinner of dragon proportions, which meant catching something in the wild. About an hour after nightfall, they went out into the yard. Thelvyn slipped into his harness while Sir George helped Kharendaen with her saddle. Minutes later, they climbed quickly into the dark sky over Braejr.

The two dragons immediately turned eastward toward the Colossus Mountains, where they planned to hunt and then wait out the rest of the night while they cooked and ate their catch before continuing northeast toward the wilderness of Norwold and the hidden city of Windreach. They needed to talk to Marthaen, and possibly other elder dragons as well, about the matter of the black renegade with the gold earring. Thelvyn remained reluctant to enter Windreach until he had recovered the collar. Kharendaen agreed. She decided she would bring Marthaen out into the mountains of the Wyrms-teeth to speak with him.

They were nearing the rugged western face of the Colossus Mountains when they saw a pair of dragons flying out to intercept them, followed at some distance by nearly a dozen others. Their presence came as no surprise. They were probably members of the band of young reds that had been left behind to keep watch on the Highlands. However, Thelvyn was afraid he wouldn't be able bluff his way past them a second time. But as the pair came nearer, they could see that the two lead dragons were quite large, obviously elder dragons by their size. The silver of moonlight glinted from their armor, revealing one to be a mature red while the other was a gold.

Thelvyn immediately sensed that this meeting was probably more important than a simple challenge by the sentries guarding the borders of the Highlands. Kharendaen followed him as he slowed and began circling in a wide arc as he waited just beyond the dark wall of the sheer mountainside. As the dragons came nearer, he was surprised to recognize them as Marthaen and Jherdar.

"Dragonking!" Marthaen called out to him as they pulled alongside him in a slow glide. Jherdar looked vaguely dissatisfied, as if he were uncomfortable with the use of Thelvyn's title.

"Find a place where we can spend the night in peace. We have something to explain to you," Thelvyn responded.

They made camp for the night in a narrow, forested valley deep behind the fold of one of the lower ridges of the Colossus Mountains, where the light of their fires would be hidden from the farmlands to the west. Marthaen instructed his bodyguards, a collection of gold and red dragons, to go hunt for their dinner. Once they were alone, Kharendaen quickly explained about their conversation with the Great One and what they had learned so far in their search for the collar. She remained silent about the matter of Thelvyn's hidden parentage, knowing that Jherdar would be upset to hear such a thing.

"A black renegade king with a gold ring in his ear . . ." Jherdar repeated slowly to himself, searching his memory. "That does indeed sound familiar."

Marthaen glanced at his old friend, quietly amused. "When the guards we had left in these mountains reported that you were on your way to Silvermist, and that you went into the Highlands the next night, we thought that we should look into the matter to see if we could be of any assistance."

"You have saved us a long journey to Windreach," Kharendaen told him. "We were on our way there to consult with you about this mystery."

"A gold earring," Jherdar repeated to himself, his neck bent in a stiff arch so that he was staring at the ground as he struggled to remember. Suddenly he lifted his head, his ears laid back. "Yes, I know of such a dragon. The black dragon in question is Murodhir, an especially nasty sort, although calling him a renegade king is flattering him. The last I heard, he had only two or three dragon cohorts, although Thelvyn probably killed one of them last year. He also has a few goblin retainers. His true strength is in his command of magic, since he hardly has much else going for him. Murodhir lives somewhere along the north shore of Lake Amsorak, on the southeastern border of the Highlands."

"Murodhir?" Sir George asked incredulously. "Why, he's the bane of every drake in Darokin and Traladara."

"Then he must be good for something," Marthaen declared, impatient with the old knight. "If you knew about Murodhir, then why were you looking for the dragon who stole the collar everywhere else in the world last year?"

"Because Murodhir is also a monumental coward," Sir George answered defensively. "He fears only one thing—other dragons—but his terror of them is so absolute that I could hardly imagine him going into Windreach after the collar. I'm still not sure I believe it."

"Then perhaps we should discover that for ourselves," Marthaen commented coldly. "I suggest we pay Murodhir a little visit in the morning. Jherdar, would you like to come along?"

"Indeed I would," the red dragon replied eagerly, anticipating the event with delight.

"You would help me?" Thelvyn asked incredulously.

Jherdar stared at him. "I am not enthusiastic about the prospect of having you as the Dragonking, and I will oppose your policies if I do not agree with them. But I am certainly no traitor, and I have no patience for any dragon who would betray his own kind. I want to see the Collar of the Dragons recovered, even if I have to see you wear it."

Thelvyn was careful to hide his amusement over Jherdar's qualified statement of support. But it was more than he had expected from the red dragon he had once defeated in battle as the Dragonlord.

* * * * *

The dragons left the Colossus Mountains well before dawn in order to pass directly over the Highlands with little concern for being seen. If they followed a straight path, the journey to Lake Amsorak was a fairly short one, perhaps three hours for dragons who were rested and eager. They came within sight of Lake Amsorak while the day was still young, and they turned to pass westward along the north shore in search of their quarry.

Amsorak was the largest lake in that part of the world, perhaps in all the world. Its vast proportions almost qualified it as an inland sea, although its waters were fresh, fed by the icy meltwater of the snows from the great range of the Amsorak Mountains to the north. Even though they knew that Murodhir's lair was somewhere along the north shore, that included a couple of hundred miles of remote territory. And the lair itself was just as likely to be somewhere in the mountains, several miles inland from the lake itself. The lair of a renegade king could be difficult even for another dragon to find.

As it happened, Murodhir's own cohorts betrayed the location of their hidden lair. The dragons were still fairly early in their search when Marthaen's keen eyes suddenly spied a pair of black dragons winging northward as quickly as they could fly, hanging low over the trees along the shore of the Amsorak River as it stretched northward toward the mountains. The blacks had seen the approaching dragons first and were sprinting for the protection of their lair, knowing that they faced an overwhelming force. Immediately Marthaen led the pursuit.

"We'll never catch them before they reach home," Jherdar said, struggling to keep pace with the gold dragons.

"We don't want to catch them yet," Marthaen said. "Let them lead us to their lair. Otherwise we might spend days searching."

The dragons pushed their pace as hard as they could, determined not to lose sight of their prey. Indeed, they were actually gaining slowly on the pair of frightened black dragons, although they were still nearly a mile behind as they came to the foothills of the mountains. Murodhir's lair was less difficult to locate than they had expected. A wide, dark cave opened beneath a broad overhang of moss-covered stone along the western shore, where the river had cut deep as it cascaded down from the heights. A high wall of dark stone, massive but crudely set, had been laid across the lower part of the entrance to the cave, leaving the upper portion open to the approach of dragons.

The two black dragons flew directly into the dark opening, landing quickly and folding away their wings as they turned to crouch behind the wall, raising their heads to peer out. They seemed to offer a poor defense, but they were not alone. A company of goblins began to file out at a run along the top of the wall, most of them still putting on their armor and helmets. There were about a hundred goblins in all, and they were armed with powerful crossbows.

Since Marthaen was still in the lead, he elected to bring their company down into the open field before the cave, landing just out of range of the crossbows. The goblins held their position, waiting. Sir George leaped down from his saddle as soon as Kharendaen settled to the ground, hurrying to get out of the way. The battle seemed hopeless for the defenders. Besides Thelvyn and Kharendaen, both Jherdar and Marthaen had their bodyguard, a dozen more young dragons. Even so, they did not fancy taking on so many crossbows.

Marthaen rose and reached over his back to draw the massive sword he always carried. If the dragons made a sudden charge at the wall, they were unlikely to take any serious harm before they were over it. Then it would be a simple matter to scatter the goblins and capture the two black dragons.

"Wait a moment," Thelvyn said. "Let me try to crack open their fort. Then you can drag them out without any bother."

"I suppose that the Dragonlord has such powers," Jherdar commented.

"Perhaps he does," Thelvyn agreed. "But I think that the time has come for us to see what the Dragonking can do. I need for all of you to be ready to rush in the moment after I strike."

"When we go in, you wait outside," Marthaen told him. "This is not work for the Dragonking. We will bring the renegade out to you."

It was all right with Thelvyn not to go into that dark, damp hole, and not because he was afraid. He was determined to scatter the goblins before they had a chance to use their crossbows. The last thing he wanted to see was the barbed bolts of those weapons penetrating Kharendaen's sleek armor. He rose to his hind legs and lifted his arms with his wings half open, reaching within himself for the powers that were his to claim as the child of an Immortal.

His own part in the battle was brief, if spectacular. His form began to glow with a soft light of pure silver as he gathered raw destructive power to himself. Then great, swift spears of lightning shot out from him, eight or ten rapid bolts of power in rapid succession, leaping across the clearing with the sound of thunder. Each bolt struck a separate part of the crude stone wall, progressing along its length in a line as they ripped apart the stone, sending great blocks and jagged splinters of stone flying along with the burned bodies of the defenders.

The last echoes of the lightning were still fading as the dragons leaped forward, crossing the clearing in long, swift bounds. Jherdar raced ahead of his companions in his eagerness for battle, but there was more of a fight waiting for him than he had expected. As he leapt over the ruined wall, he expected to face only a pair of dazed black dragons. Instead, he found himself pulled down by five renegades, who had been waiting for him. They were on top of him before he could begin to fight back. He could feel their claws pulling at his armor and their sharp fangs snapping for a death grip on his neck.

The attackers outnumbered the black dragons, and Jherdar should have had no great cause for alarm, but the tight quarters in the mouth of the cave kept his companions from assisting him. Marthaen climbed up on the highest part of the ruined wall, desperate to help his old friend before the renegades gained a hold on Jherdar's neck. The area just inside the wall was packed with blasted stone. He could barely see occasional glimpses of red armor beneath the tangle of black bodies writing below him. Hardly knowing what else to do, Marthaen arched his back and leapt down into the midst of the battle with the indiscriminate fury of a lightning bolt, crashing down with his greater weight onto the back of one of the black dragons. Not daring to pause, he pushed his way into the middle of the fight, thrusting aside the smaller black dragons to give Jherdar a chance to force his way free.

Two of Jherdar's red dragon bodyguards came over the wall and tore into the renegades furiously. Jherdar pulled free of his attackers a moment later, catching one of the black dragons by the neck and dragging it down. The three surviving renegades tried to break free to retreat into the shadowed depths of the cavern, and the remaining gold and red dragons began leaping over the shattered wall to pursue them. Marthaen paused, feeling odd points of pressure against the armor of his legs and belly. Glancing down, he was almost amused to see a small army of goblins swarming over him, trying to slip their swords and spears inside the joints of his armor. He responded by spinning quickly, his long tail scattering the goblins like vermin.

The attack was essentially over a few moments later. Marthaen followed the others into the depths of the cavern, leaving a couple of his bodyguards to chase down the surviving goblins. The bodies of two of the renegades were tossed out of the cavern a short time later, their necks broken.

But the two elder dragons did not come out, having unfinished business of their own deeper within the cave. Thelvyn hoped that they would remember how treacherous a renegade king could be in his own lair. He folded away his wings and approached the smoking, dusty ruins. Kharendaen hurried to join him. The bodyguards were already clearing away some of the wreckage, pushing the broken stones aside so that they could haul the bodies of the black dragons out into the open. Marthaen returned from the depths of the cave a few minutes later. Jherdar followed more slowly, pulling the renegade king out of his own lair by the tail. Murodhir was bleeding slowly from his ears.

"That was quite an impressive show," Jherdar said to Thelvyn as he dragged the renegade out into the clearing and released his tail. The black dragon lay limp and panting in the trampled grass.

"We seem to have made an impression on Murodhir,"

Thelvyn said as he approached and sat back on his haunches so that he could take the renegade by one horn, lifting his head. "Good day, Murodhir. You don't mind us just dropping in like this, do you? We want to have a little chat about the Collar of the Dragons."

Murodhir began to take a deep breath, but Thelvyn was too quick for him, clamping shut his snout. Black dragons breathed deadly acid rather than flame like the larger breeds, although the acid was usually an ineffective weapon against other dragons. Nevertheless, Thelvyn would have suffered grave harm if he had caught it in the face at such close range.

"Come on, now. Breathe out," Thelvyn told the renegade firmly, knowing that black dragons lacked the ability to use their breath weapons through their nostrils. "Do you want me to make Jherdar sit on you?"

Murodhir relaxed. "What difference is that to me? I don't expect you will allow me to live."

"You already owe me for the grave injury you did to my friend Solveig White-Gold," Thelvyn said. "But what happens to you depends upon what you decide. You can answer my questions now, or you can go back to Windreach to answer to the dragons for the theft of the collar."

The black dragon fell silent and began to quiver in fear. The worst of all possible fates he faced at that moment was being taken to Windreach to stand trial. The dragons would be especially inventive in punishing the greatest traitor their race had known in a long time.

"The question is really quite simple," Thelvyn continued, having given Murodhir a moment to think about his options. "Were you the one who stole the Collar of the Dragons for the Fire Wizards? Yes or no?"

Murodhir sighed loudly. "I knew the Fire Wizards from the time when they first came into the Highlands over a hundred years ago. They had always paid me well for information, especially about the dragons. Kalestraan proposed a bargain by which I would help him to gain the power he desired to rule the human races, and in return he would give me the power to rule over the dragons. He said that he would make it possible for me to steal the Collar of the Dragons and defeat the Dragonlord.

Then, when he was done with the collar, he would give it back to me so that I could proclaim myself Dragonking."

"Then you were the one who told him where the Collar of the Dragons was kept?" Thelvyn insisted.

"No. He knew that already," the renegade insisted. "He gave me an artifact of magic that allowed me to safely pass through the barriers that guarded the collar."

"Then you don't know how Kalestraan knew of the collar and its location? He did not learn of it from you?" Thelvyn asked.

"No, I swear that," Murodhir responded earnestly. "I brought the collar to him in the woods near the city of Braastar. That was the last I saw or heard of it. Some months later, he sent word of the day and the time when I was to attack the Dragonlord, but the attack did not go well. He hadn't warned me that you commanded magic other than the enchantments of the armor."

"Do you have any idea what Kalestraan did with the collar?" Thelvyn insisted.

"No. I tried to learn, so that I could still claim the collar for my own if Kalestraan tried to trick me. All I know is that I placed the collar in the back of a wagon. The wizards covered it over with a canvas and drove off into the night. I tried to watch, but after they had gone a mile or so, there was a flash of light beneath the trees and I never saw them again."

"Well, at least that's something," Thelvyn said. "You can take us to that place, I trust?"

Without warning, Murodhir suddenly panicked, as if something the others did not understand had filled him with terror. He began to twist around violently, trying to get his legs beneath him so that he could pull away, except that Thelvyn was still holding him by the horns. Realizing he couldn't get away, the renegade seemed to lose all sanity and became a snarling, thrashing beast. Unable to pull back from his captor, he abruptly thrust himself forward.

Thelvyn was not caught entirely by surprise, but he was in an awkward position. Sitting up on his haunches, he was unable to keep his balance as the weight of the black dragon was suddenly thrown against him. He crashed heavily on his back, and Murodhir was on him in the next instant, the sharp fangs of the renegade snapping inches from his throat. Moved by an instinct to defend himself at any cost, he pulled Murodhir's head to the left, since he was still holding the renegade's horn by that hand. With an effort, he reached around with his right hand until he was able to get a firm grasp of Murodhir's other horn, then twisted sharply. The renegade king instantly collapsed and went limp, his neck broken.

"A pity you had to kill him," Marthaen said as he pulled away the body of the black dragon so that Thelvyn could climb free. "I don't know if we can find the place where the Fire Wizards took the collar without him."

"I'm not sure that's really important," Thelvyn said. "If there were anything in the woods outside Braastar for us to discover, Murodhir would have found it long ago. If he had any idea where the collar is, he would have stolen it for himself after Kalestraan died last summer."

"That's true," Jherdar agreed, looking discouraged. "So now what?"

"First, we're going to search every inch of Murodhir's lair," Thelvyn replied. "We know that the Fire Wizards were paying him something for all his little chores and errands. Something they gave him might provide some clue about where to look for their hidden stronghold. Frankly, I was hoping that Murodhir had been in contact with the surviving traitor wizards since Kalestraan's death and would know where they were. But I believe that he was frightened enough to tell us all he knew."

"And what if you find nothing here?" Marthaen asked.

"Then we go back to Braejr," Sir George said as he joined them. "Alessa Vyledaar is still working on the problem. She might have learned something by now."

CHAPTER THREE

On the southern coast of the small continent of Alphatia, by the temperate waters of the Bellisarian Sea, stood the city of Archport. As its name suggests, Archport was a busy commercial port serving the trade between the great island of Bellisaria to the east, the Isle of Dawn to the west, and the scattering of lesser islands to the south. Large merchant ships from many nations could always be seen tied to the piers or anchored at wait in the harbor, ships from as far away as the sea kingdom of Ierendi far to the west or the wild and little-known continent of Skothar in the distant east.

Archport was also at that time one of the most important ports for the Alphatian navy, where many of the empire's sleek galleys and sturdy troop ships were kept and maintained. By virtue of its location, Archport was as important to Alphatia's commercial interest as it was to the island continent's appetite for conquest. Of course, the previous year's ill-advised war with the dragons had put a considerable dent in the size of the imperial navy, a fact that could be clearly seen by the unusual lack of military vessels to be found in port.

Most foreigners either did not know or else tended to forget that Alphatia was not a single nation, but a collection of eighteen semiautonomous kingdoms bound together by their shared greed and insatiable drive for conquest. Alphatia was a nation of sorcerers, a land where spellcasters were the aristocracy and common folk possessed few rights or little wealth. The land had first been settled by the ancient enemies of the Flaem, and the true Alphatians still dominated the continent. But many elves and dwarves had settled there as well in the centuries that had followed, and they now shared many of the customs and the ambitions of the original people of Alphatia.

The attack came in the deepest part of the night, and it came completely without warning. Ships standing at the piers or at anchor suddenly burst into flames, some catching fire so quickly and violently that they literally exploded. Indeed, since there was no immediate sign of any enemy, the first assumption of many was that a perfectly normal if disastrous fire was sweeping over the piers, spread by bits of burning canvas carried on the brisk sea breeze. But the fires seemed too selective, striking mostly at the swift war galleys and other naval vessels in the harbor, as well as the forts that stood guard over the port.

Defenders hurried to their stations, but there still was no enemy to be seen. No foreign warships stood out at sea, nor were any invading warriors in the streets of the city. The attack itself was swift and over in a matter of minutes. Only afterward did a few of the defenders speak of seeing vast, dark shapes passing below the stars in the moonless night sky, creatures with broad, dark wings, long necks, and tails.

Two other major ports in Alphatia were attacked that same night in similar fashion. The attack in each case was directed at, but not limited to, the ships and facilities of the imperial navy. And in every case, people spoke of seeing the dark shapes passing in the night. Of course, there was little question in anyone's mind that it was the dragons who were behind the attack. The dragons had been provoked into war with the empire the previous year; the Alphatians had treacherously broken their own truce when they thought the dragons were preoccupied with the Dragonlord in the west. But the dragons had kept to themselves since they had destroyed the last invasion force at sea, and there had been little reason to believe that they would retaliate further.

Indeed, the first thing that officials within the empire did following the attack was to make certain that their own people had not provoked the dragons yet again. Alphatians tended to be tenacious in their desire for conquest, even in the face of certain disaster. One problem with an empire of such great size as Alphatia was that one branch of the government or the military often did not know what the other parts might be doing.

Unfortunately, the dragons themselves remained very much an unknown factor. In the past, they had attacked only in just response to provocation, so that the Alphatians were inclined to wonder if they themselves were at fault. As a part of their first treaty with the Alphatians, the dragons had demanded the right to search all of Alphatia for some artifact of magic that had been taken from them. Alphatian spies reported that the dragons had made similar demands upon the Flaem in the distant west. Whatever it was the dragons wanted, they seemed to be returning for a second look. But whatever the cause of the attacks, whether in response to some threat, in retaliation for past transgressions, or merely for sport, all the Alphatians could do was to prepare themselves as best they could and wait.

* * * * *

On that same night, a cold, restless wind whipped through the narrow Sardal Pass in the mountains of southern Rockhome, the kingdom of the dwarves. The pennants above Karrak Castle snapped sharply in the breeze, the only sound to be heard in the night. But the great fortress of Karrak was not entirely asleep, for this was one of the three great fortresses guarding the only passes into Rockhome. Sardal Pass was the most direct way into the desert lands of the Ylaruam and Thyatis beyond. Sentries patrolled the walkways along the pass and manned the parapets of the massive form of the castle itself. The dwarves guarded their borders as if they were always expecting an attack, and they prided themselves upon the fact that they were almost never taken by surprise.

That night, however, even the dwarves were taken by surprise.

A great blast of intense flames seemed to explode from one of the tall, slender central towers of the castle. The blast hurled the tiles of the cone-shaped roof of the tower in all directions, great slabs of slate that were intended to deflect flaming arrows and even common dragonfire. The timbers and wood floors within the tower began to burn furiously, and even some of the stones of the outer wall began to crack and loosen from the intense heat. The sentries hardly needed to ring the watch bells to sound the alarm; the blast had shaken the castle to its core. The ranks of dwarvish warriors leapt from their beds, pausing only long enough to grab their armor and weapons as they hurried to the defense of the castle.

The top of the second tower of the main portion of the castle also exploded in flame. Then a couple of the lesser towers along the outer wall of the pass were all but shattered in sudden bursts of fire. The massive tower above the circular gate fort proved more solid than the others, withstanding three blasts before it began to burn like a great torch in the night. Only moments after the first attack, the dwarves began to rush out onto the upper walls, ready for battle. But there was no enemy to be seen; indeed, the assault upon Karrak Castle seemed to be over.

There was, of course, only one enemy who could have come and gone again so quickly in the night. The sentries who had witnessed the attack pointed to the sky and spoke of great winged shapes that had moved quickly across the stars of the moonless sky as they had hurtled along the twisting length of the pass.

The sudden and seemingly unprovoked attack was a dire mystery to Daric, son of Kuric, the young commander of the garrison at Karrak Castle. There was little he could do at first except to have the fires brought under control and repairs begun on the damaged towers. The garrison remained at full battle alert; catapults and large crossbows, at least all such weapons that were on hand, were brought out onto the walls and made ready. But Daric had to doubt that a second attack would come any time soon. This had obviously not been an attempt to capture or destroy the castle. The damage to the defenses of the castle had been minimal, and there had been no loss of life. He was inclined to believe that this had been a warning, although he did not understand the intended message.

Although dwarves considered dragons to be their special enemies, born of a certainty that every dragon in the world coveted the deep caverns and vast treasures of the dwarves, actual conflict between them was rare. Although renegades often attacked the caravans coming in and out of Rockhome, even the great renegade king Kardyer had never dared to attempt an attack on one of the underground cities of the dwarves. All raids had come to an end in the months since the Dragonlord had slain Kardyer and his cohorts. Also, the flames that had destroyed the castle's towers had been much more intense than was usual for dragonfire. Even Daric knew that much about dragons.

Only an army of dragons would dare to attack a major stronghold of the dwarves, and only the greatest of the world's dragons would command magical flames of such intensity. Daric was reminded of the time just before the coming of the Dragonlord, when Rockhome had been all but under siege from the armies of rogue dragons patrolling the northlands. Now that there was no longer a Dragonlord to maintain the peace, the dragons might be harboring new plans of conquest, encouraged by their easy defeat of Alphatia.

As morning approached, Daric had to make his decisions quickly, and he felt trapped between two duties of great importance. If the attack had been only a prelude to an invasion, he needed to do what he could to hold Karrak Castle against the dragons, as impossible as that seemed. And yet he also needed to carry his warning to Dengar immediately, so that preparations to defend all of Rockhome could begin. He decided that he was needed more in Dengar; if he left at once, he could be back by nightfall of the following day, and his lieutenant could command the castle and garrison as well as he could during that time.

Because speed was important, he elected to ride one of the few horses kept by the dwarves for delivering urgent messages. That gave him several hours during the ride to Dengar to reflect upon this new development, and for once he was glad to have Korinn Bear Slayer and the Syrklist dwarves leading

Rockhome at such a time. Daric was himself of the warrior
Torkrest Clan, but he was still fairly young for a dwarf and
had in the past been a companion, even a friend, to Dorinn,
the elder son of King Daroban and at that time the clear heir
to the throne. When Dorinn had been wounded in battle
against the orcs in the West, Daric had helped to get him
home again. Since that time, Daric had also come to respect
and trust the younger son of Daroban, Korinn, now that he
was something of a hero and the likely heir.

As he made the final climb toward the gate of upper Dengar, he saw that his warning of an attack by dragons was a little
late. Several of the small watchtowers along the massive wall
had been blasted, and some had been shattered altogether.
Crews were already at work repairing the damage, but the
greatest attention was being given to preparing the city for a
second and possibly far more serious attack. Daric had to
wonder just how many cities and fortresses in Rockhome had
been hit the previous night.

Leaving his horse at the stables of the garrison near the
inner gate, he hurried down to the lower city and presented
himself at the palace. Under the circumstances, he was not
surprised to find that the king's throne room was packed with
more than a hundred dwarves, representatives of every clan
and many leaders of the military, all talking together furiously
in small groups. His old friend Dorinn saw him as soon as he
entered and hurried to greet him, although with no joy for the
anticipated news that Daric carried.

"Karrak as well?" Dorinn asked, and sighed heavily. "You
must speak with my father at once."

Dorinn lead the way through the crowd, still walking with
an awkward limp from the injuries he had suffered in battle
years before, although he stood somewhat straighter and
looked less thin and wasted than he had. He hurried not to the
throne but to a quiet corner, where his brother Korinn and
King Daroban were talking quietly with a tall young man in
the uniform of a Thyatian officer. For a moment, Daric
noticed only that the king looked older and more frail than
ever, noticeably older than when he had last visited Dengar
the previous autumn. Although Daric was of a rival clan, he

found himself hoping that the king would retain his strength long enough for Korinn to come of age and assume the throne uncontested. Rockhome could hardly survive war with the dragons if the dwarves were fighting among themselves for the crown.

Daroban turned to him. "We had feared that Karrak Castle had been hit as well."

"The damage was only superficial," Daric said. "No worse than what I saw in the city above. But I had no way of knowing that the dragons had struck anywhere else, so I thought it best to bear the warning as quickly as I could."

"It is well that you did," the king said, then glanced up at the Thyatian. "General Daric, this is Captain Darius Glantri of Thyatis. He arrived by griffon this morning, on his way to the Flaemish realm to confer with Solveig White-Gold. He has kindly paused on his journey so that the two griffon riders in his company might survey Rockhome's damage for us."

Darius bowed politely. "This matter affects us all, I fear. The shipyards of the Thyatian fleet were attacked as well, and the damage was rather more severe. The dragons were very busy indeed last night. I wonder who else they may have attacked."

"Who indeed?" Daric asked. "My impression was that we've been given a warning, considering how little damage was actually done."

"It probably was only a warning," Darius agreed. "It's just that the warning we received in Thyatis was much sterner than the one they saved for the dwarves. But that defies explanation. If it was a warning of their intent to attack us in greater force, then why would they warn us? And if it was retribution, then what have we done to deserve it?"

"According to all our legends, dragons have their own ways, often mysterious to us," King Daroban said. "When the rogue dragons attacked just before the coming of the Dragonlord, their attacks seemed to be more a matter of harassment, as if they felt so secure in their own strength that they sought to slay their enemies by slow torment. Now that there is no longer a Dragonlord to stop them, perhaps they once more feel strong and secure. If this is a matter of retaliation, then could it be for the humiliation the dragons suffered when the Dragonlord humbled them in our defense?"

"As far as I know, there still is a Dragonlord," Korinn said. "The dragons couldn't take that away from him. All they did was incite our own hatred and mistrust, causing us to send him away from us."

"You make it sound as if the fault were our own," Daric commented, not so much in anger but in honest confusion. "Didn't the Dragonlord leave us to go back with his own kind, once he learned that he was a dragon?"

"But he is still the Dragonlord," Korinn insisted. "Remember, I was there from the first. I know that his duty was to protect all of us, even the dragons themselves, from war. And he won't let them go to war now, I'm certain of that. The dragons might have decided that he cannot or will not oppose them, but I suspect that they have a surprise coming to them."

"I agree," Darius Glantri said. "I knew the Dragonlord well, and I've never lost my faith in him. Emperor Cornelius agrees with me on that score. I was on my way to confer with Solveig White-Gold, to see if she knows how to find the Dragonlord and call him back to defend us. If King Daroban agrees, I think that Korinn Bear Slayer should go with me."

Daroban remained hesitant. "I will believe that the Dragonlord is still our defender when he has actually returned to defend us and the dragons have been sent back into the northlands. In all the history of our race, the dragons have been the demons of our waking nightmares, and I will never trust them. I cannot easily place my faith in the Dragonlord."

"Do we really have any choice?" Korinn asked. "If the dragons want to make war upon us, there's not much we can do about it. They're too strong, too fast, and too powerful in their magic. In all the history of our race, have we known any force that could stand against them except the Dragonlord?"

Dorinn frowned. "Father, Korinn speaks the truth. The Dragonlord defended us for five years, and we had no complaint. If the Dragonlord is still willing to defend us, then it is best for us that we should let him. That does not mean that we should not prepare our own defenses, or that we should not speak with our neighbors such as the Thyatians about defending ourselves against a common enemy."

His dwarvish pride stung, Daric started to protest. But the truth was that Rockhome could never hope to fight the Nation of Dragons alone, even if they locked themselves in their deepest caves.

King Daroban nodded at last, with great reluctance. "We have no choice. While my heart can find no trust in a dragon or hope that he will defend us against his own kind, I cannot deny that we need the Dragonlord. Korinn, if you and Solveig can find your one-time friend, then do everything in your power to bring him back here at once."

* * * * *

The cool, clear night was deep and silent, and the darkest shadows had filled the streets and passages of Braejr when Solveig heard the familiar sound of large, strong wings descending with powerful strokes into the courtyard. Her first thought was that Thelvyn and Kharendaen had returned for some reason, even though they had been gone barely an hour, and she hurried to the door expecting to find the dragons in the courtyard. But she heard the fierce cry of a griffon even before she stepped out into the yard, so that she knew even before she saw the beast that her visitor was a messenger from Thyatis.

Solveig saw at once that the griffon rider was Darius Glantri, but she was rather surprised and mystified to see that his passenger was a dwarf. Until that moment, she would have thought that nothing could have convinced a dwarf to mount a griffon, especially in the precarious position of holding on tightly behind the rider. Darius struggled to calm the restive beast just long enough for the dwarf to leap down from the griffon's wide rump and move aside. Indeed, the young dwarf kept moving stiffly once he found himself safely on the ground, staggering almost to where Solveig waited in the yard at the edge of the paved court.

"Korinn Bear Slayer!" she remarked once she could see who it was. "If I had been asked to wager whether any dwarf would dare to ride a griffon, I would have placed my bet on you."

"I'm not much in the mood for mirth, if you don't mind," the dwarf said, still disgruntled over the manner of his arrival. "The city looks peaceful enough. I take it that the dragons haven't attacked here yet."

"No . . . no, they haven't," Solveig answered, too startled by that statement to know quite what to think.

"I would have thought they would have struck here first," Korinn said with a shrug. "Perhaps they just don't want to seem predictable."

Solveig could only stare in shock. It occurred to her that her two old friends might be perpetrating some foolish jest at her expense. She hoped that they were, since new attacks by dragons would be the worst possible news at that time, not only to her plans for unifying the Highlands but also to Thelvyn's plans to unify the dragons. Darius began leading his griffon away to the warehouse.

She elected to follow him. Korinn had to run to keep up with her long-legged stride. After hours of sitting on the haunches of a flying griffon, his legs were reluctant to move so quickly.

"What is this talk of attacks?" Solveig demanded. "If dragons are indeed attacking, I've got to prepare the defenses of the Highlands right now."

With considerable effort, Korinn caught up to her. "Dragons attacked both Rockhome and Thyatis last night, although the damage was light enough to make it seem like nothing more than a warning. Captain Glantri has sent griffon riders to Alfheim and Darokin to discover if there have been attacks there as well."

Solveig came to an abrupt stop.

"You help Darius with his griffon and bring the captain into the den when you're finished," she said, turning back toward the house. "I've got to do something about the defense of the city."

By that time of night, Solveig had only Taeryn to carry her messages, and he could only go in one direction at a time. The best she could do was to have him saddle a horse from the stables and spread the word through the streets. She instructed him to go first to the Academy and summon Alessa, then go on to the garrison at the north gate to alert Captain Harl Geirstaan, who was now the commander of the Highland army.

Darius and Korinn came inside a short time later, having stabled the griffon for the night. They joined Solveig in the den, explaining what they knew of the attacks so far while they had something to eat and drink. Darius had sent his griffon-rider bodyguards to Darokin, Alfheim, and Traladara to discover if the dragons had attacked there as well. Solveig sat in the chair across from him and listened, staring aimlessly at the floor, obviously very deep in thought. She could only shake her head.

"This doesn't make any sense," she said at last. "I suppose that you should know that Thelvyn, Kharendaen, and Sir George have been here. In fact, they left hardly an hour before you arrived. Needless to say, they're searching for the Collar of the Dragons."

"Is it true that Thelvyn has become a dragon now?" Korinn asked.

"He's been a dragon since shortly after he left here last summer," she explained. "They really didn't say much about their affairs, except that the Great One himself has sent them to find the collar. It seems that Thelvyn is to be the Dragon-king, some legendary figure from draconic lore who is to rule all the dragons of the world. The collar was set aside for the Dragonking long ago so that the dragons would recognize his authority as their first true king."

Darius had been watching her closely. "Could that be why Thelvyn needs the collar now, so that he can order these rogue dragons back in line?"

"I don't know," Solveig replied. "Thelvyn hasn't been among the dragons, so he might not be aware of what they're doing. This situation reminds me of the attacks of the rogue dragons six years ago. The young dragons, especially the headstrong reds, might be so opposed to having Thelvyn as the Dragonking that they've convinced themselves they must do something about it while they can. These attacks might be the work of rogue dragons rather than a declaration of war from the Nation of Dragons itself."

"Does that make any difference to us?" Korinn asked sourly.

"Indeed it does," she assured him. "In fact, it might explain why the attacks seem to be nothing more than a warning. The rogues might be afraid to engage in open warfare. For that matter, they might only be throwing down the gauntlet, so to speak, to the Dragonlord, to force him to respond."

"Then Thelvyn is still the Dragonlord?" Darius asked, surprised. "How could that be, if he's now a dragon himself?"

"That was my understanding," Solveig answered. "You see, both he and Kharendaen have the ability to change form."

"Then there is really only one last question," Korinn said, looking quite uncomfortable. "Is there any possibility that Thelvyn would betray us to his own kind? Not that I'm really worried about that, but I'm sure that others will be. My father sent me to find the Dragonlord if I can and request his protection, but he doesn't hold out much hope that a dragon will take our side against his own people. Even the Dragonlord."

Solveig sat back in her chair, frowning. "Wonderful. Everyone who wanted to chase the Dragonlord away only a few months ago will be crying for him to come back to save them. But I'm sure that the Dragonlord, or perhaps I should say the Dragonking, will act as quickly as he can to get the rogue dragons back in line."

"But how can we find him?" the dwarf asked.

"He's away on business of his own right now," Solveig explained, "but he should be coming back here soon. All we have to do is to wait."

Alessa arrived by carriage a few minutes later, and Captain Geirstaan came on horseback with Taeryn soon after that. The situation was explained to them, at least as much as anyone knew. Geirstaan promised do what he could to prepare the defenses of the Highlands against yet another invasion by dragons. To help coordinate the efforts, Alessa was to have the Fire Wizards use their power to communicate with all the members of their order throughout the realm. There was still no certainty that the dragons would attack the Highlands, especially if Thelvyn could intervene in time. But it seemed best to everyone to be prepared for the worst.

"I think I will follow Solveig's advice in this matter," Darius said. "I'll wait here a few days, as long as I can, for Thelvyn to return."

Alessa had been standing off by herself, clutching her wizard's robe close to her. "Are you so certain that the Dragonlord will protect us?"

Solveig glanced at her, surprised. "What do you mean by that?"

"I was just wondering about his true motives in wanting the Collar of the Dragons," she explained. "As I understand it, it gives him the power to control the dragons. Is it to stop them from making war upon the world, or to lead them against us?"

"I, for one, trust him implicitly. Why don't we just wait and see," Darius told her, a stern note of disapproval in his voice.

"Isn't that the point?" Alessa insisted. "We have to decide before he asks for our help whether or not we can trust him once he has the collar."

"He's never done anything to earn our distrust," Darius insisted. "And I don't see that we have any choice but to take the chance. If he won't defend us, there's not much that you or I can do to protect ourselves from dragons."

Solveig shrugged. "I know I must sound as if I've been living among the Flaem too long to even think such a thing, but I have to wonder if the Alphatians might be behind these attacks in some way. They tried to fight the dragons last year and failed utterly. I'm sure that they don't much like dragons, and of course they never did like any of us. It seems that no one ever got a good look at these dragons. Every description I heard simply mentioned dark shapes against the night sky. I have to wonder if those shapes might have been Alphatian illusions."

Darius grunted in agreement. "They are air wizards, after all. They could well be able to put together something that looks like a dragon and make it fly."

Alessa had no more time to discuss the matter, since she had to return to the Academy at once to have the wizards convey the warning of the attacks and have the Highlands made ready for a possible attack. The senior wizards of the Academy would have no complaints about being turned out of their beds or away from their studies to comply, and the power of the Radiance was very effective at relaying communications between crystals attuned to its power. But a wizard had to be awake and near his crystal to know that he was being called, and it seemed that most of the rural wizards went to bed at an early hour.

At least the network of communication worked both ways. If there were an attack somewhere else in the realm during the night, the wizards at Braejr would learn of it almost at once.

Alessa's brief debate with her companions had left her feeling frustrated and angry. As Solveig had said, people would be quick to forget how deeply they had distrusted the Dragonlord now that they needed his protection, and she had little hope that she could rekindle that distrust. The voice had convinced her that the destiny of the Flaem should be in their own hands, and she was filled with quiet rage to see foreigners like Thelvyn and Solveig deciding things while she was little more than their servant, sent about her assigned tasks. She was outraged even more to see that Thelvyn was playing the part of the hero once again, while his fellow dragons created the very crisis that allowed him to presume power and authority over other nations.

Perhaps the voice of the crystal could help her to find a way to remind everyone that the Dragonlord was not a hero but a dragon and a traitor, not to be trusted. Perhaps there was some way to prevent Thelvyn from finding the Collar of the Dragons. As long as he did not have possession of the collar, he lacked the authority to command the dragons.

Once word of the dragon attacks had been relayed to the outlying wizards and things at the Academy settled down a bit, Alessa retired to her own chamber and prepared for bed, setting aside the spellbook that she had left open beside her chair. Privately, she was amazed at herself for such carelessness; usually a wizard had a fierce instinct to protect her spellbook and would never leave it lying about. That served to show just how much she was letting the problems of the dragons and the Dragonlord unsettle her. She prepared for bed, locking her door and making certain that her windows were secure. Soon she slept, and shortly afterward she began to dream.

Do you sleep? the same, familiar voice asked of her. In her dreams, she saw only the blackness of night and the vague image of the long, narrow face of a dragon.

Dream on, my sorceress, and in your dreams tell me all that you have heard this night.

Alessa reflected upon her meeting at Solveig's house with Korinn Bear Slayer and the young captain from Thyatis. There was no one in that group she could hope to claim as an ally. Solveig and Korinn had been among the original companions of Thelvyn Fox-Eyes in the quest that eventually culminated in his becoming the Dragonlord. They would never abandon their trust in their old friend. Nor would Darius Glantri, who had always thought highly of the Dragonlord. Fear of dragons seemed likely to engender new trust in the Dragonlord with everyone. People had no choice but to place their trust in Thelvyn, just as the King of the Dwarves had already, knowing that they could not hope to defend themselves against the dragons. No one had any doubts that the dragons were behind the attacks.

That was just as well, the voice reassured her. Even Thelvyn himself would not be able to deny the possibility that rogue dragons were behind the attacks. As long as he was not in possession of the Collar of the Dragons, he could not even begin to confront the dragons and learn that rogue dragons had not broken the truce. Even he could not guess his true enemy. Only the Great One could tell him that, and soon it would be too late. If everyone was blaming and fearing the dragons, then they would not be ready to confront their true enemy. Not even Thelvyn. His authority as the Dragonlord remained shattered. His authority as the Dragonking did not yet exist.

Dream, then, and in your dreams tell me of what you know of the quest of Thelvyn Fox-Eyes to find the Collar of the Dragons.

Alessa reflected upon that, but she found that she had nothing new to say. Thelvyn was seeking the renegade dragon who had stolen the collar, but that would do him no good. Alessa had told him to seek the black dragon with the gold earring, as the voice had directed her. Thelvyn might not find the dragon with the gold earring for some time, but even if he did, the renegade would not be able to give him the collar or tell him what he needed to know.

All is well, said the voice of her dreams. *The black dragon Murodhir is himself my servant. If the Dragonlord does find him, Murodhir would do and say only what is expected of him. But I know Murodhir is a coward and a fool. If he is pressed into saying more than he should, then he will die. It would be a simple matter to break his mind in a moment, driving him mad with fear. Then he would do anything to escape, or to kill his captors, forcing them to slay him in turn.*

Everything is progressing well, perhaps better than anyone could have expected. If the Dragonking is the only enemy of any potential threat, then perhaps it would be best to remove Thelvyn Fox-Eyes from the game before he can become the Dragonking. The Collar of the Dragons is the perfect bait. If Thelvyn returns to Braejr seeking more clues about where he should seek the collar, then perhaps it is time to tell him what he wants to know. Thelvyn always seems to want to know things that are not good for him.

Alessa was confused, wondering just what she should tell the Dragonlord.

He must not be told everything, the voice explained, *only enough to send him flying into the trap that awaits him. He seeks to learn the location of the secret stronghold of the traitor wizards, expecting to find only a handful of foolish old sorcerers hiding in exile, fearful and powerless. That is exactly what he should think. For all his powers, both his own and those of the Dragonlord, Thelvyn is still nothing more than an innocent and inexperienced child. It would be a simple matter indeed to pull the teeth of that young dragon.*

Do you sleep? the voice asked Alessa a final time. *Then dream, and in your dreams you will come to know all that you are to do and say when Thelvyn returns.*

But Alessa's deepest dreams were troubled, deep in that voiceless part of her mind and will that remained her own. For she understood the implications of all that she was told, and she did not see how Thelvyn could escape the trap that awaited him.

CHAPTER FOUR

Thelvyn drew himself cautiously through the tight passages of the deep cavern that had been the lair of the renegade king Murodhir, following behind his companions as they made their way out. They had spent a long day in a thorough search of the lair, and they carried with them not only Murodhir's hoard but also everything else they could find. The traitorous Fire Wizards had paid Murodhir for various services, not the least being the theft of the Collar of the Dragons and the attempt to assassinate Thelvyn and Solveig. Thelvyn had hoped that something the wizards had given Murodhir would also give some hint about the location of their secret stronghold, but they had found nothing. Of course, he had never placed much hope in that, and so he was not greatly disappointed. Byen Kalestraan had not been one to share his secrets.

The wizards had not paid Murodhir particularly well for his work, judging by the rather humble proportions of his hoard. Although Thelvyn had slain Murodhir and could now claim his treasure and his lair, it was also the custom among dragons that he should share a part of the renegade's hoard with those who had accompanied him into battle. He gave Kharendaen, Marthaen, and Jherdar each a third of the treasure. The two male dragons were both leaders of their own bands, and they shared part of their third with the young dragons who served as their bodyguards. Dragon clerics were not in the habit of accumulating treasure, nor did they often have the chance, so Kharendaen welcomed her portion. Since Thelvyn already owned the vast treasure and the lair that had belonged to the renegade king Kardyer, he was content.

"I'm done here," he said as he emerged from the entrance of the cavern, following his companions into the clearing beyond the ruined wall that had guarded the lair. "Will you be heading east now?"

"That depends upon what you plan to do next," Marthaen answered.

"Well, I certainly didn't learn very much here," Thelvyn said as he settled back on his haunches in the soft grass, facing the others. "Murodhir obviously had no idea what the Fire Wizards did with the collar. I'm not even convinced the little he did have to tell us was the truth."

"Are you sure?" Jherdar asked. "He impressed me as being too frightened to lie."

"No, I can't be sure," Thelvyn replied. "I keep thinking of how he suddenly went mad with fear and attacked me when I suggested he lead us to the place in the wilderness near Braastar. He should have been encouraged that he would not be put to death at once and might possibly have an opportunity to escape. Yet he wasn't trying to break free of me. Instead, he was attacking me."

"That is cause for wonder," Marthaen agreed. "Why would he bring the collar to the Fire Wizards there in the wilderness?"

"That's one of the few parts of his story that seems to ring true," Sir George said, moving forward to address the dragons. "When the Flaem first came into this world, they arrived somewhere near Braastar. That was where they built their first strongholds. The wizards moved to Braejr later so that they could more easily study and protect the Radiance. I've always wondered if their secret stronghold was somewhere near

Braastar."

Thelvyn lifted his head suddenly and stared at Marthaen. "Tell me about your search for the collar in Alphatia. I recall that your search was a condition of your first truce with the Alphatians, and it took you a couple of weeks to conduct it, but that hardly seems time enough for a thorough search."

"Our sorcerers conducted the search," Marthaen explained. "They have the means to detect the presence of the collar if they could come reasonably close, even if the collar were shielded magically or locked inside some interdimensional hiding place. By the same method, we've always been fairly certain that the collar is no longer in the Highlands."

Sir George looked indignant. "You mean you had me search half the world for that thing, and you could have saved me half my trouble?"

Marthaen looked down at him. "We didn't know that it wasn't in Alphatia until after we had invaded the Highlands. And you were looking everywhere except the Highlands as it was, so that hardly mattered."

Thelvyn considered that briefly. "That seems to support our suspicion that the stronghold of the traitor wizards is not in the Highlands, which is what I have always suspected. Then that decides the matter for me. I had considered going to the forests near Braastar to search for the place Murodhir described, but that seems pointless now. My only other option is to return to Braejr, to discover if Alessa Vyledaar has learned anything else."

Later that day, as the sun was setting beyond the wilderness far to the west, the dragons spread their wings and leaped into the darkening sky. While the others were returning to Windreach, Thelvyn and Kharendaen collected Sir George for their rather short flight back to Braejr. They would be passing across the vast eastern plains and light woods of the central Highlands, the most heavily settled region of the realm. While the northern frontier was the land of timber and mining, the east was a land of pastures, where cattle and sheep grazed in peace and fields of wheat were stirred by the soft winds of a gentler climate than that most of the Highlands endured.

Thelvyn hardly knew whether he dared to hope that Alessa

would be able to tell him anything that would help in his quest to find the Collar of the Dragons. Alessa was supposed to be exploring new leads, but he had no idea of the nature of her discoveries, and so he could not begin to judge whether or not they would bear fruit. All he knew was that Solveig had come to trust Alessa completely, and Thelvyn trusted Solveig. But he had to admit that his trust did not yet extend all the way to the sorceress.

As the two dragons drifted on silent wings over the lights of Braejr, Thelvyn found that his instinct for direction was finally beginning to serve him better. Although one dark building looked much the same as the next from above, he found that he was drawn unerringly to one part of the city. Kharendaen remained in the lead, guiding him to their destination, but he thought that he could have found his old house without her help.

But his delight at his new talent was brief. As the dragons descended quickly out of the night toward the paved court, they were surprised to find that the old warehouse seemed to be full of griffons. The beasts were aware of the dragons as well, struggling and calling out fiercely in fury at the approach of their one natural enemy. Sir George leapt down from his saddle at the very moment Kharendaen settled to the ground, and both of the dragons hurried to release their leather straps so that they could change form and put an end to the uproar in the warehouse.

Thelvyn tossed his harness aside and immediately began to change his form, but in his haste, he failed to recall that he needed to rise to his hind legs as the transformation began. When he assumed human form, he was rather embarrassed to find himself on his hands and knees on the dusty paving stones of the court. Kharendaen changed form a moment later, in a more dignified manner, and the griffons within the warehouse began to quiet grudgingly.

Thelvyn turned to see Solveig and Korinn Bear Slayer hurrying across the yard from the house to join him. He was more embarrassed to have them see him pick himself up from the stones, until it occurred to him to wonder what Korinn was doing in Braejr. He realized at once that good news could not come from such a remarkable event, especially with the added curiosity of a warehouse full of griffons. Apparently messengers had been descending upon the Highlands in flocks.

"I hadn't expected you back so soon," Solveig said, needlessly helping him to stand. "Did you find the black dragon with the gold earring?"

"We did, for all the good it did us," Thelvyn said a bit sourly. "Is there some kind of trouble?"

"There's trouble of the worst kind," Korinn said. "But I'm pleased to see you again, all the same. Doubly pleased, under the circumstances."

"That will take a few minutes of explanation," Solveig insisted. "It might as well be done over a quick dinner. Have you eaten?"

"Not since last night," Thelvyn said, still mystified.

Solveig had Taeryn and another servant collect the dragon saddle and Thelvyn's harness and move them to safekeeping in a storage room in the house. Since the tack smelled of dragon, they couldn't be kept with the griffons or even in the stables with the horses. Then Korinn collected Sir George's bag, and Solveig led them all into the house through the kitchen door. As they came into the soft light, Thelvyn saw for the first time that his hands and clothes were covered with a thick layer of gray dust, the result of his undignified transformation. He brushed his hands together, raising a small cloud of dust.

"What was that?" Korinn asked, sniffing the air suspiciously, as if he anticipated something magical.

"Pixie dust," Thelvyn said, disgruntled.

"Oh." The dwarf looked perplexed. "Where did you get pixie dust?"

"From grinding up dried pixies," Thelvyn answered impatiently.

"I'll have dinner for you in a moment," Solveig said, looking quietly amused. "And if our good dwarf friend will oblige, he might fetch a bottle of cherry liqueur from the den."

Sir George smiled contentedly. "Ah, child, you haven't forgotten."

Korinn returned with the bottle of cherry liqueur, plus less

distinctive drinks for the others, even before the plates were
set on the table. Thelvyn had gone to wash up, and he
returned to find that Darius Glantri had joined the others at
the table. While the others ate in silence, Darius and Korinn
told about the attacks on Thyatis and Rockhome two nights
ago. Alessa arrived on horseback before they finished their
meal. She explained quickly that most of Braejr had heard the
screams of the griffons, which she assumed to have been in
response to the arrival of dragons.

"Anyway, I sent the griffon riders in my company to check
for reports of attacks in other lands," Darius concluded.
"There were attacks that same night in Darokin and Alfheim,
although Traladara seems to have been spared. Or perhaps
ignored. In all cases, witnesses spoke of seeing the dark shapes
of dragons against the night sky."

Solveig nodded grimly. "Since no one seems to have seen
the attackers very clearly, at first I wondered if this was some
trick of the Alphatians to breed fear and distrust between the
Highlands and the dragons. But a griffon rider arrived from
Thyatis this afternoon with the report that Alphatia was
attacked at the same time."

"I can assure you that these attacks did not come from the
Nation of Dragons," Kharendaen volunteered. "From last
night until late this afternoon, we were in the company of First
Speaker Marthaen and Jherdar, the leader of the red dragons.
If something was happening among the dragons, they would
have known about it. I also don't think that this was the work
of rogue dragons."

"But we don't know for certain that dragons weren't
involved," Alessa insisted. "This could have been the work of
a band of rogues or renegades."

Kharendaen shook her head hopelessly. "No, I cannot deny
that it might have been dragons. I just don't expect it."

"We know a few things you don't," Thelvyn began cautiously, taking stock of his secrets and which ones he might
share now that it was important. "The Great One himself
assigned me the quest of finding the Collar of the Dragons,
and he told me that the dragons face a time of great trouble
from an unexpected enemy. These attacks might have been

the work of this unknown enemy."

"What were the exact words of the prophecy that the Great One related to you?" Solveig asked.

"It wasn't exactly a prophecy," Thelvyn explained. "The Great One sat down with us and told us these things in plain language. No riddles. No vague warnings that don't make sense until it happens. He wasn't yet able to tell me exactly what we face, but there was no question of his warning. All I can tell you is that the Great One has taken some pretty remarkable and drastic steps to prepare for this threat, which he has apparently anticipated for years."

"But we still have only your word," Alessa insisted.

"Thelvyn's word is enough for most of us," Korinn declared gruffly.

"That's almost beside the point just now," Sir George said. "Whoever the attackers are, only the Dragonking can stop them, and he needs the Collar of the Dragons to do that."

Alessa paused a moment, as if in contemplation. Perhaps she was only putting a rein to her own fears and suspicions, since she seemed much calmer and more reasonable when she looked up. "Yes, of course. As it happens, I have discovered just what you need to know. The funny thing is that we've always known where to look, if we had just thought about it. As you know, the Flaem traveled between worlds for hundreds of years before settling here. In some of the places our ancestors passed through, they stayed for decades at a time, but they hardly lived in tents like the Ethengar."

"The Flaem don't talk much about their time of wandering," Thelvyn remarked, having always found that curious.

"No, we put that behind us when we decided to settle here," she explained. "But the wizards did keep records of those times. According to the records, the Flaem came into this world through a gateway that was opened in the wilderness near the city of Braastar."

Sir George looked up. "That's where Murodhir said he brought the Collar of the Dragons after he stole it."

"Then that would seem to prove my suspicion," Alessa said. "The wizards had a stronghold of their own in the last world where they dwelled, near the place where they opened the gateway. That must be where Byen Kalestraan hid the collar."

"Then the missing conspirators would also be there?" Thelvyn asked.

"I suspect so," she said. "Although I don't think they would present you any serious problems in finding the collar and bringing it back with you. I have to admit that I really don't know any more than that. If you can locate the gateway, you should be able to force it to respond to your will. I don't know what you can expect to find on the other side."

Thelvyn was all for leaving at once, considering the seriousness of the situation following the new attacks. Kharendaen would have accompanied him immediately without complaint, but Sir George begged for a night in a real bed, especially since it was already late. Kharendaen was still a bit put out with Solveig over converting her lair into a stable for the griffons. Although she didn't say anything, Thelvyn knew that she preferred to sleep in her true form.

Sir George and the two dragons left Braejr at dawn the next morning, departing early because they had to go out into the street before they could change form without upsetting the griffons. Darius Glantri would be returning to Thyatis that same day, taking Korinn back to Dengar on his way. Darius intended to return once he had reported to Emperor Cornelius. Korinn would do his best to soothe the fears of the dwarves and assure them that the dragons were not preparing to make war upon them.

Still, Korinn doubted that King Daroban would be ready to place any strong faith in the Dragonlord even yet. Most dwarves would not be willing to trust the Dragonlord until that trust was proven by deeds that they could see for themselves, and they would insist that King Daroban continue to prepare for war.

The flight north along the Aalban River to Braastar was a fairly brief one. In the past, during the five years that Kharendaen had served as the companion of the Dragonlord, she had often flown this far on her morning hunt. The hilly region on the eastern side of the river was heavily forested and still quite wild, the only inhabited areas being those close to the city of Braastar. Farther south, the lands east of the river were said to

belong to the elves, although even Kharendaen had seen elves
in those rugged woods only rarely. The lands in the shadows
of the Colossus Mountains were untamed and not entirely
safe, all the more so farther south because of the ominous
proximity of the Broken Lands.

Soon they came to the wooded area south of Braastar where
they had been told to search for the worldgate. The two dragons descended until they were passing just above the treetops,
slowing their speed and drifting on the cool morning wind. Sir
George leaned well out from his saddle, looking down from
Kharendaen's neck.

"How are we supposed to find this thing?" Thelvyn asked.
"You used to fly over this forest often enough. Did you ever
sense anything unusual?"

"Not that I recall," Kharendaen replied. "You yourself
know that there are many places of old magic throughout the
continent. Some are good, some are evil, and some are simply
so old and forgotten that they are nothing more than shadows
of their former power. Dragons sense many such things in
their flights, so many that you must simply ignore those that
do not threaten you. Worldgates are rare things, best left
alone, and they are not commonly connected with the duties
of a cleric. As such, they are outside my own experience."

"If the Fire Wizards are still using it, they must have some
way of getting there," Thelvyn said. "Murodhir said he placed
the collar in a wagon the Fire Wizards had brought, and that
he tried to follow them. The first thing, obviously, is to find
that road."

After drifting back and forth over the trees for a time, they
came upon an old forest road that seemed to be the one that
Murodhir had described. Thelvyn was somewhat surprised,
since he had suspected that the renegade dragon had not been
telling the truth. They followed the road eastward for several
miles as it led deeper into the wild, rugged lands below the
towering Colossus Mountains. When the dragons caught
glimpses of the road through the trees, they saw only a simple
dirt path beaten by the hooves of horses and the wheels of
wagons, obviously little used but not yet overgrown by the forest. Since there were no settlements this far to the east of

Braastar, there was no practical purpose for having a road here.

Thelvyn suddenly felt a faint touch of magic somewhere below, and he turned sharply to circle back. Although the road continued on toward the mountains, he thought they should investigate this place before searching even farther into the wilderness. There was nothing to be seen, not even a small clearing in the forest to show that this might be the place where an entire race of wanderers had arrived from another world. Still, the gate would have been opened from the other side, and the wizards working their magic would have had no way to know where their portal would lead. It would have been just as likely to open here, in the middle of the forest, as anywhere.

"I think this might be it," Thelvyn told his companions.

He descended quickly through a break in the roof of the forest, moving quickly out of the way so that Kharendaen could follow him down. They folded away their wings and cautiously approached the area where they could sense the alien magic, pausing while they were still a safe distance away. The road made a sudden, inexplicable loop to avoid passing beneath the broad branches of a single massive oak tree. A pair of curious carved posts of gray stone, not unlike mileposts, had been set several yards apart beneath the tree, half hidden in the deep grass and the litter of leaves and twigs.

"Your flying skills are improving," Sir George observed, having no apparent interest in leaving his place in Kharendaen's saddle.

"I'm getting a lot of practice," Thelvyn said absently, then moved slowly closer to the pair of small stone posts. "If this is the gate, then those might be markers or even a part of the gateway."

"The gate would have been opened from the other side before they were set in place," his mate explained, staying back in the road with the old knight. "They might have been set to help to direct or focus the worldgate after it was opened. The first question we must deal with is to discover how we can open the gateway."

Thelvyn stepped forward a bit more boldly, standing so that

he was facing the space between the two stones. He sniffed the grass tentatively. "Someone has been through here recently, perhaps within the last few days. A Flaem, I'd say. They have a distinct scent."

"You *are* learning quickly," Kharendaen said approvingly.

"I'm still getting used to having such a sharp sense of smell," Thelvyn said, then turned his head to look at her. "I am not particularly concerned about getting through the gate. Alessa said that it would probably respond to our will, and I am inclined to trust her on that. My concern is for what we may find on the other side. If the traitor Fire Wizards are waiting for us, surely they would have set a trap in case their secret was discovered."

"What kind of trap could harm a dragon?" Sir George asked.

"I have no wish to find out the hard way," Thelvyn said as he moved to one side to examine one of the stone posts. "Considering that they probably have the Collar of the Dragons on the other side of this gateway, I imagine that they must be very concerned about dragons coming through after them."

"We could pitch Sir George through first to see what happens," Kharendaen suggested. "Or we could open the gateway and do what we can to detect any traps."

"Open the gateway," Sir George said as he dropped down from his saddle. "Remember, I was once a master thief. The ability to detect traps is second nature to me."

Thelvyn turned his head to face the area between the two gray stones. A moment later, a great oval of blackness seemed to leap out of the shadows beneath the tree. The far end of the gateway could be seen deep within the oval of blackness, as if it were a tunnel to some other place, but very distant and indistinct, as if viewed through the wrong end of a spyglass. Sir George waved the two dragons back a safe distance, then approached the center of the gateway and stood motionless before it, as if deep in thought.

After a time, Sir George began to approach the gateway very slowly and cautiously, extending his right arm before him as if he were feeling his way with his only remaining hand. Just as he was about to step within the darkness of the gate, some unseen force seemed to suddenly take hold of him and draw him sharply forward. He struggled against the force, only managing to break its hold with considerable effort, so that he was thrown backward into the deep grass. Once he was on the ground, he was content to remain there, rolling over quickly and covering his head. In the next instant, a great flash of flame shot out from the gateway, the edges of the fire curling upward into the branches of the broad oak. Fortunately the tree was too green to burn easily, although it would have soon gone up in a great bloom of flame if Thelvyn hadn't used a spell to suppress the fires licking at the ends of the branches.

"That appears to have been the only trap," Sir George declared, picking himself up and walking back to the center of the gateway. "It's safe to enter now."

True to his word, he stepped into the worldgate and allowed the mysterious force to draw him into the darkness.

Thelvyn muttered an oath under his breath and leaped into the gateway, fearful of what the old knight might face alone. That same force lifted him up and drew him swiftly forward. The sensation was so much like flying that he had to resist the instinct to spread his wings to steady himself. A moment later the darkness drew away, and he found himself in a place utterly different from the one he had left. He stepped aside quickly to allow Kharendaen to come through behind him before he dared to look about.

Only moments earlier he had been standing in the deep forest on a gentle spring morning. Now he stood in a land of harsh, barren stones beneath a night sky. A cold wind swept sheets of stinging desert sand along the ground. He seemed to be standing amid boulders and deep ravines near the rugged shore of some great lake surrounded by sharp, towering peaks and ridges of lifeless mountains. Farther along the rocky shore, perhaps three miles from where he stood, stood the dark, imposing bulk of a fortress of great size, a shadowy collection of high walls and towers that was nearly as large as a town. It was perched atop a high bluff overlooking the lake.

Surely this must be the stronghold of the Fire Wizards of the Flaem. And it seemed that the traitor wizards must be at home, for a few pale lights could be seen in the distant windows. Thelvyn noticed something odd about the lake below the cliffs that supported the dark walls of the fortress. The high waves seemed frozen in place, just as they were about to crest. He saw that the waves were in fact dunes of dull gray sand, partly hidden within a fog of wind-blown dust.

Kharendaen moved close to his side and rubbed her cheek lightly against the side of his long neck. She had in the past remained calm and brave in the face of many dangers they had shared, but this barren land was so hostile that even she found it disquieting. The cold wind whipped around them once again, so that they had to lift their heads above the sheets of blowing sand. Sir George had to climb back into his saddle to escape the worst of it.

"At least we won't have to worry where we left the gate," he said, looking back at the great archway of stone that framed the worldgate. Thelvyn released his will, permitting the gateway to close.

"My powers as a cleric have left me," Kharendaen warned her companions. "I am too far removed from the influence of the Great One."

"I don't feel any different," Thelvyn said, testing his own abilities just to be certain.

"Your powers do not come from the Great One," she explained. "They are your own. Of course, as a dragon, I also command the magic of a sorceress, and to a fairly high degree. Just the same, I fear that you alone might be able to defend us from hostile magic."

"Can we be done with this?" Sir George asked impatiently. "You armor-plated lizards might not mind this sand and cold wind, but I'm not having a very good time. Let's rout those wizards so that we can be back in Braejr in time for dinner."

Routing the Fire Wizards did indeed seem like a very good idea, although Thelvyn lacked his old friend's confidence that things would be so easy. The defenders of the dark fortress probably would have been alerted to anyone coming through their worldgate, especially since Sir George had sprung their trap. The two dragons could have simply flown to the fortress in a direct assault, but they agreed that it was best not to take for granted Alessa Vyledaar's assumption that the stronghold was probably poorly defended. They preferred that any battle be as much as possible on their own terms.

Rather than fly to the distant fortress, they elected to walk, keeping themselves hidden as much as possible in the deep shadows of the ravines and large boulders.

While it was obvious that Sir George cared nothing for the local climate, the wind-driven sand got in the large eyes and ears of the dragons, and they wanted to be done with their quest and leave this place. The land was barren and lifeless, and Thelvyn could hardly imagine the Flaem living in such a desolate place. He wondered if this fierce sandstorm was a rare event or an everyday occurrence.

Suddenly a crushing blow caught Thelvyn in the chest just below his neck, hurtling him over backward into the sand with tremendous force. He had barely caught a glimpse of his attacker, a dark shape that had suddenly leapt out at him from the shadows of a large boulder. Powerful claws caught his own wrists and forced apart his arms while the weight of his adversary held him to the ground. Jaws closed with crushing force on his neck, preventing him from recovering the breath that had been knocked out of him. He had been caught by the only enemy he had not expected to face in this place, for he had seen just enough to know that his attacker was a dragon.

Thelvyn was desperate, yet he was unable to defend himself. He would have surely been dead in a moment, but his opponent had apparently assumed he was alone. Having overcome her own brief moment of surprise, Kharendaen spun around quickly, and the whipping end of her tail caught the strange dragon hard in the side of the face. Alarmed and half stunned by the blow, the dragon released its hold on Thelvyn's neck and drew back, bracing its legs and arching its back as it snarled in rage. But Kharendaen was ready, having spun completely around so that she once again faced the enemy dragon. She caught it with a tremendous blast of flames.

Although he was still panting for breath, Thelvyn seized the opportunity to struggle to his feet. He turned to face their attacker. Although the strange dragon did not seem to have been harmed by Kharendaen's fiery breath, it was still shaken from the blow with her tail and decided that it had had enough. Obviously it had never expected to face two dragons. It turned and ran, leaping across the windswept stones toward the fortress. When it was sure that they were not following, it paused at the top of a hill and turned back, watching them.

"A dragon," Thelvyn panted at last. "Has someone gotten to the collar before us?"

"That is no dragon of our world," Kharendaen said firmly.

She paused and stared as three more dragons suddenly leapt over the top of the hill, and now all four stood in a line, their forms dimly outlined against the dark sky. Then they charged forward, rushing across the stony ground and scattering great clouds of sand from the drifts that had gathered in the lee of the boulders. Thelvyn and Kharendaen turned and ran as fast as they could back toward the worldgate.

"Stay in our tracks," Thelvyn warned as they ran, careful that he did not speak loud enough to be overheard by their pursuers. "If we can lose sight of them, they might follow our tracks the other way and lose us."

They ran as fast as they could, though running was far less natural to a dragon than flight. Within a minute, they came to a ravine that Thelvyn recalled passing through earlier. He stopped suddenly when he saw a deep recess in the wall of dull gray stone to his left, and Kharendaen nearly ran into him from behind. He pushed her desperately in the direction of the dark opening, although she acted confused.

"We can't hide in there," she protested. "We're too large. They're certain to see us."

"Not if we change form," he said quickly. "Hurry before they see us."

Kharendaen shifted form abruptly, so that the straps of her saddle collapsed about her, then hurried into the deep crevice. Thelvyn waited only long enough to toss the saddle in behind her before he changed to his Eldar form, the straps of his harness falling away. He returned to his dragon form just long enough to pass the straps of the harness into the shadows of the recess before changing form yet again.

The crevice was deeper than he had expected, almost forming a small cave in the wall of the ravine. A thick bed of sand had been blown inside the crevice, becoming steadily deeper farther back in the narrow confines of the recess. Thelvyn teleported into the armor of the Dragonlord, which had remained safe and nearly forgotten in its magical place of safekeeping in the months since Thelvyn had become a dragon. At the moment, it was a far better protection than his own powers or his natural weapons as a dragon. He drew the massive enchanted sword and turned to face the opening of the crevice. The enemy dragons rushed past only a moment later, so intent upon the chase that they did not even pause in their leaping stride.

Thelvyn moved cautiously to the opening to look out into the ravine just in time to see the last of the dragons disappear over a distant pile of large, rounded boulders. He stepped outside the opening, teleported out of the enchanted armor, and returned immediately to dragon form, reaching inside the recess to draw out the discarded saddle and harness.

"Quickly now," he told his mate. "They think that we're on our way back to the worldgate. If we hurry, we can continue on to the fortress and retrieve the Collar of the Dragons while they're still waiting for us at the gate."

"But they are sure to be guarding the gate," Kharendaen said as she slipped into the straps of the saddle as quickly as she could. "They know we have to go back that way eventually."

"That's a problem we'll have to face up to later," Thelvyn said quickly. "The power of the Dragonlord should be enough to deal with them. With any luck, they might realize that we've gone to collect the collar and abandon the gate just when we need to use it."

"If there aren't any more dragons at the fortress waiting for us," she commented sourly.

Thelvyn looked up. "What are dragons doing here, anyway? Could renegades have found this place before us?"

Kharendaen shook her head firmly. "No. Those are not dragons of our own world. The one that attacked you seemed at first to be large red, but I saw that the plates of his armor were unnatural, as if they were carved from actual ruby. And his features were different from those of any breed of dragon I know. Perhaps you were never able to see him clearly. I believe that he was not from our own world. Indeed, his appearance was so remarkable that I am not even certain that he is indeed a living dragon, but perhaps some strange creature animated by magic."

"Perhaps so," Thelvyn agreed, then glanced about. "Where's Sir George?"

Kharendaen rolled her eyes. "I must have thrown him off at the place where you were attacked, and then I forgot about him in the confusion. At least these alien dragons seem to have missed him as well."

"We can collect him on the way to the fortress," Thelvyn said. "I only hope he came to no harm during the fight."

CHAPTER FIVE

Thelvyn knew he would have only a brief time to reach the fortress and find the Collar of the Dragons. Sooner or later the four strange dragons would figure out that he and Kharendaen had circled back. He couldn't predict whether they would return at once to the fortress or stay at the gate, knowing that Thelvyn and his companions would have to return there eventually, since it was their only way home.

At least Thelvyn had not been taken completely by surprise. He had suspected that their mission would not be as easy as it had seemed, but he never expected to have to fight dragons in this world. He no longer had any idea who their true enemy was, the Fire Wizards or the alien dragons. Nor could he guess whether all the enemy dragons guarding the fortress were now somewhere in the wild behind him, or if more might still be waiting within the fortress. He would have to be cautious, but he also needed to move as quickly as he dared.

At least he had sprung the first trap prematurely. If all four of the alien dragons had attacked together, neither he nor Kharendaen might have escaped. But who were these strange dragons? Did they obey the Fire Wizards? Had they been expecting him? And had they been behind the recent attacks in his own world? He had many questions and no time to consider the answers, but he suspected that he would soon understand many things much better than he had. And if his suspicions proved true, he would demand an accounting.

Following the tracks in the sand that were already beginning to disappear under the relentless wind, he returned quickly to the place of the first attack. He paused a moment, giving Sir George a chance to see him in the expectation that he would want to be certain of his friends and enemies before showing himself. He also wanted to have a look about in the fearful possibility of finding the old knight's broken body. Sir George showed himself a moment later, emerging from a deep shadow amid the boulders.

"I'm glad you finally remembered me," he complained, hurrying to Kharendaen's side.

"You were probably safer here than you would have been with us," Thelvyn told him. "But we must hurry now. The alien dragons are probably at the worldgate waiting for us to show up, but they won't wait long."

"But won't we have to face them eventually?" Sir George asked as he pulled himself back into his saddle.

"Not if we can help it. I hope that we can raid their fortress while they're guarding the gate, then escape through the gate when they come looking for us at the fortress."

Sir George looked skeptical but said nothing. Thelvyn had to agree with his companion's cynical assessment. Thelvyn knew any number of things could go wrong with his plan, but he still hoped for the best. He paused just long enough to rise up on his hind legs and lift his head to look around. He had wondered if the alien dragons would take to the sky to search, but he saw nothing. The fortress was only a little more than a mile from where they now stood. He hoped to be inside its forbidding walls very soon.

Dragons moved in an ungainly manner on the ground, but they could move along at a very quick pace and surprisingly quietly when they needed to. The land rose slowly as they approached the high point of land where the fortress stood, and

they had to cross an open stretch of ground before the terrain
became even more rugged during the last few hundred yards. At
least it would hide their final approach. Thelvyn was both
startled and immediately suspicious to see that the main gate of
the fortress stood invitingly open, the massive wooden draw-
bridge lowered and the iron-bound portals within drawn back
so that the soft golden light of lamps spilled out into the night.

Indicating that Kharendaen should follow at a safe distance,
he stalked slowly along the last few yards of the road before
inching carefully toward the open gate, creeping like a great
cat, with his legs bent so that his deep chest was almost touching the ground. He edged forward until his slender nose was
almost within the doorway, as if he meant to poke his head
inside. Then, without warning, he suddenly leapt forward,
hurtling himself ahead with an abrupt lunge of his powerful
hind legs. His leap carried him well past any enemy that might
have been lurking just inside the gate.

Thelvyn landed on the smooth stone floor of a vast chamber
just within the gate and turned quickly to look for any enemy
that might attack after that first moment of surprise. The purpose of this chamber was not immediately clear to him. It
seemed to be like a great hall or large reception room rather
than a courtyard or enclosed stables. There were few furnishings, and the light came from magical lamps set along the
walls. Stairs at either side led up to a wide balcony on the second floor, although the stairs were exceptionally wide, long,
and shallow-stepped. But there was no sign of any defender.
Kharendaen slipped through the gate a moment later, lifting
her head to look about.

"Everything here seems to be built to the proportions of
dragons," Thelvyn explained. "Look at those stairs, the doorways, the height of the ceiling. I'm inclined to believe that
those strange dragons are the true masters of this world."

"But Alessa didn't say anything about dragons being native
to this place," Sir George said. "That's not something she
could have simply overlooked. All she said was that this was a
stronghold of the Fire Wizards."

"Yes, she did, didn't she?" Thelvyn agreed thoughtfully.
"Now, why do you suppose she neglected to mention some-

thing like that? We'll have a little talk with Alessa Vyledaar when we return to our own world. But for now, let's locate the collar and get out of here."

"The collar is straight ahead," Kharendaen said, staring intently toward a wide corridor that led directly inward from the gate. "I sense its magic, and I can remember the distinct presence of the powers of the collar from the times when I have seen it in Windreach."

"I'm almost surprised that the collar is still here, considering how the circumstances have changed," Thelvyn said, having sensed the magical presence she described. "Follow me. We still have no idea who else might still be lurking about this place."

"Not traitor Fire Wizards, at least," Sir George commented.

No attempt had been made to hide or safeguard the Collar of the Dragons in any way. Thelvyn followed the sense of its remarkable magic straight into the heart of the fortress, hurrying past many dimly lit chambers of great size. From what he could see, there seemed no doubt this was indeed a fortress or stronghold and nothing more. While everything was built to the scale of dragons, there were few furnishings, with no carpets on the cold stone floor and no tapestries or other decorations hung on the bare walls. Even the dour forts of the dwarves were more hospitable. Thelvyn smiled to himself, thinking that even the Fire Wizards of the Flaem showed better taste.

His search came to an abrupt end as the wide corridor led to the doors of the largest chamber he had seen yet, near the very center of the fortress. Thelvyn slowed to approach the doorway cautiously, then stopped just outside the chamber to look around. This chamber was truly vast in its proportions, the ceiling so high that he could have flown around it in a tight circle. Thelvyn guessed that this was a place where magic was learned and practiced, for great shelves of books lined the walls, and there were couches and reading stands much like those he had seen used by the dragons of Shadowmere. Objects he knew to be associated with magic also stood on the shelves and on stands, and on the walls hung weapons and samples of rare plants and the preserved bodies of strange creatures, the odd trophies of explorations or perhaps conquests.

In the center of the room stood a simple stand of dark stone, nothing more than a long cylinder of smooth marble supported on a heavy wooden frame. Perched atop the stand was the Collar of the Dragons. Thelvyn had never seen the collar nor even heard it described in clear detail, but he knew immediately that this was the object of his quest. The collar was made of large golden plates hinged together so that it could change shape with the movements of a dragon's neck. A row of large, hollow triangular plates along the top were shaped to fit over the ridges of a dragon's crest. The plates of the collar were adorned with a wealth of jewels.

Thelvyn refrained from rushing forward to claim the collar just yet. He had become aware that one of the alien dragons was crouching close to the wall beyond the doorway to his right, ready to spring out as he stepped through. He pretended not to notice, seeming to keep his attention focused on the collar. He waited for a long, tense moment, letting his enemy become apprehensive with uncertainty. Then he darted forward in a sudden, unexpected move, catching the alien dragon by the neck and dragging him down.

Thelvyn almost lost the battle as quickly as he had seized the initial advantage. Having little experience fighting in his dragon form, he was unaware that he should have seized his opponent's neck with his jaws and left his hands free to pin the arms of the other dragon, preventing him from thrashing and pulling free. The alien dragon was about to twist away when Kharendaen rushed forward and hauled back on his tail, pulling him off balance so that Thelvyn could get a better hold. Sir George jumped down from his saddle so that Kharendaen could help subdue their enemy without worrying about his safety.

The alien dragon acted surprised to face two intruders, and he suddenly relented, lying passively on his back and panting heavily. Thelvyn kept his entire weight on his foe's chest to prevent him from using his breath weapon. While the first of the strange dragons they had fought had possessed armor like plates of ruby, this one appeared to be made of amber. He was also larger, fully as big as Thelvyn, who was rather large for a young gold. Nor did he seem to be a creature constructed and animated by magic; they could see that he was definitely a male, and a golem would not have had a sex.

"Talk to us," Thelvyn insisted in a firm voice. "You've obviously had dealings with my world, so I suspect that you must know the language of either the dragons or the Flaem."

"I know your speech," the alien dragon said, speaking the language of the dragons with an odd accent. "I know thee as the Dragonlord who was and the Dragonking who will never be. But I may say nothing to thee."

"That's a very ancient form of the dragon language," Kharendaen said quietly, looking perplexed.

"The gemstone dragons have held no propinquity with thy coarse breed for a long age of my world or thine," their prisoner continued.

"Gemstone Dragons?" Thelvyn repeated. "Are you the masters of this place and not the servants of the Flaem?"

"In truth, are we known as the Masters," the gemstone dragon declared fiercely, seemingly offended by the suggestion that it was a servant of the Flaem. "We serve none but the Overlord. All others here are slaves."

"He's trying to delay us," Kharendaen warned. "He has summoned others to his aid. We dare not waste time on words, as important as it may be to know the answers to these mysteries."

"Nor shall I reveal to thee what thou desires most to know," the alien dragon added, glaring angrily at them. "Although such knowledge will serve thee not, for thou and thy companions will never depart from this place."

Indeed, they had already delayed too long. Thelvyn was taken by complete surprise when a fireball suddenly exploded against his shoulder and the back of his wide neck. His armor spared him any real damage, but it hurt enough to distract him, and the force of the impact knocked him off balance. In the confusion, his captive was able to struggle free. The amber dragon jumped clear and then turned back quickly to attack, leaping forward with its jaws spread wide to gain a fatal hold on Thelvyn's exposed neck. Kharendaen hurtled herself to his defense, darting her head and neck beneath the amber dragon's own neck and then thrusting herself upward with her powerful hind legs to toss her larger opponent heavily onto its back.

Kharendaen pressed her attack before Thelvyn could react, driven by a dragon's boundless fury at seeing her mate harmed. She leapt on the fallen amber dragon while it was still struggling to its feet, striking it so hard in the chest that it was hurled backward. A second fireball exploded against the stone floor where she had stood only a moment before, but she seemed not to notice as she flung herself forward to the attack once more. The amber dragon struck the floor hard, and Kharendaen was on it in an instant, landing on its chest with her entire weight, stunning it. Taking advantage of the amber's momentary helplessness, she lunged forward with her muzzle to gain a death hold on its neck.

Thelvyn had finally recovered from his fall and was rushing to his mate's side, fearful for her safety. Her full attention was focused on the amber dragon, but Thelvyn spotted another alien, a second ruby dragon, entering the chamber through a doorway on the far side of the room, followed by five human figures, who immediately took cover. Even as Thelvyn leapt across the floor, the ruby dragon arched its neck, thrust out its head sharply, and unleashed another fireball that exploded across Kharendaen's left shoulder at its juncture with the wing. Kharendaen immediately released her grip on the amber dragon and roared out in pain. The blow to her wing was a painful one, so that she lifted her head and roared.

This time it was Thelvyn who experienced the dark fury at seeing his mate come to harm. He saw the ruby dragon's companions emerge from hiding to prepare their own attack. From their distinctive, high-collared robes, he guessed they must be Fire Wizards. Desperate to protect his mate, he rushed to Kharendaen's side and turned the heavy armor of his shoulders and back to the attackers. A brief hail of magical missiles caromed harmlessly off his armor, although a couple tore through the delicate sails of his folded wings. Hardly noticing the burning pain in his battle rage, he turned his head away to protect his eyes from the missiles.

The last of the unseen bolts rebounded from his armor, and he immediately lifted his head, anticipating the next attack.

The ruby dragon had drawn back its head and was inhaling air to use its flaming breath. Roaring in fury, Thelvyn leapt up and rushed at the gemstone dragon as fast as he could move, closing his eyes and ducking his head at the last moment as a sustained blast of dragonfire washed over him. A hastily summoned spell to repel flame protected him from the worst of the fiery blast.

He ran headlong into his enemy, using his weight and speed to knock the ruby dragon back toward the stone wall behind him, even though the fierce impact stunned his neck painfully. Keeping his head lowered, he drove his horns deep into the ruby dragon's chest, finally catching between the dragon's ribs. Thelvyn was thrown off balance and crashed hard against the wall, his long neck twisted awkwardly. He righted himself with considerable effort, finally pulling his horns free so that he could press his attack, but the ruby dragon was already dead.

Indeed, the battle was over. Sir George, who always seemed to be forgotten during a fight, had quietly slipped around through the side corridors until he was able to enter the hall behind the traitorous Fire Wizards. While Thelvyn was occupied with the last of the alien dragons, Sir George suddenly appeared and slew a pair of the wizards before they even knew what was happening. The remaining three wizards had found themselves between the flames and Kharendaen's wrath. She was sitting up one her haunches with a wizard clasped tightly in each hand. The third was lying on the ground with her tail firmly over his back.

"I wish I had seen more of that fight," Sir George said. "I'm glad to be in the company of such gentle, peace-loving clerics."

"Dragon clerics," Kharendaen amended coldly, although her words were meant more for her captive wizards. The pair she held looked properly impressed and intimidated; the one under her tail seemed to have fainted. The youngest was a tall man in his middle years with white streaks in the deep red of his hair and beard. The other two wizards were considerably older and rather frail-looking.

"Now, listen carefully, Fire Wizards," Thelvyn said in the Flaemish language. "I will offer you two choices. If you tell me what I want to know, I'll let you run back to your Masters. Otherwise I'll wring your precious necks. Choose now."

"No . . . no, Dragonlord," the youngest of the wizards gasped. All three appeared to have been stricken with the greatest terror. Even the one on the ground had revived and began to cry out. "The Masters will never let us speak. They'll force us to die first, an unspeakably horrible death."

"But your Masters are not here, are they?" Thelvyn asked. "And unfortunately for you, I am. Tell me now, do all Fire Wizards serve their bidding?"

"No!" the youngest wizard shrieked, holding his head as if it were suddenly filled with searing pain. The other two seemed to be stricken as well. "The Masters see and hear all we see and hear, and they punish as swiftly. I can say no more!"

Thelvyn frowned, moved to a reluctant pity. "Let them go."

Kharendaen quickly set the two wizards on the ground, but they were already filled with such intense pain that they sank heavily to their knees, gasping for each labored breath. They could no longer suppress their cries of agony. Their faces began to turn blue, and they started to bleed from their ears, noses, and mouths.

"You . . . you must free our people," the youngest wizard cried out, then screamed as if he had been caught in a blast of dragonfire. With that, all three collapsed in lifeless heaps. The Masters had decided to silence them with a swift death.

"I think I've seen enough of this place," Kharendaen said softly, moving close to her mate's side to rub her cheek against his neck.

"Yes, we've delayed here long enough," Thelvyn agreed as he stepped over to the stand that held the Collar of the Dragons. "Since it seems that the Masters do indeed know what their servants see, then it follows that they must know where we are."

"One moment," Kharendaen interrupted when he sat up on his haunches to reach for the collar. "This hardly seems the proper time and place for the Dragonking to receive the token of his authority. But in such ceremony as we are allowed, permit me as a senior cleric of the Great One to place the Collar of the Dragons upon your neck, so that you will receive that which your father set aside for you in the half-forgotten past."

Moving quickly but deliberately, she released the clasps that held the collar closed and lifted it from its stand. Then, while Thelvyn stood motionless with his long neck extended, she fitted the crest plates of the collar over the ridges of his crest and closed the clasps. The weight felt strange to him, but the plates of the collar adjusted perfectly to follow every movement of his neck. The collar seemed to have been made to fit him. Kharendaen lowered her head to rub her cheek affectionately against the front of his deep chest.

Standing unnoticed to one side, and much to his mortification, Sir George was moved to tears. He alone, a humble mandrake, had been witness to the Dragonking receiving the Collar of the Dragons. It meant more to him than he had expected.

"Ceremony aside, we must be gone," Thelvyn said. "My hope is that the Masters are already on their way here to protect their fortress, leaving the worldgate unguarded. They will most likely return through the main gate, and that means that we must find some other way out of this place. If we must fight again, remember that I cannot change form to become the Dragonlord while I'm wearing the collar."

"From what I've seen, you don't need the Dragonlord anymore," Sir George said as he pulled himself up into Kharendaen's saddle.

"If we become separated again, you go on to the worldgate," Thelvyn told him firmly. "Any attack will most likely be directed at us, and we are better able to deal with it."

Thelvyn led the way through the doorway in the back of the hall. The small, dark back passages where they found themselves did not provide as direct a path as the corridor that had brought them into the heart of the fortress. He had no clear idea where to go at first, except to head outward until they came to a door or other large opening where they could escape from this place. The problem was that the fortress was very large, and he recalled seeing only a few windows and one main gate from the outside. But when he suddenly came upon a wide stairway leading upward, he had an idea of how he could find the quickest and possibly the most unexpected way out. He only had to trust that he would be able to discover a way out of the fortress somewhere above, or they might become trapped in the worst of all places.

They had climbed seven floors when they came upon a wide, dark chamber with windows and a doorway that stood open on the far side to an enclosed balcony. At first Thelvyn didn't recognize the significance of such a place, like a deep pocket cut in the side of the fortress more than a hundred feet above the ground. There was no rail or parapet to offer protection from attack. Kharendaen knew it at once as a ledge where dragons could land or leap out into flight. As such, it wasn't the safest place for them to be.

The two dragons moved cautiously to the front of the ledge and looked out across the desolate lands surrounding the fortress. The ledge faced toward the south, and their sharp eyes were able to locate the stone arch of the worldgate among the boulders and ravines along the top of the cliff above the sea of sand to the east. They could also see several gemstone dragons flying toward the fortress, responding to the invasion of their stronghold. Fortunately they were headed toward the main gate, just as Thelvyn had anticipated, although he noted there were more of the strange dragons than the four that had pursued them earlier.

"As soon as they're within the fortress, we'll have our best chance to escape unseen," Thelvyn said. "We'll need to fly very low and fast. Can you handle that?"

"I am unharmed," Kharendaen insisted. "But I am concerned about you. If all that flame did not burn you, it certainly left you in need of a bath."

"No, I'm not burned," he said, bending his neck to examine himself. The portions of his armor that had endured the blasts of dragonfire did indeed look singed, although it was apparently only soot and dust. "I have a few small holes in the sails of my wings from those magic darts. Is that likely to interfere with my ability to fly?"

"It shouldn't, as long as it's not too painful."

Thelvyn had been too distracted with the business at hand to notice his pain, although the small tears in his wings did sting somewhat. Cautiously he extended his head well out from the opening of the ledge, but he could no longer see any of the gemstone dragons outside the fortress. "We must go, and quickly. Stay close behind me."

His wings half spread, Thelvyn leapt out from the ledge, then nosed over so that he was descending almost straight down, allowing his fall to build speed. Although his experience and trust in flight was growing quickly, he still couldn't do something like this without feeling a rush of fear. At the last possible moment, he spread his wings and came out of his steep dive, hurtling just over the tops of the dunes in the shadow of the cliff. Glancing back briefly, he could see that Kharendaen was following about two lengths beyond the end of his tail, while Sir George was holding on for his very life with the hook on his left wrist caught over the front edge of his saddle.

Thelvyn had forgotten about the fierce winds that constantly howled across the dunes, and the two dragons had to fight the sudden, fitful gusts that threatened to smash them against the face of the cliff. Fortunately their flight was a short one, at least at such a speed. Following his instinctive sense of direction, Thelvyn lifted his wings to catch the wind beneath the sails, lifting him sharply up over the edge of the cliff, where he looked down upon the stone arch below.

He had been hoping that his speed would give his attack the element of complete surprise, since he had guessed that the gemstone dragons wouldn't leave the worldgate completely unguarded. His instinct had proven true; he hurtled up over the cliff almost as close to the stone arch as he could come, rising steeply to give himself room for an attack run before descending sharply toward the pair of alien dragons left to guard the gate. The nearest of the two, a gemstone dragon with armor like jade, saw Thelvyn only at the last moment as he plunged from the sky like an eagle swooping toward its prey, all four of his legs braced stiffly for the impact. The weight of the gold dragon crashed squarely into the middle of the jade dragon's long back, snapping his spine and crushing his ribs. Thelvyn pressed his attack just the same, learning from his recent mistakes, and he lunged forward to take the jade dragon's neck in a death grip.

Kharendaen followed through Thelvyn's attack as best she could, although she could not descend upon the second of the alien dragons as Thelvyn had while she still had Sir George in her saddle. Instead, she passed swiftly just over his head, snapping him in the face with the whip of her tail. The blow was enough to cause the crystal-plated dragon to stagger back on his haunches, holding his face in his claws during that first moment of blinding pain. That gave Kharendaen the time she needed to circle back and land a short distance away, folding her wings tightly while Sir George leapt down from his saddle and ran for the protection of the nearby boulders.

The crystal dragon blinked, finding it hard for a moment to focus on her. She stood facing him a few yards away, crouching low on all fours with her head held low, a deep growl rumbling in her throat. Responding to the threat, the crystal dragon dropped down from his haunches to stand on all fours, but he was still dazed and unsteady. The gold dragon seized the moment to dart in, driving her head beneath his chest and heaving him up across her shoulders, then using the power of her hind legs to toss him backward, a tactic that she had used with success only a short time earlier. Dragons were vulnerable for a moment just after being thrown onto their backs, and that held true for this alien race of dragons as well. The crystal dragon struggled to roll away, but Kharendaen threw her own weight across his chest to pin him down. Unseen and forgotten during the last desperate moments, Thelvyn darted in from behind to crush his neck.

"Ah, thank you," Kharendaen said as she gingerly climbed off the body of the crystal dragon and stepped away. She looked very tired.

"Sir George! It's time to go home," Thelvyn called, then turned his head when the old knight stepped out from behind a boulder. "How can I close this gate so that they can't use it again?"

"You can't," Sir George explained. "You can destroy this particular worldgate, of course. But they can always open another one to take its place."

"I suspect they already have many gates into our world," Thelvyn said. "But it will make me feel better to close this one behind us, even if only for a short time."

"Can you destroy it from the other side?" Kharendaen asked.

"I can try," he said. "Go on through. I'll be just behind you,

I promise you."

He glanced toward the stone arch, and the gate responded at once to his will, a pit of black opening swiftly in the center of that great oval of carved gray stone, showing them a remote view of spring sunlight dancing on grass beneath trees. Kharendaen stepped into the darkness and was drawn away, suddenly emerging as a distant image beneath the trees. She glanced back only briefly, then quickly stepped out of the way.

Alerted by some vague sense of danger, Thelvyn glanced over his shoulder to see at least half a dozen gemstone dragons approaching, driving themselves swiftly over the stony, wind-swept land with long, powerful thrusts of their wings. They would be upon him in moments, which meant that he would be given only one chance to close the worldgate and escape pursuit. He impressed his will even more firmly upon the gateway, until he felt that the innate magic which cause it to function had become his own. Then he stepped into the gate.

The passage fought him from the first moment, not actually pushing him back into the world he had just left but seemingly reluctant to permit him to pass through. For a moment, he felt a twinge of panic as he wondered if the gemstone dragons were trying to hold him back with magic, but then he became increasingly certain that the hesitation was in the gate itself as it fought being torn apart behind him. Now he could only wait and fight back the fear that the passage would collapse too soon and leave him trapped between worlds.

Then, in the final moments, he was suddenly thrust forward with violent force, almost as if the worldgate sought to expel him. He was hurled out into his own world so powerfully that he was tossed a short distance across the grass beneath the trees before he lost his balance and fell heavily. A great flash of flames exploded just over his head, and fragments of broken stone were hurtled through the forest for nearly a hundred yards. The collapse of the worldgate had shattered the stone arch, drawing the debris through the gate as it closed.

Thelvyn opened his eyes and looked upward, not yet daring to move. The large oak that stood over what had been this end of the worldgate had been caught in the flash of fire, and the leaves of the nearest branches were already burning furiously.

Kharendaen cast a spell to suppress the flame. After this second assault on it, the tree was beginning to look the worse for wear. Thelvyn sat up on his haunches and shook his head, then glanced back at his mate. Fortunately she had stepped to one side of the worldgate to make room for his arrival, and the destruction had missed her.

"Well, it worked," Sir George said as he dropped down from his saddle. He looked no less worn and abused than the two dragons.

Thelvyn took a deep breath and sighed heavily. "I believe we should remain here for a time, to be certain that the gemstone dragons don't attempt to pass through into our world."

"I haven't the strength to fly anywhere in any event," Kharendaen agreed, sitting back on her tail with her long neck sagging wearily.

"If I could find the strength, I'd hunt down Alessa Vyledaar and skin her alive with a dull knife," Thelvyn said darkly, his ears laid back. Then he shrugged helplessly. "Not that it matters. Considering what we saw of those wizards that attacked us, my suspicion is that she had no will of her own."

"I wasn't certain if that wizard was trying to answer your question or if he was simply crying out," Kharendaen said as they walked slowly together to sit in the shade of a nearby tree. "Clearly the wizards were under the will of the strange dragons they call the Masters. But didn't he say not all the wizards are under their command?"

"He did say that," Thelvyn replied. "I'm sure Byen Kalestraan was under their influence as well, whether he was aware of it or not. That alone now explains his strange, often contradictory actions, which I could never begin to understand before. I think the destruction of so many of the wizards and the escape of the rest brought a serious interruption to the schemes of the Masters, since they no longer had anyone in Braejr under their influence. As near as I can tell, Alessa didn't come under their control until fairly recently, just in time to lead us into a trap they had prepared for us."

"How do you figure that?" Sir George asked. He was still shaking sand out of his clothes.

"Because that explains the other mystery," Thelvyn said.

"Solveig swore to us that Alessa had come over to our side, and I have no reason to doubt Solveig's judgment. But later we found Alessa to be as suspicious and sneaky as any Fire Wizard ever was."

"But why didn't they try to control us?" Sir George wondered.

"The only reason I can think of is that we are all three dragon-kin," Thelvyn said, looking perplexed. "I find myself with certain suspicions about the true history of the Flaem. I suspect that some time in the distant past, they wandered into the world of the gemstone dragons—or were brought there—and came under the influence of the Masters. And I also suspect that the Flaem didn't continue on into our own world through their own will. I think they were sent by the Masters as advance scouts to establish a presence, to secure and evaluate the power of the Radiance, and to evaluate the strength of their enemies in our world."

Kharendaen shook her head slowly from side to side. "The Masters knew an ancient form of the language of the dragons. Obviously they had some past contact with our world long ago."

"Can you guess how long?" Thelvyn asked.

"Not accurately," she admitted. "At least three thousand years ago. Possibly as long ago as five thousand years or more."

"That is bothersome," Thelvyn agreed as he stared aimlessly at the ground, lost in thought. He frowned. "That leads me to wonder if the gemstone dragons were once related to the dragons of our own world, but then they were changed by the magic of an alien world. Except for their rather remarkable armor, their general shape was more or less the same as ours."

"That seems unlikely, but not impossible," Kharendaen said, obviously troubled by the idea. "I think they've changed too much in a short time for that to be likely. Unless something very strange has happened to them."

"Obviously the Masters know a great deal about the dragons of Mystara," Sir George commented. "Since it was never used in any way, was the theft of the collar meant primarily to forestall the coming of the Dragonking? That dragon did refer to you as 'the Dragonlord who was and the Dragonking who never will be,' at least if his kind has their way. And they directed all of Byen Kalestraan's efforts to destroying you. It seems obvious to me that they want to prevent you from uniting the dragons. Why? Because the dragons alone have the power to stave off their invasion of our world?"

"That seems obvious now," Kharendaen agreed. "The Great One himself warned us of this, didn't he? He said that the Dragonking alone could unite the dragons against an enemy only they can fight. It would seem that he has anticipated the coming of the Masters since he created the Collar of the Dragons for the Dragonking more than three thousand years ago, which is also about the time the gemstone dragons might have come into our world."

"We're beginning to understand a lot of things now," Thelvyn said. "We seem to have two choices now that I have the Collar of the Dragons and can claim the authority of the Dragonking. Should we go at once to Windreach and have the dragons begin preparations for war immediately? Or should we go back to Braejr while we're still so near, to reveal the conspiracy of the Masters, break their control of the Flaem, and set to rest the fears that the recent attacks were the work of dragons?"

"I suggest that we go to Windreach at once," Kharendaen said. "The time has come for the Dragonking to establish his own following, so that you will have the power and authority to face the Masters. And I believe that we should be very sure of ourselves before we return to Braejr. The Masters have used the Flaem to surprise us once already. Perhaps the Great One will speak to us again and tell us more that we should know."

Thelvyn nodded, if with some misgivings over facing the dragons in their own element. But that was a confrontation he could not avoid much longer, now that matters had suddenly become so desperate.

"Then we go on to Windreach tonight. But first we must rest and hunt. I'm so hungry I could eat a horse," he commented, then realized what he had said. He turned his head to glare at Sir George. "Don't you dare say a word."

The old knight closed his mouth and tried to look innocent.

CHAPTER SIX

Marthaen opened one eye reluctantly, then closed it again and turned his head away. It was still the middle of the night, and he was in no mood to drag himself out of his warm bed. But Daresha, his mate, pushed at him again, and he opened his eyes to see her narrow face peering down at him.

"Dragons are landing on your ledge," she explained.

"Tell them to come back in the morning," he complained sleepily.

"Tell them yourself," Daresha insisted, pushing at him even more insistently. "Get up, you lazy lizard. The world is about to go to war again. Would someone come knocking at your door at such a time if it weren't urgent?"

Indeed, there came an impatient knocking at the door at almost that same moment. Marthaen lifted his head and yawned hugely, then climbed out of his bed and ambled into the main chamber of his lair. He opened the back door just enough to peer out onto the ledge, and he was rather startled to see Sir George Kirbey staring back at him.

"Oh, honestly," the dragon muttered, sighing. "You're the

last person I expected to find loitering on my ledge. I suppose your companions must be just behind you."

Marthaen stepped back so Sir George could hurry inside with his travel bags, followed closely by Kharendaen and Thelvyn. In spite of his outwardly inhospitable mood, Marthaen recognized it was important to get the Dragonking inside before he was seen. Kharendaen paused a moment to rub her cheek against her brother's, as if trying to put him in a better humor before she stepped quickly aside. Thelvyn entered last, bearing himself with the pride and dignity befitting the king of the dragons. Marthaen was so startled to see Thelvyn wearing the Collar of the Dragons that he could only stare.

"Dragonking," Daresha breathed softly from the doorway leading into the bedroom. She lowered her head in a gesture of respect.

"So you found the collar," Marthaen said, then hurried to close the door. "I know it's the middle of the night, but did you have to come here to Windreach unannounced and wearing the thing like some kind of conqueror?"

"I don't seem to have a pocket large enough to carry it," Thelvyn remarked.

"Still, the dragons are going to have to become accustomed to the idea that there really is a Dragonking before they can easily accept your being here," Marthaen said. "I realize Jherdar already knows you have been seeking the collar, but I would have preferred some time after you found it for him to get used to the idea and to try to gain his support before you came here."

"I agree with what you say," Thelvyn said. "But things have changed, and matters are far more desperate than you know."

"I'm aware of the attacks that appear to have been by dragons," the First Speaker answered impatiently. "That makes our situation here all the more uncertain. The dragons are ready to explode into war as it is, and your sudden appearance is only going to upset things all the more."

"I no longer have the luxury of time," Thelvyn said firmly, speaking with a calm authority that put an end to the disagreement. "I'm not here for the sake of power or fame. I have always been a protector, and that is all I remain."

Marthaen paused as he suddenly understood. He bowed his own head as a sign of respect. Thelvyn was no longer the awkward outcast under Marthaen's guidance as he had been since first becoming a dragon the previous year. He was now the Dragonking, wise and confident, and he meant to claim the authority that was his right. He might trust Marthaen as his advisor and friend, but he was now the master.

"There is much that you do not yet know," Thelvyn told him. "The warning that we received from the Great One has proven true. Our world faces a war that only the dragons can fight, and we must move quickly. Kharendaen and I fought and slew four dragons to claim the collar."

"Dragons?" Marthaen looked up sharply, alarmed. "Renegades?"

"We found the Collar of the Dragons in another world, one where the Flaem dwelt for a time before coming here," he explained. "We found it in the possession of dragons who were not of our own race."

Thelvyn and Kharendaen quickly related the events of their brief journey into the world of the Masters, telling Marthaen all that they knew, all that they could surmise or even only suspected about the gemstone dragons. The older dragon listened in silence, staring at the ground with his ears laid back.

"I understand your concern," he admitted when they were done. "And I agree that these strange dragons must have had some contact with our own people at some time in the distant past. But if the clerics remember nothing of such a thing, then I do not know what to say."

"I will speak with Saerna about it as soon as I can," Kharendaen said. "She is the oldest living dragon in the world. Perhaps there are some things she might recall that are not recorded in any book, some legend out of the days of her own childhood about strange dragons. Anything might help."

"It would help more if the Great One would speak with me plainly on this matter," Thelvyn said. "He obviously knows much more than we do."

"Of course, we can't count on his being willing or able to do that," Marthaen said, then looked up at the Dragonking. "I share your need for haste, but I still recommend some caution.

Many of the leaders among the dragons may still be reluctant to give you their support if you declare yourself Dragonking in one breath and call upon them to follow you into war with the next. Especially since you ask them to go to war in defense of a world that fears and rejects them. I will call them to parliament in the morning to give them a brief time to consider what has happened."

Thelvyn had to agree that Marthaen's plan made sense, partly because he no longer had the strength to argue the matter any further. The time that he and his companions had spent in the world of the Masters had been quite brief, actually little more than an hour, yet both Kharendaen and he were very tired from their battles with the alien dragons. They had rested only a brief time before making the desperate flight all the way from the Highlands to Windreach in distant Norwald, beginning that long journey just after noon and arriving a couple of hours after midnight.

Unfortunately, Marthaen was at something of a loss to know where he could keep them in hiding for the remainder of the night. Kharendaen hadn't kept a lair of her own in Windreach for more than a hundred years. As it turned out, Daresha was honored to have the Dragonking and his mate spend the night in her lair, which was only a short walk through the deep inner passages of the ring wall of the city. Sir George had to be content with a cushion thrown on the floor of the main chamber of the lair, but a dragon-sized cushion was easily large enough to serve him for a bed.

The two dragons were awakened by a knock at the inner door the next morning, fortunately not too early. They were both a bit surprised to find that Sir George had gone out somewhere; he had caught some sleep in the saddle during their journey, and had arrived not much the worse for wear. Since he was gone already, they could only hope that he would be able to keep himself out of trouble. It seemed best for Thelvyn to remain discreet about his own presence in the city, so it was Kharendaen who went to open the door.

Their visitors were not dragons but elves, of a race that Thelvyn had once believed to be his own. They were both males and quite tall for elves, or even humans, with powerful builds, black hair, large, dark eyes, and slightly pointed ears. He realized immediately that they must be Eldar, the most ancient race of elves in the world. He had worn their form until the time when he had first taken his true form as a dragon. The younger of the two was pushing a large cart that bore trays of roasted meat, bread, cheese, and drink.

"Your brother Marthaen sent us," the older one explained simply. "We know of your secrets and will respect them."

Kharendaen stepped aside, and the two Eldar entered, bringing in the cart. They paused a moment and bowed in deep respect when they saw Thelvyn farther back in the room, recognizing him even though he no longer wore the Collar of the Dragons. The younger elf bowed once more, this time to them all, then departed in silence.

"I am the wizard Alendhae, a longtime friend of Marthaen's," the remaining Eldar explained. "I am also honored to serve from time to time as his advisor, so he thought it best to send me to attend to your needs while he is occupied with the parliament."

"Yes, I remember you," Kharendaen said. "I was very young when I last saw you. It must have been nearly a hundred and fifty years ago."

"Gold lady, you are still very young," Alendhae told her with the gentle amusement of the old. He turned to Thelvyn. "Dragonking, I am of the Eldar, the ancestors of the elves. Perhaps you have heard of us."

"I had not heard of the Eldar until recently," he said. "But in a way, I know your people well, since I wore the body of your people until recently. You are all but forgotten in the outside world."

"Yes, even the elves remember us only as a vague legend of their forgotten past," Alendhae said sadly. "We are all that is left of a dying race. There are very few of us remaining, but it has been thus for a very long time. All that remains of our people have lived here in Windreach since the founding of the city three thousand years ago."

"But why do you choose to live with the dragons?" Thelvyn asked.

"Don't you know?" Alendhae asked. "It is said that there is

a very ancient tie between the Eldar and the dragons."

Alendhae insisted upon serving the two dragons before he related the legend of the Eldar and the origin of the dragons, setting their trays before them. While they sat and ate, he poured them large cups of fruit wine as he began the tale.

"It is a very ancient legend and may or may not be true," he began. "The Eldar lived many thousands of years ago. We built great kingdoms of our own at a time when we were alone in the world, long before the coming of men or dwarves. Ours was a race of powerful wizards, far stronger in our magic than the modern elves. In time we became beings partly of magic and partly mortal, like the dragons themselves.

"Then, at the very height of our civilization, our race became so strong in magic, our wizards so infused with power, that we could no longer contain the magic within ourselves. A time of great turmoil came upon us, and our entire race was ripped asunder by our own magic. Many of our more powerful magic-users evolved into the race of dragons, that being the reason why the higher dragon forms retain the ability to assume the Eldar form, just as many Eldar can take the form of a small gray dragon. This would also seem to explain the origin of the drakes, an intermediate form.

"But while a part of our people became dragons, the magic was ripped away from other members of our race, and those became the modern elves, diminished in power, in stature, and in their span of years, for modern elves live only a few hundred years, while the Eldar, like the dragons, live for thousands. A small core of our race remained unchanged from what we were before, and that core still survives here in Windreach. I cannot say if this legend has any truth, although there is much evidence to support it. Both the draconic and elven inhabitants of Windreach are very fond of this tale, and most prefer to believe it, since it binds the civilized dragons and the Eldar in almost brotherly ties."

"The Great One himself acknowledges the strong possibility of that tie, although it happened long before he became an Immortal," Kharendaen added. "But the ties between the dragons and the elves remain until this day. That is why many elves recognize the patronage of the Great One and some even serve as his clerics. It is also why the dragons stay out of the lands and the affairs of the elves. Even the renegades usually leave them alone."

Once the two dragons had eaten, Alendhae led them to the bathing pools deeper within the mountain. Each of the pools was more than large enough to hold three or four dragons, so there was plenty of room for the two of them to recline in ease. Kharendaen immediately submerged herself up to her nose, but Thelvyn lowered himself gingerly into the steaming water. The gentle warmth of the water needed several minutes before it began to penetrate his tough armor, soothing muscles that still felt the strain of his recent battles and long flights.

Thelvyn had never before had a warm bath, at least not as a dragon. He could never have imagined heating enough water, so he had resigned himself to cold dips in icy mountain lakes. While life encased in armor had been less bothersome than he had feared, having a hide that could turn arrows was still uncomfortable, and the warm bath was very soothing. After some time, he retreated to a corner of the pool where the water was deep enough for him to sit up on his haunches with his head just above the water. Kharendaen drifted over and pressed herself close against him. He gathered her in his arms and held her tightly.

"Do you still have any complaints about being a dragon?" she asked.

"Did I ever complain?" he asked in turn. "It meant being with you. I always thought you were the most beautiful, graceful lady I had ever seen. Of course, such feelings were a matter of some confusion to me for the five years we were together before I knew that I was a dragon."

Kharendaen smiled teasingly. "Even if I don't have long legs like Solveig?"

"Well, she doesn't have your long neck."

Thelvyn suddenly raised his head and lifted his ears, turning his head as if listening to some distant voice. Kharendaen fell silent, and she lifted her own ears as if she, too, could catch the sound of that voice, even if she did not understand the words.

"We are called," Thelvyn said at last, turning to face his

mate. "There is much that the Great One wants me to know before I face the Parliament of Dragons. Sir George is requested to come as well. I wonder where he has gone off to."

"He went out early to bathe," Alendhae answered, approaching from where he had been standing near the door. "He is with my own people presently, but he can be summoned at once."

The dragons pulled themselves out of the pool and dried themselves quickly before they hurried back to Daresha's lair. Kharendaen hastened to slip back into her saddle, while Thelvyn thought it best to put on the Collar of the Dragons. By the time they were ready to leave, Sir George was escorted in by a couple of Eldar who had been assigned to serve him.

"Where are we going?" he asked as he collected his hat and climbed into the saddle.

"We are on our way to meet with the Great One," Thelvyn said, then paused and looked perplexed. "But where? I just realized that I have no idea where we should go."

"The Great One's sacred place here in Windreach is at the top of his own hall," Kharendaen explained, glancing over her shoulder at Sir George. "You might not be very happy about going there, but we will try to keep you safe."

"Try?" Sir George asked, but the dragons were already on their way out to the ledge before he could question her further.

They paused for a moment on the ledge, taking a moment to look about. This was Thelvyn's first chance to have a good look at the hidden city of Windreach, since they had arrived late the previous night. Most of the lairs of the dragons who lived or regularly visited the city were located along the steep inner wall of the dead volcano, and he could see at least a couple of thousand ledges like the one where they now stood. The lairs themselves seemed draconic enough, but the great city, with its many tall buildings in the floor of the volcano, was far different from anything he had expected.

Later, when he had the time for a tour of Windreach, he would learn the names and functions of many of the buildings he saw. In one part of the city stood perhaps the largest university in all the world, in size if not in actual attendance, which was also a school of magic, where wizards of other races would have given all they had to study under dragon mages who knew disciplines of magic far in advance of their own, if they had only known that such a place even existed. There was a great library with books that had been gathered for thousands of years, many from the time before the Rain of Fire, ancient texts from a hundred or more nations that had risen and fallen again throughout history, some already forgotten to the outside world.

Perhaps what surprised Thelvyn most, at least at first, was that Windreach, like all cities, had large areas devoted to shops and markets. The elves of Wendar in the wild, forested mountains surrounding Windreach were under the protection of the dragons and traded with them freely, not only food but also wood, metals, and gems for a variety of uses. Dragon craftsmen kept workrooms throughout many parts of the city, where they made such things as furnishings for their lairs, weapons and leather harnesses, and other goods that dragons needed or fancied. One of the most common professions practiced here was the making of jewelry, since dragons throughout the world often brought parts of their treasures here to be reworked from human, elvish, or dwarvish forms into jewelry of their own styles and proportions. The jewelers of Windreach were among the most skilled in the world, many having practiced their art for hundreds of years.

Several hundred dragons were in residence at Windreach at all times. Due to the wishes of the Great One, even the shape-changing dragons remained in draconic form at all times while they were here. Windreach was a place of rare honor and trust among the dragons. Many of the permanent residents kept their hoards here under only a minimum of security, without fear of theft, and fights or duels between dragons were strictly forbidden. Only rare battles of supreme political dominance were tolerated, and those fights had to be taken outside the city.

Drakes and other dragon-kin were permitted as long as they were of intelligent breeds, but the dragon-kin typically found the company of true dragons intimidating. Renegade dragons were not trusted and were never permitted; they would almost certainly be slain if they tried to enter, especially after the theft of the Collar of the Dragons, for dragons who did not conform to draconic law were not tolerated. No other races were permitted. Humans, elves, dwarves, gnomes, and halflings approaching under innocent circumstances would be turned away, while thieves and mercenary adventurers and any evil humanoids would be slain. The only exception was the Eldar. The wild elves of Wendar were left to themselves.

The most outstanding and remarkable feature in all of Windreach was the Hall of the Great One. Standing more than twelve hundred feet above the floor of the extinct volcano, that towering edifice of smooth white stone was the tallest in all the world. The two dragons leapt out from the ledge, passing over the roofs of the city as they gathered speed before they began to climb steeply in a wide circle around the Hall of the Great One. The lowest floors comprised the Treasury of the Dragons, where the most important and valuable artifacts and treasures of their race had been gathered through the years. The Collar of the Dragons, the greatest of all their heirlooms, had been kept there through the centuries since the time of the founding of Windreach. Several floors above the treasury were occupied by the Parliament of the Dragons, including the private chambers of the members of the parliament.

The entire top half of the Hall of the Great One had been reserved as the stronghold of his clerics, with their own lairs and their places of training and research. Kharendaen led the way, climbing higher and higher until they were far above the outer wall of the city. The winds here were almost always strong, so that the two dragons had to fight increasingly fierce crosswinds. They took special care not to be thrown against the wall of the great building. Level after level, the Hall of the Great One became steadily narrower as they continued to climb, their circle becoming tighter and tighter.

Soon they neared the top, flying swiftly in and out between the highest of the great spires and towers of the Hall of the Great One. As she moved nearer to a group of the highest towers, Kharendaen suddenly darted toward a wide ledge of white stone set in the outer wall just beneath the steep, cone-shaped roof of the highest tower. She turned sharply to land on the ledge, which was barely large enough for Thelvyn to land as well. He made a desperate leap at the other end. The ledge was nothing more than a simple shelf of smooth stone, without rail or parapet. There was a small recessed area in the back of the ledge that offered slight protection from the treacherous winds, with a large door leading into the tower, flanked by large glass windows.

Sir George dropped down from his saddle and retreated into the minimal safety of the recess, as far from the edge as he could get. The bulk of the two dragons offered him some protection from the cold wind, which threatened to pull them from the ledge. Even the dragons had to fold their wings quickly and crouch low.

Moving cautiously, Kharendaen approached the door. There was no handle or latch visible on the outside, not even a keyhole, although the door began to open by itself as she stood before it. They passed through the door into a chamber of vast size, large enough that it filled that entire level of the tower, although its exact proportions were difficult to gauge. Most of the hall was filled with deep shadows, as dark as night, broken by shafts of light that poured in from a few widely spaced windows. Great columns of smooth, white stone stood like ghostly sentries at the edge of the darkness. The dragons slowly descended the wide steps into a large recessed portion in the center, the only area that was well lighted.

"Come along, Sir George," a voice said. "There is nothing to fear."

They turned abruptly to see that the Great One awaited them patiently on a small area like a simple stage above the recessed area where they now stood. He appeared not in his more authoritative guise of the great three-headed dragon, but in his less threatening form of an older dragon of some small, dull goldish gray breed that had long since disappeared from the world. This form was probably close to what his appearance had been in life. Sir George made a helpless gesture and descended the steps to join his companions.

"You have found the collar and unmasked your true enemies," the Great One began. "Indeed, you could not have done better. Unfortunately, the gemstone dragons will have learned from this that they do not dare take the Dragonking lightly. Nor are they likely to underestimate the dragons of this world, whom they have looked upon as far beneath themselves. I fear that you must expect them to be better prepared in the future."

"You seem to know a great deal," Thelvyn observed.

"Do not expect that I have special knowledge of such things," the Great One explained. "I know only what you know, what I have heard you say between yourselves and to Marthaen, for I am often with you even if you cannot see me. I know these gemstone dragons, for I fought them long ago. But my awareness cannot extend into their world."

"But there was obviously much that you knew or expected," Thelvyn said, with a note of impatience. "You could have spoken a bit more plainly when we talked with you in Silvermist."

"Yes, I could have," he agreed. "Indeed, I would have preferred to have given you better warning of what to expect. But I have not been acting alone in preparing the champion who will defend our world. Many Immortals are allied to my cause, but it has always been necessary for us to act circumspectly, remaining cautious of the limitations that we must respect to maintain the balances of good and evil."

"It has always been best for us to proceed cautiously in dealing with mortals," a woman's deep, resonant voice spoke from out of the darkness. The voice was that of the Immortal Terra, although the dragons could see only an indistinct form standing in the deepest shadows. "Thelvyn, you must not forget that you are still young, especially for one of your race. I still believe that it was better to be safe with you."

"Safe?" Thelvyn asked incredulously, although his two companions were obviously apprehensive that he was being so direct with the Immortals. "You allowed us to be sent completely unprepared into a stronghold of the gemstone dragons."

"The time has come when I can speak plainly to you on this matter," the Great One said. "All that you know and have concluded about the gemstone dragons is correct, although the situation is far more complex than you may think. For one thing, although they are called the Masters, they are not the true masters behind these events."

"One of them said the gemstone dragons serve someone called the Overlord," Thelvyn replied. "Unfortunately, I do not know anything more."

"Nor do I. They do indeed control Alessa Vyledaar, and as you suspected, they achieved that control only recently. Nor is she the only one in this world whose will they control. But you must be aware that they can control the will of any dragon just as they controlled Murodhir and his henchmen, although it was the traitor, Byen Kalestraan, who helped the Masters entrap them. You must also be aware that they have controlled the Flaemish people in the past, and it is within their power to seize control of the Flaem once again. Fortunately, they are not yet that strong in this world."

"But who are the gemstone dragons?" Thelvyn asked. "They know an ancient version of the language of the dragons, so we suspect they must have had some contact with this world long ago. Is it possible this isn't the first time that they have tried to conquer Mystara?"

"Indeed it is not the first time," the Great One answered. "Have you been told of the Eldar and the origin of the dragons? That will help you to better understand the gemstone dragons."

The Great One paused a moment to recline along the length of the stage, still facing them. "The time has come that you should learn the true history of the first Dragonlord, which even the dragons do not know. For in the time of ancient Blackmoor, there was no dragon Immortal to guide and protect the dragons. The dragons had been gaining in power and in knowledge, and their breeds continued to evolve, becoming larger and wiser. Magic became even more a part of their very being.

"In this time, there was a fellowship of powerful dragon sorcerers who had observed the slow advancement of their race and wished to gather and direct the magic they would need to accelerate that natural process. They wished to evolve into higher forms rather than be content to wait for their descendants to inherit the power and wisdom that would be their birthright."

The Great One paused a moment, turning his head to look away. "I must confess that I was a part of their band at first, for I was a cleric in the service of the Immortal Terra, and I supported anything that might benefit the dragons. At first their desires were pure and noble. But in time they came to believe that they could become Immortals, and that became their ultimate goal. I argued with them, warning them that they expected too much, but they would not listen. And so I withdrew from their company.

"In time, these dragon sorcerers worked great magic upon themselves, but their experiment failed. They did not become true Immortals but were instead transformed into the gemstone dragons, far more powerful than any dragon that lived at that time, even more powerful that most modern golds and reds. Believing that they had the right as the most powerful beings in the world to rule the world, they began to force lesser nations to their will. Eventually they made war upon Blackmoor.

"That was when the first misunderstanding began, since the men of Blackmoor believed that all dragons were at war with them, not understanding that it was only the gemstone dragons. And Blackmoor was slowly being defeated, so that in desperation they sought to create a weapon the dragons could not hope to fight. Eventually the wizards of Blackmoor created the first Dragonlord, who mistakenly made war upon all dragons and nearly destroyed them, while the gemstone dragons withdrew and continued their own war in secret."

The Great One rose, sitting up on his haunches as if the memory of that time still filled him with concern. "At that time, the Immortals, especially Terra, became convinced they must intervene to save the dragons and stop the war. I had withdrawn to the ancient forests as a cleric of Terra. Terra conceived a plan that seemed to her the only hope to put an end to the conflict. Terra sponsored me, and in a relatively short time, she succeeded in making me the first dragon Immortal. To make a long story short, I eventually defeated the first Dragonlord, that being the only way to force him to listen, and then we joined forces together with the wizards of Blackmoor against the gemstone dragons. Subsequently the gemstone dragons were defeated and escaped through a world gate.

"We were aware from the first that the gemstone dragons had only retreated, and we suspected that they would withdraw for a time to gather new strength, then return. We had to be certain that the dragons would always be ready to face them. The wizards of Blackmoor had created the Collar of the Dragons, and I created a prophecy so that, if the gemstone dragons did indeed return, my chosen hero could use the collar to claim the unquestioned support of all dragons."

"I would not yet call their support unquestioned," Thelvyn remarked.

"No, I fear not," the Great One agreed regretfully. "We had always anticipated that when the time came, both a Dragonking and the new Dragonlord would be chosen, but unforeseen problems necessitated that you should be both Dragonking and Dragonlord. I had been suspicious of the Flaem since they first came to Mystara. When I became certain that they were secret agents of the gemstone dragons, and after enlisting the aide of Terra and other sympathetic Immortals, I made the arrangements to bring my chosen hero into the world. You possess nearly Immortal powers: those that you have inherited from me, the most powerful enchantments of ancient Blackmoor, and the authority of the Dragonking.

"Ever since the gemstone dragons left our world, they have been regaining their strength, gathering new powers, and collecting slaves from many worlds. They must have captured the Flaem during their wanderings from world to world, and they hoped to use the rivalry between the Flaem and the Alphatians as the means to prepare for their invasion of Mystara and to secure the power of the Radiance. They had known of the Radiance for some time, and were disappointed to find that its power is quite limited in range."

The Great One paused and rose to his hind legs so that he stood above them. "Sir George Kirbey, I summon you to stand before me."

For a moment, Sir George looked like a child who had been caught doing something wrong. The two dragons stepped aside so that he could approach the Great One, but he did so with obvious reluctance and considerable apprehension.

"Do not fear," the Great One said. "You have served very well indeed, but you represent a problem as you are. You cannot accompany Thelvyn among the dragons in human form, nor are you of much use as a flightless drake. Therefore I have a gift for you, which you may consider payment for services above and beyond what was expected."

Suddenly Sir George became aware of a strange sensation

in his left arm, at the end of his wrist, where his hand had been
severed long ago. The feeling was not one of actual pain but
rather an intense tingling, a nagging sensation such as had
often driven him to distraction in the first months after he had
lost his hand. Fearful that something was wrong, he struggled
to release the buckles and pull loose the straps that held the
leather cuff and its attached hook to his wrist. Then, as he
watched in amazement, the end of his arm began to grow
longer, eventually forming a new hand. Once the moment of
discomfort had passed, he watched his hand with wonder and
delight as it slowly began to respond to his will.

"Now you must go," the Great One said to Thelvyn. "The
parliament is expecting you. Now is the time to declare yourself as the rightful Dragonking. Be resolute in your claim, for
the time of compromise is past."

* * * * *

Marthaen stood at the front of his ledge before the assembled
parliament, watching the dragons as they argued fiercely among
themselves. As First Speaker, he knew he should do something
to maintain order, but the parliament was almost beyond his
control, and he thought it best to allow the members to vent their
fury before he called them back to order. He was aware of his
sister Kharendaen standing behind him; he had tried his best to
ignore her for as long as he could.

But he knew that he would be forced to relent eventually.
At last he turned and followed Kharendaen down the short
passage from his ledge to the main corridor beyond. Thelvyn
waited there, boldly wearing the Collar of the Dragons within
the Hall of the Great One itself. Sir George Kirbey stood
nearby, looking both startled and very pleased with himself at
the same time.

"I don't know if this is the proper time," Marthaen said
before any of the others could speak. "As I expected, the dragons are hesitant. They still fear the Dragonking, who is still
also the Dragonlord and to them their most dangerous enemy.
And they are reluctant to go to war in the defense of others.
Since the Masters appear to be dragon-kin, that also causes

them some concern. I'm afraid I will need more time to convince them to accept you as Dragonking."

"I'm not sure you could ever convince them," Thelvyn replied. "If they are ever going to accept my leadership, it will have to be me who convinces them."

"Perhaps so," Marthaen agreed with great reluctance. "Go down the stairs and follow the passage almost directly below where we stand. That will lead you out onto the floor of the Hall of Parliament and directly to the speaker's dais. You can address the parliament from there."

He turned and strode back out onto his ledge, leaving Thelvyn to find his way to the parliament floor. The dragons were still arguing furiously, and Marthaen despaired of ever getting them to set aside their fear and suspicion long enough to listen. But time had become too critical for such nonsense. If the Immortals had invested so much effort in making Thelvyn Fox-Eyes the Dragonking, he was not about to argue.

"Silence!" he declared, startling the dragons. They turned to stare at him. "Silence, I say! I demand that you stop chattering and screaming like frightened wyverns and maintain the dignity and wisdom that befits this assembly."

The dragons muttered among themselves but finally fell silent, staring in astonishment when they saw Thelvyn step out onto the floor below them and advance toward the speaker's dais. He was wearing the Collar of the Dragons, and that by itself was enough to leave them shaken and uncertain. One of the oldest and most important legends of their people had indeed come to life, for the Dragonking stood before them. Thelvyn carried himself with the supreme dignity and confidence that dragons instinctively respected, as if to prove that he had earned the right to wear the collar.

Marthaen sat back on his haunches, smiling to himself with grim satisfaction. Now that they could actually see Thelvyn standing before them, the dragons could see that the legend of the Dragonking was no longer a matter of debate but a reality. They could no longer find it easy to deny his existence. Marthaen watched the red dragons carefully, certain that Jherdar would never allow the issue to be resolved easily. The red dragon would undoubtedly think that the hated Dragonlord was trying to usurp the place of the beloved Dragonking.

Thelvyn advanced to the speaker's dais and seated himself in a pose of great dignity, sitting upright with his long tail curled around his legs. His neck was drawn back in a proud, graceful curve. He paused for a long moment, then began to speak. "Marthaen has spoken to you of the gemstone dragons, who were once of our own kind. The Great One has told me about how he and the first Dragonlord fought the gemstone dragons long ago and drove them from our world. He has told me how the gemstone dragons have prepared their invasion for centuries, and how the Immortals have planned to counter it by having me serve as both Dragonlord and Dragonking and lead the dragons in the defense of our world."

"You know that I fought with you against the renegade Murodhir," Jherdar said, growing impatient. "I told you then that I would rather see you wearing the Collar of the Dragons than have it remain missing. But I cannot lightly accept that you seem so eager to lead us into war when we do not yet know even the strength or the intentions of our enemy."

"I have not yet summoned the dragons to war," Thelvyn replied. "But we must prepare for its likelihood."

"These gemstone dragons may have attacked our world, but they have not yet done us any harm," the red dragon responded.

"Haven't they?" Thelvyn demanded. "The Masters have tried to implicate us for their attacks on other lands, with the intent of forcing us into war with those who are not our true enemies. The Masters were behind the theft of the Collar of the Dragons. There was a time when you were very eager to punish those who stole the collar, but you do not seem so eager now. Are you in sympathy with our enemies now that you know who they are, or is it that you fear them?"

There was a loud muttering among the dragons when they heard Thelvyn's bold accusations. Marthaen watched apprehensively. Thelvyn wasn't about to compromise himself to placate the red dragon. He couldn't afford to. He had to earn the loyalty of the dragons even if he must fight Jherdar for it.

"I am not in sympathy with our enemies," Jherdar answered coldly. "Nor do I fear them. You are young and hardly even know what it means to be a dragon. You are too eager to go to war."

"I am not eager for war," Thelvyn insisted. "And I am not proposing that we carry the battle into their world. We would be at a distinct disadvantage if we tried to fight them on their own ground. But at the same time, we can put them at a disadvantage when they invade our world. We must be prepared to defend not only ourselves but our world, wherever the Masters attack. If we wait until our enemy brings the war directly to us, we will have already lost."

"Never!" Jherdar shouted, crouching in fury at the front of his ledge. "If the enemy comes to us, then we will fight in our own defense, but never for a world that hates and despises us."

Marthaen tensed, moving closer to the front of his ledge. He could see that Jherdar, caught between his anger at the other races of the world and his fear of the Dragonking, was desperate enough to challenge Thelvyn for the leadership of the dragons. Dragons were forbidden to fight within the city of Windreach and were required to take their challenges into the wild, but Jherdar looked furious enough to forget the law. It had happened before in the past, and Marthaen's duty as First Speaker was to insure that there were no fights on the floor of parliament.

"Yes, we will fight to defend the other nations of the world," Thelvyn said patiently but firmly. "We have no choice. What hope do we have if we allow the Masters to turn people who should be our allies into their slaves? Are we to wait until they besiege Windreach? What would you have us do?"

"We are fools to fight in the defense of those who hate us," Jherdar insisted stubbornly.

"And do you believe that I am eager to do so?" Thelvyn demanded. "I was their champion for five years before they chased me away in contempt, and now they beg for my protection. If anyone has cause to be angry with our world, surely it is I. But I will defend them just the same, because in so doing, it is my best chance to defend the dragons as well."

"Then defend them alone," Jherdar said coldly. "That is your appointed task. The Immortals supposedly gave you all the power you need as both Dragonlord and Dragonking."

"If I must fight alone, I will," Thelvyn answered in a voice that was as cold and hard as ice. "Do you think that I have forgotten the injuries I received from the dragons when I was forced to oppose you for your own good? I will defend you if I can, but if you prefer to act like a coward, then you deserve to be enslaved."

Jherdar was obviously stung. The dragons tended to forget the price that Thelvyn had been required to pay for the sake of his duty, especially the grief and pain they had caused him. But Jherdar could not allow Thelvyn's attack on his pride to pass unchallenged. He drew himself up in cold fury. "Even you may not talk to me that way."

"Then stop wasting my time with your foolish talk," Thelvyn answered him boldly. "You have said nothing but words of cowardice and irresponsibility. Challenge me now, or follow me as your rightful king. I will accept no other choice from any of you."

The silence that followed was absolute as the dragons waited tensely. All arguments were at an end, for Jherdar could do nothing now but accept the Dragonking or challenge him. Thelvyn had seen that this debate could lead nowhere but to compromise on his own part or a challenge of his authority, and so he had issued the challenge first, a bold move that surprised the dragons and impressed them tremendously. Thelvyn had fought and defeated gemstone dragons, and he knew that he could defeat Jherdar.

He waited calmly for his answer. In the end, it was his obvious confidence in himself that convinced Jherdar. The red dragon laid back his ears and sat back. "I am not a coward, and I will not be disloyal when the Great One calls me to serve his chosen one. If you will lead well and wisely, I will follow you. Tell us what we must do."

Jherdar's capitulation startled the other dragons, and they lifted their heads and moved out to the edge of their ledges to stare in astonishment. But their fear and anger had passed, and they waited in curiosity to hear what the Dragonking had to say.

"You have said that I do not know the strength of our enemy," Thelvyn began. "But I can infer at least this much: The Masters tried to conquer this world once before, and only the combined power of the Dragonlord and the Immortals succeeded in driving them into exile. They've had thousands of years to gather their strength, and they've returned at a time of their own choosing. Our only advantage is that they have to bring the battle to us, coming into a world where they have no strongholds of their own. We don't dare allow them a single victory."

The dragons once again muttered anxiously among themselves, but Marthaen thought Thelvyn had finally gotten them to face the full implications of the danger they faced. The Immortals had chosen them to defend their world because they alone had any hope of defeating this enemy. Their only choices were to do their best to fight an enemy that might yet prove too powerful for them, or to be defeated by their own stubbornness.

"With any luck, we can still be ready for them," Thelvyn continued. "To be prepared for the worst, I propose an alliance between the dragons and the other nations of our world against the invaders."

Jherdar opened his mouth to protest, then laid back his ears as he reconsidered and sat back on his haunches. He glanced over at Marthaen.

The gold dragon nodded slowly. "He is the Dragonking. I will follow him."

Jherdar considered Marthaen's words and nodded. The crisis of confidence was over, and the dragons would follow the Dragonking's leadership. They had doubted that he knew how to be a dragon, and he had proven himself by facing down Jherdar's challenge as one dragon to another. Marthaen realized now that the very confrontation he had been trying to avoid had been the only way that Thelvyn could have convinced the dragons that he was capable of leading them.

He decided that he would never tell Thelvyn that Jherdar had been under pressure from the representatives of the red, green, and black dragons to challenge him in combat. Then again, Marthaen wouldn't be surprised if Thelvyn had known after all. The new Dragonking seemed to know more about being a dragon than even Marthaen had expected.

CHAPTER SEVEN

Kharendaen helped Thelvyn remove the Collar of the Dragons and return it to its stand in the Hall of the Great One, where it had waited for the coming of the Dragonking for centuries. Marthaen, Jherdar, and Sir George Kirbey watched in silence from just beyond the two-stepped dais leading up to the stand. By nature of being first speaker, Marthaen, like Kharendaen, had the right to approach the collar, although neither of his two companions dared to pass the magical barriers that guarded it. The spells of protection were said to bring instant death to anyone who was not allowed access to the collar.

"I would feel better if you kept the collar with you," Marthaen said to Thelvyn. "I have no idea what powers it is supposed to bring you, but I would prefer that you had its protection."

"If I wore the collar, there would be times when I might need to remove it to change form. If that happened, I would never feel the collar was safe. This is the only place I would ever dare to leave it. I still have the powers of the Dragonlord to protect me."

Having secured the collar on its stand, Thelvyn and Kharendaen descended the steps. They planned to leave for the west at once, and they were both ready for travel. Kharendaen was already wearing her saddle, since Sir George would accompany them. Thelvyn wore his harness, which now included a double-edged sword of draconic proportions, with a blade more than five yards long, much like the one Marthaen always wore when he traveled. Indeed, it had been Marthaen who had insisted upon giving it to him, saying that such a weapon was fitting for a true leader of dragons. In his Eldar form, Thelvyn was well trained in using a sword, but he had no idea if this ability held true in his dragon state.

"We expect to reach Braejr late tonight," Thelvyn explained to Marthaen and Jherdar as they walked together toward the stairs. "Matters being what they are, it will be best for us to enter the city in the dark. It would probably be best to summon representatives of the various nations to Braejr using the Thyatian griffon riders, until we can convince everyone that we are not their enemy."

"For all the good this alliance is likely to do," Jherdar grumbled. "I'm still not sure what the other races can do to help us fight the Masters."

"If nothing else, they'll have to bear the responsibility of defending themselves," Thelvyn said firmly. "If we send out dragons to guard every city and large town in this part of the world, there won't be anyone left to fight the Masters. Our first concern is to make it clear to everyone who their true enemy is, so that the dragons are free to move about wherever they want without worrying that the people we are trying to defend will attack us."

They all fell silent while they descended the wide spiral staircase leading down to the ground level of the Hall of the Great One. Dragons were not built for going down stairs, so they had to descend carefully in single file.

"We will begin to summon and instruct the dragons at once," Marthaen said when they finally reached the bottom and started toward the main door. "The bands of dragons in the wild will be told to watch for any sign of our enemy, and an army will be gathered and prepared. However, the dragons would be more eager to serve if they could see the Dragonking for themselves."

"Kharendaen and I can go to Braejr in your place," Sir George suggested to Thelvyn.

"Thanks for the offer, but we still have a traitor to turn out," Thelvyn said. "I want to try break the influence the Masters have over Alessa Vyledaar so that she can tell us what she knows. And that might be something that only I can do."

"Be careful," Marthaen warned him. "Until you break their influence, the Masters are going to know where you are and what you are doing. You will be most vulnerable to them at that time."

"Didn't you say the dragon-kin are immune to their influence?" Jherdar asked.

"We thought so at first," Kharendaen answered. "The Masters made no attempt to control any of us when we were in their world. But they did control the renegade, Murodhir."

"I suspect that the Masters had the Fire Wizards trap him somehow," Thelvyn added. "I'll have to be wary of traps as well."

They all fell silent again as they filed out the main door of the Hall of the Great One, descending the broad steps down into the court paved with large, smooth stones. Thelvyn lifted his head and sniffed the cool morning air. The sun had not yet begun to climb above the rim of the crater, and the city remained in deep shadows. He saw a few dragons drifting on the morning wind above the towering buildings and halls of Windreach, their smooth white stone still appearing pale gray in the shadows. Other dragons could be seen sitting or reclining on the ledges of their lairs along the inside wall of the old volcano.

"I know you need me here," Thelvyn said, turning back to the others. "We'll be back in just a few days, I promise you."

He crouched low and then leapt into the air, his wings snapping out and catching the wind with long, quick strokes. Within a couple of moments, he had gained enough speed to turn and begin to circle while he waited for his mate to join him. Kharendaen moved in close beside him, and they turned to fly westward over the city, building speed before they began to ascend in a wide spiral as they climbed over the outer wall of Windreach. They were just coming over the ragged edge when they moved into the morning sun, warm and bright above the ragged expanse of white clouds that hid most of the wilderness of Wendar far below.

By leaving early in the morning, they hoped to reach Braejr about two or three hours after nightfall. It was a long, difficult flight, especially since they had made the same journey in the other direction only a couple of days earlier. The two dragons had eaten their fill of venison and warm bread before they left, so they shouldn't be hungry.

Thelvyn had to admit that he would have liked a little more time to explore Windreach, having had only a portion of the previous afternoon to look about the city. He found that he liked the company of dragons more than he thought he would, at least now that they were coming to think of him as something other than their deadly enemy. Indeed, dragons of every breed were now eager to serve and to please him, even if most of them had still had to hide an almost instinctive fear of him. He even had his own lair now, not in the outer ring of the city but high in the towers of the Hall of the Great One, near the lairs of the clerics of his order. In fact, his accommodations were quite kingly, with an entire suite of apartments and young dragon clerics and one of the Eldar at hand to serve him and his mate.

Now that Thelvyn was more or less officially recognized as Dragonking, he was beginning to feel the weight of that responsibility, just as when he had been the king of the Highlands the previous summer. He didn't much feel like the lord and master of a nation as much as he felt like what he had always been, a defender. He saw his duties as the Dragonking as being not very different from what he had known as the Dragonlord, except that he now had far greater authority to direct others in assisting him. He certainly wasn't about to attempt to rule the Nation of Dragons himself, even if that authority seemed to be inherent in his rights as the Dragonking. He had already made it clear that he expected the parliament to retain its authority as the governing body of the

Nation of Dragons, although he would now become a part of the parliament.

He appreciated the enormity of the task before him, arranging the defense of his world against an enemy even the Immortals feared. Having convinced the dragons to follow his leadership, he now had to convince all the other nations of the world to defer to him as well. He felt daunted to have to begin his reign as the Dragonking in such dire times, but that was the nature of his duty, the chosen defender in a time of desperate need. Becoming the Dragonking had never been intended as a gift that was his to enjoy, but a grave responsibility that he had been born to fulfill.

Night had long since fallen when the two dragons descended over the city of Braejr. Thelvyn led the way down, trusting in his developing sense of direction, and he landed quietly in the dark street just outside Solveig's house. He had hoped to avoid disturbing any griffons that might be stabled in the warehouse. There was indeed a griffon in the stables, and it made a few angry noises as the dragons landed, but nothing compared to what had occurred on earlier occasions. In fact, their arrival had so quiet that Solveig didn't come out of the house to investigate until they were almost finished removing their saddle and harness. Darius Glantri joined her a moment later.

"Have you finally moved in here?" Thelvyn asked the young Thyatian.

"No. Actually, I've been waiting for you to return," Darius explained. "I expect that you have a great deal to tell us."

"Far more than you could have ever expected," Thelvyn said, pausing a moment to leave his sword and harness in a safe place before he changed form. Only a dragon could have lifted that sword. "But we can talk about it inside. We've spent the entire day in flight, and we could use some hospitality."

"Yes, of course," Solveig agreed, hurrying to assist Sir George with his travel bags. "Let me give you a hand."

"I appreciate the thought, but you're actually too late for that," Sir George said, showing her his newly acquired left hand.

"My word," Solveig said, obviously surprised. "How did you manage that?"

"As it happens, it was a gift from the Great One for having made myself so useful to the Dragonking."

Solveig led them into the den and had Taeryn fetch something from the kitchen. She even located a bottle of cherry liqueur for Sir George in the cabinet. He was greatly pleased, complaining that the real problem with a life of adventure was being required to do without so many civilized comforts. He had actually enjoyed a great many comforts while in Windreach, since the Eldar had been pleased to fetch anything that the companion of the Dragonking wanted, but there had been no cherry liqueur.

"Then you did succeed in finding the Collar of the Dragons?" Solveig asked impatiently as soon as everyone was seated.

"Oh, yes. We finally found the collar," Thelvyn said. "I left it in the care of the dragons for now."

"Was it where Alessa said it would be?"

"Yes, it was," Thelvyn answered guardedly. "However, she sent us right into a trap. Fortunately for us, the trap was sprung a little too soon. We were able to find the collar and escape, although we had to fight for it."

"A trap?" Solveig was obviously confused and concerned. "Alessa set a trap for you? Is she working for the traitor wizards?"

"We discovered who was behind the attacks throughout this part of the world a few nights ago. They control Alessa's mind and will, just as they controlled Byen Kalestraan before her. In fact, before the Flaem came into this world, the entire race were their slaves."

Thelvyn saw that it was time for some detailed explanations of all they had discovered during the last few days, although he was satisfied to leave the tale for Sir George to tell. He felt the old knight related the events of their battles with the gemstone dragons in overly heroic terms, but he resisted the temptation to interrupt. Both Solveig and Darius saw the full implications of what they had learned. They looked very concerned, and even a bit frightened.

"Well, that certainly explains a lot," Solveig remarked when she had heard the full account. "I suppose the first thing to do is to send the city guard to arrest Alessa and the other senior wizards before they can disappear."

"No, I want to wait on that," Thelvyn insisted. "The Masters don't regard Alessa as an ally but as a slave, a resource to be exploited for as long as she might be useful and then tossed aside. They'll undoubtedly want her to discover everything she can about what I learned about the Masters and what my plans are. With any luck, I might be able to use her to feed the Masters a little false information that might work to our advantage. Then I want to try to break their control over her, to see if she can tell us anything else that might prove useful."

"I'm willing to go along with whatever you want," Solveig agreed. "What are you planning?"

"I want you to call Alessa and Captain Geirstaan here for a meeting right away," he explained. "That might catch both Alessa and the Masters off guard. I'll tell the story you've just heard over again, except that a few details will be considerably different. I need for you to go along with it and act like you're hearing it for the first time. Then we'll see how Alessa reacts."

"Is there anything else we can do now?" Solveig asked.

"Are there any spare griffon riders available?"

"No, but at least one should return sometime tomorrow," Darius said.

"I'll need enough griffon riders to relay my message to every nation in this part of the world," Thelvyn said. "Even Alphatia. I want everyone to know who our real enemy is and that the dragons will help to defend them, but they'll also have to do everything they can to help themselves. I want representatives of each nation we contact brought here in a few days for a general council of war."

*　*　*　*　*

Captain Geirstaan arrived in a matter of minutes, having ridden a horse from the gate stables, and Alessa came by carriage a short time later. She looked confused and uncertain, as if she had been caught off her guard. Thelvyn wondered if she was surprised by his sudden return, having expected that the Masters would have dealt with him. He also wondered if the Masters had bothered to tell her that he had evaded their trap and reclaimed the Collar of the Dragons. He thought his return to Braejr was an obvious next step, but apparently Alessa had not anticipated it.

He related the events of their recovery of the Collar of the Dragons through their escape from the world of the Masters and the destruction of the worldgate. He could hardly change that part of his tale, since the Masters would be familiar with those details. Even so, he was careful not to reveal just how much he had been able to infer about the Masters and their abilities from what he had seen. And the Masters would not know anything about his time in Windreach, or at least he hoped not. He had already considered the possibility that they had other dragons under their control, although that seemed unlikely. If they did control other dragons, the Great One probably would have been aware of it and told Thelvyn about it.

"Perhaps I was a fool to go among the dragons at once," he continued more slowly, as if he regretted this part. "All I knew was that there was little time to prepare, and I needed the dragons to help me defeat these invaders. In any event, the dragons were not impressed. They have refused their assistance for now. Moreover, they forced me to depart, and they insisted that I leave the Collar of the Dragons with them. They may be planning to use the collar to nominate a Dragonking of their own choosing."

"They are fools," Kharendaen said in disgust, playing her own part to the hilt.

"But what can we do?" Solveig asked, catching on quickly.

"I'm not sure what we can do," Thelvyn said helplessly. "I still have the powers of the Dragonlord. I know the rest of the world doesn't trust me much more than the dragons do, but they need my help as much as I need theirs."

Darius shrugged in frustration. "All I can do is to send a griffon rider to Emperor Cornelius in the morning. If he's willing to offer his support, then messengers can relay your proposal to anyone who will listen."

"I think you can count on the Flaem to support you," Alessa offered, watching Thelvyn carefully. "Since it seems that Byen Kalestraan was in league with these creatures, it seems only fair that the Fire Wizards should do anything in their power to counteract his treachery."

"Now that you know what Byen Kalestraan was up to, does that give you any ideas where to look for more clues?" Thelvyn asked. "I know practically nothing about these Masters, so anything you might learn would be a great help."

"I can only try," she agreed, rising to leave. "If you will excuse me, I want to start searching at once. I'll do everything in my power to help, even if I have to stay at it all night and enlist every wizard at the Academy to help me."

Taeryn hurried to fetch her shawl and met her at the door of the den to escort her to her carriage. Sir George began to discuss plans with Solveig even before Alessa left the room. He had reasoned that it would help to make their meeting seem more natural. Alessa seemed to suspect nothing so far, and he wanted to keep it that way.

"That was easier than I thought it would be," Thelvyn commented when he finally heard the front door close. "I was afraid we might have to play out this game well into the night, but Alessa seems to be in quite a hurry to get home. Either she's planning to talk to the Masters right away, or they've been seeing and hearing everything she does and they want to instruct her before anything else can happen."

Captain Geirstaan looked up in surprise. He was the only one who was not in on the plan, but he could guess already that Alessa was suspected of being in league with the Masters.

"And now what?" Solveig asked.

"Now I have to follow her," Thelvyn said. "And I don't want to get too far behind, in case she does something unexpected. Sir George, I need your skills as a thief to get me into Alessa's apartment unseen."

"That should be simple enough," Sir George replied, rising quickly to accompany Thelvyn.

"I'll bring Alessa back here when I'm done," Thelvyn explained quickly. "For now, I think someone should fill in Captain Geirstaan about what has been going on here."

* * * * *

Sir George came up with a simple plan for getting inside the Wizard's Residence of the Academy unchallenged. They would enter through the main door as unobtrusively as possible and walk through the corridors and up the stairs as if they belonged there. After all, they were all supposed to be friends and allies, and no one was likely to attack them or sound the alarm even if they were seen. Thelvyn was pleased they wouldn't have to skulk about like thieves. His Eldar form was no longer completely familiar to him, and he wasn't as agile as he used to be. Sir George pointed out that it was getting quite late, so no one was likely to be moving about in the dimly lit passages.

Thelvyn was concerned that there might be trouble when he tried to break the control of the Masters over Alessa. For one thing, they might force her to fight him. He was also concerned that they might try to control him as well, although he felt his powers as a cleric were probably enough to protect him. As both a dragon and the Dragonlord, there was little that the Fire Wizards could do to hurt him. His biggest concern of all was that the Masters might destroy Alessa rather than risk letting her go free, which would permit her to reveal any of their secrets she might know. When Thelvyn broke their contact with her, he would have to move quickly to protect her.

Sir George brought him unopposed and apparently unseen to the door of Alessa's chambers. The old knight stayed just long enough to pick the lock on the door before Thelvyn sent him away to guard the hall and do whatever he had to do to prevent anyone from approaching. There was too much danger that Sir George would himself be vulnerable to the control of the Masters, or to any vengeance they might force Alessa to take upon Thelvyn. It was safer for Sir George and better for Thelvyn that he kept his distance.

Thelvyn listened at the door for a moment, certain that he heard voices speaking softly somewhere inside. Cautiously opening the door just a crack, he paused a moment more to listen. He could hear Alessa's voice and also that of someone else, a soft voice that almost purred in a deep, throaty rumble, a voice he had learned to associate with dragons. But the strange voice also seemed dim and remote, muffled somehow, which was not surprising, since there could hardly have been a gemstone dragon in the room.

Opening the door a little more, he looked inside. As he had expected, Alessa was alone. The room was fairly dark, the only light coming from a single lamp, beside which Alessa was standing still and motionless, as if staring out the window into the night. Her right hand was raised so that she was lightly touching a red jewel that was pinned to the breast of her wizard's robe. Thelvyn couldn't see it clearly, since she was turned mostly away from him, but he recalled that it was a wizard's token, a cheap broach made from what appeared to be colored glass. She had been speaking, her own voice lifeless and remote, and then the strange voice answered her from out of the very air somewhere near her. To Thelvyn, it seemed as though it were speaking inside his head somehow.

There is no cause for alarm, the voice was telling her. *You have done your best. It was not your fault that he escaped our trap.*

"It is my duty to serve," Alessa said. Her voice was flat and emotionless, and Thelvyn could not tell if her words were intended as a promise or a plea.

Unfortunately, your service to us must come to an end, the unseen speaker continued. *I thought they had no suspicion of your involvement, but it seems I was wrong. The only way that you can serve me now is by preserving my secrets.*

Thelvyn understood what that meant, having seen wizards put to death so that they could not betray the Masters. He knew that he would have to move quickly. He had planned to find some magical way to break the hold the Masters had over Alessa, but now he decided, like Sir George, to use a much simpler solution. Several years ago, Sir George had taught him a spell, a form of protection that he had never found a use for because it required him to be in physical contact with the person he wanted to stun. Moving with the quickness and grace of a trained swordsman, he leapt across the room and grabbed Alessa by the neck. At the same moment, he uttered the words to the spell. She collapsed into unconsciousness, never even aware of his presence.

Not trusting that the spell would be enough to isolate Alessa from the command of the Masters, he took hold of the jewel and ripped it free of her robe. At the same time, he flooded the jewel with his own will, forcing back the presence that occupied it until he was able to employ another spell to isolate the crystal from all other magical influences. The pale light inside the red crystal flared brilliantly for a moment, then died quickly as he clutched it in his hand.

He braced himself, knowing the attack would come. A moment later, the alien presence returned to the crystal, trying to force its way past his will. Thelvyn had expected something like that. If they could control him, they could force him to betray himself and his friends, or they could even destroy him as they had slain the enslaved wizards in their own world. He had been aware of the risks from the first, but he had to test his will against that of the Masters so that he would know if he could fight them on their own terms.

The attack surged forward with such confidence that Thelvyn prepared himself for the worst, concentrating firmly upon his own willpower. Even so, he was barely able to hold his own in those first moments by devoting the full power of his resolve to fighting the vague presence. Finally the deepest magic of his very being seemed to respond on its own, raising an insurmountable barrier of power to shield his mind from his mysterious attacker. For a brief instant, he could feel the alien will pressing against his own, and he sensed that his unseen opponent was struggling to summon every last iota of its power to throw against him. Suddenly the force of the alien will faded quickly and was gone.

"Are you quite finished?" he asked the crystal, not quite sure what else to say.

I am finished with you . . . for now, the strange voice echoed inside his head. *Perhaps I have underestimated you. You are surprisingly clever.*

"And lucky," Thelvyn said, refusing to be taunted into any debates.

And most assuredly lucky, the alien voice agreed. *It would seem we are both at a disadvantage, since each of us knows little about the other's situation. But I know a good deal more about you than you know about me. I have been watching you since long before you ever became aware of me.*

"That may be true," Thelvyn answered cautiously, "but as

you are also well aware, everything about me and all that I am was designed to fight you. Your return has been anticipated for centuries. You are not going to find me unprepared."

True in part, perhaps, but only in part. You try to threaten me, and yet your words only prove how little you actually know and how unprepared you really are.

"You sound very sure of yourself," Thelvyn said evenly. "You seem determined to keep making that mistake, and I don't see it as my place to correct you. But I must remind you that the Dragonlord and the Great One defeated you once before."

Whatever happened long ago did not involve me and is not my concern, the voice replied scornfully. *You cannot oppose me without the support of the dragons. And you have no idea of my strength.*

"We can only see," Thelvyn answered vaguely. He was growing suspicious of new traps, especially since his enemy was willing to speak for so long after losing control of the red crystal. This seemed like a good time not only to break the contact but also to destroy the jewel before it could do any more harm. After looking about the room quickly, he carried the jewel over to the dark fireplace and set it on the cold metal grate, then stepped back. While he had little experience in trying to direct his will, he had found the crystal easy enough to control so far. A strong response was probably essential to such a magical artifact, which had to link the minds of its users across worlds. The small crystal flared with a sudden brilliant red light before flashing a blinding white. The crystal itself was shattered into dust, and the gold broach was half melted.

Responding to the sudden flash of light, Sir George rushed into the room to discover what had happened, then paused just inside the door. Thelvyn was bent over the fireplace, prodding the remains of the crystal with a poker. Alessa remained in a crumpled heap on the floor.

"Are you all right?" Sir George asked.

"I'm fine," Thelvyn insisted, setting aside the poker. "Let's see if our slumbering beauty is ready to wake up and talk to us."

Alessa was slow to come around. Sir George bent over her

and worked at her for a couple of minutes. When she finally started to respond, she recovered fairly quickly. Sir George helped her to sit up, and she rubbed her eyes.

"My word, I feel dizzy," she said.

"That should pass quickly enough," the old knight told her. "How does your head feel otherwise?"

"Not too bad," she insisted weakly. "Did someone hit me?"

"It was the only way to save your life," Thelvyn told her. "The Masters somehow have a way to command their victims to die—very painfully, I might add. I've seen it happen with some of the missing members of your order. I had to get you instantly into a state where you were unresponsive to their commands."

"Oh, my," Alessa said, surprised and contrite as she began to realize what had been going on. "I suppose I should thank you."

"If you don't mind, I think we should go back to Solveig's house," he said. "We can explain a few things to you on the way."

Alessa's carriage was brought around again, and Sir George used the ride back to Solveig's house to explain things from their own perspective. The more Alessa learned about the situation, the more furious she became. She had grown to take her role as the defender of the Flaem very seriously. Sir George and Thelvyn hadn't yet had a chance to see that for themselves, since she had already been under the control of the Masters by the time they had returned to Braejr. But Alessa now seemed every bit as fair and conscientious as Solveig had insisted, and the awareness that the Flaem had been enslaved and manipulated by the Masters distressed and enraged her greatly.

They brought Alessa into the kitchen, where they could sit her down at the table and give her something warm to drink. She was beginning to get a headache, and Sir George hurried to fetch a small bottle from his collection of medicines and magical potions. He brought back a small brown bottle that he popped open, then instructed her to sniff the white vapor that rose from the container. She felt better almost at once.

"That's a hangover potion I got from Perrantin a few years

ago," he said. "I've never needed it myself, but I thought it would work for your problem."

"I should be grateful it wasn't poison," Alessa remarked sourly.

"Nonsense. We want you to talk before we kill you," Thelvyn said teasingly. "Tell us about the Masters."

"I wish I could tell you more," she said. "Unfortunately, I was never privy to their secrets. They had no need to explain anything to me, only to ask me for information and give me their instructions. I never thought to question anything. I only wanted to serve him, because he spoke to me in ways that made that seem like the right thing to do."

"Who is the Overlord? I know about the Masters, and one of the wizards mentioned this Overlord, but that's all I know. I suspect I may have talked with him tonight."

"Possibly," Alessa said. "I know almost nothing of the Masters because my dealings were never with them. I suspect the Masters serve the Overlord, since he speaks as if everyone serves him."

"Is he one of the gemstone dragons?"

Alessa shook her head firmly, her eyes wide. "No. I've seen the gemstone dragons in my dreams, when the Overlord usually spoke to me. When he spoke in my dreams, I sometimes saw a vision that looked vaguely like a dragon, but far more horrible."

Kharendaen looked confused. "What's horrible about a dragon?"

"In your dreams?" Thelvyn asked, ignoring Kharendaen's question. "Did you dream of a desert world where a cold wind always blows and the sky is always dark?"

"Why, yes," Alessa agreed, surprised. "I believe that's the world where the Flaem lived before we came here. Where we lived for many years as slaves with other races and strange beasts gathered from many worlds. We were forced to tend fields sheltered from the wind and the sand by tall mountains, and we built many strange devices of metal in dark fortresses. I've seen such places in my dreams. They seemed more like memories that were blocked from our minds when we were sent here as unwitting slaves to make ready for the invasion."

Thelvyn nodded. "I've suspected as much."

"This fortress that you described, where you found the Collar of the Dragons," Alessa continued. "It's nothing more than an outpost. In my dreams, I've seen far greater fortresses somewhere north and west of there . . . a vast complex of massive stone buildings, where the Masters live among their armies of slaves. That is the place of the Overlord."

"That could be a useful thing to know," Thelvyn said. Sir George looked somewhat concerned.

"There are a few other things I can tell you, but you must understand that I am only guessing now," Alessa said. "I suspect there is an even larger worldgate somewhere in our world, one that corresponds to the gate in the main stronghold of the Masters, from where they will launch their invasion. I suspect they have many gates opening into different parts of our world."

"I thought as much," Thelvyn said. "That explains how they were able to attack so many places in our world at the same time and disappear again. The Masters must have scouted this world thoroughly before they made their first attack. I've always wondered why the Fire Wizards spent so much time and effort assembling that huge library. It never seemed to do them any good. Now I wonder if the real purpose was to provide information to the Masters."

Sir George shrugged. "That seems reasonable. Did you learn anything from your little talk with the Overlord?"

Thelvyn looked smug. "Yes, I think I did . . . more than the Overlord intended, at any rate. He told me a couple of things that didn't make sense until just now. He said that he had no involvement in the first attempt of the gemstone dragons to conquer our world, and Alessa suspects that he himself is not a gemstone dragon. I wonder if, when they fled this world, the gemstone dragons met up with the Overlord and fell under his control. They might be just another of his race of slaves and, like Alessa, don't suspect it even yet."

"Could we find some way to break his control?" Solveig asked. "If we could do that, perhaps we could turn his own armies against him."

"That could be," Thelvyn said cautiously. "If we can block his will, or if I can destroy him, then our worries are over. Otherwise, I doubt we can do anything to stop him short of defeating his armies."

"How can we possibly fight the gemstone dragons?" Alessa asked, obviously still unsettled over what had happened. "Especially without the support of the dragons."

"As it happens, we do have their support," he told her. "When I told you the dragons had rejected me, it was only because that was what I wanted the Masters to hear."

Alessa sat up straight, staring at him. "What are you saying?"

"Thelvyn is the Dragonking," Kharendaen explained. "He has the support of the Nation of Dragons, and they are preparing for war. The Masters have underestimated us, and we prefer to keep it that way."

"We'll have to move quickly to make use of any advantage," Thelvyn said, then glanced over at Solveig. "I don't want to be a bother, but can you put those griffons somewhere else and convert the warehouse back into a lair for Kharendaen?"

"I can have it done tomorrow if you want," she agreed. "Why?"

"Because the time has come for me to be a dragon. After tonight, I won't be taking this form except when I must."

CHAPTER EIGHT

The first hint of trouble came from the sentries along the northern border of Rockhome, where from their posts in the mountains they could see out across the steppes of Ethengar. They thought at first that the steppes might be on fire, in spite of the spring rains. They could see a haze of dark smoke just beyond the horizon, and after a time, herds of frightened horses thundered over the plains, fleeing some terror from the north. Not far behind the herds, the clans of the Ethengar were retreating across the steppes as well, setting aside their old rivalries with one another in their desperation to escape a common danger. They were still many long miles out on the steppes, but they were fleeing as quickly as they could. And there was no indication that they would stop until they left the grasslands behind, heading straight into the mountains.

Soon a delegation from the Ethengar appeared out of the steppes, seven young warriors, each from a different clan but riding together in a common cause. Each of the riders led two horses in reserve, so that their mounts would always be rested and able to keep a quick, steady pace. They rode directly up

the trade road to the main dwarvish stronghold of Fort Denwarf and requested permission to ride on to Dengar. They
claimed to bear important news for the dwarves as well as a
plea for their own people. After speaking hurriedly with the
captain of the fort, they were issued special papers of safe conduct and allowed to pass.

The Ethengar rode well into the night, changing their
horses frequently until none of the poor beasts could run any
farther. Only then did they stop for a time, making a simple
camp through the deepest part of the night. They were on
their way again well before dawn, so that midmorning found
them approaching the gate of Dengar. Crews were still at
work on the walls, repairing the damage from the night of the
attack. The riders presented themselves to the guards at the
gate, showing the papers they had been given at Fort Denwarf the day before. They were led through the city at once
to the stables of the main garrison, where their horses would
be tended to. Most of the riders chose to stay with their
mounts, but their spokesman and two of his companions
were immediately escorted down the long, winding passage
to the lower city.

The deep passages of Dengar seemed very dark and close to
the Ethengar, who were riders and warriors of the open, wind-
swept grass, used to the sun and the stars. The only roofs they
had known in the past were no more solid than the canvas and
skins of their tents. The nomads were not actually frightened
to find themselves in such an alien place, but they did look
about the tunnels nervously for a time. But mindful of their
pride, they marched behind their escort, trying to appear calm
and unconcerned as they were led across the length of the
lower city to the palace.

As they were led into the throne room, they found that they
had arrived at a busy time. King Daroban was seated at his
throne. Both of his sons stood close at hand, while many gen-
erals and advisors were gathered as well. They had all been listening to a report from a foreign messenger, a Thyatian
captain to judge from his uniform, while the king was glancing
at a written report at the same time. They all turned to stare as
the escort announced these new visitors to the court.

The Ethengar spokesman approached the throne, bowing upon one knee in the manner of his people. "Great King of Rockhome, I am Kaihatu of the clan of the Red Horse. My companions and I have left our people in their time of greatest need to bring you news of great danger. We are all of many clans, once enemies, now brothers brought together by urgent need, for invaders have come among us, and the steppes have been overrun.

"The first attacks came three nights ago, when dragonlike creatures fell upon our clans like eagles descending upon their prey, scattering our herds and setting fires among our wagons and our yurts. I say that they were like dragons in shape and size, and yet they were unlike dragons in appearance. They did not hide themselves by the light of day but flew swiftly over the steppes, spreading their terror and destruction. Their armor is like the facets of costly jewels, some like rubies or sapphires, or like amber, or white crystal or dark onyx. Never before have we heard of such dragons."

"The gemstone dragons," King Daroban said, nodding slowly. Then he glanced at the Thyatian. "The Dragonking spoke true. Not that I was inclined to doubt the message you brought from the Dragonking, but I'm certain that even he never expected an attack so soon."

"Perhaps not," the Thyatian answered. "The Masters know that they have been unmasked, and their attempt to sow fear and distrust of the dragons has failed. Now that the time for secrecy has passed, they might believe they would be best served by moving quickly, before we can gather our defenses. The Dragonking may have anticipated such a thing, but what more could he have done?"

"True enough," Daroban agreed, then turned back to the Ethengar. "This is Darius Glantri, who left Braejr this very morning on his way to Thyatis, bearing the Dragonking's warning of these gemstone dragons. He has been kind enough to pause for a brief time to share that news with us, unaware just how relevant that news would become. At least now we know many things that might have otherwise remained a mystery to us for days yet to come."

"You call them the Masters," Kaihatu said. "The name

suits them well, for they were soon followed by other invaders, men and also many strange creatures who are not like men or elves or dwarves. Hordes of terrible monsters have been released upon the steppes to spread their own terror. The Masters guide and command all the others."

"Those would be slave races subject to the will of the Masters," Darius explained. "Do you have any idea of the number of these Masters and their warriors?"

Kaihatu could only shake his head. "They move too swiftly and they are spread all across the northern steppes from east to west, but they are strong and the clans have no choice but flee before them. Their numbers are like the blades of grass. There are scores of the gemstone dragons but not, I think, more than a hundred altogether. Their warriors are gathered in armies of perhaps five thousand, and we know of at least five such armies. There could be even more farther to the east and the west, beyond sight of our clans."

Daroban sighed. "What can we do? Your enemy is the enemy of all the people of our world, and we stand with you against them. Even so, we do not have the strength to help the clans drive them from the steppes."

"The steppes are lost already," Kaihatu answered. "The clans flee before these invaders. I have come only to bear you this warning, for we cannot say yet whether they will be satisfied to hold the steppes, or if they will drive on south into your land. The best that you can do is to prepare all the strength you have to protect your border. I bring only this one plea, for in truth, the clans cannot remain in the steppes or they will die. Allow our people to flee into your own wild lands, to hide themselves in your northern mountains."

The king considered only for a moment, then nodded. "So be it. Take your people into whatever safety they can find in the mountains. It may be that soon we will be standing together against these enemies."

"The dragons have pledged themselves to fight this same enemy," Darius assured them. "By your leave, I will be returning to Braejr at once to warn the Dragonking. He will need some time to gather the dragons and lead them here, so you must be prepared to hold out on your own for a few days."

The Ethengar thanked the dwarves and left with Darius Glantri, returning quickly to upper Dengar. King Daroban hardly waited until they had left the room before he rose, leaving his crown on his throne as he began to pace nervously while he considered the problem of the defense of Rockhome.

"I see no hope for it," he said after only a moment. "These gemstone dragons can come and go as they please, and I fear that they will be our chief problem from the first. Their wings can take them anywhere swiftly, and their flames can destroy our fortresses. But they cannot easily get at our underground cities. In our tunnels, their size is against them. We must prepare to close all the upper cities at once. All the goods that can be moved, all the children and those too old or too weak to fight, even the foreigners who live among us and choose not to flee, must be brought down into the tunnels at once. We will not surrender our upper cities and fortresses without a fight, but our main defense will be below ground."

Korinn nodded. "That will give us time to hold out until the dragons come."

Daroban turned to him. "You still trust that your old friend can convince the dragons to fight for us? Do not mistake me; I hope that you are correct. But I only hope, and nothing more. I cannot yet bring myself to trust in dragons until I have seen such a thing for myself."

"They will come," Korinn insisted. "But there will be whole armies following these Masters, and they might be able to crack open our defenses and invade our underground strongholds. When these armies come down from the steppes, they will have to enter Rockhome through the Styrdal Pass. Better, it seems, to keep them out of Rockhome as long as possible. I would like to take all the soldiers we can spare to strengthen Fort Denwarf."

"Yes, that was my own thought," Daroban agreed. "You must go there at once. We will send all the soldiers and supplies we can spare as soon as we can. But we must also give some thought to Fort Evekarr to the northeast, and to the undefended pass on the Hrap River. Your brother Dorinn will prepare the defenses of Dengar."

Dorinn looked surprised to hear that, and quietly grateful.

He hadn't commanded a military force since his injury several
years before, having served as an advisor to his father in Dengar while he recovered. Commanding the defenses of Dengar
spared him the need to make swift rides or long, hard marches,
which his disabilities would not allow.

Needing to reach Fort Denwarf as soon as possible, Korinn
sent a messenger to ask the Ethengar to wait a brief time so
that he could ride north with them. No one but a dragon or a
griffon rider could travel more quickly than the warriors of the
clans, even in the mountains of Rockhome. Korinn hurried to
put on his armor and collect his weapons, and then he all but
ran up the passages to upper Dengar. So it was that he reached
the garrison stables only shortly after the Ethengar.

As it happened, the young warriors were pleased to have
him in their company. They considered it a remarkably generous gesture on the part of the dwarves to allow the clans to flee
into the mountains of Rockhome, and they had come prepared to be refused. And so they were very grateful and would
have taken him anywhere, although Korinn knew that they
were desperate to return to the defense of their own people
and he promised not to slow their ride. He selected two of the
best courier horses from the garrison for his own, and he rode
away with the Ethengar only minutes later.

Unlike most dwarves, Korinn was not only used to riding
but was also quite good at it, skills he had learned during his
travels with Solveig White-Gold and Sir George Kirbey. Just
the same, he wasn't used to keeping such a swift pace, and riding with the nomads required more concentration on his part.
But he still had several hours of riding that day alone with his
thoughts and his concerns.

Thelvyn Fox-Eye's finding of the Collar of the Dragons and
his ascendancy as the Dragonking had come just in time for
the dwarves. Korinn completely trusted Thelvyn to gather the
dragons and come to the aid of Rockhome, but he still had to
wonder if even that would be enough. The Ethengar had been
forced to flee before this new enemy, and they had no idea of
the full size and strength of the invading force. Korinn wondered how many dragons there were in all his world to
respond to the Dragonking's call. Surely no more than a few

thousand at most.

For that matter, he had to wonder just how soon the Dragonking would be able to gather his army of dragons and bring them to Rockhome. A few days at least, and Korinn was no longer certain they had a few days to wait. The defense of the Styrdal Pass was a hopeless effort, he realized now. He might be able to delay the invading army for a while, but the Masters would inevitably prevail. The gemstone dragons could descend upon Fort Denwarf and leave it in ruins in a matter of minutes if they chose to. He was beginning to agree with the king that the only hope for the dwarves would be to secure themselves in their underground cities and do anything they could to keep the invaders out until the dragons came to their rescue.

Korinn spent the day thinking of anything he could to slow the invasion of Rockhome, but he couldn't come up with anything special. His enemies simply had too many advantages. His only real hope now was that the Masters would be delayed in securing their domination of the steppes before they pushed on into Rockhome. They might not even push on to the south but turn eastward instead, into the Flaemish realm, reclaiming the people who had once been their slaves. But he had no real hope of that.

They didn't reach Fort Denwarf until well after nightfall, although Korinn was pleased to have made the ride in only one day. The sentries at the gate recognized him before he had the chance to identify himself, and the commander of the fortress hurried out to greet him. Korinn requested supplies and accommodations for the Ethengar and fodder for their horses, turning over his own mounts to the garrison stablehands.

Korinn stood in the lamplit yard of the fortress while he explained the situation quickly to the commander of the fortress, a solid older dwarf of the Torkrest Clan, Balar, son of Balic. After riding all day, Korinn needed to walk around for a time before he tried to sit down to dinner.

"We really haven't learned anything new," General Balar told him. "The clans have continued to retreat in our direction, and some have even reached the mountains by now. I was loath to permit them to cross over our border unchallenged, and I'm not completely at ease with the king's decision to grant them safe passage into our lands."

"It suits our purposes," Korinn told him, answering in a manner that the general would appreciate. "Right now no one hates these invaders more than the Ethengar, who have already lost their land and herds. If the invaders try to avoid the Styrdal Pass and slip through the mountains, they'll have to answer to the Ethengar."

The preparations to make Fort Denwarf ready for battle had already begun. The fortress had taken only light damage during the first attack of the gemstone dragons several nights earlier. The highest tower was still missing its top, since the height of the tower made repairs difficult. Korinn wished there were more catapults at Fort Denwarf, remembering that those were the only weapons proven to have any effectiveness against dragons during the assault on the Highlands the previous year. Everything about this fortress had been designed to discourage invasion by more conventional enemies—particularly raiding parties of Ethengar warriors. The gemstone dragons, however, would be nearly impossible to fight.

Early the next morning, Korinn went through the pass to a high rise, where he could look out from the mountains across the rolling hills of the steppes. A shroud of dark smoke lay over the plains for as far as he could see, as if the Masters were trying to burn off all the steppes in a single vast wildfire. The clans themselves had apparently already reached the safety of the foothills, since he could see no movement out in the steppes anywhere along the southern border. There was also no clear sign of the enemy to the north, although Korinn wasn't sure whether he saw glimpses of the distant forms of gemstone dragons through the wall of smoke.

That seemed to suggest that they had a couple of days before the invaders reached the mountains of Rockhome. The first of the additional supplies and warriors being sent to reinforce the border fortress arrived later that same day. Unfortunately, there were few catapults or heavy crossbows that might have the power to penetrate a dragon's hide. Actually, he had no idea whether the gemstone dragons had the same armor as the dragons of his own world. The dwarves had many cleverly designed ballistae and similar devices for hurling stones and heavy weights, but such things were unlikely to hit a dragon in flight.

By that night, the reddish glow of the fires marching southward across the steppes could be seen clearly from the fortress's higher towers, and all through the next day the great wall of dark smoke grew steadily larger. The wind was from slightly west of due north, driving the flames before it and carrying a great curtain of black smoke southward over the mountains of Rockhome. Smoke scuttled like storm clouds overhead, casting a deep shadow over the mountains, broken only occasionally when the sunlight penetrated fitfully through rents opened by the wind. The smell of smoke was thick and heavy.

More troops and supplies arrived during the day. Recognizing that his plans for the defense of Rockhome had changed, Korinn elected to send a part of the new troops and most of the supplies back to the south, where they would be needed more. He sent with them written orders stating his reasons why nothing more should be sent. Once the gemstone dragons attacked in earnest, Fort Denwarf would have to be abandoned, no matter what the strength of the defenders or their weapons.

By that night, the fires that were consuming the steppes seemed to march steadily like an incoming tide toward the foothills of the mountains of Rockhome. The angry light of the flames flickered on the bare stone of the peaks and ridges, and on the walls of the fortress. When dawn came, the black wall of smoke stretched across the horizon from east to west and loomed higher than the mountain peaks of the nearby Altan Tepes. Fires flared in many places as the line of flames began to push into the bracken and stunted trees of the lower foothills. But there was still no sign of the invaders. Apparently their army marched hidden somewhere behind the wall of flame and smoke, fanning the line of fire and driving it before them.

Korinn ordered the defenders of Fort Denwarf to don their armor and make ready their weapons, for the invasion of Rockhome could come at any time now. Their only hope was that the invaders would turn aside at the last minute. The line of fire began to push upward into the foothills, feeding greedily on the lightly wooded lower slopes and almost as quickly breaking into many smaller fires and dying away. The mountainsides were too rocky and barren, the stands of wood too sparse and stunted. There had been a great deal of rain in the mountains that spring, even along the northern slopes, and the trees were reluctant to burn.

The wall of dark smoke grew thicker, like a dark cloud that hung over the mountains. Finally the smoke began to lift grudgingly as the last fires faded. Now the dwarves had their first look at what the flames had done to the steppes. They were shocked to see a dead, barren land, the gently rolling hills black and bare where there had always been a sea of grass. A dull gray haze of smoke hung over the devastated land. Near at hand, several small armies were gathering into a single invasion force of great size and strength along the banks of the Styrdal River, obviously preparing for an assault on the pass.

Korinn went down beyond the pass for a closer look, to try to get some estimate of the size of the force that he would soon face. Four separate companies of soldiers, each some five thousand strong, were approaching from the west with their supply wagons and siege weapons, and at least five more companies were strung out in a line to the east for as far as he could see. He was even more alarmed to discover that their forces were assembled from many different races, some unlike any he had ever seen, not even vaguely human.

At least Korinn now had answers to all his questions. The invasion of Rockhome had become a certainty, and he knew now that an invasion force of perhaps fifty thousand was being directed at this pass alone. He felt reasonably certain they would not be attempting to storm the pass that day, and possibly not the next. The enemy forces were still scattered, and he could imagine with grim satisfaction that they must be in poor condition after marching the breadth of the steppes in all that ash and dust and choking smoke. Korinn also felt reasonably certain he could keep them from taking Fort Denwarf for many days, as long as the Masters themselves did not take a hand in the assault on the fortress. But the gemstone dragons remained curiously absent.

Korinn was concerned about those missing dragons, fearful that they had already passed secretly over the mountains and were raiding with impunity in the cities and settlements of Rockhome to the south. His question was answered later that night, when gemstone dragons began to fly swiftly, alone or in small groups, through the center of the pass, just beyond the reach of the weapons of Fort Denwarf. Their business was obviously to the south, and for now they seemed content to completely ignore the border fortress.

This was Korinn's first opportunity to actually see the gemstone dragons. He had been wondering how much they were like the dragons of his own world. He thought that they were larger than most dragons he had seen, the shapes of their heads and ridges different from that of any breed he knew. Their jewel-like armor gave them a very remarkable appearance, as if they were not living creatures at all but statues carved of stone or cut from facetted jewels that had been brought to life. He watched them hurtle past in the night, wondering where they were going and what they were planning, and he could only hope that the dwarves of Rockhome were already secure below the ground.

The fearful night passed, but the new day only brought the dwarvish defenders that much closer to the inevitability of invasion. By midmorning, the sentries had left their posts farther down the pass, retreating back to the fortress. They brought the warning that the invading armies were beginning their slow march along the road into the mountains, even though a couple of the companies from the east had yet to join the main body of the army. Fort Denwarf would be under siege by nightfall.

For the dozenth time, Korinn reviewed his plans for the battle to hold the Styrdal Pass. He had one plan of defense if the invading armies attacked first, and a second, very different plan if the gemstone dragons attacked. He had to take for granted that he would have to face the Masters sooner or later, especially if he was successful in holding up their army. The only plan he did not consider was that Thelvyn Fox-Eyes and the dragons would come to his rescue at the last moment. He had no doubt that the dragons would come, but he knew they needed time. Thelvyn was too clever to go to war unprepared; he would wait until he had a force of dragons powerful enough to face the Masters and their army.

Late that afternoon, as the sun was sinking behind the mountains to the west, the front ranks of the invaders came up through the pass and halted a short distance from the gates of Fort Denwarf. They stopped just beyond the range of most longbows or light crossbows, and they moved their siege weapons and many of their supply wagons to the front to provide added protection. Then, to all appearances, they began to make camp for the night, as if they had no wish to begin battle in the darkness. They were at some disadvantage in bringing their forces against the fortress, since there was only a small open area before the gate.

Indeed, the invaders were required to camp on the road itself, since the last three miles of the approach to Fort Denwarf had been cut into the rocky eastern wall of the deep ravine formed by the Styrdal River. There were sheer cliffs or unclimbably steep slopes on the east side of the road. The west side of the road, bordered by a high, massive stone curb, fell away into the darkness of the ravine. While the design of the road appeared to be a simple matter of convenience, dwarves seldom left anything to chance that might prove important to the defense of their cities and treasures.

Korinn waited until well after nightfall, giving the invaders time to make their camp and settle in for the night. He had been standing on the wall of the fortress watching them for some time, and he could easily believe the report that they were slaves whose minds and wills were under the control of the Masters. They seldom spoke, or at least when they did they spoke too softly to be heard, never singing or laughing or taunting the defenders but going about their tasks with a lifeless, almost mindless intensity.

"How are you at ninepins?" Korinn asked General Balar.

"My boys are very good at it," the older dwarf answered. "Shall we have a game tonight?"

"Right now would seem to be a good time, while the Masters aren't here to interfere."

The defenders of Fort Denwarf began their "game" only a few minutes later. A large ballista released its load with a dull, heavy snap and creak of timbers, and a large stone lifted deceptively slowly over the wall of the gateyard. The dwarves knew their business well, and the stone sailed out over the road over a hundred yards before it crashed into the nearest of the siege engines the invaders had brought forward. The impact crushed the base of the small tower, which gradually tilted, then fell forward as if it were in slow motion. The heavy stone itself continued on, gathering speed on the steep incline of the road, brutally battering aside supply wagons.

Dwarves were meticulous in their plans, and they had anticipated circumstances such as this in their designs. Over the years, they had cut stones, ranging from a hundred pounds to several tons, into perfectly round shot for the ballistae. Of course, even the dwarves could not hurl a stone more than a couple of hundred yards or so, and the road disappeared around a turn in the pass not much farther beyond that range. But the dwarves had devised a way that allowed their weapons to have a much greater effective range. The road was wide, bordered by the wall of the cliff on one side and a high stone curb on the other, and it descended steadily to the sentry post on the far side, nearly three miles away. The descent was just steep enough to keep a large stone rolling at a deadly pace for the entire distance.

During the day, the dwarves had moved all their ballistae into the gate yard along with a generous supply of shot, so that they were able to fling stones over the wall as quickly as they could reload. The first three dozen shots reduced the barrier of siege weapons and supply wagons to shattered ruins. Most of the stones continued to roll along the road, scattering the encamped invaders. Indeed, the first stone caught a large portion of the army by surprise; many of the soldiers failed to understand their situation until three or four stones had rolled through in rapid succession. They scrambled desperately to get out of the way, but there was nowhere for them to go. They were trapped on the road, left trying to dodge as best they could while the stones bounced back and forth between the inner wall and the curb.

For the moment, the defenders of Fort Denwarf had every advantage, their enemy trapped in the path of destruction of their weapons, unable even to protect themselves, much less fight back. But Korinn knew how quickly fortune could turn against the dwarves. They kept up their attack for as long as they could, as teams of dwarves cranked back the arms of the ballistae and loaded another stone as quickly as they could. Suddenly, without warning, one of the higher towers of the fortress exploded in flames and crashed down in burning wreckage. The defenders looked up to see dark shapes moving swiftly through the night sky, darting in to strike swiftly with fire and destruction.

But the dwarves were hardly caught by surprise. Korinn had known that if he gave the invading army any trouble, the Masters would return quickly to deal with the problem. Except for the crews working the ballistae, he had already sent all the defenders out of Fort Denwarf by secret ways, beginning the inevitable retreat southward toward Stahl and Evemur. That made the final retreat much quicker and easier now that the fortress had to be abandoned in a hurry. The dwarves released their final shots and hurried into the depths of the main keep, descending into deep tunnels cut into the mountain. In a matter of minutes, the last of the defenders were filing quickly and silently through the underground ways, careful to leave no trace of their passage. In time they came to a secret door in the shadows along one wall, and one by one they disappeared inside.

Korinn Bear Slayer and General Balar were the last to arrive at the hidden door. In honor of the older dwarf's years of service at the fortress, Korinn passed inside first, permitting Balar to close and seal the door behind him.

"A week ago I wouldn't have believed that we would ever be forced to abandon Denwarf to an enemy," Balar said, pausing a moment to listen at the door. "It galls me to leave while the walls are still standing and the gate is still intact. But with those dragons blasting at the towers, it's no use trying to defend the fort. I just hope those beasties don't tear the place apart."

"I doubt they'll spend the time and effort," Korinn assured

him. "We'll rebuild whatever is left. I fear we'll have a great deal to rebuild before this is done."

They quickly set the final traps, which would bring down massive blocks of stone to close the passage if anyone tried to come through from the other side. Then the two dwarves hurried along the dark passage. About a hundred yards down the tunnel, they came to a chamber where a small company of soldiers waited for them with their packs. The others were already far ahead. The soldiers bore magic lanterns to light the way, although a dwarf's night vision was sufficient to find his way in almost total darkness. Once Korinn and Balar had pulled on the straps of their packs, the company filed out through the passage on the far side of the chamber.

Korinn wondered what was happening back at the fortress. Had the Masters already discovered that the dwarves had abandoned Fort Denwarf? He hoped they would notice that the fortress was empty soon in order to hold destruction to a minimum. The only thing Korinn really regretted leaving behind was his courier horses. Being young and strong, he had no complaints about marching, but the horses would have gotten him back to Dengar far sooner. But unfortunately the horses were not a safe option. The roads were unsafe for travel with the Masters already within Rockhome, and the cities were probably under siege by now.

He understood that there was little he could do. The dwarves of Fort Denwarf had probably fought the last battle in the protection of Rockhome that very night. From now on, their only for survival was to lock themselves as securely as they could within their underground cities and strongholds and wait for the Dragonking to arrive with reinforcements. But how long would that be? With any luck, the dragons could already be on their way, although it seemed more realistic not to expect them for another three or four days.

Even if there was nothing else he could do, he wanted to return to Dengar immediately. If the lower city was in danger of falling to the enemy, he wanted to be there.

The dwarves marched at a swift and steady pace for nearly two hours before they came to another small chamber, where they paused to rest. They didn't dare wait long, because soon they would have to take to the open. Dwarves were industrious and patient tunnelers, but cutting tunnels took a great deal of time, even small passages such as the one they were in.

After resting a short time, they followed a side tunnel for several hundred yards before it brought them to a hidden door deep within the ravine of the Styrdal River. Korinn paused a moment to look toward the north, fearful of seeing Fort Denwarf in flames. When he saw only a few tiny yellow lights flickering in the distance, he was reassured that the fortress itself was not burning. His companions were already filing across a simple rope bridge that had been erected only days before. It was cut down again once they were all across. When daylight came, there was to be no trace of their passage.

After that, they disappeared into the mountains to the west of the Styrdal Valley, following narrow, hidden paths through the wilderness. Keeping in deep ravines or beneath the cover of trees, they weren't likely to be seen by a passing dragon. The distance from Fort Denwarf to the city of Stahl was nearly forty-five miles, and even the sturdy dwarves couldn't march that far in one night. The sun was peeking above the summit of Denwarf Spur on the east side of the river when they came at last to another hidden door leading down into another tunnel. They paused to rest for some time before they went on. They would march another ten miles through the tunnels before they reached Stahl.

They did not move on again until noon, having reached the end of their endurance. After a final determined march through the tunnels, they entered the remote passages of the lower city of Stahl late that afternoon. Soldiers from Fort Denwarf had been arriving all day. One of the commanders of the city garrison was there to meet them as they emerged through the hidden entrance to the tunnel.

"Korinn Bear Slayer," the soldier said, recognizing him. "Then it's true that Fort Denwarf has fallen?"

"We've been forced to leave Denwarf to the Masters," Korinn said as he moved aside so that the door of the tunnel could be closed. "What about Stahl? Have you sealed the entrance to the upper city yet?"

"Just about. The Masters have been battering at our

defenses since the night before last, but we're still trying to move needed supplies down here between their attacks. We hope we won't have to abandon the upper city until the actual siege begins."

Korinn was taken to the residence of the governor of Stahl, where he was able to wash and had his first real meal in some time. What he wanted most was news of the invasion of Rockhome, but there was little to hear. For the most part, the only things moving between the cities and towns of Rockhome were the Masters. Because the roads were closed, the cities themselves were effectively already under siege.

Having the garrison from Fort Denwarf at hand could make a good deal of difference to the defense of Stahl. The invaders would most likely attack here first, so it appeared that Stahl would have to endure the longest siege of any of the cities of Rockhome. Korinn feared there might be another army of invaders coming through one of the passes to the northeast, which would place the eastern cities, perhaps even Dengar itself, in immediate danger. He suspected that the Masters might pass by some of the lesser cities to attack Dengar first, and so he sent part of the Fort Denwarf garrison on to Dengar at once.

The invaders began to descend from the pass the next morning. The road crossed the Styrdal a few miles beyond Fort Denwarf, and their army could be seen marching down from the mountains on the west side of the river. Standing on the wall of the city near the north gate, Korinn could see them clearly. They appeared to be entirely lacking in siege weapons. That might help slow down the assault of Stahl, unless the gemstone dragons arrived.

"They should be here by tonight," General Balar said. "I wonder if they've learned to keep their distance after the welcome we gave them at Fort Denwarf."

"They'll be more wary of traps," Korinn replied. "The only question I have is whether they'll attack right away, or if they'll wait for the Masters."

"Stahl is a difficult place to defend," Governor Konar said, stroking his long, white beard. Although he was not a soldier, he seemed eager for a fight. "Our problem is having no less

than eight gates to defend, seven crossing the rivers on the east
and west sides and one facing south."

Korinn was aware of the problem. Stahl sat on a hilly point
of land at the fork of two rivers. While the rivers made the final
approach to the walls difficult, there were simply too many
gates to defend. If the Masters did level the place, he thought
grimly, the city would be rebuilt a little differently.

"Will you be staying here at Stahl?" he asked General Balar.

"That was my plan," the older dwarf said. "I want to stay
with my lads through this. And if I stay here, you can head out
to Dengar right away. You might as well go now, before the
Masters arrive."

Korinn nodded. "I suppose I should be on my way. Even if
I leave now, I won't reach Dengar any sooner than the day
after tomorrow. With any luck, the dragons will be here to
help us about the same time."

CHAPTER NINE

Thelvyn and Kharendaen approached the hidden city of Windreach boldly, for the first time unconcerned about what kind of welcome they would receive. But when dragons began rising swiftly out of the city of Windreach, Thelvyn wondered if their opinion of him had taken a bad turn during his absence. Kharendaen remained unconcerned about the reception. In fact, she actually looked rather pleased, so he ignored his apprehension and continued his approach toward the city. He was still a bit confused when a dozen dragons of every breed began to circle around quickly to move ahead of him and his mate. More dragons soon joined them.

Only then did he realize that this was an impromptu honor guard to welcome the return of the Dragonking. To his even greater surprise, he realized that he was actually rather touched by the gesture, and also quite impressed. He had always found dragons to be solitary and aloof creatures.

Following their honor guard, Thelvyn and Kharendaen began a slow descent into Windreach, dropping down into the deep late-afternoon shadows of the wall of the city. Looking enormously pleased, Sir George was all but standing in his saddle. He looked as if he would have waved a flag or blown a trumpet if he had one. Thelvyn was beginning to wonder just where he was being taken, but a moment later he saw First Speaker Marthaen moving up to fly close beside him.

"I assume that the dragons have already learned about the invasion of the steppes," Thelvyn said, looking over his shoulder at the gold dragon.

"News arrived last night," Marthaen answered, dropping his sails to slow his flight. "I felt certain you would arrive soon, and I ordered the dragons to begin to prepare for war this morning."

"Good thinking," Thelvyn said. "They no longer seem averse to the idea of going to war."

"They've had a few days to think about it since you were here last," the older dragon replied. "The full extent of the danger we face has become much more apparent to them. You can see for yourself that they've finally begun to understand that you are no threat to them."

Marthaen suggested that they retreat to Thelvyn's lair in the Hall of the Great One, which was large enough to accommodate a hasty council of war. That proved to be a wise course of action. Jherdar joined them while they were still circling to land, and a number of other dragon leaders continued to arrive over the next half hour while Thelvyn and Kharendaen rested briefly, dining on roast elk, bread, and cheese.

"We tried to get a look at the invaders on our way here," Thelvyn told the dragons a short time later. "I cannot say how many gemstone dragons there are, since we had to be careful to keep our distance, but they've brought an army of perhaps a hundred thousand with them into this world. As you know, they're burning off the steppes in a single, immense wall of fire. I've never seen anything like it. By tomorrow night, they will have left the steppes completely destroyed."

"I've sent scouts to do some judicious spying," Marthaen said. "We have already heard that there may be as many as two hundred gemstone dragons. The Ethengar and the wild herds of the steppes have been fleeing into the mountains of northern Rockhome, so they should survive. But I don't believe we can be ready to face the invaders before they have moved on into Rockhome."

"I agree," Thelvyn said. "For one thing, I want to wait for accurate reports of their numbers. If we can destroy the Masters or force them to retreat, dealing with their army should be a matter of sport."

"Do you really expect it to be that easy?" Jherdar asked. "The Masters have to know that we can overwhelm their invasion force. And now that the Dragonking has returned with the collar, they must know that we will be coming after them."

"Not necessarily," Thelvyn explained. "We have one very unexpected advantage. The Masters believe that the dragons have refused my rule and will not go to war. As far as they know, the Dragonking is an exile begging for support wherever he can find it. I suspect that's why they've chosen to attack now, while they believe there's no one in this world willing or able to fight them."

Jherdar looked impressed. "How did they arrive at such an inaccurate impression of the situation?"

"Do you recall that spy in Braejr I went to flush out? I fed her some misleading information before I broke her tie with the Masters. I've learned that she actually served someone called the Overlord, who seems not to be a dragon at all. I suspect the Masters are only slaves to the Overlord, but they don't know it."

"We seem to possess more advantages than I would have expected," Marthaen remarked.

"We must not deceive ourselves," Thelvyn warned. "I may have them fooled, but they may only be leading me to think that I've fooled them. The Masters are experts at conquering worlds. Whole races may be enslaved to serve as their armies. They could open a worldgate and send through a hundred thousand soldiers any time and place they choose. We must be very careful, even if it means that Rockhome must endure a long siege while we gather our strength. If the element of surprise is indeed in our favor, then we must be careful that we do not give ourselves away."

The others looked thoughtful, even a little subdued. Now that Thelvyn had their support, he wanted them to understand just how serious a threat they faced. Although he didn't speak of it, he knew the dragons weren't used to working together in large numbers, even though they had cooperated reasonably well in their war with Alphatia the year before. But his greatest concern was that they would be overconfident. Except for the Dragonlord, the dragons had never known an enemy that was a serious threat to them, able to stand up to them on their own terms.

"How large a force of dragons can we expect to assemble and take into Rockhome within in a week at most?" he asked.

Jherdar lowered his head, considering his answer. "We have been gathering an army here since you returned to the west several days ago, and we summoned the kingdoms of the dragons when we first became aware of the invasion of the steppes. Even so, we have little more than a thousand fighting dragons at Windreach. We can have another thousand in three, perhaps four days. Given a full week, perhaps a thousand more."

"Of course, we cannot have so many dragons assembled in one place for very long," Marthaen added. "It is impossible to feed so many."

Thelvyn nodded. "Jherdar, do you know the location of the ancient city of Darmouk?"

"No," Jherdar replied, looking confused and rather surprised at the question. Darmouk was Thelvyn's lair, his property and the stronghold of his hoard, won in battle from the renegade king Kardyer. Another dragon would not dare violate the privacy of his stronghold.

"You'll be able to find it easily enough," Thelvyn said. "It would be a very good place to establish our stronghold. I'm considering having you take a force of dragons there in a couple of days."

"It may be too near Rockhome," Kharendaen said.

"That's true, but it makes it a very convenient place for a stronghold," he said, then noticed that the others still looked uncertain. He smiled wryly. "I appreciate your concern for my rights, but it cannot be helped. We may win this battle, but we still have a long war ahead of us, and the worst is yet to come. We need strongholds for several hundred dragons throughout this part of the world, from the Highlands to

Alphatia. Wherever the Masters might appear, we must be able to get a company of dragons there quickly. They must not catch us by surprise."

Jherdar bowed his head. "It will be as you say. And you may be assured that my own bodyguards will stand watch over your treasure."

"That won't be necessary, I'm sure," Sir George commented. "Is anyone likely to try to steal from the Dragonking?"

As soon as their plans were finalized and duties assigned, most of the others hurried away to attend to the preparations for battle. Sir George retired to his own room, one of the spare chambers of the Dragonking's lair that the Eldar had furnished to suit his needs. Thelvyn felt better about the problem of gathering an army, since everything was proceeding much more swiftly and smoothly than he had expected. He was also beginning to have a much higher opinion of his dragons; he had always been under the well-founded impression that dragons could usually be counted upon to be stubborn, contrary, and determined to do everything the hard way. He needed to be able to trust them to serve him willingly and wisely.

Both he and his mate were exhausted after the long flight from the Highlands, and they needed to rest. When Marthaen returned to the chamber after seeing the other dragons on their way, he found that his sister had moved close to Thelvyn's side so that she could rub her cheek along the side of his chest and neck.

"Must the two of you be so boundlessly affectionate?" Marthaen asked, sighing loudly.

Thelvyn knew the older dragon was jesting with him. "Do not deprive me of my only comfort. What about the dragons? Are they still willing to follow me?"

"I honestly believe you can trust them to follow you," Marthaen said, sitting back on his haunches and facing the other two. "They have had a little time to consider what they have learned about the Masters, and they have been forced to admit that they must defend their world in order to defend themselves. The knowledge that the gemstone dragons were responsible for the near destruction of their race at the hands of the first Dragonlord has awakened their desire for vengeance. And they fear that the gemstone dragons look upon them as inferior, easy victims for enslavement. Jherdar and the red dragons are ready and eager for war, and the golds will be responsive to your call."

Thelvyn nodded, looking weary. "We have a hard time ahead of us. I wish I could keep my people safe rather than lead them into a possibly hopeless war."

Marthaen lifted his head. "Your people?"

"I find myself becoming quite comfortable with the thought of being a dragon," Thelvyn admitted. "I wish I had more time to enjoy it, but the dwarves are waiting. Korinn Bear Slayer is sure to have told them we will be coming."

"You seem certain that the Masters will push on into Rockhome," Marthaen observed.

"Have you ever wondered why they struck first in the steppes and their next move appears to be to invade Rockhome? Certainly not for the sake of an easy victory; they have to know that they'll have a hard time routing the dwarves from their underground cities. But by taking the steppes and then Rockhome, and possibly pushing on into Alfheim and Traladara, they'll break this part of the world into two parts, with them in the middle. Thyatis would be on one side, while Darokin and the Highlands would be on the other. Neither would be able to work together in a common defense."

Marthaen nodded. "What do you think will happen when we attack? Will the Masters retreat, or will they open their worldgates and pour through their reserves until they overwhelm us?"

"I honestly do not know what will happen," Thelvyn had to admit. "That's why we must gather our strength before we attack. We have to hit them so hard from the outset that they have no choice but to flee. I just hope we have no traitors in our midst telling them our every move."

Marthaen looked overwhelmed for a moment with surprise and indignation. "Surely the Masters cannot control dragons," he said finally.

"You forget that they controlled Murodhir," Kharendaen told him. "We must never underestimate them, especially since they seem so willing to underestimate us."

* * * * *

Korinn Bear Slayer left Stahl at dawn in the same manner in which he had arrived the previous day, by the secret underground passages. But this time he went alone, since all the troops that had been sent on to Dengar had left the day before. He wished now that he had left the previous day, slipping out with a pair of courier horses before the invaders besieged the city. Now he would be required to walk, and he couldn't hope to reach Dengar before the end of the next day no matter how hard he forced his pace.

The hidden passage leading east from Stahl toward Dengar was one of the most remarkable tunnels in all of Rockhome, and one of the most difficult feats of engineering the dwarves had ever attempted. The passage ran for nearly eight miles beneath the northern end of Lake Stahl, buried a hundred yards deep in bedrock in a clay-lined tunnel to prevent flooding. Korinn had never taken this tunnel before, and he found the thought of passing beneath the lake itself to be a bit daunting, but in the two hours he spent in that part of the tunnel, he found it the same as the rest of the passage.

He didn't emerge from the tunnel until it ended in the rugged, forested land more than a dozen miles east of the lake, where a small passage brought him up through a hidden door in a rocky outcrop. The secret path led him quickly to the top of a low, moss-covered cliff where he could look back toward the west through an opening in the trees. It was now the middle of the day, and he could see that a brisk battle was being fought over the city of Stahl many miles across the lake. He was too far away to see much detail, and so he could only judge from the dark haze and the trails of smoke that rose from the city.

Looking closer, he saw that an army was moving along the main road, having already passed the bridge over the Styrdal River. Indeed, their vanguard was now hardly more than a couple of miles northwest of where he stood. When the invaders had prepared their siege outside Stahl the evening before, he had assumed that they meant to capture that city before they pressed on into Rockhome. Instead, they had divided their forces, sending perhaps half of their army on toward Dengar. His decision to leave Stahl had been the correct one, since he would now be bringing news of the attack to Dengar only a day or so ahead of the invaders.

With an army following him, Korinn knew that every extra hour he could gain in reaching Dengar ahead of the invaders was important. Dengar was far more defensible than Stahl, and the upper city might hold out for days against a conventional army, but not against an attack of gemstone dragons. Following the trail south through the woods just below the mountains to the east, he marched as rapidly as he could through the rest of that day and well into the night. Reluctantly he gave up the race a couple of hours before midnight, when the night became so dark that he was having trouble finding the trail at times.

Korinn hurried on again early the next morning, just as the sky was beginning to grow light before the rising of the sun beyond the mountains to the east. He walked only another hour before he slowed, looking about when he came into a land he recognized from past visits. After a short time, he found a tumble of gray, mossy stones almost hidden in a steep fold of the wooded hills. He realized he never would have found it in the darkness of the night before. He had to take off his pack before he could push back behind the stones, but he found the hidden door and the dark, narrow tunnel that ran as straight as an arrow beneath the mountains to Dengar. The underground passage cut more than a dozen miles from the overland journey around the southern spur of the mountains at Evemur.

Because the underground passage was so straight and level, he was able to move along at a quick pace. All the same, many long hours passed in the deep darkness of the tunnel, lit only dimly by the pale silver light of his lamp. When at last he came up through a hidden door into the back passage of Lower Dengar, night had long since fallen in the world above. He was careful to secure all the hidden traps as he approached the door and opened it cautiously. A trap or two was always set in the secret ways, even in times of peace, in the unlikely event that an old enemy or a band of thieves found the tunnel. Even then, only commanders of the highest rank knew the secrets for setting the traps and opening the doors.

The city itself was relatively quiet, with few people about, so that he passed unnoticed as he made his way to the palace. Dengar hadn't been besieged within living memory, but he thought that the city seemed unusually tense, as if no one dared to speak loudly or show themselves. As he passed through the silent streets, he began to see people peering out at him out from windows and from behind narrowly opened doorways.

The palace itself was especially dark and quiet, as if it were the middle of the night. The hour was indeed a bit late, but Korinn thought that someone should be around. He wondered if the siege had already begun. While he was certain the invading army was still behind him, other forces could have approached Dengar from a different direction. He was beginning to wonder if he should make the journey to the upper city when he saw Dorinn emerging from their father's chambers.

"Korinn!" his brother exclaimed, surprised to see him. "Have you just returned?"

"I just arrived through the hidden tunnel," Korinn explained. "Is the city under siege?"

Dorinn nodded grimly. "Three days ago, an army of about fifty thousand came through the pass of the Hrap River. They moved into the valley below the city earlier today, but so far they've been content to remain there. What about Stahl? The troops you sent here finished coming through the tunnel only hours ahead of you, which was why I hadn't expected to see you back so soon."

"I've had to hurry," Korinn said as they walked slowly toward his room to stow away his gear. "The invaders—their western army, I should say—laid siege to Stahl two nights ago. When I left yesterday morning, I found half of their forces following me."

Dorinn frowned. "Were they headed here, or to Evemur?"

"I assumed they were coming here," Korinn replied, pausing a moment while his brother held open the door to his room for him. He slipped the straps off his shoulder and set down his pack just inside the door. "Of course, with fifty thousand invaders already here, they might be headed for Evemur instead. The battle has already begun in Stahl. I could see smoke rising from several parts of the upper city. Of course, Stahl isn't very easily defended against a large force, and there isn't much of a lower city. Whether or not the upper city has fallen by now depends largely upon whether or not the gemstone dragons have attacked."

"My greatest concern about our situation here is that the invaders are waiting for the Masters to crack open our defenses," Dorinn said. "That's what I would do in their place. An army of fifty thousand seems large, but they could suffer enormous casualties trying to reach the gate of the upper city."

"If the Masters attack, they attack," Korinn said philosophically. "There's nothing we can do about it. We can't hold the upper city for very long against them in any event. My hope is that the dragons will come before the Masters attack, or soon after. They should be here any time now."

"Yes, the dragons," Dorinn said, staring at the ground uncomfortably. "I should warn you that our people have no faith in receiving help from the dragons. The senate has forced Father to shape our policies on the assumption that the dragons will never come. I've been told that the upper city must not be taken at any cost."

"That's foolish," Korinn declared hotly. "The dwarves have always been ready to close the inner gates and wait out an attack underground, where our greatest safety lies."

"The assumption is that we cannot hope to wait out the Masters," the older dwarf explained. "Most people fear that, given time, the Masters can simply dig us out like a hound after a rabbit. And no one believes that the dragons are going to help us. You'll find yourself very unpopular if you insist that the Dragonking will keep his word. I think that even Father no longer has any hope of that."

Korinn had to retire for the night, in order to be rested enough to face the next day and the coming battle with all his strength. But he was dismayed by what he had learned. When he considered it, however, he had to admit that he wasn't surprised to find that the dwarves had no faith in the word of the dragons. Nothing had ever happened to make them believe the dragons would come to their defense. The one point that disturbed him most was that the dwarves seemed to have lost faith not only in the dragons, but also in their once unshakable belief that they could always hold their own in the underground.

When he thought about it, he had to face the unsettling truth. He knew the enemy as well as anyone. He had seen the burning of the steppes, and he had seen the Masters at Fort Denwarf. And he had to admit that the dwarves could never hope to win this war on their own. The only difference between him and the other dwarves was that Thelvyn Fox-Eyes was his friend, and he trusted the Dragonking.

Korinn donned his armor and gathered his weapons before dawn the next morning. After speaking with his father, he began the long climb to the upper city. His brother Dorinn had gone up before dawn, in order to be on hand if the enemy began to move against Dengar. King Daroban would remain below, trusting the defense of the upper city to his sons, and ready to assume command of the defense of the lower city if they did not return.

Korinn found his brother standing on the wall over the gate. The sun was still behind the mountains to the east, and the valley far below remained in deep shadows, as if night lingered in the woods. He could see thousands of flickering yellow campfires amid the trees, as distant and small as the stars in the predawn sky. He could also see that the invaders were preparing themselves for the steep climb to the gates of Dengar, gathering their companies in a long column along the road below the ramp. He surveyed the sky quickly, but there was no sign yet of the Masters.

"This would seem to be the day," Dorinn commented. "I should pass the command of the upper city to you, considering your experience."

Korinn shook his head firmly. "You've prepared the defenses of this city, and you know best what to do. I don't know what strength of arms or weapons you might have at hand. And you've had your own share of experience."

"I appreciate your confidence," his brother said sincerely. "But to speak candidly, I have other reasons for giving you command. If the Masters come, I see no reason to waste the lives of our soldiers trying to hold the upper city when the passages below are far more defensible. My intention is to defy the senate's orders and abandon the upper city, but my concern is that I will be branded a coward and the defense of the city will be given to someone more willing to make foolish and hopeless gestures. They will be less willing to call you a coward. They would accept your actions as inevitable."

"I appreciate your concern," Korinn said pensively, "but I will not accept your command. I will support your decisions completely. They will not dare to call both of us cowards."

He turned away, but Dorinn stopped him. "We both know which of us is to be the next king. You should have the command of our defenses so that you will have the honor of the victory."

"It remains to be seen which of us will sit on the throne," Korinn told his brother firmly. "I believe that the throne would be well served by your patience and wisdom. But since dwarves often see valor above wisdom, you would do well to earn such an honor for yourself."

The invaders began the slow climb up the steep approach to the gates of Dengar in the middle of the morning, but they seemed to be in no hurry. Perhaps having learned a lesson at Fort Dengar, they placed a heavily armored fighting force in the lead. They pushed before them sturdy barricades to turn aside any boulders and carried large shields over their heads to protect themselves from projectiles hurled from the cliffs above. Korinn watched them from the wall above the gate, trying to guess what they would do when they came within striking distance. He wondered if they would spend their own strength on an assault when the Masters could tear away the city defenses so much more quickly and easily.

He also kept in mind that a second army could arrive as soon as that very evening. That left him with some difficult questions in guessing the intentions of his enemies. The enemy force below Dengar gave every appearance of preparing for an immediate attack, while a second army was only hours away. Either the invaders wanted to initiate a siege of the city by getting a force to the top of the plateau, or they expected the appearance of the Masters to turn this first assault into an inevitable conquest of Upper Dengar. Korinn thought it wise to be prepared for the worst.

He waited a moment while his brother spoke briefly with a messenger, relaying orders to move troops to the front wall. Once the soldier had left with his assignment, Korinn moved closer so that they could speak quietly.

"I may be guessing, but I believe that the Masters will be here soon," he explained. "When their troops got in trouble at Fort Denwarf, they were ready to move in quickly. Of course, when Stahl was besieged, I never saw any of the Masters above the city. Then again, I was miles away by that time."

"I won't argue with you," Dorinn said, glancing briefly over the wall at the approaching invaders. "What do you think?"

"I suspect that these forces are advancing up the ramp to be ready to move in when the Masters drive us from the wall. That places us in a very difficult situation. We can't allow those forces to come up the ramp, but the Masters are going to intervene if things go badly for their boys."

Dorinn nodded. "Then we must do all the damage we can as quickly as we can, but we also must be ready to withdraw to the tunnels. I think we can handle that."

Dorinn left at once to put the new plans into action. With the enemy already on the march, the defenders of Dengar had only a short time to make any changes in tactics. Since his brother was more familiar with the forces at hand, Korinn was satisfied to leave such matters entirely to Dorinn. Instead, he remained at the wall watching the advance of the enemy, trying to anticipate what would happen in the next few hours. He expected the Masters to appear at any time, probably as their army neared the gate. Once the dwarves began their attempt to repel the enemy's advance, he knew that the gemstone dragons were likely to come in a hurry.

When the first of the invaders had come halfway up the long ramp, Korinn began to feel the rising tension not only in himself but in all the grim dwarvish warriors stationed along the wall. The ramp twisted back and forth on itself, with first one side and then the other looking out over the steep slope of the escarpment. The first of the defensive traps was located just

beyond the army's present location, at a point where there was
no room to turn and no place to run. The invaders came on
until their vanguard moved slowly, steadily up the longest
straight length of the road in the very center of the climb and
was nearing the next sharp turn.

A deep rumble shook the wall where Korinn stood, as if the
spine of the mountain itself had suddenly snapped, reverberat-
ing for a long moment through even the deepest caverns of the
lower city. The invaders on the ramp paused for a moment,
waiting in apprehension as the vibration in the stones on
which they stood died away. Then, just as they began to feel
that the danger had passed and began to resume their climb,
the seemingly solid stone of the mountainside crumbled and
the entire middle length of the ramp broke free and began to
slide away. The long line of soldiers, including their beasts and
their armor and their great war machines, fell away in a cas-
cade of broken stone, sweeping down the steep slope in a
deadly avalanche, carrying away even more segments of the
invading army on the slopes below.

Within moments, the lower half of the escarpment disappeared beneath a great cloud of brown dust, billowing out
across the valley below, so that Korinn was unable to see the
bottom. Even after the lower half of the ramp disappeared in a
spreading cloud of dust, he could hear the cries of the injured
and the shouts of terse orders. The dwarves along the wall
began to cheer and to call out fierce challenges, greatly heart-
ened by the swift, devastating rout of the first assault.

Korinn knew that any other army would have just been
dealt a serious setback. The invaders had lost at least several
thousand soldiers, but they had tens of thousands waiting in
the valley below. A large portion of the middle of the ramp
had been destroyed, creating an obstacle that would bring
most armies to a stop for days. But he was certain that the
Masters were out there somewhere, watching and waiting.

Indeed, the answer was at hand almost at once. The
dwarves fell silent as the dark, menacing forms of dragons
passed almost directly overhead, the unearthly forms of gemstone dragons as they moved down from the upper slopes of
Point Everast. With all their attention focused on the invaders

below, the dwarves hadn't even seen them approaching. They flew swiftly over the city, passing just over the wall in an almost contemptuous gesture, then circled around tightly as they braced their wings to drop toward the forests below.

Following their line of flight, Korinn leaned out over the parapet, but he couldn't see the gemstone dragons once they had dropped down beneath the cloud of dust created by the avalanche. Even after the cloud of dust began to settle, he couldn't tell for certain just what the Masters intended. For the moment, they seemed to be devoting their full attention to restoring order among their troops and preparing for a new assault. Companies of soldiers had been gathered into precise columns and stood ready, although Korinn could not imagine what they proposed to do next. The ramp was closed to them, unless they were reckless enough to swarm over the wreckage of the center loop while the dwarves sent a deadly hail of stones and arrows down upon their heads.

Many long, anxious moments passed while the invaders reorganized. Their new tactics seemed to defy reason: they were not gathered on the road at the base of the ramp but in two large groups well to either side. A pair of alien dragons moved behind each of the two large companies of soldiers. Standing at the parapet of their high walls, the dwarves were utterly silent as they watched and waited in apprehension. Then the Masters stood up on their hind legs, their long, proud necks held high and their wings spread out behind their backs for balance. Facing the wall of the escarpment, they lifted their forelegs in a gesture that was clearly a part of some invocation of magic.

The jewel-like armor of the strange dragons began to glow, two like ruby, one with the clear light of crystal, and the last with the deep green of emerald. Then, with a sudden flash of light, brief but so intense that Korinn had to look away, they disappeared. The light faded away slowly from that first blinding glare, but then the light surrounding each of the gemstone dragons reached upward toward the city in a long, graceful curve like the arc of a rainbow. The companies of soldiers began to hurry forward in orderly columns, forming into long, narrow lines of two abreast as they stepped into the streams of light.

An instant later, they began to stream out of the far ends of the arcs of light before the walls of the city. During the first moments, the invaders spread out across the open fields unopposed, swinging grappling hooks at the ends of looped ropes to the top of the wall. The dwarves began to recover from their surprise, raining down arrows and stones and cutting away the ropes even as the enemy was climbing the walls of Dengar. But the dwarves were in a desperate position from the outset, since they had hardly expected to have the battle at their very walls so soon. Many of the dwarven soldiers were still away from the wall at the hidden defenses designed to keep the invaders off the ramp.

And yet the assault had only just begun. Many of the invaders were not even vaguely like men, but rather strange beings who could leap up the ropes faster than the dwarves could cut them down, or strange, hulking warriors whose natural armor could resist almost any arrow or battle-axe. In addition, there were swift, slender swordsmen who towered over the dwarves, with arms so long that it was difficult to penetrate within their reach to slay them. And then the Masters arrived, sweeping down from the mountains in great waves.

Korinn fought desperately to hold his own on the wall over the gate, standing with a dozen soldiers to drive back the hordes intent upon sweeping over the wall and opening the gate. He could no longer spot his brother, who was off somewhere trying to muster reinforcements to man the walls. For his own part, Korinn thought it was already too late to hold the wall, perhaps even too late for the defenders along the wall to retreat back to the passage to the lower city. Still he fought on with grim fury, sweeping his ax from side to side to snap the ropes of the hooks that were being flung over the parapet, then turning to engage in fierce battle with some alien warrior.

Suddenly the attackers fell back from the gate wall so abruptly that Korinn and his fellow defenders glanced about in surprise, so caught up the fierceness of the battle that for a moment they did not understand what had happened. Korinn turned sharply and saw that one of the largest of the gemstone dragons, a jade, was approaching the gate of the city, snapping its broad wings in quick, powerful strokes as it landed at the top of the ramp. The dragon waited for a long moment, folding away its wings while it was joined by the terrible creatures that served as its bodyguards, slender creatures not unlike wyverns. They were quick, darting flyers but could also stalk swiftly on their long hind legs, bearing broad-headed spears in their claws.

Rising to its hind legs, the jade dragon suddenly hurtled itself forward toward the gate. Korinn and his dwarven companions leapt aside. The parapet over the gate had suddenly become a very unsafe place to be, and consequently they failed to see the jade dragon's actually attack. A tremendous blow crashed like thunder against the timbers of the gate. The crossbars snapped, and the portals were nearly broken free from their hinges. The walls of the city shook from the impact, and the parapet above the gate cracked and collapsed in a shower of splintered stone.

Two more gemstone dragons arrived, and they rose to their hind legs to take hold of the shattered portals and force them open, sweeping aside the broken stone of the crumbled parapet. The jade dragon forced its way through into the gate yard, intent upon tearing open the inner gate as well. It had only just stepped through the gate when the floor suddenly broke open, dropping the creature into a deep pit filled with sharp spikes. The pits had been built with the intention of trapping enemies on the central bridge, but both of the pits were more than large enough to contain a dragon. Dorinn had ordered the supports holding the retractable platforms to be deliberately weakened. The jade dragon disappeared into the darkness of the pits and fell screaming upon the spikes far below.

Some of the dwarves cheered, but the celebration was half-hearted at best. They had managed to slay one of the Masters almost by chance, but the upper city would fall in a matter of minutes. Korinn did not wait to see how the remaining gemstone dragons would respond, hurrying the remaining defenders off the wall back toward the city. Now that the gate parapet had fallen, they could easily find themselves trapped, with no way to retreat back to the main wall. Glancing briefly over his shoulder, Korinn had the impression that the Masters were everywhere, at least a score of them crawling over the front of the escarpment and physically tearing away the defenses along the wall so that their forces could pour into the city.

Then the sounds of battle died away, and Korinn paused at the doorway of the wall tower to stare. The Masters had stopped short in their destruction, lifting their long necks to stare toward the north. They roared in fury and frustration, a final, futile challenge before they reluctantly drew back from the walls of Dengar to face a new challenge. Moments later the first of wave upon wave of dragons hurtled down from the north and east, red, black, and gold dragons of their own world rushing into battle with swift strokes of their wings.

Holding aloft their shields and weapons, the defenders of Dengar shouted encouragement to their unexpected allies. For the first time in the history of their race, dwarves cheered and laughed to see dragons descending upon their city, and wept with joy to see as if for the first time the grace and beauty of those warriors of the wind.

CHAPTER TEN

Less than a score of gemstone dragons were gathered either above or below the escarpment of the city of Dengar, and yet they seemed determined to stand their ground, even though whole companies of dragons, several hundred strong, were approaching swiftly from the north and east. At least the assault on the walls of the city had faltered while the invading army was left without direction, unable to decide on their own whether to continue with their assault or stand by their Masters.

Leading the advance of the dragons, Thelvyn, once more wearing the Collar of the Dragons, made use of his sharp eyes to search out the scene of battle ahead. Making his decision quickly, he turned his head toward Marthaen, flying a short distance away to his right, and nodded. The First Speaker nodded in response and then turned to head swiftly over the mountains to the west. The largest part of the combined force followed him, some eight hundred dragons in all, leaving Thelvyn with only two hundred. Marthaen would lead his forces quickly against the invaders in western Rockhome; Jherdar was leading an army of a thousand more dragons into

Rockhome from the east. Thelvyn's first concern was to liberate Dengar and help the dwarves to begin to restore order to their land.

The attacking dragons circled out over the valley before turning again so that they could descend in a rapid glide toward the escarpment, soaring on stiff wings with the sails of their tails dropped slightly to reduce their speed. Kharendaen began to drift to one side, prepared to lead a contingent of dragons against four Masters in the valley below. Thelvyn led the remaining forces against the rest of the Masters on the escarpment above, selecting as his own target the largest of the amber dragons, a proud warrior easily his own size who stood just before the ruined gate.

Thelvyn dived down to land at the very top of the ramp, intending to turn the remaining speed of his flight into a swift run that would carry him into battle. For the first time in weeks, he was betrayed by his lack of experience. Dragons were not quite as agile on the ground as he had anticipated. Because his forelegs were shorter than his powerful hind legs, he slipped on his second stride and collapsed heavily onto his deep chest. The amber dragon stepped forward to catch him, tossing him backward with such force that Thelvyn was almost tumbled backward off the escarpment. Even while he was struggling to rise, he lifted his head to see two of the younger gold dragons in his company hurtle themselves upon the amber dragon, who caught them with astonishing ease and easily tossed them aside.

That was enough to make Thelvyn pause, crouching low in a menacing gesture and hackling to discourage his opponent from an immediate attack. He needed an instant to think. Something seemed very wrong. When he had fought them in their own world, the Masters had seemed no more powerful than his world's dragons, either in their magic or in their native strength and speed. Yet now they were easily three times stronger. He reminded himself that Mystara was in fact their true home, the world where their kind had originated centuries before. Whether it was because they were home, or perhaps because of some enchantment, the gemstone dragons were suddenly far stronger, and far more dangerous.

Thelvyn began to wonder if he had come to trust too much in his fighting abilities as a dragon, forgetting his inexperience. Still crouching low in a menacing pose, he began to circle slowly around the amber dragon to buy a few moments more to consider his next move. The first thing that came to his mind was a trick that Kharendaen used successfully to put a dragon on his back. Suddenly he sprang forward toward his opponent. At the very last moment, he ducked his head low, driving his neck and shoulders under the chest of the amber dragon and then thrusting himself upward.

He had no idea what happened next, except that he was abruptly hurtled to the ground with such force that his breath was torn from his chest and his sight turned dark for a long moment. He hardly even recalled what he had been doing until the amber dragon's jaws suddenly fastened tight about his throat, seeking a death grip. For now, he could do nothing more than struggle weakly, still fighting for breath. At that moment, he could not have saved himself.

A pair of gold dragons in Thelvyn's bodyguard suddenly leapt upon the amber dragon from either side, desperate to protect the Dragonking. They should have been able to overwhelm the gemstone dragon easily, even though it was somewhat larger than either of them. As the golds ripped into its folded wings, it reluctantly released its death grip and arched its long neck to roar in pain and fury. Then it shook free from the two attacking dragons and tossed them aside easily, hurtling them across the plain before the gate of Dengar. Finally the gemstone dragon turned back to the Dragonking, determined to destroy its principal enemy while it could.

Thelvyn had been struggling to regain his breath and rise to a standing position, but suddenly he relaxed and lifted himself purposefully. For the first time since he had taken possession of it, the Collar of the Dragons began to surge with power, filling him in turn with renewed energy. He recalled that the collar was said to enhance the powers of its wearer, but no one had been able to tell him just what it could do or how he might command it. Now he understood that the collar had been created in anticipation of this very need, enhancing his abilities to make him more than an equal to the greatest of the Masters.

The amber dragon paused, as if puzzled by Thelvyn's sudden confidence. Then it elected to attack immediately, hoping perhaps to catch him off his guard, leaping forward with its head down in a tactic intended to strike him in the chest and sweep him backward over the edge of the escarpment. In response, Thelvyn rose abruptly to his hind legs and struck the amber dragon with a backhand smash against the side of its head. The blow had force enough to halt the creature's lunge and send it tumbling heavily onto its back, stunned by the impact.

The amber dragon struggled feebly for a moment, then shook its head and tried to rise. But even as it turned back to face him, Thelvyn struck the alien dragon a second blow that left it almost senseless. This time Thelvyn did not wait for his enemy to recover, but stepped forward to grab the amber dragon by the tail. Half-dragging the alien dragon, he carried it to the edge of the escarpment, its weak struggles unable to break his crushing hold. Commanding all his enhanced strength, Thelvyn tossed the amber dragon well out over the edge of the steep cliff, then drew a sharp breath to release a blast of dragonfire. The amber dragon disappeared in a tremendous explosion of fire, and its broken form fell in a fiery trail into the forest far below.

Thelvyn turned quickly, fearful for the safety of his fellow dragons, but he saw that he had little reason to be concerned. The other gemstone dragons seemed to lack the tremendous power of their leader, and the dragons had them vastly outnumbered. The Masters were getting the worst of it, and the death of their leader convinced them that they had had enough. Fighting to break free from the packs of dragons harassing them relentlessly, they leapt into flight and retreated to the north. But the dragons were not about to give up the battle so easily, and a dozen of them pursued the fleeing gemstone dragons into the sky.

For a moment, Thelvyn watched the retreating aliens and wondered whether he should follow them. His plan was to catch the Masters by surprise, which he seemed to have done, and drive them not only from Rockhome but from his world before they could summon forces to organize a counterattack. He decided instead that he could spare a minute more to speak with the dwarves. The dwarven defenders looked as if they needed some reassurance, still struggling to throw the last of the invaders from the wall.

When he turned back to face the city, he was surprised to see Korinn Bear Slayer waving to him from the north wall of the ruined gate. Dwarves built the highest walls in the world, and Thelvyn had to stretch his hind legs to lift his head level with the young dwarf. The soldiers along the wall cheered loudly.

"Everyone seems happy to see me," he commented wryly. "Did they perchance think I would not come?"

"Not for a moment," Korinn declared. "Not to complain, but you might have arrived just a bit sooner."

"Not really," Thelvyn replied. "I had to wait until I had gathered the numbers necessary to destroy the Masters or drive them from our world before they can get organized to strike back against us. I must go after the Masters as soon as possible, but you still have a large army to deal with here. Do you think you can handle the problem if I leave a few dragons behind with you?"

"Of course," Korinn said without hesitation, realizing that the dragons would be doing most of the work. "Your dragons do understand that the dwarves are now their allies, don't they?"

"I think so."

Korinn laughed to himself; he had asked the question in jest, and he hoped Thelvyn had been jesting in turn. Then he turned to see his brother, who had made his way through the tower where the gatehouse joined the main wall. Dorinn was moving with even more difficulty than usual, obviously nearing the end of his strength, and his abused armor was mute testimony that he had seen his own share of fighting. He paused, a bit shaken to see the head of a gold dragon only a few yards away.

"Thelvyn Fox-Eyes, you recall my older brother, Dorinn," Korinn said quickly, to remind Dorinn that this dragon was an old friend. "I take it the city is secure once again?"

"We're rounding up the last of the invaders who made it over the wall," Dorinn explained, still somewhat hesitant. "I was coming to look for you. I was concerned for your safety when the gate wall collapsed."

"I need to gather a large force of fighters and lead them down through the secret ways," Korinn explained quickly. "The dragons are helping to destroy our enemies, but we must still help them in any way we can."

"Yes, of course," Dorinn agreed without hesitation. Dwarves always wanted to play as large a part in any fight as they could. "I must begin to set things in order here, especially the repair of the road. And I should send a message to the lower city so that father will know that the danger is over. It is over, isn't it?"

"It should be over by nightfall," Thelvyn answered. "We still have to hunt down the remaining Masters and either slay them or drive them from this world. They seem to have entered our world somewhere in the mountains north of the steppes. We might have to chase them all the way back there. If you can manage things here yourself, I'd like to take Korinn with me."

"Me?" Korinn asked, confused.

"Every city in Rockhome has been under siege. They might be pleased to see the dragons destroying their enemies, but they might need to be reassured about their new allies."

Dorinn was obviously pleased to continue his duties as the leader of the defenders of Dengar, even if it meant going into battle once again with his warriors. Making himself useful at such a time of need was very important to him, important enough that he was able to overcome his physical limitations by will alone. Aside from the ruined gate, the upper city had suffered little damage during the battle, although the gemstone dragons had once again inflicted damage on a number of the highest towers.

As it happened, the battle in the valley below was well on its way to being over. The dragons had already destroyed or driven away the Masters, and Kharendaen had led a score of red dragons against the invading army. By surrounding the invaders, the dragons were steadily driving them into a trap in a blind canyon a few miles north of Dengar. So far, Kharendaen's chief concern had been struggling to prevent the red dragons from being needlessly cruel. All the gold dragons except for Thelvyn's bodyguards had left in pursuit of the Masters, since their greater size, speed, and magic were needed to fight the gemstone dragons.

Thelvyn selected one of the gold dragon clerics among his bodyguards to take command of the young reds. Then Korinn Bear Slayer mounted Kharendaen's saddle, which she had brought along in anticipation of this very need. Flying as swiftly as they could, Thelvyn and Kharendaen made a complete circuit of the cities of Rockhome, beginning in the east with Kurdal and Smaggeft on the shores of Lake Klintest, then crossing the mountains to Evemur and on to Stahl. The dragons had already driven the Masters from all the cities, leaving behind a small force to deal with the invading forces abandoned by the gemstone dragons. Korinn spoke briefly with the leaders of each city and the local commanders, and then they hurried on.

By late afternoon, they arrived at Fort Denwarf. Korinn had been concerned about the safety of the fortress he had been forced to abandon, but the invaders had done no great damage in their haste to push on into Rockhome. Korinn planned to summon a small force under General Balar from Stahl in a couple of days to secure the fortress and begin necessary repairs. The dwarves would feel better once their borders were secure once more. The dragons had already slain more than twoscore of the Masters. The rest had fled across the steppes back toward their base somewhere in the Wendarian Range to the north, with over a thousand dragons in close pursuit.

The Ethengar were in a worse situation, scattered in the forests of the foothills of the mountains of Rockhome. They had witnessed the flight of the Masters and the pursuit of the dragons, but they didn't understand what was happening. They remained as fearful of the dragons as they were of any other enemy, and so they were unwilling to come out of hiding to speak with Thelvyn and Korinn. There seemed to be no way to get news to them until the dwarves returned to Fort Denwarf, and Korinn knew that they would have to remain in the lower mountains of Rockhome for some time to come. The steppes had been completely destroyed from north to south and across its full width from the Northern Reaches in the east to the Highlands in the west. Weeks or even months would pass before the deep grass and the herds would return to the blackened hills of the plains.

Night had long since fallen by the time they had returned to Dengar. The upper city seemed to glow under the golden light of hundreds of lamps and flickering torches, for the dwarves were already hard at work on repairs. Their first concern was with restoring the damaged portion of the gate ramp and the gate itself, since there was no way to carry goods in and out of the city while that access was blocked. Dragons had already lifted the body of the amber dragon out of the trap in the gate fort and were helping to fix the collapsed platform.

"Now, there's something I never expected to see," Korinn said as they circled down to land. "Dragons working alongside dwarves. How were you able to manage that?"

"I told them the dwarves would pay them a hundred gold crowns each for their trouble," Thelvyn said, staring straight ahead as he spoke. Finally he couldn't help smiling, and he turned his head to see if the dwarf was taking him seriously. "Actually, the dragons are genuinely concerned about the Masters. And being helpful to someone else is such a novelty to them that it piques their interest."

Kharendaen glanced at him briefly, as if she wanted to dispute his last remark about dragons, but she found that she could not. The gold dragons would, on rare occasions, offer some help to adventurers of other races if their quest and their motives seemed worthwhile. But for the most part, dragons were seldom helpful, even to each other.

Thelvyn circled wide, giving Kharendaen a moment to drop down quickly and settle onto the paving stones of the market square before the entrance to the lower city, a scene of great activity as the dwarves worked to restore Dengar. Everyone hurried out of the way as the two dragons approached, giving them far more room than they actually needed. Thelvyn dropped to the ground just as Korinn was climbing down from his saddle. The dwarves cheered loudly, and most of them rushed forward as soon as both of the dragons had folded their wings, but others paused to stare in awe and mutter among themselves when they saw that Thelvyn wore the Collar of the Dragons. He was privately amused to wonder if their admiration was for him or for the wealth of gold and jewels in the collar.

Korinn lifted his fist to the crowd in a triumphant salute. "The Masters are gone, their armies scattered. Rockhome once more belongs to the dwarves. The dragons have brought us victory!"

The dwarves cheered again, then began to chant his name rhythmically. Thelvyn was grateful that dragons lacked the capacity to blush. Kharendaen poked him gently with her nose, reminding him to sit up straight.

Then the crowd parted, and King Daroban himself stepped out to greet the dragons, together with his eldest son. Daroban still wore his armor, but Dorinn had changed to more casual dress and appeared to have rested some, possibly against his will. He was leaning on a cane and walking stiffly. The crowd fell silent as Daroban came to stand before Thelvyn.

"Greetings, Dragonking, lord of the winds," he declared.

"Greetings, Daroban, lord of the caverns," Thelvyn responded. "I have no wish to speak dark words at a time of celebration, but I cannot forget that we have won only the first battle in what will be a desperate war. Now that the Masters have seen what the dragons can do, they will be far better prepared for us next time. We have to be ready for them."

King Daroban nodded gravely, while the dwarves listened in silence. "I appreciate your warning, and I pledge to you all the assistance the dwarves have to give. We know now that if the dragons fall, then Rockhome must also fall in time. What can we do?"

"I have already called a council from all the nations of our world to meet with me in Braejr," Thelvyn explained. "I need for you to select a representative to attend that council, someone you trust well enough to vote on important matters and whose judgment must be binding. You must be prepared to set aside all past differences with those who must now become your allies, at least until our common enemy is defeated. We must all stand together, dwarves and elves, men and dragons, or we will surely be defeated."

Daroban nodded grimly. "So be it. I understand that the Immortals themselves have selected you to be our leader. You have proven yourself devoted to your duty, and I defer to your authority in matters of our common defense. I hereby appoint my son Korinn to be our representative to your council, and to serve you in any way he can as your companion and advisor."

"Good," Thelvyn answered. "I will leave behind a small force of dragons until all the invaders have been hunted down. A couple of dragons will remain here at all times, to carry important messages and patrol your mountains for any sign of the invaders. I must now divide my force of dragons into equal parts and garrison them in different parts of the world so that we are ready to move quickly in response to the next attack, wherever it might come. But enough of grim words. It is time for a little more celebration and a great deal more work."

The dwarves cheered once again, and then the crowd began to break apart as they hurried back to their tasks. Thelvyn felt a great sense of relief. If dwarves could work side by side with dragons and even defer to his authority, there was good reason to hope for the success of the alliance.

"Will you be coming below?" Korinn asked.

Thelvyn shook his head. "As Dragonking, it befits my new station to remain in dragon form. I must seek my chief advisors, and then I will leave for Braejr at dawn. Will you be ready?"

"You will find me here."

The dwarves drew back, cheering once again as the two dragons leapt into flight. Thelvyn led the way, climbing quickly into the night sky above the lights of the city before he turned to glide slowly beyond the edge of the escarpment. During his approach, he had seen in the valley the lights of large fires, where the dragons remaining at Dengar were making their camp for the night. He hoped to find Marthaen or Jherdar there, although he had to be satisfied to wait when he did not find them. While he waited, young dragons eagerly brought roasted meat for both him and Kharendaen.

Marthaen arrived several hours later, near the middle of the night. Kharendaen had been lying curled in sleep, but Thelvyn had been sitting up on his haunches staring at the moon, lost in thought about the challenges he still faced. He moved quickly aside so that the older dragon would have room to land in the clearing.

"The Masters are gone," Marthaen reported simply as he folded away his wings. "They are swift and gave us quite a chase, but we had a force of a hundred dragons waiting in the Wendarian Range to intercept them. Only seven of them escaped us in the end, destroying their worldgate behind them. Apparently they were using only that one gate, since they had a large supply base hidden in a deep valley nearby. There was evidence of tens of thousands of soldiers spreading out from that one base to establish lesser camps in the foothills before they pushed into the steppes in a single line more than three hundred miles wide."

Thelvyn nodded slowly. "The dwarves thought there were a couple hundred of the gemstone dragons, but they had to admit that they had no way of knowing for certain."

"I would say they overestimated the number in their excitement. We found no more than some fourscore in all. As long as we have them completely outnumbered, we have no cause for concern."

"We don't dare count on that," Thelvyn said. "How many dragons did we lose?"

"We suffered a couple of hundred injuries, but few of them were serious," Marthaen answered, obviously pleased. "But I don't believe we lost a single dragon. As I say, we overwhelmed them with our numbers and caught them off guard. I am curious about one thing, however. When you and Kharendaen fought them in their own world, did you find them so strong? If you did, then I've underestimated not only you but my little sister as well."

Thelvyn laughed quietly, but Kharendaen looked fierce as she puffed out her chest proudly. "You must not forget that the clerics of the Great One are trained warriors. But to satisfy your curiosity, I found the Masters as swift and powerful in a fight as any mature gold dragon, but no more so."

"They seem to be stronger here in this world," Thelvyn said. "Their leader was at least three times as powerful as he should have been, although the others didn't seem as strong. And I would very much like to know why they are stronger here—if it is the result of some enchantment, or if they draw power in battle from the one who is called the Overlord. I also

wonder if their enhanced strength is somehow due to their
return to their true home world. Remember that the gemstone
dragons came into existence when they tried to raise themselves to the level of the Immortals. They failed, but we don't
know just what they might have done to themselves yet."

He paused a moment, then glanced at Marthaen. "At least I
know now what the Collar of the Dragons is supposed to do
for me. It enhanced my strength and powers tremendously
when I faced the Masters."

"Legend always said the collar would enhance the powers
of the Dragonking," Kharendaen pointed out.

"Yes, but no one could ever tell me how it works," he
insisted, then frowned. "Tomorrow I must fly to Braejr to try to
convince a group of people who normally do not get along that
they must work together. I also must convince them to allow
several hundred dragons to be garrisoned in their countries."

"Let Korinn Bear Slayer tell them about the invasion of
Rockhome," Marthaen suggested. "That should improve their
opinion of dragons."

* * * * *

Thelvyn and Kharendaen left early the next morning, flying
directly across the mountains of the Altan Tepes and the
northern Broken Lands to Braejr. All during the flight, Thelvyn
was concerned that this journey might be a waste of time. When
he had left Braejr days before, Darius Glantri had been trying to
use the considerable influence of Thyatis to arrange for a first
meeting of parties to join in an alliance. Unfortunately, he had
no idea of how much success the Thyatians had. He could
only hope that a number of representatives had gathered and
begun to work through their differences, setting aside past
rivalries and complaints.

It was possible that the invasion of Rockhome had given
them something to think about. Thelvyn now had the almost
unquestioned support of the dwarves, and he had expected
them to be among the hardest to convince. Of course, they
now had experienced the danger of the Masters firsthand, and
they had reason to be grateful. Thelvyn expected most of the
other delegates to be far more reserved in their support. He

wondered if he were beginning to think too much like a dragon, but he had to admit that it was far simpler to slay an enemy than to argue with an ally.

Their appearance over the city failed to raise any cries of alarm. That worried him, since he knew the generally bad opinion that the Flaem had of dragons. He had yet to prove that his armor was heavy enough to turn aside an arrow. He was apprehensive as he descended toward the yard of Solveig's house, waiting for the shrill challenge from a griffon. When he had landed in the yard and folded away his wings without hearing so much as a squawk, he began to hope that the griffon stables really had been moved to another part of the city.

Thelvyn moved aside quickly so that Kharendaen could land as well. They were both surprised when the door of the warehouse opened and a young gold dragon poked his head outside to stare at them. Thelvyn needed a moment before he recognized the young male as an old friend, the cleric, Seldaek, who had journeyed with Sir George the previous year in search of the Collar of the Dragons. Sir George himself emerged from the front door of the house a moment later, followed by Solveig White-Gold and Darius Glantri.

"Korinn!" Solveig called when she saw the dwarf climbing down from his saddle. "Then the invasion of Rockhome is over?"

"Aye, thanks to the Dragonking," he declared. "The Masters were nearly all destroyed, and their armies are broken and scattered. But our good dragon here is quick to remind me that the war is far from over and the worst still ahead."

"It seems I have no need to remind you," Thelvyn commented, watching while Kharendaen slipped out of her saddle. He turned to Darius Glantri. "We have indeed won a battle, mostly because I was able to trick the Overlord into believing that the dragons had refused to follow me. Now he knows better, and I expect that his next attack will come very soon and with far greater strength. We must be ready. I hope you can tell me you've had some luck in calling together a council to discuss an alliance."

"Then I can indeed contribute something to your good mood," Darius replied. "If Korinn Bear Slayer is here to represent the dwarves, then we now have delegates from all the major nations and a few minor ones. Even the Alphatians have sent a delegate—an affable chap, very eager to please, if a bit nervous at finding himself in the Flaemish realm."

"I want to talk to them as soon as I can . . . within the hour, if possible," Thelvyn said, turning to the door of the old warehouse where Seldaek still sat. "I assume you moved the griffons somewhere else."

"We have them in the stables near the north gate," Solveig explained. "We had reached the point where we had too many griffons on hand to stable them all here. I've had the lair restored to the way it was when you left last year. The bed might be a little small for the two of you."

"We don't need a great deal of room," Kharendaen said succinctly. "But there is most certainly not room for three. Sir George, you will have to do something else with your friend."

"We've been preparing some lairs for dragon messengers in a warehouse near the palace," Solveig explained. "This place has been reserved for the private abode of the Dragonking and his consort. Do you need anything? A moose for lunch? A couple of virgins, perhaps?"

Thelvyn looked surprised. "What would I want with a pair of virgins?"

"To eat them, of course," Kharendaen said eagerly, licking her chops.

Thelvyn looked even more alarmed for a moment before he realized that Kharendaen was making a jest at his expense. He looked disgruntled over the matter, which only amused the others even more.

"You've never heard that old legend about dragons and virgins?" Darius asked.

"There aren't many virgins to be found around here, I assure you," Thelvyn replied, then paused at the entrance to the lair to glance back at Kharendaen. "I don't say that from personal experience, mind you."

The light banter matched Thelvyn's positive mood. Things were progressing better than he had dared to hope. Most of the delegates of the proposed alliance were not only gathered but apparently in a mood to talk. Only a year before, King

Jherridan had striven desperately to organize an alliance against the Alphatians, and later against the dragons. Now both Alphatia and the dragons were a part of a new alliance against an unexpected enemy. Thelvyn himself had been more or less run out of civilized lands the year before, and now the world was ready to defer to his leadership. He was not so surprised at how much things had changed but at how quickly it had all happened.

A short time later, he and Kharendaen walked through the streets of Braejr to the palace, where the representatives were housed in the guest chambers. This was the first time he had seen the palace since the previous summer, when the extensive damage from his battle with the traitor wizards had not yet been repaired. The restoration was nearly complete, although Thelvyn was only able to enter as far as the main hall for a quick look about. So much of his past had been spent in this place, as the advisor to King Jherridan during his time as the Dragonlord, and then later when he had served as king. He had to resist the urge to change form so that he could take a more complete tour of the building.

Solveig had gone to the palace ahead of them to summon the representatives. Since the dragons couldn't enter any of the meeting rooms within the palace, they had elected to meet in the garden near the main gate. Thelvyn sat in the center of the paved court, like a broad patio outside the doors of the reception hall, with stone benches for the other delegates. Kharendaen lay beneath the trees near the wall. Once the meeting was assembled, they all spoke together for some time, although it was more accurate to say that Thelvyn explained everything he knew about the invaders to the representatives and answered their questions.

For his own part, Thelvyn watched the representatives closely and weighed their words with care. He was trying to judge the extent of the commitment their nations were able or willing to make. He also wanted to determine just how much the various nations would comply with the decisions made by their own delegates. The only representatives he could be certain of were Solveig and Darius Glantri, who already had broad authority to make binding decisions in this council.

Korinn seemed to have that same authority, but Thelvyn was
not yet certain that the dwarves would continue to be so willing to cooperate once their memory of the invasion had faded.

Of the others, King Celedril of Alfheim could decide his
own counsels without challenge at home, and he was obviously supportive of the alliance. Lord Derrick of Darokin was
also supportive, as Darokin had been during the previous
summer. The Traladaran representative didn't seem to understand all of what he heard, but he was willing to vote with the
majority, perhaps to spare himself the strain of making decisions in matters that were mostly beyond him. The delegates
from the Emirates of Ylaruam and the Jarldoms of the Northern Reaches were still alarmed that the burning of the steppes
and the invasion of Rockhome had occurred so near their own
lands. Their lands were controlled by loosely allied factions
that were often at odds over old feuds and rivalries, and
Thelvyn wondered how much of an organized defense they
were capable of assembling.

The Heldannic Freeholds had failed to send a representative,
giving the Thyatian messenger a rather haughty reply about
their confidence in their ability to defend themselves. The
Ierendi representative was cautious in his support, believing that
his island kingdom was far from the actual danger. The delegate
from the Minrothad Guilds was also disinterested, but he followed the Thyatian vote as a matter of politics.

Which was all very much just as Thelvyn had expected. The
only unpredictable element in all of this was Ambassador Serran, the Alphatian representative. Thelvyn found his position
on the alliance to be most surprising. As he had been warned
earlier, Ambassador Serran was very friendly and eager to
please, and insisted that his people were willing to follow the
Dragonking without hesitation. Thelvyn wondered if the
Alphatians simply found it easier than most of the others to
understand just how desperate the situation really was. They
had fought the dragons the year before, provoking a long war
that they had no hope of winning. Thus they saw any enemy
the dragons feared as being very fearsome indeed.

Under the circumstances, Thelvyn had no problem con-
vincing the council to follow his plans for the defense of their

world. They had already known that they would have to arrange for their own defense as much as they could. That meant they needed to be ready to endure a sudden invasion at any time and hold out long enough for the dragons to gather an army and respond. The places where Thelvyn wanted to establish garrisons of hundreds of dragons were in the very lands where they would be most welcome. The northeast garrison was the city of Windreach itself. The garrison in the forgotten city of Darmouk was also convenient, and another garrison in the mountains of western Thyatis was no problem. Only a couple of hundred dragons could be spared to give Alphatia some peace of mind.

Thelvyn felt certain that the next attack would come in the west. The Masters had been active in the Highlands in the years since the Flaem had first come into this world. He was suspicious that the Flaem would once more play some key part in the Masters' plans for a major invasion. For that reason, he planned to move several hundred dragons into the mountains of the Highland Frontier and southern Wendar. Yet another garrison would be located in the wilds of northern Darokin, near Lake Amsorak. The delegate from Darokin said that he would try to have soldiers from his own country moved into their northern forts, to aid the Highlands when the invasion came. King Celedril of Alfheim promised a couple thousand elvish rangers, to be stationed in the elvish holdings in the southern Highlands.

"Then you really do believe that the Masters will attack here next?" Solveig asked quietly after the council concluded and the other delegates were left to speak among themselves.

"Perhaps not next," Thelvyn explained. "They could make other, lesser attacks in other parts of the world, to draw away our strength and throw us off our guard. But I feel certain that the Masters will invade the Highlands soon. The Highlands have been central to their plans for more than a hundred years, even before they sent the Flaem into this world. And the Highlands have been central in my own destiny since before I was born. The Masters have to deal with me before they can secure any conquests in this world, and this is where they will find me."

"That's very reassuring," Solveig commented sarcastically. "The Highlands seem to be your chosen battlefield. Now I remember why we threw you out a year ago."

"The Flaem need me," he insisted. "They remain especially vulnerable to the control of the Masters. They can't escape deep involvement in this conflict, and only the dragons and I can protect them. Even if I leave, the Masters will use the Flaem to draw me back. I feel sure of that."

"Then I know what I have to prepare for as well," Solveig added. She glanced up at the dragon. "Considering how we've seen the Masters operate, I have good reason to suspect that we have at least one traitor in our midst—probably not in our company, but near enough to report any plans we begin to implement."

Thelvyn nodded. "I agree. In fact, I'm counting on it. I'm playing the same trap that has worked for us once already, saying things I want the Masters to hear whenever I suspect the presence of any possible spy. I am baiting them to attack here in the Highlands. Why subject other lands to needless destruction when the final battle must be here anyway? I want the Masters to know that I am waiting for them."

"Do you have any idea who the traitor could be?"

He glanced around at the delegates, talking together in small clusters near the open outer doors of the reception hall. "I suspect Ambassador Serran, or at least someone of high authority in Alphatia. Remember that, like the Flaem, they are not originally of this world. Many of their policies of conquest can now be interpreted as a prelude to the invasion of the Masters. Have you asked yourself why they were so determined to wage a hopeless war against the dragons last year, even to the point of launching a doomed invasion fleet after they had been forced to surrender once before? They drew the dragons out of hiding. The dragons have always kept to themselves, and their gathering places have always been closely guarded secrets. Because of their war with the Alphatians, most of those secrets were betrayed."

CHAPTER ELEVEN

Daylight faded slowly, the brilliant sapphire blue of day growing deeper and deeper, becoming a dark indigo that in turn faded slowly to black as the first stars of night appeared in the east. The light seemed to draw back from the rugged, forested hills below the Colossus Mountains, as if retreating after the sun, already set beyond the wild lands of the west.

The deepest shadows of night gathered first beneath the trees, turning the still, almost mysterious silence of the day to the brooding, fearful darkness of night. But in the wilderness east of Braastar, to one side of a crude, long-forgotten road, a single point of light shone with a soft, silver radiance like a star that had fallen from the sky. Hidden in the darkness beneath a spreading oak, lost in the shadows, a pair of small, carved stones stood an equal distance to either side of the small light. Other pieces of shattered stone lay half hidden in the grass and fallen leaves; the tree itself was only beginning to recover from being damaged by fire in some recent disaster.

Suddenly the point of light flared and rushed outward in a luminescent ring, like the wave from a stone dropped into a

pool of liquid silver. The ring of light raced outward, expanding quickly to form a wide oval like a doorway into the night.
The cold wind of an alien world whipped through the portal,
dry and heavy with dust. Then, with a sudden rush of icy air, a
dark form hurtled out of the depths of the portal, at first only a
blurry shape that expanded rapidly. In the final instant, it leapt
out from the passage, fully formed, an amber dragon of great
strength and stature, with plates of armor almost like translu-
cent gold.

The dragon stepped forward, making room for a ruby
dragon that followed close behind. Then, while the second of
the pair stood guard at the gate, the amber dragon stepped
forward to stand in the partial opening in the forest beside the
road. For a moment, it paused, its head cocked as if listening,
and then it rose up on its hind legs with its great neck
stretched to its limit, lifting its head as high as it could. It
looked first one way and then the other, searching the night
sky. Satisfied, it dropped back down and turned to face its
companion, nodding its head. The ruby dragon disappeared
back inside the portal, drawn away in an instant, while the
amber dragon turned back to watch and listen.

Only a moment passed before other gemstone dragons began
to come through the portal, one by one in rapid succession.
They separated at once, moving out quickly in all directions, as
if they were desperate to hold and protect the worldgate from
discovery and danger. A vanguard of more than twoscore gemstone dragons came through in a short time, many leaping into
flight to take their positions in the region surrounding the gate
for five miles around. Then companies of soldiers began to
appear, marching out of the gate in neat rows before spreading
along the sides of the road. Supply wagons began to file through
as well, small groups of heavy wagons drawn by massive horses
nearly as large as the dragons themselves.

Now the leader of the Masters stepped away from the
worldgate, moving quickly a short distance down the road
until it came to a rise where it could look back through a break
in the trees. The worldgate and all the activity surrounding it
was now several hundred yards behind the creature and no
longer a distraction. It sat up on its haunches, its forelegs off

the ground and bracing the bulk of its body with its tail for balance. Then, in the quiet, remarkably understated way of dragons, it began to work great magic.

Strange things began to happen in the night, as deep, elemental forces began to move through the world in response to the amber dragon's magic. Or perhaps it was that the world fought to resist the dragon's magic, which reached from beyond that plane of existence. But the spells were powerful and carefully prepared well in advance, so that the amber dragon needed only to invoke the magic that waited to be summoned. The darkness of the night began to gather deeper above the hill that stood just beyond the worldgate, like a well of shadows that seemed to draw the fabric of the night in upon itself.

Then, when the spells had gained their greatest strength, the well of deep darkness suddenly rushed outward again. And when the blackness faded into ordinary night, the face of a massive cliff now stood above the forest, and a great fortress stood at the point of the cliff. It looked remarkably like the same fortress in which the Dragonking had found the Collar of the Dragons, but if indeed it were, the entire fortress had been transported with the rock upon which it stood from one world to the next.

The fortress stood silent and empty. While stone and timbers could be magically transported between worlds, living creatures could not, not even the gemstone dragons. The Masters and their many slaves had been required to come through the gate one by one, abandoning their great fortress for a brief time while it was shifted between worlds. Now they had a ready-made stronghold in the land of their enemies, a place where they could stage their invasion of the Highlands with certainty and precision. And with a stronghold of their own, they could stand against the fury of the dragons of Mystara. The soldiers and supply wagons that had been gathering in the road were now moved quickly toward the fortress, making room for more fighters, who continued to file through the worldgate.

And yet the Masters were not yet done with their preparations. The amber dragon and several of its companions spread their wings to lift themselves into the night sky, flying quickly to the fortress to post guards within its massive walls and prepare it

for occupation. One of their first duties would be to complete
the opening of a second worldgate, one that was hidden deep
within their own stronghold. In that way, they could maintain
contact with their own world, even under siege, bringing in
more soldiers, weapons, and supplies as needed.

This time they would not make the same foolish mistake of
underestimating the Dragonking. They intended to prove to
him that his bands of half-wild dragons were no match for
their great powers and careful planning.

The Masters and their servants labored through the night,
knowing that their fortress had to be secure before the dragons
discovered it. Now that there were dragons in Braejr less than
a hundred miles to the south, they knew it was inevitable that
they would be discovered soon, perhaps that very dawn. The
Masters took every precaution they could, moving their forces
and wagons through the night without light. Above all, they
had to be careful that there were no lights visible within their
fortress, especially from the tower windows that faced west
toward Braastar. Since they could plainly see the lights of the
city only a few short miles away, they needed no other
reminder of the need for caution.

The strategies and policies of the Masters had recently been
unsettled, for the Dragonking had surprised them and frustrated their plans, and they still did not understand how that
had happened. All they knew was that the Overlord had
informed them that the dragons had rejected their king, yet
somehow the Overlord had been mistaken in that, as impossible
as that seemed. Or perhaps matters had changed more quickly
than the Overlord suspected, and the dragons had pledged their
support to the Dragonking after all. The latter explanation was
easier for the Masters to accept, but they knew for certain that
such mistakes must not happen again. This time they would be
a step ahead of their enemy.

Only two days before, the Overlord had warned them that
the time had come. Whole armies of soldiers and supplies had
been moved immediately from the nearest strongholds to the
fortress that had served to guide the settlement of the Highlands, built in the time when the Flaem had been held as
slaves in the world of the Overlord. The Masters had always

intended to transfer their stronghold into the world of Mystara, to serve their needs when they finally came into the world they planned to conquer.

Word had been sent that the Dragonking was assembling an alliance against the invaders and that he would soon be bringing hundreds of dragons into the Highlands. The Dragonking seemed to anticipate that the next invasion would come in the Highlands; now it had become a race between the dragons and the Masters to assemble their forces in the Highlands first, and so far the Masters were ahead. The dragons were on the way, however, and the Masters and their armies had to be in place before the dragons arrived.

When morning came, the Masters were careful to remain with their slaves inside the fortress, closing the worldgate in the forest so that from now on they would rely only upon the one hidden within their own walls. By being as unobtrusive as possible, they hoped to evade discovery for as long as they could. There was always the vague hope that any dragons who saw their fortress would be new to the Highlands and unaware it had not always been there. Just the same, they would be forced to act soon, even if it meant an end to secrecy and the element of surprise. They no longer had enough room to keep their considerable forces hidden within their stronghold, and they would have to launch their attack before they could bring through more of their own people.

The Masters liked to believe they were prepared for the worst, and their plans were put to the test within the first hour of daylight. The land was still in the deep shadows of the mountains when a dragon was spotted riding the winds northward, a young gold who was drifting and soaring back and forth over the forest as he hunted. He seemed to not even see the fortress of the Masters at first, or else he was unconcerned by the great edifice of gray stone standing dark and silent over the woods, seemingly abandoned. But the young dragon's interest began to grow as he came nearer, although he was careful not to approach too closely as he circled warily. Suddenly he turned and flew back toward the south at great speed, obviously carrying a warning to Braejr.

The Masters had to let him go, knowing from their experience in Rockhome that they were not as swift as the sleek gold dragons. They were running out of time, but they still had several hours left to them, perhaps even a day. There still weren't enough dragons in the entire Highlands to challenge them, although there might be a few hundred as near as Rockhome. The Masters had no way of knowing with any certainty just where the Dragonking kept his forces at that time, or what numbers he had been able to gather. They had only a brief time to act, but they would not be easily stopped once their plans were set into motion.

Hardly an hour later, the invasion of the Highlands was launched. The main gate of the fortress flung open, and armies began to march out to war, joining with the additional forces that had already filed through the old worldgate. They followed the forest road west toward Braastar, a ready-made path of invasion. When the Flaem had first come into this world, the Masters had intended for them to establish their greatest city near the gate, so that the Masters could move quickly to seize control when they finally launched their invasion. Later, the Flaem had been permitted to move their capital to Braejr to protect the secret of the Radiance, which had been in danger of discovery by the elves. The Masters had never anticipated that Braejr and the Radiance would fall into the hands of their most powerful and determined enemies, but that was only a minor inconvenience. They had tried to find answers to all problems.

Now the Masters began their second invasion, one that was not waged with swords or arrows or even the terrible natural weapons of dragonkind, but with magic. The Flaem had been their slaves in the past, and there remained embedded in their minds an instinct for obedience, the same instinct that the Masters employed to control all the races and strange creatures that were enslaved to their will. Now they invoked that same magic to a far higher degree than usual, to awaken the instinct for obedience in the Flaem and summon the lost flock back into the Masters' fold.

The army that marched toward Braastar did not expect to fight for possession of the city. The Flaem would most likely freely open their city to the invaders, or at least be too distracted fighting for control of their own minds to defend themselves. By nightfall, it would be too late for the dragons to attempt to regain the city in battle. And as the Masters gained new strength, they would extend their control to other parts of the Highlands. In time, the people of Braejr would help to expel the dragons from their own city. Once the Masters had control of the Radiance, they would command all the power needed to launch armies that would subdue the entire world. Even the dragons would be powerless to stop them.

* * * * *

Seldaek hurried back to Braejr to report to the Dragonking, telling Thelvyn of the mysterious fortress and the gathering army that he had seen to the east of Braastar. Thelvyn sat in silence for a long moment, deep in thought. The young cleric waited patiently, sorry that he could not have made a clearer report of what he had seen. Kharendaen sat up on her haunches nearby in the yard of Solveig's house, listening attentively, with Sir George at her side. Solveig had already gone inside the house to find Taeryn and have him hurry to the Academy to summon Alessa Vyledaar. When she hurried back out to the court, Thelvyn roused from his private thoughts to watch her.

"I don't suppose there can be any question," he said at last. "When great fortresses suddenly appear out of nowhere, we can guess easily where they came from. Its location must be near the old worldgate near Braastar. And from the description, I suspect that I visited this same fortress not long ago."

"Inventive devils, aren't they?" Sir George commented.

"Despite the fact that I anticipated the Masters would strike here next, they were still able to surprise me," Thelvyn complained. He glanced over at Seldaek. "How many dragons are in the Highlands at this time?"

The young dragon could only shake his head. "Only those who came to serve as couriers for the delegates of the Grand Alliance. Ten or eleven, perhaps, not counting the three of us."

"Not enough," Thelvyn said bitterly, considering his limited options. "We have to send messengers at once to Rockhome,

Darmouk, and Windreach, which are the only places where we have concentrated forces of dragons at this time. Each is to send one third of its total strength here at once, especially the most powerful of the dragon sorcerers. The rest must continue with our plans for establishing garrisons. If we divert too much of our strength here, they'll simply attack somewhere else."

Kharendaen frowned. "You apparently guessed correctly on one account. We must have a traitor somewhere in our company. You announced only two days ago that you would expect an invasion here and that you would be bringing in a large force of dragons."

"And now I have fallen in a trap of my own making," Thelvyn said, frowning. "I baited the Masters into invading the Highlands, but I never expected that they could move so quickly after we repulsed their attack on Rockhome. The dragons I planned to have ready to defend the Highlands are still in the east."

"Does it make any difference?" Sir George asked. "Just because the Masters are here doesn't mean that they're ready to attack. Are they going to be ready to fight before an army of dragons can get here?"

Thelvyn considered that and shook his head slowly. "I have no way of knowing that. I just wish we had some idea of the actual numbers of the army the Masters already have at hand. I don't have any way of knowing how long they need to bring through an army of several tens of thousands, such as they had at Rockhome."

"Do they really need such a large army?" Kharendaen asked. "The Masters must have learned their lesson in Rockhome. They know they cannot hold on to any conquered lands until they have dealt with the Dragonking and the dragons."

"I haven't forgotten that," he said. "We must be very careful not to place ourselves in any traps they may have set for us. That's made all the more difficult because we have no prior knowledge of the kind of traps they're fond of using."

"That must be why you want the dragon sorcerers," Seldaek remarked.

Thelvyn turned his head to glare at the young cleric. "You have your orders, Seldaek, and every minute counts. I need at least five hundred dragons here by this time tomorrow."

Seldaek hurried across the court to the front gate and leapt over the wall. The young cleric hurried through the streets toward the palace and the lairs of the dragon couriers. He needed to find a couple of recruits to help him carry the Dragonking's summons to different lands.

Thelvyn turned to his mate. "Is he some relative of yours?"

Kharendaen lifted her ears in surprise. "Not as far as I know. Dragons don't always keep track of such things. Why do you ask?"

"He seems to be an eager young pup. I was wondering why he keeps turning up."

"Because your mature and competent advisors are always needed somewhere else," Sir George pointed out. "Except for myself, of course."

Thelvyn glanced down at the old knight. "You are going to stay here and help Solveig to beg or bully Alessa Vyledaar into finding some way to put the Radiance to use against the Masters. The Radiance is the best weapon we have to prevent the Masters from taking control of the Flaem, at least until the dragon sorcerers can get here."

Solveig looked perplexed. "You're not going to be here?"

He shook his head. "I must gather all the dragons willing to fight with me and go at once to Braastar. Our presence might spell the difference in whether the city can hold out until the dragons arrive."

"Do you really think you'll stand a chance?" she asked. "There won't be more than ten of you in all."

"I don't expect to be able to hold out for very long," Thelvyn said. "We might even have to retreat back here before the day is out. Frankly, I don't have much hope for saving Braastar, beyond giving the people there time to escape if they can. My greatest concern right now is that Braejr is not endangered before the dragons can arrive."

Since Seldaek and two of the dragon couriers had already departed for the east, Thelvyn and Kharendaen gathered together the eight remaining couriers and flew north toward Braastar at once. Thelvyn was fearful of taking Kharendaen into great danger over and over again, remembering that she was a cleric. But the simple fact was that he needed her. She had proven herself to be a fierce fighting dragon as well as a capable leader in her own right.

Although they found it difficult to speak while flying at high speed, Thelvyn and Kharendaen spent the brief time discussing possible magical or clerical spells that might help isolate the people of Braastar from the influence of the Masters. While there were various ways to dispel magic at the source, by turning it back onto its source or by shielding potential victims, no conventional spells would be very useful, considering the scale of the attack and the distance from which the Masters could influence their slaves. There was really only one answer. Unless the Great One or possibly some other Immortals were willing to channel their own powers through Thelvyn, there wasn't much he could do.

* * * * *

In the city of Braastar, matters had long since taken a turn for the worse. The bells of the city had begun to ring early that morning, signaling an attack, and the word quickly went through the streets that an invading army had been spotted several miles to the east. The people of the city began preparing for an attack, sealing the heavy shutters of their windows and quickly filling buckets and barrels with water in anticipation of damage caused by dragonfire. Soldiers strapped on their armor and collected their weapons, hurrying to defend the east wall.

The first attack came only minutes later, and in a way unlike anything the people of Braastar could have anticipated. Everyone of Flaemish descent became aware of some odd presence forcing itself upon their minds. Most found the sensation vaguely uncomfortable and compelling, speaking to them in a voice that was too soft and distant to understand. But to some, the words were clearer, so that they understood yet could not easily refuse the commands spoken to them by the mysterious voice. Pain grew steadily more intense with each passing minute until some people could no longer resist the voice's will. Others endured the pain, as if they were being punished for fighting for the possession of their own minds.

Even so, there were still many people in Braastar who were willing to try to defend their city. One such defender was Mayor Kervaal. Upon first hearing news of the impending attack, he hurried through the chaos of the streets of his city, desperate to find soldiers to man the east gate. The confusion in the stricken city made it impossible to hail a carriage, and he found it faster to go on foot. The strange voice calling to him inside his mind made it difficult for him to think clearly, but he knew that somehow he had to reach the main garrison and find the captain of the city guard. With any luck, the garrison was already on its way to the east gate, but the mayor had to be certain.

"Look! It's the mayor!"

He stopped and turned abruptly toward the caller, thinking that perhaps it was someone who could help who had found him. Then he hesitated, sensing trouble. Several yards away, a young man was staring at him through the confusion in the crowded street. The face was one that the mayor did not recognize, although he could tell from the person's mad stare that he had fallen under the influence of the mysterious voice.

As the young man stood and pointed like a hound flushing its prey, a couple of his companions turned and stared as well. They, too, had the look of madness about their eyes. Then they slowly began to advance. Mayor Kervaal drew the sword that he had belted on hastily; he doubted his ability to outrun these young pups, so it seemed wisest to stand and fight. The Flaem were not in the habit of wearing heavy weapons such as swords. These three carried nothing more than a couple of knives and a heavy stick that could be used as a club. The mayor had been a soldier in his younger days, although he hadn't used a sword in a real fight in almost two decades. Still, his past training and the fact that he had a real blade gave him some advantage.

People began clearing the street, wanting no part of a fight. The mayor realized, with some misgivings, that he was going to be on his own in this encounter. Suddenly one of the young attackers shouted a battle cry and rushed forward, holding his knife out before him. It was a bold but utterly foolish tactic. Kervaal had one tense moment as he feinted to one side and

then darted away from his opponent's naive attack, then
placed the point of his sword firmly against his attacker's
shoulder, just enough to penetrate his skin, to force him to
drop his knife. The young man cried out, seemingly more in
fury than in pain, but his cry turned to one of astonishment as
the people in the crowd swarmed over him and pulled him
down now that he was disarmed and wounded.

Now the remaining pair of attackers began to move in, but
with far greater caution after they had witnessed the fate of
their companion. They seemed to sense that they were at a
disadvantage with only a knife and a small club between them.
But the mayor could not count a victory just yet. His long,
two-edged sword was not a proper weapon for taking on two
widely spaced opponents, and his older muscles did not
respond as fast as they would have in former days.

The young attacker with the knife suddenly lunged at him,
and the mayor drew back quickly from the glinting point of the
small blade. He responded by raising his sword and driving it
directly at the knife-wielder, forcing the young assailant backward so quickly that he almost tripped and fell. The mayor
knew he was exposing his back to the man with the club, and
he could hear him advancing from behind. But the man to his
rear had forgotten that a hostile crowd was behind him; someone tripped him from behind, and he went down. That was
just what Kervaal had hoped for. He continued to force the
last attacker backward until he finally lost his balance and fell.

Leaving his attackers to be dealt with by the crowd, Mayor
Kervaal sheathed his sword and then stood for a long moment
leaning against the wall of a building to catch his breath. In
spite of the attack, he was encouraged about one thing. Most
of the people of Braastar still retained command of their will,
and in spite of the stress of fighting for possession of their own
minds, they were still able to defend themselves. He might
save his city yet. Suddenly he heard the ring of heavy boots on
the cobblestones and turned to see the crowd parting to allow
the passage of the city garrison. The soldiers stopped, and the
captain of the city guard hurried over to him.

"Mayor Kervaal, are you all right?" the captain asked.

"I'm fine," the mayor insisted. "I was just coming to make

certain that you were taking the garrison to defend the east gate. Do you have all of your soldiers?"

"Only those I could find," the captain answered. "Some were too distracted by the voice to be of any use in a fight, and a few have already disappeared. I was hoping the wizards could protect us, but they seem to have fallen victim to this magic as well. What is happening to us, anyway?"

"It must be the gemstone dragons," the mayor said ruefully. "Come on. We have to secure the east gate and hope we can hold on until the Dragonking can get here."

The mayor strode along beside the captain of the guard as they led the company of soldiers through the streets. It gave the mayor a chance for a quick assessment of the condition of the city. In spite of the apparent chaos, many people of Braastar were preparing their homes and shops for battle. Windows were tightly shuttered and doors were being locked and boarded; wooden roofs were being drenched with water, and every container that could be found was being filled with water that might be needed to fight fires started by the invaders. The mayor was reminded of the previous summer, when the cities and towns of the Highlands had to be prepared for the possibility of attack by dragons. The irony was that only the dragons could save Braastar now.

The captain of the guard brought his troops to a halt the moment they came within sight of the east gate, gesturing for his men to remain quiet. A battle was already being fought here; the small gate garrison was quickly being overwhelmed by a crowd of people from the city itself, men of all ages as well as women and even children. Already they had the gate partway open and were attacking the hinges and locks, trying to damage anything they could in at attempt to prevent the gate from being secured. At least for the moment, the gate still seemed to be intact, mostly because this crowd lacked the heavy tools or weapons needed to destroy such massive metal parts.

"We have to get that gate shut!" the mayor exclaimed. "Whatever it takes, get those people away from there!"

The captain frowned. "I don't much like the idea of fighting our own people."

"It can't be helped. We'll lose the entire city otherwise."

The captain turned to his soldiers and issued several terse orders. As one, they drew their swords and lifted their shields, then marched in an ordered line down the street toward the gate, deliberately putting on a bold show in hope of frightening away the attackers. If possible, the captain of the guard wanted to avoid fighting as many of his own people as he could.

Fortunately the crowd of attackers drew back quickly from the approaching soldiers. Several turned to flee back into the city immediately. While the crowd was most certainly under the command of the gemstone dragons, a number of them still possessed a mind of their own when it came to self-preservation. Some of the attackers, perhaps two dozen in all, tried to make a stand before the open gate, but they were neither armed nor trained to fight real soldiers. The city garrison marched directly into the band trying to hold the gate, scattering them in a matter of moments. Some of the stragglers tried to circle around and harass the garrison from behind, but the soldiers immediately spread out to either side of the gate to begin forcing the remaining attackers to draw back.

Now that the east gate was once more in the hands of the loyal forces, Mayor Kervaal hurried to check the condition of the gate itself. The attackers had beaten the lower hinges and the crossbar with stones and clubs, but the damage was probably not enough to prevent them from closing and barring the gate. The captain of the guard walked over to the half-open gate, rubbing the back of his neck. They were all feeling the stress of resisting the relentless voice in their minds.

"The gate seems to be in good shape," he said, turning to a group of soldiers. "Let's get this gate closed and secured."

"Wait a moment," the mayor interrupted, stepping out through the gate. "Look! It's the dragons."

Led by the Dragonking, a small band of dragons circled down from the north to land in the field just beyond the east gate. The invasion force had not yet reached the city, although Thelvyn could see narrow columns of soldiers and lines of wagons hardly five miles to the east, stretching back toward the mountains in the distance. The mayor and the captain of the city guard hurried to meet with Thelvyn as soon as he approached.

"Will the dragons protect us?" the mayor asked, almost pleading. The nearby Flaem appeared distracted, and most were obviously in varying degrees of pain. The will of the Masters was already like a storm raging in their minds.

Thelvyn shook his head sadly, hating to refuse such a desperate plea. "The Masters were warned before I could summon a force of dragons from the east. The dragons won't be here any sooner than dawn tomorrow, and your city will not endure that long. But we will defend you for as long as we can."

"We'll fight beside you!" the captain of the guard declared vehemently.

"I appreciate your spirit, but you mustn't," Thelvyn insisted. "Tell me quickly how bad it is in the city. How far does the influence of the Masters reach?"

"Not too many yet," the mayor said. "Our problem is that their influence is becoming stronger, and it's becoming harder for us to resist."

Thelvyn glanced at Kharendaen, who was frowning. "It will only get worse, especially when the Masters themselves arrive. The city is indefensible, even with the help of myself and my dragons. I suggest that all those who still command their own minds flee Braastar at once. Even your garrison force, which should follow as a rear guard. We will hold this gate until the Masters themselves force us to withdraw."

"But where should we go?" the mayor asked.

"South, to Braejr. I'm hoping that the Fire Wizards can make use of their special powers to break the influence of the Masters, and the dragon sorcerers will be gathering there tomorrow. Our best hope to protect your people from domination rests in Braejr."

The defenders of Braastar hated to abandon their city, but they were quick to agree to Thelvyn's plan. The mayor left to make preparations for the retreat of all those who still were in control of their wills and desired to leave. Fortunately many of the people could be placed on barges and small boats to float down the Aalban River to Braejr, arriving considerably sooner than those who would walk or ride. The soldiers of the city garrison closed and barred the east gate, then hurried to assist with the evacuation of the city.

As soon as the gate was shut, Thelvyn prepared to do what he could to buy some time for the evacuation of the Braastar. The other dragons in his company stayed close beside him, lying on the ground near the wall of the city so that they could not easily be seen across the couple of miles of open fields between them and the distant forest. So far, Thelvyn had yet to see the gemstone dragons themselves, and that led him to wonder if they even knew that he had arrived with his small force to defend Braastar. They were bound to know soon enough, once he attacked their army. That was why he was holding back, buying every possible minute for the evacuation of the city.

Even if the Masters didn't know he was at Braastar, he would soon be forced to reveal his presence. Moving out a short way from the gate, he sat upright with his head lifted and his tail looped around his legs. Then he closed his eyes and tried to open himself to the powers of the Great One. He knew he was asking for something the Immortals might not be able or willing to grant him, powers far beyond those commonly extended to their clerics. And yet he had to chase all thoughts that he might not succeed from of his mind, believing with all his heart that he was asking for powers that were within his right to possess. He was, after all, the Dragonking, and nearly an Immortal in his own right.

"What are you going to do?" Kharendaen asked quietly.

"I'm going to try to fight the will of the Masters," he answered. "If I can dispel their magical influence over this city, then the people of Braastar will be able to evacuate much easier and faster."

She looked uncertain. "Can you cast a spell to dispel magic on such a vast scale?"

"I have no idea," he admitted. "Perhaps, if the Immortals are willing to add their powers to my own, I might be able to cast such a spell."

Thelvyn stared toward the east with the intent, penetrating gaze that was unique to dragons, as if he faced the Masters directly and was locking his will against their own. Then he concentrated all his powers upon his spell, as if weaving layer upon layer of magic upon that one spell until it had grown many hundreds of times greater than usual. When he released the spell, it was as if it pulled away a large part of himself as it was cast, leaving him so empty and weak that he felt dizzy and could hardly lift his long neck for several moments.

Then the Masters recovered from their surprise and began their own attack, increasing the force of their summons. They couldn't break Thelvyn's defense, and yet he could not completely shield the people of Braastar from their summons. Because Thelvyn had cast the spell on so many people at once, it had affected them all to different degrees, failing entirely on some of them. While this spell was ordinarily a permanent one, the massive scale at which it had been cast made it weak and vulnerable to the influence of the Masters, so that it would fade over several hours. At least he was able to give many of the Flaem some relief from the distraction and the pain, freeing some who had not previously been able to flee and making it easier for others to escape from the city.

For now, Thelvyn could only wait, resting while he could, as the invading army drew slowly but steadily closer. His spell of protection wouldn't last very long, and he had poured so much of his own energy into working his magic that he would have to regain his strength before he could cast another spell.

"Are you well?" Kharendaen asked, concerned.

He nodded slowly. "I just need to rest. Can you go into the city and find the mayor? Tell him to keep his people together in one group when they leave the city. I can protect them better with my magic if they're close together."

Kharendaen looked dubious. "If they remain together, we're going to have a difficult time protecting them from the gemstone dragons."

"Actually, it should be easier," Thelvyn said. "There aren't enough of us to confront the gemstone dragons if we have to divide up to protect the people of Braastar."

The dragons waited patiently, remaining hidden by lying flat in the deep grass while they awaited the approach of the invading army. Kharendaen returned a few minutes later, reporting that the evacuation of the city was proceeding quickly, although it was not particularly well organized. Most of the people seemed to have decided on their own to flee the city once they heard that the invading army was only a few miles away. Consequently there was a great deal of chaos, which hampered the Mayor's efforts to organize an orderly evacuation. Many of the refugees were already on their way south on horseback, in carriages, or even in farm wagons. Since they seemed to be moving along fairly quickly, they probably weren't in much danger from the Masters, and so they would have to be on their own. The rest were heading to the river a few miles to the west, where boats and barges would transport them directly to Braejr.

The problem for the dragons would be to hold the city long enough for everyone to get away, then guard the disorderly fleet of boats and barges as it drifted along the river. It would be a tall order for only ten dragons, and their success would depend greatly upon whether or not the gemstone dragons moved against them in numbers they could not fight.

By late that morning, the army of the invaders was only about two miles from the city. For the first time, they could be seen fairly clearly as they followed the road through the scattered woods just beyond the open fields. Thelvyn guessed that there were at least twenty or twenty-five thousand troops in all, and he was privately amazed that the Masters had been able to summon such a large force through the gate in such a short time. Beyond an occasional draconic form riding the winds in the distance, there was little to be seen of the Masters, a tactic that made it hard to guess their numbers or their intentions.

Thelvyn considered his options quickly and then had his dragons withdraw back inside the city. If the invaders attacked, ten dragons were more than enough to keep an army of soldiers from scaling the wall. If the Masters themselves attacked in superior numbers, the dragons might be able to hold their own briefly by using the protection of the wall. Next he sent Kharendaen back through the city a final time to check the progress of the evacuation.

Kharendaen returned a short time later with her report. "The last of the barges and boats have just set out. More people are on the road to the south. There are only a few stragglers still leaving the city."

"After we are forced to leave, I will still have to do what I can to shield those who are fleeing south from the summons of the Masters. I only hope that Alessa can find some way to use the Radiance to help me."

"Do you think we will have to fight?" she asked.

Thelvyn considered that. "The invaders are still two miles or so away. They won't be near enough to challenge us for another hour, and there is no reason for us to be concerned until the Masters come. We must fight them for as long as we can, to keep their attention on us rather than the people fleeing south."

The invading army began to move out into the fields just to the east of Braastar shortly after noon. They gave every indication of preparing for an immediate attack. Thelvyn left the wall of the city briefly to make final preparations. He found that the ragged collection of boats and barges had already drifted several miles down the river. He began to hope that they might actually escape. He stayed just long enough to renew his spell of protection over the citizens of Braastar, although he had to rest a few minutes before he could fly back to the city to rejoin the dragons waiting to defend the east gate.

Thelvyn was surprised and rather alarmed to see that the invading army had already organized itself for attack. Rank upon rank of soldiers waited in a strange silence in the fields, the closest lines barely a hundred yards out from the wall. Either they did not yet know that a force of dragons was waiting for them or else they had lost all fear of the dragons. The Masters were still only distant forms flying over the treetops in the distance. As he watched, they broke into four groups that slowly circled around to attack from different directions. Thelvyn could see that there were at least a score of gemstone dragons in each of the four groups.

"Pass the order quietly," Thelvyn said. "Have the dragons spread out about a couple of wingspans or so apart, so that we can try to hold as much of the wall as possible. Remind them to listen for my orders. If the Masters come in force, we might have to get away from here quickly."

Because he had not been watching over the wall, he was surprised when grappling hooks and ladders suddenly appeared at the top of the gate, scraping and rattling as they

were set into place and the ropes pulled tight. He took a deep
breath to prepare his flame, then stood up on his hind legs to
lift his head over the wall. The moment his head appeared,
dozens of arrows began snapping and bouncing off the armor
of his face so that he had to close his eyes and drop back down
behind the protection of the wall. The invaders had been waiting for the dragons, with companies of archers standing ready
to drive them back.

Unfortunately Thelvyn already had his flame ready, and all
he could do now was to turn his head and let the blast of
dragonfire wash over the paving stones of the street behind him.
He couldn't risk lifting his head over the wall to use his dragonfire on the attackers. While he had survived the first volley of
arrows unscathed, he was fearful of an arrow or crossbow bolt
penetrating the light armor of his face. At least the invaders
would be vulnerable to the dragons the moment they tried to
come over the wall. He moved back from the wall and waited,
ready to attack anyone coming over the parapet with his flaming
breath. His companions on either side of him did likewise.

Thelvyn paused, waiting and listening. The assault on the
wall had grown curiously silent, and no one had climbed the
scaling ropes that were already hooked over the wall. Moving
closer to the massive timbers of the gate, he could hear only
faint sounds from the vast army that was gathered outside the
wall. Then he heard the sound of some large beast running,
and a moment later, he leapt back in alarm as the gate was
struck with tremendous force, nearly bursting the crossbars.

The other dragons hurried to help him hold the gate, but
Thelvyn knew that the battle to defend the wall was already
lost. He was certain the gemstone dragons were attacking the
gate, and he was just as certain that they must have come in
overwhelming numbers. When Kharendaen rushed up to him,
he sat up on his haunches and turned her to face the middle of
the city.

"Trying to hold this gate is pointless," he told the dragons.
"We have to save ourselves to protect the people fleeing."

He leapt forward, leading the way. He turned sharply as
soon as he came to the first side street in order to get his dragons quickly out of sight from the main street in case the gem-

stone dragons broke through the gate in the next few moments. The last of the dragons had only just darted down the narrow side street when they heard a tremendous crash as the Masters hit the ruined gate a second time. Timbers splintered, and huge shards of wood were sent hurtling into the walls of the surrounding buildings.

Thelvyn's only interest was in leading the dragons far enough away that the Masters wouldn't see how few of them there really were. Braastar still had not been completely abandoned. There were still people of Flaemish descent who were too far under the influence of the Masters to seek escape. They wandered the streets in bands, seeking out enemies who had been their own countrymen only hours before. The enslaved citizens elected to keep well away from the dragons.

Thelvyn led his companions diagonally across the city until they came at last to the south wall. Although there was no gate in this section of the wall, the dragons simply leapt over it. Then they flew quickly west toward the Aalban River, so low over the fields that the tips of their wings brushed the high grass. Only when they reached the banks of the river and turned south did they dare to fly a little higher.

They followed the river for several miles before they came to the drifting mass of boats and barges filled almost to overflowing with refugees. The people cheered loudly when they saw the dragons; Thelvyn wondered if they realized that the dragons had retreated to the river only because the city had fallen to the invaders. He was circling around to land on the nearest bank when he became aware a young gold dragon was struggling to overtake him. He locked his wings to drift over the river, waiting for the young dragon to move up beside him.

"The Masters are not far behind us," the dragon reported. "I was the last of our company, and I could see them following us across the fields from the city."

"How many were there?" Thelvyn asked.

"I could not tell for certain. Many more than us, I am certain."

Thelvyn nodded, and the young dragon turned and circled back to join the rest of their company. Thelvyn realized he had to make a quick decision. He had to decide whether to stay

and defend the people fleeing Braastar or to save himself and
the other dragons for more important battles rather than risk
all their lives in a battle they could not win. It was the most
difficult decision he'd had to make in some time, since he
knew what the answer had to be. He didn't dare chance losing
his own life needlessly, even to save the population of an entire
city. His loss might well mean the defeat of his entire world.
After a moment, he turned to land on the grassy east bank of
the river, waiting while the others joined him.

"This is a battle we cannot afford to fight," he told the dragons simply. "Once the Masters discover how few of us there
are, they will surely force their advantage against us. Our only
hope is to try to bluff them. Follow my lead closely, but be
ready to retreat in a moment."

"What about the people of Braastar?" Kharendaen asked
quietly.

Thelvyn could only shake his head. "Perhaps the Masters
will leave them alone."

Thelvyn knew had badly it stung a dragon's pride to run from
a fight, but there was no other choice. Hopping out to the edge
of the bank, he spread his wings and leapt into the air, then
waited for his companions to join him. Once all the dragons
were in flight, he led them close to the east bank of the river, flying barely over the dark water of the river almost within the
shadows of the forest that hugged the riverbank. With any luck,
they would remain unseen until the last moment.

Luck was with them. Thelvyn was unable to see the gemstone dragons until they suddenly passed almost directly overhead, yet even then they were so intent upon their attack that
they failed to see the dragons just below them. There were at
least two dozen of them, their company composed mainly of
large amber and ruby gemstone dragons. The gold dragons
angled up sharply, and their swift flight carried them abruptly
into the rear of the pack.

Following Thelvyn's lead, the dragons attacked quickly and
furiously, using claws, fangs, and flames to inflict all the damage they could in the first few moments of their attack, ripping
into the vulnerable wings of the gemstone dragons to knock
them out of the fight. The rest of the gemstone dragons circled

around to attack as soon as they could, but by that time, Thelvyn had broken off the attack and led the dragons back down almost to the surface of the river before they turned and darted beneath the cover of the forest on the east bank. They weaved tightly in and out among the trees, their wings crashing through the smaller branches. Heavier and less agile, the Masters could not fly among the trees and were forced to follow the dragons above the tops of the trees.

Thelvyn planned to lead the Masters away from the river as far as he could, realizing that his only hope to save the people of Braastar was to get the Masters to pursue him. He wondered how long he could lure the Masters into following them. If he had to, he would send the other dragons away; he was the one the Masters wanted, and he would lead this chase into the Colossus Mountains if he had to.

After a few miles, the dragons had worked their way eastward to a very old, dense part of the forest, where it was easier to fly beneath the lower branches of the tall trees. The foliage in the forest's canopy was still too thick for the Masters to see them from above. Thelvyn spotted a particularly shadowy vale and landed. Flying in and out between the trees was tiring, and the dragons needed a rest. Thelvyn also needed a few moments to consider his next move. He posted a couple of the younger dragons on the perimeters of the vale to watch for danger.

"How long can we keep this up?" Kharendaen asked, sitting close beside her mate. "Can you really hope to stay ahead of the Masters indefinitely?"

"I'll do whatever I must to save those people on the river," he told her. "But when we leave, I want you to stay hidden here until it's safe to leave and then return to Braejr. Tell Solveig that she has to do something about getting ready for all those people, and Alessa has to find some way to get the Radiance to protect her people."

"You know that I won't leave you," she answered simply.

"Dragonking!" one of the young dragons called. "The Masters are flying back to the west, toward the river."

For a moment, Thelvyn looked utterly defeated. "The Masters know how to play this game as well as we do. They know they can draw me back to them by threatening the people on the river."

"But what can we do?" Kharendaen asked worriedly.

"We're out of choices now," he said, rising. "We have to fight them."

The dragons followed Thelvyn as he hurried through the forest, seeking an opening in the trees large enough for them to return to the sky. After a few hundred yards, Thelvyn came to a small clearing and spread his wings, then leapt almost straight up with long, quick sweeps of his wings. He circled slowly just above the trees, waiting for the others to make the difficult climb out of the clearing.

The Masters were about two miles away and moving toward the west. They were flying slowly enough that Thelvyn guessed they were waiting for the dragons to show themselves. Almost as soon as the dragons began to rise above the trees, the gemstone dragons circled and turned back to attack. Then, inexplicably, they suddenly turned once more and began to fly away as quickly as they could in yet a new direction, not toward the river but north, back toward Braastar. Thelvyn did not attempt to pursue them, suspicious that they were trying to lead him into a trap. He could hardly imagine that they would be foolish enough to think he would follow them back to the city, where other gemstone dragons would be waiting to join the fray.

This time the Masters did not hesitate when the dragons failed to pursue them. Thelvyn was beginning to get the impression that they were fleeing, and since he doubted that they were trying to escape the wrath of the Dragonking, he could think of only one thing that would cause the Masters to flee. Looking back, he saw that the sky behind him was full of dragons. A small army of dragons was approaching from the southeast, part of the garrison that had remained at Rockhome. Seldaek had wasted no time in his mission, finding the nearest force of dragons and returning with them in a matter of hours.

Thelvyn circled widely until he found a large clearing where he could land and wait to speak with the leaders of this company of dragons. He was trying to anticipate which of his chief advisors, Marthaen or Jherdar, Seldaek might have located in

Rockhome. He needed to have Marthaen at hand, but he was not surprised when he saw a red dragon leading his companions as they circled down toward the clearing. Most of his companions, some four hundred in all, remained aloft, flying wide patterns to discourage the Masters from returning.

Jherdar circled tightly to slow himself as much as possible, then dropped down into the clearing. Once the red dragon had folded away his wings, he paused a moment and then bowed his head as a gesture of respect to the Dragonking. Thelvyn was still secretly surprised by such loyalty from the red dragon who had challenged him ever since he first became the Dragonlord.

"I came as quickly as I could," Jherdar said almost apologetically.

"I have no complaint," Thelvyn insisted. "I didn't really expect help until tomorrow morning. Now I feel certain we can keep Braejr and the refugees from Braastar safe until the dragon sorcerers can arrive."

The red dragon looked surprised. "Then we will not attack now? Surely we must now have the advantage of numbers."

Thelvyn shook his head firmly. "We dare not. The Masters know that they cannot hold their conquests in this world as long as we are here to fight them. They have to deal with us, specifically with me, as soon as possible. I suspect a trap, and I'm reluctant to attack until we have a better understanding of the situation. For that, I need our sorcerers. I doubt that a delay will make any real difference, since Braastar has already fallen."

Jherdar turned his head aside, looking rather disgruntled. Like all dragons, he wanted to face all challenges with direct action, attacking his enemies immediately and with unrestrained fury. But he would not question the Dragonking, having come to understand the need for restraint and careful planning. Thelvyn was glad of that, since he had been afraid the dragons might have become overconfident from their relatively easy victory in Rockhome.

CHAPTER TWELVE

The arrival of the first group of dragons made Thelvyn's problems a little easier to handle, since in effect it brought the invasion of the Highlands to a stalemate. The Masters were content to concentrate on trying to secure their own position in Braastar and the area around the city, leaving the refugees from the city in relative peace. That made it easy for the dragons to protect the refugees and help them on their way south, both the people on the river and those traveling by the main road. But the Masters were relentless in expanding their influence over the minds of the Flaem. They extended their mind attack beyond the refugees to towns and cities as far south as Braejr.

Thelvyn was able to continue to relieve much of the pressure that the Masters were exerting against the refugees by maintaining his spells of protection. But the spell that he used to dispel the magic of the mental summons demanded a great deal of his strength, especially since he was required to renew the spell every two or three hours. The demand upon him became almost too much to handle when he was also required to employ the spell to protect the people of Braejr. Nevertheless, it was something that only he could accomplish. Not even the greatest of the dragon sorcerers could command even a portion of the powers that were his by right as the son of an Immortal.

Another company of dragons arrived during the night, and that insured the dominance of the dragons in the Highlands. Even so, no one could help ease the burden of Thelvyn's burden of defending the Flaem from the control of the Masters. He slept when he could at night, but he was required to renew one of the two protective spells he was maintaining every hour or so. By daybreak, he was so tired he could hardly rise.

He had one turn of good fortune the morning after arriving back in Braejr. After Alessa's Fire Wizards had experimented with the power of the Radiance for a day and a night, they had finally discovered a way to use its power to partially block the power of the Masters. He was able to speak briefly with Alessa Vyledaar that morning, and she had told him something of the search to find a way to use the Radiance against the Masters. Mostly, she had made certain that he understood its two main limitations. The power of the Radiance was great but limited; she had to be careful that the wizards maintaining the shield used its power no faster than it could renew itself. In addition, as he had known previously, the Radiance lost its strength steadily with distance. The limit of the shield was just barely enough to protect Braejr.

But Thelvyn still had to maintain his spell to protect the refugees. He spent most of the next day in the wilderness with the dragons guarding the retreat of the people from Braastar, shielding them from the cold, demanding will that kept trying to force them to turn back toward the north. The struggle was even greater than it had been the day before, since the Masters had grown somewhat in their own powers during the night, and they became even stronger during that third day of the invasion of the Highlands. Yet another company of dragons arrived late in the morning. There were now over a thousand dragons in the Highlands, and the latest arrivals brought the news that armies from the dwarves, the elves, and Darokin were already on their way.

As Thelvyn was returning to the lair at Solveig's house that evening, he noticed with some interest that every lamp and lantern from her home had been brought out to illuminate the court. The area around the house was full of dragons and people. Indeed, the court was so full that Thelvyn had to land in the street outside the gate. When he peered through the gate, he saw that Marthaen had arrived, together with a couple of older dragons he hoped were the sorcerers he had been anticipating. They were discussing something with Alessa Vyledaar, who looked rather sullen.

Thelvyn was surprised and delighted to see Perrantin, mage and former adventuring partner, standing with Solveig and Sir George. The wizard hadn't returned to the Highlands in the last six years, and Thelvyn had never really expected to see him again. Perrantin looked much the same as ever, more like a baker or a street vendor than an experienced wizard, both in his appearance and in the way he dressed. Thelvyn was wearing the Collar of the Dragons, and the wizard realized that it was him at once.

"Thelvyn!" Perrantin exclaimed, hurrying to greet him as he entered the court. "My word, it's been a long time."

"It certainly has," Thelvyn agreed, laying back his ears. "And it has also been a long day for me. Did Sir George bring you here?"

"No, I commandeered one of your dragon couriers who was passing through Traladara bringing news of the invasion," Perrantin explained. "I thought you might need me, since I'm sure that Sir George is of no possible use to you as an advisor."

"Now, why should I suddenly no longer be of my usual incalculable worth to the lad?" the old knight asked indignantly.

"Possibly because you are so insufferably pleased at getting back your missing hand that you can't possibly appreciate just how desperate the situation really is."

"If you don't mind, the two of you can argue your alleged worth later," Thelvyn interrupted, although he was privately amused. Watching those two eccentric older men reminded him of the days he had lived with Sir George in the small frontier village of Graez, making him feel almost like a child again. He had matured enough lately that he no longer resented feeling young. "Is this a party to welcome old friends, or is this a serious discussion?"

"Alessa is having a problem with her Flaemish suspicion of strangers," Sir George explained. "She has some strong objections to allowing the dragon sorcerers to study the Radiance."

"We don't have time for this," Thelvyn remarked. "Come with me."

He walked slowly over to where Alessa Vyledaar was arguing quietly but firmly with Marthaen and the two dragon sorcerers. She was wearing a Flaemish wizard's robe with a high, stiffened collar, and Thelvyn was impressed by how much her appearance and demeanor reminded him of Byen Kalestraan. He sat back on his haunches facing them, sitting upright so that he was looking down at Alessa in a manner designed to be intimidating.

"What is the trouble?" he asked simply.

"The Radiance belongs to the Flaem," Alessa declared sullenly. "When the war is over, it is to be left in our control."

"And I keep reassuring her that it will be," Marthaen insisted. "It's not something that we can take with us, even if we wanted it. We just want to help you use it to defend yourselves. Did you discuss this with the other members of your order?"

"None of us are happy about this," she answered. "But they've left it up to me to decide."

"Then will you listen to Perrantin?" Thelvyn asked. "He's come all the way from his dark hole in Traladara to advise you in your time of trouble. Perrantin is a wizard and scholar of great renown. When the renegade dragons were attacking six years ago, he took on the task of finding an answer when no one else knew what to do. They ended up making me the Dragonlord. I've never forgiven him. You can tell your young colleague what she should do, can't you, Perry?"

"Yes, I believe so," Perrantin agreed, nodding vigorously. "You have to let the dragons help you or the Masters are going to toss your pot, as the saying goes."

"How pithy and direct," Thelvyn commented. "How can you refute such wisdom?"

Alessa had been glaring more and more fiercely with each

passing moment. "You're getting to be as bad as Sir George."

Thelvyn feigned surprise. "I think I've just been insulted."

"You can take that the way it was intended," she told him, with a stern glance at the old knight that made him shut his mouth before he could comment. Then she frowned. "Very well. Better to have the Radiance in the hands of the dragons than let the Masters take it. But you have to promise me that you will tell us everything that you learn about it."

"I promise you will be told," Marthaen assured her. "What you do with such secrets will be up to you."

Watching Alessa, Thelvyn was certain she was still rather suspicious, or at least angry. He hadn't understood the real problem at first, until he realized that her annoyance was not with the dragons but with herself. The Radiance was one of the greatest heirlooms of the Fire Wizards, much as the collar had been for the dragons. Alessa's instincts told her to refuse to allow the dragons to work with the Radiance because she very much wanted to uncover its secrets for herself. She might need a little more persuasion in the morning, but she would be more agreeable once the dragons had actually begun their research.

"If that's the last problem I need to handle tonight, then I plan to have my dinner and go to bed," he said, turning his head to look at Kharendaen, seated patiently behind him. "I've been fighting the will of the Masters all day, and frankly, I've had enough. Is there anything to eat around here, or do I have to hunt for my supper?"

"You've earned your dinner," Solveig told him. "It took some work, but we managed to scare up three virgins for you."

"I don't find that amusing," Thelvyn said as he rose slowly and began to move toward the warehouse.

"Wait in your lair," she called after him. "We'll have something brought to you right away."

The next day brought new problems in need of answers. Thelvyn had been afraid from the first that the Masters would press their attack on Braejr as soon as they could, and he was not prepared for that. That was why he had resented the two days he had spent getting the people of Braastar to safety while he had needed to be making preparations for war. Of course, he was able to remind himself that there was little he could have done while he waited for the dragon sorcerers to arrive, and Marthaen had brought them only the previous evening. But while the time lost had been unavoidable, it had allowed the Masters to move ahead in their plans while he had accomplished nothing of real value in the interim.

Nor had he forgotten the mysterious voice that was the true master behind the Masters, the powerful will he had fought to rescue Alessa when her mind had been held captive. By necessity, he had been forced to fight the underlings of the true leader behind the invasion, dealing with the Masters and their armies first and often forgetting that his greatest enemy had not yet challenged him directly. That was why he found it so important to discover the secret to commanding the full power of the Radiance.

At least he had been able to enlist spies who kept him informed of the situation in Braastar, now a stronghold of the enemy. His dragons didn't dare fly near enough to the fallen city to see anything for themselves, but dragon messengers were able to secretly carry elvish scouts to within a few short miles of Braastar. They reported that an army of some fifty thousand was gathered in and around the city, and that perhaps two hundred gemstone dragons were gathered there as well.

The scouts also brought back reports of strange creatures that had been set loose in the woods and hills of the Highlands, terrifying, unworldly creatures that posed strange and unexpected dangers. Thelvyn had heard such reports during the invasion of Rockhome, tales of monsters with many eyes on short stalks, eyes that did not see but which possessed various magical weapons that could slay from a distance; flowing, formless creatures that hid in the shadows to trap the unwary; and huge insects with deadly bites and stings. Many types of monsters had been seen, creatures that had never before existed in Mystara, gathered by the Masters from many strange worlds.

Unfortunately, the release of such monsters was the least of the problems that Thelvyn and his allies faced right now. Just after dawn, the will of the Masters increased, so that many of the people of Braejr now struggled against the call of that strange distant voice. It was not yet so great that anyone was in danger of being enslaved, but it was enough to leave many of the Flaem troubled and distracted. The wizards tried to compensate by increasing the power of the Radiance, but they did not dare exhaust its reserves.

Thelvyn knew that he could no longer spend all his time fighting the will of the Masters. If he did not prepare to fight the Masters themselves, he would ultimately lose the Highlands to them. But he thought he might have one answer to the problem of combatting the relentless call of the Masters. Early that morning, he requested that six large stones should be brought to him. He didn't specify the shape of the stones, but they had to be of a certain type, a dense, dark stone with the sparkle of crystal, at least the size of a large trunk but not much larger. Within the hour, workmen had found building stones that suited his needs perfectly and brought them in a wagon to the court of Solveig's house.

Thelvyn had never tried to use his unique powers to create artifacts of magic, so he could only try his best and find out the hard way whether or not he could do such a thing. Setting one of the stones on the ground before him, he sat upright with his tail wrapped around his legs and closed his eyes while he opened himself to his inner powers. As he had once relied upon the enchantments of the armor and weapons of the Dragonlord, now he was learning how to make use of the unique powers that were the legacy of his remarkable heritage as the son of an Immortal who had briefly taken mortal form.

After some experimentation, he was able to convert the first stone into an artifact of magic. He began by making it the focus of an opening to a plane of natural magical force, like a well or spring where magic was drawn out at a controlled rate. This was the most difficult part, since without an actual knowledge of the many unseen planes of existence, he had to feel his way. His next step was to divert most of that native magic through a spell of his own that created a shield against the will of the Masters. Finally he set most of the spells of protection against magical tampering that he knew into the stone, so that it could also protect itself against any hostile magic used against it.

Thelvyn was able to complete only four of the ward stones before he needed time for his powers to recover, but he hoped to prepare more stones later that day. When he was done, dragons carried the stones out into the wilderness north of the city. The effect of the four stones was limited, but together they nearly doubled the power of the Radiance. That spared him the need to use his own spell of shielding when he should be working on other problems, and it also spared the need for the Fire Wizards to overtax the powers of the Radiance.

And that was all for the best, because Thelvyn now found himself in a race to find a way to fight the Masters before they defeated him. Not only did the power of their will gain slowly but steadily in strength, but also the army they were gathering at Braastar was obviously intended for an attack on Braejr. He knew he didn't dare attack the Masters in their own stronghold, so the most obvious tactic seemed to be for him to wait until the Masters moved against him, then strike swiftly and with overwhelming force. As far as he knew, he had enough dragons to deal with the two hundred or so gemstone dragons thought to be at the stronghold. But he would not easily be able to summon more dragons if he needed them; the Masters had made certain of that, attacking at random in many parts of the world so as to present a constant threat. Because of these attacks, he was forced to keep most of his own dragons scattered among other garrisons.

For the moment, the most immediate problem was finding a way to make certain that the people of Braejr were not in danger of falling under the control of the Masters, even if the siege came to the very walls of their city. If the Flaem were enslaved, the dragons and all other allies would be forced to abandon Braejr and, for all purposes, surrender all the Highlands to the domination of the Masters.

Late that morning, the dragon sorcerers asked to speak to the leaders in charge of the defense of Braejr, or at least those who were aware of the existence of the Radiance. For now, that meant Thelvyn, Kharendaen, Perrantin, Sir George, Solveig, and Korinn Bear Slayer. Marthaen had been elected to speak for the dragon sorcerers, while Alessa Vyledaar stood by in case she was needed.

"We've confirmed something the Fire Wizards always had strong reason to suspect," Marthaen began. "We've located the source of the Radiance. We know that it's a magical artifact or device of some type located far below the city."

"Is it a Blackmoor device?" Thelvyn asked.

"That would seem the most obvious answer," the older dragon agreed. "We don't know that for certain yet, but I can't think of anyone else except the dragons who could have constructed an artifact of such power, and we know that the dragons didn't create it. The only part that mystifies us is the depth that thing is buried beneath the city. It doesn't seem possible for something to become buried so deep in three thousand years, even considering the effect of the Rain of Fire and the shattering of the world."

"That suggests it was put there on purpose," Sir George remarked. "If you wanted something to stay buried, the best place would be beneath the joining of two rivers. The city itself is almost a marsh in places."

"But the Masters could have it dug out if they're determined and resourceful enough," Marthaen said.

Thelvyn frowned, then glanced up. "I hate to speak of such things, but the problem must be faced. I'm not even sure if we can hold Braejr, and therefore I'm concerned that the Radiance could fall into the hands of the Masters. Can we destroy it, or perhaps force it to destroy itself somehow?"

"That may not be advisable," Perrantin interrupted. "I suspect that this is a Blackmoor device of great power. The elves who once inhabited this land found a similar device centuries ago. We know almost nothing about the object they found, except that they caused it to explode with such force that the northlands were devastated. The evil lands surrounding the World Mountain in the steppes were created as a distant result of that same explosion. I don't think we dare try to destroy the Radiance ourselves, or we may do worse damage to our world than the Masters could ever do. For that same reason, however, the Masters must not be allowed to capture the Radiance. I fear what they may do with such power, whether accidentally or deliberately."

Thelvyn considered that briefly and sighed. "I agree. Unless we come to understand the Radiance well enough that we can shut it down for all time without risk, then we must defend it at all costs. Unfortunately, that also means that the dragons might have to turn on the people of Braejr and either destroy them or expel them from the city if they fall under the control of the Masters. I'd rather send the Flaem away to the south before that happens."

Solveig nodded. "I've been thinking the same thing. Perhaps we should evacuate the people of Braejr while we can. Alessa, what do you think? If anyone should speak for the Flaemish people about this matter, it's you."

"The Flaem seem to be caught in the worst possible position," Alessa said bitterly, not looking up. "Now the dragons who came to defend us might have to destroy us in order to defend our world. Our protectors could suddenly become our enemies, and our true enemies could enslave us. But I agree. I would rather see the Flaem leave the Highlands than have them become slaves in their own lands. Until we can understand the Radiance enough to know that it can protect us, then we should begin evacuating the city. The Masters must not capture the Radiance, no matter what. I would rather lose it than have it used against us."

"I'm aware that this is an extremely hard and dangerous time for your people," Thelvyn assured her. "But why are the Masters so determined to possess the Radiance when its powers are so limited in range? Do they understand it better than we do, or are they ignorant of its limitations?"

"I cannot say," Marthaen answered. "Perhaps the Masters themselves came into our world and probed the secrets of the Radiance before they sent the Flaem here to guard it. I cannot guess what the Radiance can or cannot do, but I can say this: Our dragon sorcerers believe the Radiance can be made to reveal its secrets to us very soon, perhaps in only a matter of hours."

Solveig hurried to prepare for the evacuation of the city, and the boats and barges that had brought the refugees from Braastar once again made ready to take the people of Braejr farther to the south. If necessary, the Flaem could be sent on into Darokin, although they would need the protection of the dragons to safely pass the bands of orcs and goblins in the Broken Lands. It was also possible that the barges would not survive the rapids.

The race to find a way to defend the Highlands soon became even more desperate. That same afternoon, reports arrived that the invasion army being gathered at Braastar was already marching south, with the Masters accompanying their forces in great numbers to insure that their army was not harassed by the dragons. Their pace was difficult to guess, but the invaders seemed likely to arrive at Braejr and begin their siege some time on the fourth day of their march.

Now Thelvyn had some difficult choices to make. With the Masters and their army moving out from their strongholds, they were now much more vulnerable to attack from the dragons. Thelvyn could attack at once in full strength and hope to defeat the Masters quickly, or he could organize a series of quick hit-and-run strikes designed to draw the Masters away from their army. Or he could simply wait, summoning all the dragons that could be spared from other lands to assemble an overwhelming force. The dragon sorcerers might unravel the secrets of the Radiance in the meantime and finally turn it into an effective weapon of magic.

He elected to discuss the matter with Marthaen, who had firsthand experience with what dragons could do in battle, since he had led the dragons in war against both Alphatia and the Highlands the year before. Marthaen had to admit that the problem was a difficult one, mostly because they could not accurately predict just what the Masters could do in battle. He pointed out that, unlike opposing the Dragonlord, fighting Alphatia had been relatively enough.

That reminded Thelvyn that he was still the Dragonlord, a fact he had been overlooking lately. The first Dragonlord and the Great One together had defeated the gemstone dragons once before, and Thelvyn possessed a combination of the powers of both. The Great One had never said he would lose the powers of the Dragonlord when he made the decision to remain in dragon form. He couldn't afford to overlook the tremendous powers he possessed as the Dragonlord.

For the time being, Marthaen agreed with Thelvyn that he

should wait at least a day to give time for the invaders to move away from the protection of their strongholds in the north. Once the Masters and their army were well away from their strongholds, Thelvyn and the dragons would attack, cautiously drawing out and slaying the gemstone dragons a few at a time. If the invaders couldn't be stopped before they reached Braejr, then Thelvyn would probably assume the form of the Dragonlord and face the enemy in a final battle in the fields north of the city, where there would be no woods or hills to conceal the enemy from him.

"I would like to suggest one other alternative," Marthaen added. "My sorcerers have been working hard at probing the nature of the Radiance. They have been exploring it in visions, which seemed the best way to delve into its secrets without exposing their minds to traps or other dangers. They've been making significant progress, and they hope to know the nature of the Radiance and learn how to control it very soon."

"How soon will they know?" Thelvyn asked. "If I am to wait for the Radiance, I need to know that it will work by tomorrow morning. Otherwise, I must make plans that do not include its powers."

Marthaen nodded. "I understand. I will have your answer by morning."

In addition to his many other concerns, Thelvyn had to be careful that only his most trusted friends and advisors were aware of his true plans. He hadn't forgotten that there was a proven traitor somewhere in the city, a spy who had somehow relayed the details from his first meeting with the Grand Alliance to the Masters. He knew the spy must be a delegate to the meetings of the alliance, and he strongly suspected he was the representative from Alphatia. Thelvyn wanted to give the Masters the impression of being less prepared for battle than he actually was, a tactic that had worked well for him once before.

So far the only delegates who had left Braejr were Korinn Bear Slayer, Lord Derrick of Darokin, and King Celedril of Alfheim, who had returned to their own lands to prepare armies for the defense of the Highlands. The other delegates remained in Braejr for now, although they would most likely leave if a siege threatened. Thelvyn kept them informed of his plans, but only those matters he wanted them to know. If the Masters appeared to know only what he told the delegates, he would know for certain where his spy was hiding. At the same time, he hoped to be better prepared to face the Masters than they expected him to be.

Of course, he said nothing of the Radiance or made any suggestion that the dragons and the Fire Wizards were seeking special magic to defend the city. The Masters knew of the Radiance and possibly already knew more about its true nature than he did, and they could easily guess that he might be trying to find ways to use it as a weapon against them. He knew that he could not hope to be fully successful in tricking them, but he still hoped to give the impression that the dragons were having no luck in probing the secrets of the Radiance.

The dragon sorcerers were indeed making progress in understanding the Radiance. As he had promised, Marthaen came to the lair early the next morning to report all that he had learned so far. The discoveries of the sorcerers were so remarkable that both he and Alessa agreed that no one should hear what they had learned except a few who really needed to know. The only others admitted to their meeting were Kharendaen, Sir George, and Perrantin.

"At least we have a very good idea of what the Radiance is," Marthaen began. "I admit that we cannot completely understand what we have found, and perhaps we never will. As we had expected, the source of the Radiance is not an artifact of magic or a portal into another plane, but a great machine that generates tremendous amounts of power. Although it is similar to the devices of ancient Blackmoor, it is obviously alien in origin."

Thelvyn lifted his ears in surprise. "Could this be something that the Masters made for their own use long ago?"

Marthaen shook his head firmly. "The device is very old, older than the origin of the gemstone dragons. In fact, it predates even the dragons themselves. It might be a relic of the forgotten First Age of the world, the time of the civilization of the Eldar, before the coming of men and elves. And we suspect that it might not be from this world at all."

Thelvyn thought he had never seen Mage Perrantin look so pleased since they had first discovered the Citadel of the Ancients. The discussion of the Radiance excited his curiosity so much that he appeared ready to take a shovel and start digging for it. Thelvyn also wondered why Alessa looked so sullen and angry, even disillusioned.

"Can the Radiance do anything to help us?" he asked, wondering if that was the cause of her concern.

"I believe that it can," Marthaen answered. "One thing we have discovered is that the Radiance device, as powerful as it is, has only been waiting idly. It is capable of producing far greater power in service of anyone who can command it. The mortal wizards are unable to control the function of the device itself. They can only channel its powers into other forms of magic. But the dragons can control the device."

"And the Masters as well, no doubt," Sir George commented.

"Unfortunately so. We still dare not attempt to destroy it. We can at least shut it down, but it could easily be brought back to life again by the Masters if they were able to capture it."

"But the dragons can use it to defeat the Masters," Alessa said. Thelvyn now understood the cause of her discontent. The Fire Wizards claimed the Radiance as their own, but they could never fully command it. Only the dragons could do that, which seemed to give them a claim as the rightful owners of the Radiance.

"We cannot defeat the Masters with the power of the Radiance alone," Marthaen was quick to explain. "The range of its power remains limited even to us. But we could use it to drive the Masters from the Highlands and prevent them from ever returning here. And that might be the key to their ultimate defeat, since their plans for invasion seem to have been built around their control of the Flaem."

Alessa sighed deeply, apparently coming to some kind of a decision. "That's why I decided to surrender the control of the Radiance to the dragons, so that they can use it to protect us at a time when we cannot save ourselves. The people of Braejr are feeling the pull of the Masters very strongly now, in spite of the protection of the wards that the Dragonking has set, and it causes us great discomfort. I would not have my people suffer an hour longer than can be helped."

"We will do all that we can for you," Marthaen assured her. "If we can vanquish the Masters from the Highlands, they will never be able to return. Only one or two dragon sorcerers could then use the Radiance to keep all our lands secure from their influence."

Thelvyn looked up suddenly. "Are the Masters aware of your experiments with the Radiance?"

"They must be," the older dragon agreed. "When we manipulate magic of such proportions, they must surely sense it. And as our control of the Radiance grows, they will be aware of that as well. I cannot guess how they might respond to that, except that there is nothing much that they can do to stop us."

"How they respond is an important consideration," Thelvyn remarked, almost to himself. Then he saw the others watching him. "If they anticipate defeat, they might salvage what they can by retreating back through their gate at Braastar. Or they might still believe that common dragons are foolish and weak, no match for them even with the power of the Radiance. I don't know them well enough to anticipate an answer."

"They have proved to be very cautious and calculating so far," Marthaen reminded him. "I can only believe they will continue to be so. If they sense that we are using levels of magic that could be a threat to them, they will certainly proceed more cautiously, possibly even withdraw."

"Then we must respond accordingly," Thelvyn agreed. "I need to know when you plan to use the Radiance to break their power. At that time, I want to have somehow moved most of our dragons between them and their gate, and I will be there as the Dragonlord to face them. And no one in this city must be able to guess our plans."

"If they retreat, is it wise to stand in their way?" Sir George asked.

"We have to win battles, not avoid them," Thelvyn insisted. "We must try to avoid fighting the Masters when they have the advantage, but we must fight them when the advantage is our own. If we allow them to escape, they will only return at a time of their own choosing."

Marthaen bowed to his king and hurried to rejoin the dragon sorcerers. Alessa accompanied him, looking very tired and unhappy about the situation. Only recently had Thelvyn learned that the Flaem with the greatest talent for magic were also the most vulnerable to the call of the Masters, so he realized how much she was really suffering. Of course, she was also still dissatisfied over turning control of the Radiance over to the dragons, although she had to admit it was best, considering the way things had turned out. The dragons could command the full power of the Radiance, but they could not take it away with them. The Fire Wizards claimed the Radiance, but they had access to only a small part of its true power. That helped to insure that neither party would be tempted to misuse it.

Within the hour, Thelvyn had a final meeting with the remaining delegates of the Grand Alliance. He explained to them that the evacuation of Braejr was continuing and that the time had come for them to leave as well. Although he was cautious with his information, he tried very hard to imply that he didn't expect to be able to hold the city. He was somewhat surprised when they all agreed to leave immediately. If there was a spy among them, apparently the Masters thought that his work was done.

To his dismay, Thelvyn discovered that the Masters had outguessed him once again. Later that same morning, a dragon hurried to Braejr with the warning that he had seen a dragon of tremendous size, a strange, wingless dragon that appeared to have metal armor. The metal dragon had apparently come through the worldgate near their stronghold east of Braastar and was moving quickly overland, heading south to join the invading army. The young dragon had to admit that he had few details to offer, since the Masters had prevented him from coming closer than several miles. But he had certainly seen something odd and alarming.

Thelvyn decided he had better see this thing at once. He took along with him enough bodyguards to force their way through the defenses of the Masters long enough for a close look at the metal creature. To keep the element of surprise as long as possible, they began by flying west from Braejr. After many miles, they came to the hilly, wooded lands of the central Highlands and began a long circle northward that brought them across the Aalban River from the northwest, just above Braastar. They continued to fly swiftly over the forest east of the city, over a hundred dragons in a tight column as they searched the wilderness for the mysterious metal dragon.

Finding the strange dragon in the wilderness proved to be easy, even from miles away, since it stood taller at the shoulders than the tops of many of the trees. It was like some strange, alien draconic form, with a long, serpentine body carried on four sets of legs. Its extended face had eyes that burned like red jewels from the deep shadows of protective horns and spikes, and its long tail was armed at the end with a massive weight like a crushing club, lined with ridges of sharp-edged plates that glittered like metal. The very size of the metallic beast was alarming. It was easily a hundred yards from its nose to the end of its tail and twenty yards high at the shoulders, making it several times the size of even the largest gold dragon.

Keeping just above the trees, Thelvyn led his dragons in as fast as they could fly. As he came closer, he began to have serious doubts about what he saw. Whatever this strange creature was, the massive shell of dark bluish silver metal was almost certainly not its natural armor. But if the creature was wearing a suit of protective armor, then it had to be carrying more than its own weight in metal. Thelvyn had seen dragon armor at Windreach, but only partial pieces that usually covered only the wearer's neck, face, and chest and could be easily carried in flight. Of course, since this beast didn't fly, it was free to bear far more weight. As massive as it was, it was moving along at a rapid pace and would probably overtake the invading army by the next morning.

Thelvyn led the dragons in for a swift attack, taking a chance that the armored creature lacked flames or other deadly weapons. The beast didn't even hesitate in its ponderous stride, seemingly unconcerned by the flood of dragonfire that the scores of attacking dragons directed at its back. Thelvyn quickly realized that he would have to reconsider his tactics. He had thought that dragonfire was enough to penetrate any thickness of armor in moments, but the armor of this creature had to be enchanted in some way to resist the flames. He warned the dragons to keep their distance and then landed in a clearing some distance ahead of the armored creature.

That gave him a moment to change to human form and teleport himself into the armor of the Dragonlord. He found that he moved a bit unsteadily because of the long time since he had taken this form. He stepped out into the south end of the clearing and turned to face the armored dragon as it pushed through the trees with the lumbering ease of some massive beast crashing through the underbrush. As it came into the clearing, Thelvyn drew and lifted his sword, directing the power of the enchanted blade toward the heavy armor of the alien dragon. It didn't even react to the first several strikes, even though the bolts were powerful enough to have slain a red dragon. Pausing a moment to summon the full power of the sword, he aimed a final blast of tremendous strength directly at the chest of the armored beast in the last moment before it was upon him.

The blast was fierce enough that it caused him to turn his head aside, and the force of the explosion echoed through the hills like thunder. The front end of the creature was lifted from the ground by the impact, but it hesitated only momentarily in its stride, the thick metal of its armor not even dented or scorched, even though the grass was seared for some distance around it. Then it reached out with one massive foreleg and swatted the Dragonlord aside almost casually.

Only the magical armor saved Thelvyn's life, since the force of the blow lifted him from the ground and sent him flying more than a quarter of a mile over the top of the forest. The panic of falling awakened newly learned instincts as he struggled to spread his wings and fly, forgetting that he was no longer in dragon form. Then he crashed heavily through the branches of the trees, landing on the soft humus of the forest floor on his back. For the moment, he was stunned by the blow and ached fiercely in spite of the protection of his armor.

All he could do was lie moaning in pain amid the wreckage of torn leaves and broken branches. After a time, he stirred and lifted himself painfully, shifting out of the armor of the Dragonlord and returning to his draconic form.

Moving slowly, he found an opening through the trees where he could show himself to his concerned dragon body-guards, already flying back and forth over the forest searching for him. He seemed to have no serious injuries, although he needed several more minutes to recover before he dared to spread his wings and trust himself to flight. The massive armored form continued to move quickly through the woods with single-minded determination, its brief encounter with the Dragonlord seemingly forgotten. A small band of gemstone dragons had joined the fantastic creature.

Now Thelvyn understood why the Masters believed from the first that they could fight the Dragonking and the dragons and win. Their armored beast was impervious to attack, having taken the worst the Dragonlord could throw at it and had emerged unharmed. Thelvyn had no idea how he could fight such a thing, but he was now certain there was no living creature inside that armor.

CHAPTER THIRTEEN

Many years had passed since Thelvyn had faced an enemy he could not fight. There had always been a great deal of security in knowing that if things got out of hand, he could always win any argument that came to blows. Even when he had faced the dragons a year before, desperate to find some way to save them by avoiding battle, he had always had the assurance that he could defeat them. Of course, Marthaen had known that the dragons could not fight the Dragonlord, and he had never had any intention of trying. The Masters had found a very different answer to the problem of fighting the Dragonlord, by building a device so big and solid that it could simply walk right over any opposition.

Thelvyn was glad the evacuation of Braejr had continued uninterrupted, since the metal beast was moving along quickly enough to be there some time the next day if it did not slow down to march with the invading army. Thelvyn believed there was a way to defeat the giant war machine, but at the moment, it was unavailable. He returned to Braejr as quickly as he could, calling together his chief advisors for a hasty discussion. Above all, he wanted Marthaen to be there.

"At least now we know why the Masters were willing to have their spy leave the city," Sir George commented when Thelvyn had related the events of his brief encounter. "Obviously they believe they already have the answer to any problems they may encounter."

Marthaen sat for a moment in silent thought. The news that the Masters had a weapon that even the Dragonlord could not face up to had shaken them all, since they had always looked upon the Dragonlord as the most dangerous force of destruction in the world. The gold dragon looked up at last. "What manner of beast could be locked inside that armor? No true dragon-kin, certainly."

"I'm fairly certain there is no living creature inside the armor," Thelvyn replied, to everyone's considerable surprise.

"A giant automaton?" Perrantin asked.

Thelvyn shook his head from side to side. "I also doubt that there is any machinery inside that armor. The reason why I believe it's impervious to attack is that it's nothing more than massive pieces of metal joined together by heavy hinges and set in motion by the will of the Masters. The heat of dragonfire doesn't harm it and explosions do not damage it because it is nothing more than solid metal. The Masters stayed clear of their device as long as the dragons were attacking it. But after my battle with it, the gemstone dragons returned. Obviously their will animated the thing."

"Do you think the power of the Radiance can shut down this armored device?" Marthaen asked.

"If you can protect the Flaem by cutting off the will of the Masters, then you can block their control of this thing as well," Thelvyn stated. "I see no other way of defeating it. Of course, the Masters must know that as well, and I suspect they'll send their armored device here as quickly as they can before we learn how to use the Radiance against it. I think you have until tomorrow afternoon sometime to learn to command the full power of the Radiance, or the city is lost."

Marthaen considered that statement briefly, his ears laid back. "I think you're right. If we can break the will of the Masters, we will solve any number of our problems. Whether or not we can do it by the time that monster gets here remains to be seen. Do you have any idea how you might slow it down?"

"It might just slow itself," Thelvyn said. "Can you imagine how much that thing must weigh? I'm interested in seeing how the Masters plan to get it across the river."

Keeping track of the siege device was no problem, even from such a distance, since they could frequently see it moving through the forests and clearings east of the river from as far away as twenty miles or more. As they watched it come closer that day, they found that Thelvyn's estimate had been fairly precise. Unless it was slowed down somehow, it would reach Braejr by late the next morning, a full day ahead of the invading army. And it probably did not need an army to help it.

Finding a way to slow the metal beast was one of Thelvyn's most pressing problems, and he was unable to find any good answer. Trapping it in a pit or some other obstacle was too impractical because of the size of the thing. Its only vulnerability seemed to be that it required the will of the Masters to keep it motion, but he doubted that his own spells would be enough to break their will. If he was to try, the best time would be when it tried to cross the Aalban River. With any luck, it might become stuck in the soft mud. Just the same, he thought it best to continue the evacuation of Braejr, knowing that only a fraction of the Flaemish population could withdraw from the city in the time that remained.

When the reports came in early the next morning, the news was not good. The metal beast had turned west late the previous afternoon to intercept the main road, and it had made even better time during the night by staying on the road. It had passed the army of the Masters in the middle of the night while the invaders were camped on the side of the road, and dawn had found it less than ten miles from the bridge.

All of Thelvyn's previous plans were now of no use. He sent Kharendaen to find her brother and have him engage the full power of the Radiance as soon as he could. Then Thelvyn hurried to the near side of the bridge over the Aalban River to do anything he could to prevent or delay the armored creature from crossing the river. He had dragons stand ready in the fields on either side of the river, with firm orders that they were to stay well back from the road and avoid the metal beast. Their part was to force the Masters to keep their distance, making it as difficult as possible for them to maintain their control over their metal warrior.

When all other preparations had been made, Thelvyn could only sit in the field beside the bridge and wait. Since the powerful enchantments of the Dragonlord had failed him already, he elected to remain in dragon form. His real weapons would be his own remarkable powers and those granted to him as a cleric of the Great One, the same ones he had used to fight the will of the Masters in the first few days of their invasion of the Highlands. He was certain that the metal beast would try to wade across the river itself. The bridge would never support its tremendous weight. His part would be to keep it from gaining the west bank.

Near midmorning, he could see the dark silver-blue of the metal monster's back just over the tops of the trees to the northeast. Minutes later, the immense war machine stepped out from the trees into the last long stretch of open land on the east side of the river. At a signal from Thelvyn, Jherdar led the dragons against the score of gemstone dragons that accompanied their warrior. Spreading their wings, four hundred dragons climbed steeply into the morning sky from both sides of the river, more than enough to encourage the Masters to make a grudging retreat back to the northeast.

The metal beast paused momentarily in its stride, briefly lacking the full attention of the will that animated it while the Masters withdrew. But after a few moments, it began to move forward again, more slowly than before but with purposeful resolve. Thelvyn glanced up. The Masters were doing everything they could to evade the packs of dragons who harassed them and still stay within sight of their metal servant. Watching them, Thelvyn knew that their control of the fighting machine would now be at its weakest.

He hadn't seriously considered trying to fight the Masters for control of their warrior, but there was nothing he could do to slow down the armored monster otherwise. Once again he sat back on his haunches and opened himself to his deepest powers, and then he reached out with his will to seize control of the metallic warrior. In almost the same moment, his will was forcibly rejected, as if his mind had hit against an unseen wall. In that brief instant, he had witnessed the intricate network of spells that gave the massive device both the strength and direction that set it into motion. It was far more complex than he had anticipated, but it was also strongly warded against the intrusion of any will except that of the Masters, fiercely protecting itself from any hostile influence.

But it was also dependent upon the eyes and minds of the gemstone dragons for guidance, and the nearest of the alien dragons was now almost five miles away. Thelvyn was now fairly certain that the Masters could see through the metal warrior's jewel-like eyes, but from this distance, they could not see the land about it well enough to guide the creature accurately. While dragons had the sharpest vision in the world, five miles was a long way to try to guide the steps of a machine with eight legs. The warrior had already begun to wander somewhat north of the road, although that might have been to avoid getting itself entangled with the bridge.

Thelvyn watched with interest as the warrior's jeweled eyes began to glow bright red within the deep shadows of their protective brows. His first thought was that the Masters must be enhancing the device's vision, since they were obviously too far away to direct the creature themselves. Then he realized his mistake and leapt aside, running as fast as he could in an erratic, zigzag course. That alone saved his life. Suddenly beams of power shot out from the eyes of the warrior, striking the ground with explosive force where he had stood only a moment before.

Desperate to escape, Thelvyn scrambled over the ground, his dragon's claws digging into the deep sod to give him purchase for tight turns. The beams of ruby light followed him, ripping through the ground like some immense plow, then suddenly jumping ahead or sharply to one side to cut off the young dragon's escape. There was nowhere for Thelvyn to run, caught as he was in the open fields north of the city without protection from the searing beams. In growing fear, he turned back toward the river, seeking the uncertain safety of the water.

The attack was so swift and relentless that Thelvyn could not even begin to plan ahead, running blindly a short distance and then leaping aside to elude certain death. Suddenly one of the beams flashed across his lower back, not quite touching it but so close that it felt like raw fire. The pain caused him to stumble and crash heavily to the ground. The armor on his haunches and the base of his tail was still smoking as he struggled to rise, aware that he would be dead if he did not resume running. For the moment, the burning pain was so intense that he could hardly even walk, let alone run. But the Masters had been so intent upon their attack on Thelvyn that they had not been watching the steps of their animated servant. It continued to march toward the bank and out into the river without slowing its stride.

It was already too late for the gemstone dragons guiding the warrior to correct the problem. The front legs of the device slipped in the soft mud, and it fell down the surprisingly steep bank of the river channel, hurtled forward by its own tremendous weight. Carried by the momentum of its fall, the warrior was thrown completely over on its back and fell heavily, upside down, in the middle of the channel, creating a tremendous splash. Several hundred yards away, Thelvyn had to close his eyes and duck his head as he was caught in the sudden deluge. At least the cool water eased the burning pain of his scorched back.

He blinked and shook himself dry, glancing over his shoulder to see Kharendaen approaching. There was no sign of the metal warrior, which was probably lying on its back at the bottom of the river. It seemed to be making no effort to free itself. The Masters were apparently resigned to leave it where it was for now, perhaps finding it impossible to direct their warrior precisely from such a distance. Kharendaen landed in the field a moment later and hurried over to inspect his singed armor.

"I would not have missed that for anything," she remarked as she folded away her wings, then moved closer to his side. "Are you well?"

"I seem to be," he assured her. "It doesn't hurt anymore."

"I will tend to your damage when I can," she said. "Marthaen reports that he will be ready to command the full power of the Radiance any minute now."

"Not a moment too soon," Thelvyn commented. "Tell him, if possible, to close all the worldgates in the Highlands that he can locate."

Kharendaen nodded. "I will tell him at once."

She turned and spread her wings, lunging twice across the field before leaping into flight to return quickly to the city. Thelvyn turned back to the east, watching the dragons as they continued to chase the Masters back toward the northeast. Many of them were now many miles away, darting back and forth after the persistent gemstone dragons each time they tried to turn back. But Jherdar had wisely kept a large part of his forces near the city, at least a hundred, where they were available to help the Dragonking if he was forced to fight the metal warrior. Thelvyn stepped out to the bank of the river, lifted his long neck, and took a deep breath, as if he were about to release a tremendous blast of flame.

"Jherdar!" he called as loudly as he could, which turned out to be a great deal louder than he had expected. He had never had cause to use his full voice as a dragon.

The nearest dragons turned sharply at the sound of his voice and stared. Thelvyn suspected that he had been heard halfway to Braastar. Then one of the large red dragons turned and began to fly swiftly toward him, crossing the distance quickly. Jherdar circled tightly over the river and landed in the field, folding away his wings before he bowed to the Dragonking.

"Marthaen will engage the full power of the Radiance any moment now," Thelvyn explained quickly. "Things are going to turn bad for the Masters very soon now, and they are going to have to flee. We're going to try to close their gates here in the Highlands. I need you to have a force of dragons ready to follow them when they retreat. Hunt down as many of them as you can, but don't kill all of them."

"Why not?" Jherdar asked. "If we allow some of them to escape, why bother to close the gates?"

"I'm very interested in discovering where they go," Thelvyn said. "I suspect they have a large base somewhere in the western wilderness where no one dwells, and the Masters might flee in that direction. Find it for me if you can, but try not to let them know you're following them. With any luck, the next move will be to our advantage."

"It will be done," Jherdar promised. He was agreeable now that he understood the reason for such plans. "Am I to follow the Masters myself when they flee?"

"Yes. I'll be ready to assume command of our main forces when you leave."

Jherdar bowed again before he left, returning quickly to the dragons scattered in the sky east of the river. He called the nearest dragons to join him, landing in the fields east of the river so that he could divide them into companies and give them their orders. Thelvyn watched them from a distance. He had decided that he should stay close to the metal warrior in case it tried to pull itself from the river before the Radiance could be used to overcome the will of the Masters. So far, he had yet to see any sign of movement from the place where it had disappeared into the dark water.

A moment later Thelvyn was caught by surprise when the dragon sorcerers engaged the full power of the Radiance. He had never experienced such a wash of latent magic, moving rapidly outward from its source like a sudden blast of wind. If dragons had hair, his would have been standing on end. Across the river, Jherdar immediately launched the dragons into the sky and led them quickly to the north, rising steeply with long, powerful strokes of their wings. They turned as a group to fly swiftly toward the north, rushing to attack the invaders during the first minutes of confusion after the will of the Masters was broken.

Thelvyn waited as long as he dared, knowing that he needed to be with the rest of dragons in Jherdar's absence. Suddenly he saw Kharendaen flying swiftly from the city to join him. She didn't bother to land but circled him tightly, and he understood that he was to join her in flight. A few moments later, they were flying side by side only a few miles behind the ranks of the fighting dragons.

"Marthaen promises that the dragon sorcerers can maintain the Radiance at this intensity for as long as you need them to," she reported. "If fact, they will have to use nearly this much power for the foreseeable future to keep the Highlands secure.

But he says we will have to determine how much the influence of the Masters has been broken."

"As long as the Flaem are protected from their control and that metal beast remains in the river, we'll be fine," Thelvyn said. "If we can count on that much, we can chase the gemstone dragons right out of the Highlands."

Thelvyn was still concerned that the Masters might have some deadly defenses or traps at their strongholds in Braastar or near the old worldgate. This was the main reason he had been reluctant to face them on their own ground from the start. He couldn't count on the power of the Radiance to counteract any such traps. He was determined to be the first to enter their strongholds, so that he might be able to detect and disable any nasty surprises left by the Masters before his dragons got into trouble.

Jherdar had planned his counterattack well. Leading his force of dragons swiftly northward, he sent a quarter of his dragons to deal with the invading army while the rest continued on toward Braastar. With the collapse of the power that commanded their will, the many strange races of slave warriors were turning on their former Masters, forcing the gemstone dragons to retreat from their own armies. Those that had remained on the ground rose into the air just in time to flee desperately before the fury of the army of dragons. Some were trapped as they tried to climb into the sky, forced down under the weight of an overwhelming number of attackers and slain on the ground. Still other gemstone dragons found themselves overtaken in flight by the swifter gold and red dragons, finally giving up their hopeless flight to turn on the pursuing dragons for a last desperate fight.

Once the gemstone dragons had fled, many of the former slaves of their invading army were now either too interested in fighting each other or escaping into the wilderness to care about the attacking dragons. Still others welcomed the Dragonking and his warriors as their rescuers. The dragons Jherdar had left behind to deal with the invaders were mostly concerned with breaking up fights between different factions of the invading army, hunting down those who had fled into the forest.

The main body of the army of the dragons flew as swiftly as

they could toward Braastar, only to find that the Masters had already been forced to abandon the city and the enslaved Flaem had turned against them. Leaving behind a small force to help secure the city, Jherdar led his remaining fighting dragons into the east, toward the stronghold near the worldgate, where he expected the Masters to stand and fight. Thelvyn had been thinking the same thing, which was why he hurried to arrive ahead of the dragons and probe the defenses of the invaders. But his concern proved to be needless.

When he came to the wild lands east of Braastar, he was surprised to find a seared, smoking area of blasted ground where the old worldgate had been. The stronghold of the Masters was shattered and burning. Marthaen had directed the full power of the Radiance against the worldgates, blocking the retreat of the Masters. Apparently the power used to destroy the gates had been far greater than anyone had expected, and the destruction of the gates had been devastatingly violent. The Masters themselves, more than a score in all, were circling warily, but they turned to flee to the west when Thelvyn and Kharendaen approached.

The gemstone dragons were not as swift as the true dragons, and many were overtaken and slain as they tried desperately to flee. Only a couple of dozen that had accompanied their army had escaped to join the score or so that had survived the annihilation of the stronghold. These were all that remained of at least two hundred gemstone dragons that had invaded the Highlands. Cut off by the destruction of the nearest gates, the Masters turned and fled swiftly to the northwest, just as Thelvyn had expected. Jherdar followed, leading a couple hundred of his own dragons in pursuit.

Once again Thelvyn had waited until he seemed to have a clear advantage, and once again the Masters had been forced to flee after a brief battle. But Thelvyn's problems were far from over. While the Masters had left behind an army in their haste, this time their army was not being forced to fight to its inevitable destruction. Suddenly he had to deal with a main army north of Braejr and a secondary force at Braastar, well over sixty thousand beings of numerous races, some not even remotely human, who were now eager to join the fight against their former masters. The only problem was that, like the Flaem, they did not dare leave the Highlands and the protection of the Radiance.

For now, at least, the Flaem were happy to have a well-supplied army on hand to help protect their homelands, and Solveig was already arranging for them to be given land to settle in the eastern and far northern portions of the realm. Of course, Thelvyn hadn't forgotten the natural Flaemish suspicion of foreigners, which he had endured often himself. He suspected they would be less willing to have people from various off-world races sharing their land once the threat of war was past. His only comfort was knowing that the problem would be left for someone else to resolve, probably Solveig White-Gold.

There was considerable celebration in Braejr that evening when Thelvyn and Kharendaen returned to the city with news that the Masters had either been destroyed or had fled into the wilderness. He could appreciate the relief of the Flaem, who had been living in fear not only of conquest but also of enslavement. Those who had already been evacuated to the south would be returning the next day, and the people who had fled Braastar were eager to go home again. Thelvyn regretted how much the city of Braastar had suffered in the invasion, for there had been much damage by fire and the Masters had looted the city.

Of course, few people even knew about the existence of the Radiance. The general assumption was that the powers employed by the dragon sorcerers had been their own. It seemed best that the Radiance should remain a secret, so that people of other lands would not someday be tempted to try to invade the Highlands to capture it for themselves. The only way to protect that secret was to continue to allow most people to believe that the dragon sorcerers alone, under the guidance of the Dragonking, had been responsible for vanquishing the will of the Masters. Alessa Vyledaar was somewhat annoyed at having to allow the dragons to take the full credit, but she had to admit that it was better than revealing the secrets of the Radiance.

Now that the invasion of the Highlands seemed to be

settled, Thelvyn was already thinking ahead to the next problem. Every time that he had fought and defeated the Masters, they had responded quickly and in even greater strength than before. This time was no different. He knew that they would strike again, and soon. His problem now was anticipating their next move, and he needed more information before he could guess what it might be. Fortunately Jherdar returned early that night, having pursued the surviving gemstone dragons as far as he could. Thelvyn quickly called together his chief advisors to meet with him in the lair at Solveig's house.

"I was not able to learn all the answers you would have liked," Jherdar began, pausing as he devoured a roasted haunch of elk that had been brought for him. "We followed the Masters who fled into the wilderness of the northwest until we were perhaps a couple hours west of Wendar. I had my fastest golds and young red dragons after them, so the gemstone dragons had to push themselves hard to stay ahead. But then we began to see other gemstone dragons coming toward us, more than we could hope to fight."

"More of them?" Thelvyn asked. He was trying to maintain his dignity while Kharendaen rubbed oil into the scorched armor on his lower back and rump, having already washed him thoroughly in the court outside the lair a short time earlier.

"At least another hundred, probably more," the red dragon said. "I followed as long as I dared, trying to discover where they were coming from, but I never saw anything."

"At least we know they must have a base somewhere in that direction," Sir George observed. "It might have been only a few miles ahead."

"I've learned all that I hoped to at this time," Thelvyn said. "There is a vast area west of Wendar and the Highlands where few seldom go, not even many dragons, and all the kingdoms of dragons in that region have long since been summoned to war in the east. I was fairly certain the Masters had a stronghold there somewhere."

"What good does it do them?" Solveig asked. "You don't fortify a stronghold if you never expect the enemy to come."

"The Masters have some very serious problems to solve before their plans of conquest can proceed," Thelvyn said, although he seemed mostly to be thinking aloud. "They didn't expect the dragons to fight them. They didn't expect me to be a serious problem. They didn't expect the Flaem to fight them, and they thought the Radiance could be easily taken, and now both are lost. Now they have to deal with me and with the dragons, and they have to stop losing battles. Obviously there aren't enough gemstone dragons to take on the dragons directly, or they would have done that by now."

"How do you think they expect to fight us effectively?" Marthaen asked. "The only thing that seemed to work for them was that metal monster."

Thelvyn stared at the ground for a long moment while he considered that carefully. "They have two options. If they can, they might try constant, random attacks everywhere at once and divide our strength. Or they can assemble everything they have to throw at us, even if they must empty the resources of their own world, and force us into a battle we cannot win. I suspect that the second plan is the more likely one. I have to know, and I must have that answer now."

Sir George frowned. "You mean to find that stronghold of theirs, don't you?"

Marthaen lifted his ears in alarm. "You must not take such a risk. I can find dragon scouts willing to take that chance. They could plant elvish scouts as close to their hidden stronghold as possible, as we have done here in the Highlands."

"You are forgetting that I am still the Dragonlord," Thelvyn said. "As a dragon, I have the speed to avoid their metal warriors. As the Dragonlord, I can hold my own against any number of the Masters."

No one was happy with such a plan, but there was no dissuading Thelvyn. His best hope of an effective reconnaissance of the secret stronghold of the Masters was to go alone, getting in and back out again as quickly as he could. He agreed to allow Kharendaen and several of his bodyguards to accompany him partway. Once he had made his plans, he dismissed his companions for a well-earned night of rest. He thanked them all for their efforts as they filed out the door of the lair into the yard.

"You need rest more than anyone right now," Solveig told

him. "We're still trying to find you a virgin or two, if you still want them. Do they taste better?"

"I have no idea," Thelvyn said, frowning fiercely. "I haven't had a virgin recently."

Kharendaen put on a very innocent expression. "I have."

"Oh, enough," Thelvyn declared. "Is this any way to show respect for the Dragonking?"

"Perhaps you are unfamiliar with the ancient prophecies of the dragons," Marthaen remarked. "Thus it was said: 'Verily shall you know the true Dragonking, for he shall be the butt of many jokes.' "

After a good laugh, the others all left. Marthaen was about to depart as well when Thelvyn asked him to wait a moment. "I haven't forgotten that you are still the First Speaker of the parliament, or that you are the lord of your own kingdom of dragons. And I certainly haven't forgotten how capable you proved yourself to be as a leader last year. Perhaps it has seemed that I have usurped your authority, but I do not claim power for its own sake."

"You are the Dragonking, chosen by the Great One to lead us," Marthaen assured him. "You have done things to lead and protect the dragons that I could never do. Do not forget that you have called upon me to support you from the first, or that you turned to me to find a way to drive the Masters from the Highlands when you could not. I am content with my role."

"Perhaps I am concerned that you should remain content," Thelvyn admitted. "As much as you have done, this war is far from over. If you or Jherdar should come to begrudge me your support, we are doomed."

"You must never fear that my support will waver," the older dragon said. "I believe the trust and support you have from all the dragons is absolute. They have seen that the Masters are an enemy that will destroy them if they are not entirely committed to this fight. As for Jherdar, he is happy as long as he has enemies to slay. I think that you have taught even the red dragons the value of being patient and wise."

"The dragons have always been wise," Thelvyn remarked. "Their problem has always been that they forget their wisdom when it matters most. I have never understood that."

"Perhaps you have never been angry or frightened enough," Marthaen said. "A frightened or angry dragon knows only what it feels, and the most basic instincts seems like wisdom. That is why I feel you should not try to fight all the battles and take all the risks yourself in your need to protect your people. Do not forget that, above all else, you are our only hope to defeat the Masters. Do not risk unnecessarily the weapon that the Great One has prepared for us for our defense."

Thelvyn took that advice very much to heart. He had to admit to himself that his inclination was always to do anything he could to protect the dragons and take the greatest risks himself. He still believed that the greatest risks were his to take, simply because he possessed the greatest ability to defend himself. If nothing else, he could always retreat into the armor of the Dragonlord, which left him invulnerable to nearly any attack.

But not invulnerable to every attack, he reminded himself. The Fire Wizards had once used the power of the Radiance to inhibit the enchantments of his armor and had nearly defeated him, an attack he now knew had been directed by the Masters themselves. Possibly the Masters commanded such power that they could overcome the enchantments of his armor. And there was nothing he could do about their metal warriors, assuming they had any more of the hulking war machines. At least he was quick enough to stay out of their way.

He was glad when he finally got to bed that night. Although he had been a dragon only a short time, his neck had been hurting him these last few days from all his long journeys and his many fights. Kharendaen's bed wasn't as comfortable as those he had slept in during his brief visits to Windreach, but far better than sleeping on the ground. And while the bed was somewhat small for the two of them, that kept his mate close beside him during the night. He was content.

That night he dreamed that he and Kharendaen were riding the cool winds over a rugged, deeply forested land between tall, rocky mountains. The place reminded him so much of the wilds of Wendar that for a brief time he thought he had returned to those happy weeks they had spent together in Shadowmere and the Foxwoods, when he had still been learning what it meant to be a dragon and war and desperation were forgotten. Then he realized that this was a dream, one of those rare dreams he had experienced in the past in which he would receive instructions from the Great One.

The two dragons turned toward the mountains, guided by some strange instinct rather than any actual instructions. They were flying high over the forest with tremendous speed and yet with almost no effort, hardly even feeling the pull of their own weight on their wings. Moments later they were hurtling over the ridges and slopes of the mountains, sailing on the ever-shifting winds. Circling tightly to break their speed, they descended quickly into a high meadow of deep, green grass surrounded by a forest of tall, narrow pines.

They stood for just a moment staring out across the meadow into the distant forests below the mountains. Then Thelvyn saw Kharendaen start and turn quickly, and he turned as well to see a gold dragon sitting in the soft grass a short distance away. She was tall and lean, long and slender but well muscled, and her narrow face and large blue eyes gave her an expression of grace and wisdom. He realized that this was his mother, the dragon cleric Arbendael.

"We have met so I can warn you to change your plans," she told them. "You propose to seek the main stronghold of the Masters to judge their strength. You search for knowledge that the Great One already possesses and can share with you. Have his clerics forgotten that they can ask?"

Kharendaen bowed her head, but Thelvyn was undaunted. "The Great One has been reluctant to speak with us in the past. Perhaps we can be forgiven for not expecting him to answer now."

"That was never by his own choice," Arbendael told him. "Your time is short, and you must not waste it. Do you wish to know the true strength of the Masters and their army? They have built themselves a fortress as large as any city in your own world in the wilderness. The dragons could hardly hope to stand against them, and they have not yet gathered their fullest strength. But that is not your most immediate concern. Have you forgotten that the Masters serve an even greater master of their own?"

"I have not forgotten," Thelvyn insisted. "But I must face my challenges as they come. It has been all I could do to keep the Masters at bay. I'm afraid that left me no time to concern myself with the mystery of the one who calls himself the Overlord."

"And yet the Overlord is your true enemy," a deeper voice said, speaking from behind him. "You cannot ignore him."

Thelvyn turned quickly to see that the Great One himself now stood in the meadow behind him, wearing his common guise of an older dragon of some ancient breed. Apparently he was impatient to speak his mind about such important matters and was no longer content to leave the discussion to his servant.

"What can you tell me of the Overlord?" Thelvyn asked plainly.

"There is very little that I can tell you," the Great One said. "Neither my own powers nor those of any of the Immortals can extend into his world, and so he remains a mystery even to us. I suspect that his powers rival those of a lesser Immortal, although I doubt that he is an Immortal himself. I know that his powers can be channeled to his servants in this world, or else his slaves would no longer be under his will. You have seen that for yourself, with the crystal that was used to control the mage, Alessa. That is why the Masters possess greater powers than they should have."

"Can we block his influence from our world?" Thelvyn asked.

"Unfortunately, no," the Great One said. "The power of the Radiance, or perhaps the combined magic of the dragon sorcerers, might accomplish that, but then the Overlord would only come himself."

"What must I do?" Thelvyn asked, confused. "You seem to be telling me my true enemy is one whom I cannot hope to fight."

"Your true enemy is one you know nothing about," the Great One corrected him. "When the first Dragonlord and I fought the gemstone dragons long ago, they had not yet fled into the world of the Overlord and fallen under his will. I know nothing about him, and so I cannot guide you. And you cannot afford to continue to fight an enemy you know so little about. The time has come for you to go secretly into the world of the Masters to learn all that you can. Unfortunately, the Immortals cannot help you, because our powers do not extend into that world."

Thelvyn lowered his head. "I think I understand. That is why the Dragonking exists, is it not? To go where you cannot, to act when you are forbidden to?"

"You must be very careful," the Great One cautioned. "You must have the dragon sorcerers open a worldgate for you in a place where the Masters will not suspect it. And you must not go alone. Kharendaen will accompany you."

Thelvyn looked surprised. "I believe I would be able to move more swiftly and safely alone."

"Perhaps in many ways you are right," Arbendael said, moving around to stand closer to the Great One. "Your powers might be far greater than Kharendaen's, but they are still different. Kharendaen is a true cleric. If the Immortals are to have any contact with that world, it will be through her."

Arbendael sat close at the Great One's side and rubbed her cheek gently against his breast, a gesture that he accepted graciously. Thelvyn was surprised. Suddenly he realized that, for the first time in his life, he was in the company of his parents, even if it was only in a dream. They had never seemed particularly real to him before now. They had been like two strangers he had never known in life, their mating a mere matter of necessity. He felt much better in knowing that they were still together in this extraordinary dream world. In some odd way he could not define, he felt better about himself.

"Under no circumstances is the old drake to go with you," the Great One added. "Learn what you can without risking capture and then return at once. Remember above all else that the most important thing is to return safely, even if you learn nothing. Without you, there is no hope for this world."

CHAPTER FOURTEEN

Marthaen was beside himself when he went to the lair early the next morning and learned that Thelvyn and Kharendaen would be leaving at once for the world of the Masters. He tried hard not to show his disapproval, since the instructions had come from the Great One himself, but he wasn't able to completely hide his agitation. He obviously considered the whole thing ill-advised. He did not believe that the Dragonking should subject himself to such a risk, not to mention his own sister.

"There is only one good thing I can say about it," he grumbled at last. "With Kharendaen along, you might be more careful to stay out of trouble."

"I'm not happy about bringing Kharendaen along," Thelvyn insisted. "I'd still prefer to go alone, but I dare not second-guess the Great One. For now, I need to know if you can open a worldgate someplace where the Masters will not suspect it."

Marthaen considered that briefly. "I believe it can be done, but I must consult with my sorcerers before I can promise anything. Opening such a gate is one thing, but knowing where to send the other end is quite another matter. Perhaps one of the sealed gates at Braastar can show us how to create one of our own."

Marthaen went out into the yard and leapt into the air, flying quickly across the city to join the dragon sorcerers at the Academy. Once he was gone, Thelvyn retreated into the lair. He sat for a time staring down at a platter of roasted elk that had been brought for him. Dragons did not commonly eat more than once a day; he had dined late the previous night after his return from battle, and he wasn't particularly hungry yet. But ahead of him was a long journey, during which he may not be able to hunt for his fare, so it was best to eat while he could. Kharendaen sat on the other side of the table nibbling quietly at her own breakfast, also without great interest.

After a long moment, Kharendaen looked up at him. "What are you thinking about? Are you worried about the task ahead?"

"I suppose I should be," Thelvyn answered, "but actually I was thinking about last night—about my mother and the Great One."

"Your mother and your father," she corrected him.

Thelvyn shook his head slowly. "In these last few weeks, I've found it difficult to think of the Great One as my father. It seems presumptuous somehow, although I admit I find it easier after last night. Do you suppose that there might be some real affection between my mother and father?"

"It is common for dragons to mate for reasons that have nothing to do with affection," Kharendaen said. "But my impression was the same as yours, that there was real affection between them. I always wondered why the Great One brought the spirit of Arbendael into his realm to be his chief servant and advisor. I suppose that being an Immortal must be a very lonely thing."

Marthaen returned within the hour with the word that the dragon sorcerers could open a gate into the world of the Masters at any time or place required. They had already probed the structure of one of the collapsed gates and knew just what to do to open a gate of their own. Now they were waiting for word that the Dragonking was ready to give them final instructions. There were still a few unanswered questions, plus a few things they wanted Thelvyn to be aware of.

"We know already that a worldgate establishes two gateways, one in each world, which serve to anchor either end of the passage," the gold dragon explained. "In that way, even while the separate worlds might be moving through their own orbits, the gates always open in the same place in each world."

Thelvyn said nothing, since Marthaen's explanation had gone somewhat beyond his limited knowledge of astronomy. He understood the magic well enough, but the idea of worlds moving in orbits escaped him. As far as he was concerned, the world was the most stable and motionless thing in existence. Of course, he lacked the education of most civilized dragons, who spent the better part of a hundred years in school. As a human youth in the Highlands, he had been lucky to receive ten.

"For that reason, we have guessed that distances and locations in one world correspond to those in the other," Marthaen continued. "Therefore you can probably find your way around the world of the Masters by judging directions and distances from where you have entered."

"I see no reason that we should not open our own gate right here, in the core of our greatest power," Thelvyn said.

"That's what we thought," the First Speaker said. "But for the sake of your own security, we dare not leave our worldgate open a moment longer than we have to. If the Masters detect its presence, then they will know that spies have entered their world and they will be on their guard. The best suggestion I can offer is that we open the gate again for brief periods of time every few hours. If the Masters do find our gate, we can prevent them from passing through it. How you get past them to return home, however, may be quite another matter."

Thelvyn was already well aware of how things could go wrong in the cold, dry world of the Masters. The Masters had been able to surprise him nearly every time he had to deal with them so far, and he considered it more a matter of good fortune than any cleverness on his own part that he had managed to get the best of them. He knew he would be facing an enemy he could not fight and that the risks would be enormous.

Marthaen led Thelvyn and Kharendaen to the city park, located in a wooded, rather marshy area in the center of Braejr. The park existed mostly because the land was unsuitable for buildings, its only real virtue being that it was the location of the tomb of Jherridan Maarstan, the first king of the Flaemish realm. It was also the only part of the city where the dragons could gather in large numbers and a fair amount of privacy. Marthaen had insisted that privacy was important. Aware of the concern it might cause, he thought it best that even the dragons didn't know that the Dragonking had subjected himself to great danger. There was also a possibility there were spies in the city.

The moment that the two dragons were ready to leap through it, the worldgate was opened. It was closed again at once, to keep it from being detected by the Masters in either world. Thelvyn went through first, hurtling through the void ready to fight, his back arched and his neck held low, bounding forward on the opposite side to make room for Kharendaen just behind him. They emerged into a dark, colorless world, their legs sinking into the soft, dry sand of gray dunes. A cold wind stirred the dull gray dust into what seemed like a dense fog. They could see only that they stood in the middle of a cluster of boulders and jagged pinnacles of stone that rose like a half-submerged island from the dunes.

"This must be the sea of sand that we could see to the southwest of the stronghold when we were here earlier," Thelvyn observed.

"Either the days are very dark here or the nights are fairly bright," Kharendaen said, looking around. "I've never been sure which."

"I suspect their nights are much darker," Thelvyn said, blinking from the dust in his eyes. "Let's move away from this place, in case the Masters detected the opening of the gate."

"Where do we go?" she asked.

"I think we should scout out their main stronghold, then get away while we can."

Thelvyn spread his wings and leapt upward, trying to get above the tricky crosswinds that raced over the dunes as quickly as possible. He had expected to rise above the dust fairly quickly, since most desert sandstorms remained fairly close to the ground, but the dust was still as thick and dark as ever three hundred feet above the ground's surface. The winds were even stronger and more fitful. He had been climbing only a few seconds when a vast, dark shape suddenly loomed out of the dust just ahead of him. He almost had to stand on his tail to slow himself in time to avoid flying directly into what he now recognized as a massive wall of stone.

Kharendaen had been far enough behind him that she was able to dart to the side. The two dragons turned and began to move slowly along the edge of the wall. The clouds of dust made their gold armor nearly impossible to see. Soon they realized that they were circling around the high keep of another great fortress like the one that had seen earlier. Their caution seemed unnecessary, since the stronghold appeared to be deserted.

After a time Thelvyn, turned back to the northwest, deciding to continue on without pausing to explore this stronghold. While it appeared to be abandoned, he thought it best not to risk discovery. He climbed slowly into the air, waiting for his mate to move close beside him.

"We know the Masters were able to transport that other fortress into our world," he explained. "My guess is they prepared this one for that same purpose. Once Braejr had fallen to their control, they would have brought their forces through this fortress to enforce their domination of Braejr and the Highlands. Now that the Highlands have been secured against them, they have most likely moved their resources to another stronghold."

"It's fortunate for us that they are gone," Kharendaen agreed. "Otherwise we might have leapt through right into their claws."

"I should have thought of that," Thelvyn said. "I don't think much of our chances if I make such stupid mistakes right from the start."

Kharendaen was prepared to argue with him, but at that moment, they finally rose through the clouds of dust into the clear sky above, or at least as clear as the skies of this world

ever were, since a fine dust filled the air higher than a dragon
could fly, drawing a pale, thin shroud over the cold, distant
sun. Thelvyn knew that they could have remained hidden if
they had stayed within the thicker dust, but their large eyes
could not bear the relentless assault of grit and sand. Instead,
they flew low over the thicker clouds of dust, watching the
skies around them for any sign of movement, trusting that
their burnished gold and deep brown coloration made them
hard to detect.

They flew for over an hour in the direction that, in their
own world, would have brought them over the western Highlands near the village of Graez, where Thelvyn had grown up.
He was not concerned about failing to see anything that might
have been below them, since the very fact that the dust storm
remained thick and unbroken almost certainly meant that they
were still over the open desert. According to Jherdar's report,
they would fly in a straight line for several hours before they
approached the area where the main stronghold of the Masters
was likely to be.

The hazy image of the sun was advancing steadily toward
the west, and night would be falling in another hour or so. The
day had still been young when they had left Braejr, indicating
that the passing of day and night in this world did not correspond to their own. Thelvyn welcomed the approach of night,
with its promise of deep darkness to keep the two dragons hidden as they flew farther into the lands of the enemy. He began
to hope that they might be able to scout the stronghold of the
Masters and withdraw from their lands by morning.

After another half hour of flight, they began to realize that
what they had thought were bulges in the clouds of dust below
them were in fact hills and ridges of rugged land. The final
miles of open desert passed swiftly beneath them, although
they never saw the windswept dunes. Now the clouds of gray
dust were confined to the valleys between the barren ridges,
like the sea reaching to form deep fjords. The clouds hung
thick even in places that were largely sheltered from the restless winds. The rugged land, with its rocky, barren ridges and
stark cliffs gave the impression that they were higher in the
mountains than they were.

Now the two dragons had to be more careful than ever, hugging the deeper valleys and ravines as they moved steadily toward the northwest. They had wondered previously how such a lifeless world could support the armies of men and monsters of the Masters, but as they moved away from the sea of sand, they finally began to spot the first signs of native life. At first they saw only small patches of dry, tough grass or stunted bushes or twisted trees hidden in sheltered place among deep dells or behind huge boulders, protected from the harsh, dry wind. While their first impression was that this bleak land must never feel the soothing touch of rain, they soon saw signs of floods brought by sudden, violent storms, the raging waters ripping through the ravines.

The long miles passed swiftly below them, and they began to see even more signs of life. The rugged heights were too blasted by cold winds to support more than the smallest and most hearty plants, but many of the sheltered valleys began to harbor ragged stands of stunted, stiff-leaved trees and tough, dry ferns. Thelvyn had the impression that the weather was less severe and the ceaseless winds not quite as strong and relentless as they flew farther from the sea of sand. He tried to picture in his mind the place that Alessa Vyledaar had described from the visions in her dreams when she had been under the control of the Masters. Her description of a world that was always dark, hidden beneath a haze of dust, with winds that were cool even in the height of summer had proven extremely accurate so far.

Night had nearly settled when Thelvyn spotted something in the distance, dark shapes that were too regular to be natural in a broad valley ahead of them. Thelvyn's remarkable night vision, which he had possessed all his life, was even sharper in dragon form. He was certain he had seen something unusual, and Kharendaen agreed when he pointed it out to her. They paused in their flight, circling cautiously while they searched for any sign of life. There was no light to be seen, no trails of smoke rising into the night sky, nor any scent of burning wood or coal on the wind. After discussing the matter briefly, they decided to detour from their journey long enough to take a quick look. They approached with great care, aware that any sign of life in this world could mean danger.

As they came nearer, Thelvyn saw no hint of fields or orchards. Instead, there were wide, low dikes and ditches nearly choked with sand, running in straight lines or smooth curves of obviously artificial constructions. In places, he saw lines of tumbled stones, the tops of ancient fences protruding through the sand, and even the broken walls of old houses. Ahead, the dark, irregular shapes he had seen from the distance became the crumbling, wind-blasted remains of a large town, the dry bones of a place that must not have seen life for centuries.

The two dragons crossed the last couple of miles slowly and cautiously, flying low over the ground. Already they could see clearly, even in the gathering darkness, the crumbling remains of the buildings of a small city. The roofs had long since fallen in, and many of the walls were broken. Parts of the city were nearly buried in sand, while other parts, swept clear by some trick of the endless winds, stood open down to the stone-paved streets. There was no light anywhere, nor any sign of life.

Since there was no apparent danger, they decided to enter the city, flying slowly between the ruins of the ancient buildings. They found no signs of life except the tracks of strange animals in the sand. Since it seemed to be safe, they landed in a large paved square in the center of the ruined city, folding away their wings, then taking a few minutes to explore. The first thing they noticed was that the buildings didn't seem to have been made for men. The doorways were large and wide and the ceilings high. However, they were still too small for the dragons to enter.

Kharendaen extended her head well inside one of the doorways, but Thelvyn was more interested in something he saw on the walls. At first it appeared as a faint haze of blackness on the rough stone, so that even his sharp eyes did not detect it immediately. He stared intently, to make certain that what he saw wasn't merely paint nearly blasted away from centuries of sandstorms, although his eyes were made for distance and had difficulty focusing on anything so near. But when he began to look around, he quickly discovered that all the stone had a similar haze of darkness, especially thick in the deep cracks.

"The Rain of Fire," he said softly.

Kharendaen swiftly drew her head back from a doorway to stare at him. "What did you say?"

He turned toward her. "This place was destroyed by flame. At some time in the distant past, this town was consumed by fire. I wonder if perhaps this entire world was enveloped in flame, changed forever into the cold, dark, dry place that it is now."

The female dragon walked over to join him, staring intently at the wall that had caught his attention. Then she turned, inspecting the walls of a nearby building. She brought her head through one of the doorways to search the interior, but it was too dark inside for even for a dragon to see. The time of fire had been so long ago that any scent of smoke had long since vanished, even for her sensitive nose.

She brought her head back out through the doorway after a moment and turned to her mate. "Could this be the home world of the Flaem?"

Thelvyn shook his head. "I don't think so, for three reasons. For one thing, Sir George has taught me a few tricks about judging the age of ruins by their decay as a result of time and the elements. This destruction is far too old to have been the world of the Flaem and the Alphatians. Also, the shapes of these doors and the sizes of the buildings suggest to me that they were made to serve the needs of some creature considerably larger than a man or elf. And the histories of the Flaem all state that their world was utterly destroyed, not merely ravaged."

"Indeed?" Kharendaen cocked her head, curious. "I've never heard how they managed to destroy their world."

"Even the survivors of that time never knew exactly what spell of magic was involved," Thelvyn explained. "They describe a wall of flame that moved across the land as fast as a dragon can fly. Behind it, the land itself broke apart. Great pieces of earth, from dust and sand to fragments the size of small towns, rose into the sky and drifted toward the stars. Water turned to spray and flew off into the sky. Even the air itself grew thin and cold. Whatever the cause, their very world shook itself apart."

"No wonder they don't like to talk about it," Kharendaen commented.

"Only the senior Fire Wizards know as much as I've told you," he said. "I only learned of it when I became their king."

"Quickly . . . quickly!" a voice suddenly spoke out of the night.

The two dragons turned, realizing they were no longer alone. Some distance behind them, standing in a passageway between two large buildings where they could quickly retreat, were three tall, slender creatures that looked vaguely like wyverns. Thelvyn had already seen their like in his own world in the form of the fierce, swift warriors fighting alongside the Masters in the siege of Rockhome and again in the wild of the Highlands. They somewhat resembled the wyverns of his own world, although they were more delicate. Nevertheless, they were strong and alarmingly swift. Their greatest difference from true wyverns was that they had both wings and arms like dragons, although they walked only upright like wyverns.

Another important difference was that these slender dragon-folk were apparently intelligent, while wyverns were nothing more than wild beasts. Recalling what fierce warriors they were, Thelvyn's first thought was that he and Kharendaen were about to be attacked, or perhaps called upon to surrender. Certainly these three were a delegation of some type, although they were hardly enough to take on two gold dragons.

To Thelvyn's surprise, the three bowed their heads to him, and their leader stepped forward. When Thelvyn turned to face him, the leader cautiously came a few steps closer and bowed his once head again before looking up and speaking earnestly. "Please . . . we must speak . . . quickly . . ."

"Do you understand him?" Kharendaen asked quietly.

"Somewhat," Thelvyn answered. These dragon-folk spoke a language of their own unlike any that Thelvyn knew, but he was able to understand some of their words by the means of some latent magic of his own. Clerics often had the ability to understand unknown languages and sometimes to be understood by those who did not speak their own tongue.

"Do you know what I am saying?" Thelvyn asked, speaking slowly.

"Yes," the leader answered, although he spoke a great many words that Thelvyn didn't recognize. "Are you . . are you an enemy of the Masters?"

"I am," Thelvyn replied, taking the chance that the dragon-folk were also their enemies. "I am the Dragonking, chosen by prophecy to fight and defeat the Masters."

"You have come to fight them?"

He thought he recognized a note of cautious hope, although it was difficult to be certain. "I have come to try to learn their secrets, so that I can fight them in my own world where my strength is greatest."

"I am Long Spear, leader of my clan," the speaker said, introducing himself at last. He seemed at last to have grown to trust these strangers, as if had to overcome long-held suspicions and resignation. "My people are called the Veydran. Once this world belonged to us alone. Then, in a forgotten time some five thousand years past, the Overlord came upon us."

"He is not of your own world?" Thelvyn asked.

"We do not know. If we ever knew, it has long since been forgotten. All we know now is that he came to us long ago. At first, he was our god and protector, and we prospered. Then the Overlord's heart turned to the blackness of utter evil. He told us that we lived only to serve him, that we had no life or thought of our own. But he could not control us, and so he tried to destroy us with a great Wind of Fire that swept through the world, turning the seas to sand and the sky to dust. Our land turned cold."

"But he could not control you?" Thelvyn asked.

"He cannot control us, for we know his name," Long Spear explained. "Some of us were taken away. Their children were stolen from them and never allowed to learn his name, and so they must serve him. But they were not enough to satisfy his ambitions. He began to conquer other worlds where he could control others who do not know His name."

"Is that when the Masters came?"

Long Spear stared at the ground sadly. "The Masters came and shared with him the visions of the world they had left, the world of the dragons. The dragons had sent them away. Their black hearts were bitter, and they hated this cold, dry world just as the Overlord hates it. The Overlord could never pass through his own gates to leave this world, but now the Masters had a way to lead him into their world. They have waited a long, long time, gathering their strength so that they could defeat and control the dragons. Then the Overlord would depart, but we would still not be free."

"I will destroy the Overlord if I can," Thelvyn promised. "But it is beyond my power to make your world the way it was."

"It would be enough for us to be free." Long Spear took another step forward, cocking his head to stare up at the gold dragon. "The Masters are very busy. They fly constantly between their strongholds, but they do not have the time to bother us. They are fighting you, and you are here. Take a look at their great places, but be careful not to go too close, not unless you are ready to fight them."

The three Veydran bowed their long necks once again, then turned and disappeared quickly into the shadows. Thelvyn guessed they never dared to stay out in the open for very long, a lifetime habit that kept them alive in a hostile world that had not belonged to them in a very long time. He suspected that it would also be wise for him to avoid open places for very long.

"That was the most interesting chat I've had in some time, whatever language it was in," Thelvyn commented, then turned to look at Kharendaen. "Did you understand any of it?"

"I caught enough to understand the gist of it. The Veydran seem to consider the Overlord a god. I don't like the idea that he has enough power to completely devastate a world. You may find yourself fighting one who has powers greater than those of an Immortal."

"No wonder the Immortals themselves seem to fear him," Thelvyn said, preparing to launch himself into the air once more. "Come on. If we hurry, perhaps we can reach their main stronghold and get back again before morning."

The two dragons spread their wings and leapt into the sky, leaving behind the ruins of the ancient town. Once again they passed swiftly through the night, keeping as much as they could to the deep shadows of the valleys as they made their way steadily northwest. For a time, Thelvyn felt so distracted by his thoughts that he wasn't being as cautious as he should have been in such a strange, hostile land.

He was beginning to form a full understanding of the situation. What impressed him was not how desperate it already was but how much worse it could yet become. Perhaps the Immortals had chosen him as their champion, but he wondered now if even they had fully appreciated what they expected of him. He suspected they had not. The Great One had apparently known only that the Overlord was a being of tremendous power. Under the circumstances, Thelvyn realized he couldn't completely trust in the knowledge and the judgment of the Immortals. The fact that they had prepared him for the task of fighting and defeating the Overlord did not mean that he could assume he would win.

Like the Immortals, he needed to know just how powerful his true enemy actually was, to judge how best to fight the Overlord . . . if fighting him was even a real possibility. The fact that he had devastated this world with fire was intimidating on the surface and made the Overlord seem very powerful indeed. But that was not necessarily so, Thelvyn knew. Such magic could have been prepared carefully, the power behind it drawn from many sources or gathered over a long period of time. The Overlord was still a very powerful being, but as long as he was less powerful than the Immortals, then either they or their champion could still defeat him. Thelvyn needed to know just how powerful the Overlord really was, and he could think of no way to judge that except in combat.

He had already learned a few things about his enemy, but not enough to do him any good. He could guess already that the Overlord wasn't a true god, an all-powerful enemy he could never hope to defeat. So far the Overlord had acted only through his servants, channeling his magical power to the Masters and leaving the actual fighting of his wars to them. And although he had long waited for the chance to leave behind the world he had nearly destroyed, he apparently needed the magic of the Masters to make that possible. Perhaps at the Overlord's own stronghold, Thelvyn would see evidence from which he could infer just how powerful his true enemy really was.

Another hour or so brought the two dragons near the lands where they expected to find the greatest of the strongholds of their enemy, and their progress was slowed by the need of being more cautious than ever. It was a remarkably rugged, mountainous area, and many of the larger open areas were lakes of drifting sand. But a few deep valleys offered enough protection from the harsh wind to be carefully cultivated. In these remote valleys, even the smallest bit of land was used for fields of crops or pastures for animals. The dragons had been weaving a path in and out of the valleys to keep themselves hidden from sight, but now they were forced to fly over the barren heights.

Thelvyn hoped they would be mistaken in the darkness for gemstone dragons even if they were seen. His image of the true size of dragons had changed somewhat over the last few months, so that he no longer thought of them as being as large as they had once seemed to him. All the same, he reminded himself, a dragon was a very big creature and not very easy to hide. As they traveled deeper into inhabited regions, his apprehension continued to grow. He knew that he was taking a tremendous risk, and he would have preferred to turn back at once, but that would mean his quest had ended in failure. He knew now that he could not hope to win this war until he found a way to defeat the Overlord.

The zigzag course that had helped to keep them from being seen had made the actual distance of their journey difficult to judge, but he was certain that they must be nearing their destination. They were entering an area of more hospitable land, highland plains divided by scattered ranges of low, steep mountains. As before, every small piece of reasonably level ground was neatly laid out in meticulously cultivated fields and pastures. They were even surprised to see terraces built into the eastern sides of the ridges and peaks, apparently the direction that caught what little rain might be carried on the seasonal winds.

Thelvyn had never seen anything quite like this. The fields had been laid out with absolute attention to detail for efficiency, perhaps from many long years of preparing the terraces, dikes, and the high, thick stone walls that served as windbreaks, with enclosed tubes atop the walls that apparently served as aqueducts to carry precious water. He was surprised to see no evidence of villages or towns, or even farmhouses scattered among the fields. The only buildings he saw appeared to be barns and sheds and occasional barracks, all built of heavy stone.

The dragons flew as fast as they could and as low as they dared over the fields, two dark forms passing swiftly in the dim starlight through the haze of dust. Mile after mile streaked past below them, all neatly laid out in dark squares. From time to time, they would rise quickly to pass over a ridge of low mountains, or drift to one side to fly around a lone peak of stone rising like an island out of the patterns of fields. So far they had seen no living creature except for the beasts in the pastures. At first Thelvyn found it odd that, in a nation of armies, there were no forts or guard stations to protect the fields. Indeed, it seemed that no watch whatsoever was kept over the fields. Finally he realized that since this was a land with no real enemies, there was no reason to guard the land.

He could only hope that meant the Masters held no fear of invasion or the intrusion of spies, but he knew better than to feel a false sense of security. He had invaded their world once before, and he seemed to have caught them less prepared than they would have liked, but he was surprised they hadn't taken more precautions after his previous incursion into their land.

The dragons were caught completely by surprise when they climbed steeply to pass just above an especially high ridge and found themselves almost within the main stronghold of the Overlord. Circling around sharply and dropping the sails on the bases of their tails to slow themselves, they darted back into the protection of the deep shadows among some massive boulders alongside the ridge. Only then did they dare to look around to check whether or not they had been seen and take a closer look at the fortress.

The stronghold had been built within the protection of a natural ring of stone, at a place where the three different ridges joined to form an almost complete circle around the encampment. From inside the ring, the valley vaguely resembled a vast crater, twenty miles or more across, but formed in an irregular shape that was more square than round and open on the corners facing to the southeast and southwest. The floor of the valley within the ring was perfectly flat, although there was no way to know if it had been made that way by natural processes or by deliberate design. The entire surface within the ring appeared to be either paved or occupied by some imposing structure.

The stronghold itself was actually an entire complex of great fortresses, neatly arranged in the same carefully laid grids as the fields, centered around an immense paved square that was probably nearly a mile long on each side. The fortresses were all nearly identical in form, solid, almost featureless structures built of gray stone that had been cut into vast, smooth-sided blocks. Distance was deceptive because the fortresses were so simple in design, being nothing more than massive straight-sided buildings without towers or turrets. When Thelvyn considered the size of the valley itself, he realized that each fortress was nearly the size of a small town, covering an area of nearly a square mile.

But it was the activity in the central square that caught his attention. A great arch of black stone stood in the very middle of the square, an oval that was large enough for both Kharendaen and he to have flown through side by side. The archway opened into a pit of utter darkness. Thelvyn could make out little detail because he could see the arch of stone almost directly from one side, but he had no doubt that this was a worldgate of tremendous size. Whole armies had gathered in the square, neatly arranged in silent companies as each awaited its turn to advance to the gate. Scores of gemstone dragons were stationed between the companies scattered about the square, or stood about the gate itself. The gate was so large that, even as he watched, three of the Masters came through one after the other, passing on the wing just above a line of freight wagons passing through in the opposite direction.

As he watched from his place of hiding, Thelvyn began to despair of ever being able to fight the army of the Masters, even if he had every dragon alive under his command. The Masters had already lost perhaps a hundred thousand warriors and fighting beasts in their sieges of Rockhome and the High-lands. Ten times that number were gathered in the square below and in hundreds of companies waiting in lines miles long on the roads leading through the two main passes of the ring of mountains. Thelvyn counted at least a score of the immense metal warriors like the one that he had tried to fight outside Braejr. One of the warriors advanced slowly toward the worldgate, following closely behind a line of freight wagons. As impossibly vast as that walking mountain of steel was, the gate was large enough that the metal monster could simply step through the passage.

Thelvyn could not even begin to guess how many fighters and weapons and how many supplies had already been sent through the gate. Companies of warriors and lines of wagons continued along both of the approaching roads for as far as he could see in the dusty darkness. Nor did he have any idea of the true numbers and strength of the Masters themselves. He knew that his own world could not hope to put together an army large enough to face this one, certainly not in the short time available.

"Now I know how they've been able to conquer whole worlds," Thelvyn whispered in awe.

"Remember, they've never had to fight dragons before," Kharendaen remarked, trying to be encouraging. "Or Immortals, for that matter."

"I know now why the Great One thought we were wasting our time trying to fight a defensive war," he said, sitting up. "We can't hope to fight such an awesome army. But if we can defeat the Overlord, all the rest should simply fall apart."

"As easily as all that, Little One?" a strange, deep voice asked, speaking to them as if from the air.

The dragons started, alarmed to realize they had been discovered. In the first instant, they obeyed their fierce instincts, arching their backs and necks as they prepared to fight their unseen enemy. Then Thelvyn's heart sank into despair as he realized he had heard that same voice once before. It was the voice of the Overlord.

Already he realized his mistake. He had underestimated his enemy. The Overlord was said to have the powers of an

Immortal, and here, in his own world, his powers would be at their greatest. Here he was secure, a being of magic rather than mortal form, his mind and will able to be anywhere and everywhere in an instant. In this place, he was indeed almost a god, and Thelvyn's powers as both Dragonlord and Dragonking were very slight in comparison.

In the next moment, Thelvyn and Kharendaen felt almost as if some great, unseen hand had reached out to take them up, drawing them in an instant into the very heart of the Overlord's innermost stronghold. The ridge where they had been hiding was left behind; suddenly they found themselves standing on the smooth stone floor of what seemed to be some vast chamber. The walls and ceiling of the chamber were hidden from them, lost behind the cold, dark mists that surrounded them. But they knew that they were not alone. Standing back to back, they guarded each other as best they could, their heads darting back and forth as they watched the creeping mists. After a moment, they became aware of the large, glittering eyes of the gemstone dragons peering at them out of the darkness.

A portion of the dark mists began to move and take form, slowly becoming the long, horrible face of the Overlord glaring down at them, still mostly hidden in the mists. He gloated over the easy defeat of his greatest enemy, captured with little more effort than a thought.

CHAPTER FIFTEEN

Thelvyn had to force down a sense of panic. He had to suppress the instinct of a dragon to react with fear and a sudden snap of desperate fury when pressed too closely by another, amplified many times over by the terror that faced him. He knew little of the legends and superstitions of the dragons, but he felt certain that the great, horrible creature that confronted him was the very image of the worst monster that could possibly haunt a dragon's nightmares.

The moment of his capture had been so abrupt, the method so swift and absolute, that he was thrown off his guard. He knew he did not dare give in to a dragon's battle rage. The time to fight had come and gone before he could respond. Now was the time to remain calm and think, to guard his own secrets carefully while he tried to learn all he could. If he was ever to escape from this place, it would be by cunning and stealth.

The mists were beginning to draw back, and the pale light in the center of the chamber where he stood with Kharendaen grew subtly brighter, although the deep gloom didn't lighten much. Even so, he found that they were in a chamber of tremendous size, the walls and ceiling lost in the distance and the heavy darkness. All he knew for certain about the place was that he was in the middle of a large but shallow pit, the sides so low that he could have simply stepped out if he had dared. Surrounding him were scores, if not hundreds, of the gemstone dragons, waiting half hidden in the mists beyond the edge of the pit. With their strange, faceted armor, watching him quietly with their large, dark eyes, they seemed like alien creatures, hardly something alive. They never spoke or indeed made any sound, giving no hint of their thoughts or mood, standing as silent witnesses to his defeat.

Before him stood the Overlord, a commanding and terrifying presence who moved slowly out of the darkness to confront his prisoner. He was a being of immense size, so that Thelvyn, standing before him, looked as small as a man appeared next to a dragon. Indeed, Thelvyn saw to his surprise that the Overlord was in size and shape very much like his metal warriors, a draconic form perhaps as much as a hundred yards in length, his slender, sinuous body carried on four pairs of legs. But the metal warriors were merely plain, stylized representations of the Overlord, whose armor was a nightmare patchwork of spikes and horns and elaborate frills.

Thelvyn drew back a step in instinctive fear, suddenly aware that his mate was also retreating to stand behind him when she bumped against him. Neither dared to take his or her eyes away from that image of terror standing before them. Clearly the Immortals had not known the true nature of the Overlord, or else they would have never expected him to fight such a monster. But then he forced himself to gather his ragged courage and stand his ground, although his thoughts at that moment did not go beyond the seemingly hopeless possibility of finding a way to save himself and his mate.

"You have come," the Overlord said, staring down at him in amusement. "Dragonlord. Dragonking. Pale hope of desperate Immortals, who dare not act for themselves for fear of risking defeat. I knew that you would come to me. You are too clever and too bold for your own good. You had to have answers. You knew you were lost if you did not try. Now your trials are done, and I have prepared for you a place where you can rest from your hopeless labors."

"The Dragonlord and the Great One defeated you once before," Thelvyn retaliated, realizing how weak it sounded as he tried to gather his thoughts.

"You know that is not so," the Overlord corrected him. "I played no part of the battle to which you refer. The Dragonlord and the Great One fought the gemstone dragons, and even then only at a time when their race was young and inexperienced. But that has become irrelevant. You know now that you could destroy the Masters, yet even then you would be a long way from winning your war. You cannot fight me."

"I must try," Thelvyn insisted. "You offer me no choice."

"I have given you no choice," the Overlord repeated. "In truth, I can hardly fault you for opposing me, and for that reason, in all fairness, I should not punish you for the harm that you have done to my servants and my plans."

Thelvyn looked up in surprise, but he saw no compassion or tolerance in those cold eyes.

"But I have no concern with what is fair," the Overlord continued. "I must punish all my enemies when they have been conquered, except those who have been fortunate enough to die in battle. I know a special punishment for you, so that you will long for the escape of death until, in the end, your shall will yourself to die."

The Overlord continued to move slowly forward until he stood just beyond the edge of the pit, staring down at his captives. "They say that you spent most of your life unaware that you were a dragon. Do you still feel a bit uncertain of your dragon identity? I will show you just how much a dragon you are. I will show you what you fear most. I will show you despair such as you have never known."

Thelvyn prepared himself for the assault, expecting to be confronted with visions of horror, or perhaps with pain or longings that were unique to dragons. He was to be shown the worst that a dragon could endure, yet he was not yet dragon enough to anticipate the form that fear would take. The Overlord surprised him by doing nothing. Instead, he moved a few steps back into the dark mists.

"Attack me," the Overlord ordered him after a long moment.

"I promise the Masters will not interfere, no matter what happens. And I will not attack you in turn. I have no wish or need to harm or slay you just yet, I promise you. Come now. Show us first the terrible powers of the Dragonlord."

Thelvyn wasn't certain if he acted by his own will, although he wondered why he responded without hesitation. He changed form, teleporting himself into the armor of the Dragonlord as he did so. The weapons and armor, even the body that he had worn for so much of his life, now seemed strange and awkward to him. The Overlord merely stared down at him with vague interest as he drew the sword and held it out before him, commanding the tremendous powers of the enchantments of ancient Blackmoor.

But his weapon refused to respond to his will, remaining cold and lifeless in his hands. Instead, the weight of his armor seemed to settle heavily about him. He knew what was wrong at once, recalling too well the time that the renegade Fire Wizards had used the Radiance to nullify most of the powers of his armor and weapons. Clearly the Overlord was strong enough in his own magic that he could defeat the powers of the Dragonlord by the most direct means, by simply stripping away those enchantments.

For a long moment, Thelvyn could only stand motionless in surprise as he realized what had happened. Then he slowly lowered the heavy sword. In the next moment, he was struck squarely in the breastplate of the armor by some massive force, as if he had been struck a blow with a mammoth, unseen club. The usual protections of the armor had failed entirely, so that he took the full force of the impact. It lifted him entirely from the ground and hurled him backward against Kharendaen's chest. The dragon was so startled that she jumped back in alarm. By then it was too late for her to catch him as he fell.

Thelvyn struggled to move, but he had had the breath knocked from him in his fall, and he hurt all over. The weight of the armor was too much for him to lift. When Kharendaen tried to help him up, she found herself gently but firmly pushed aside by some unseen force. As the moments passed, Thelvyn found himself struggling for breath more than ever. In the past, the helmet had always supplied its own cool, fresh air by means of its native enchantments. Now even that power was subdued, and he was beginning to suffocate within the sealed armor.

Realizing he had only moments to save himself, Thelvyn rolled over so that he could push himself up against the dead weight of the armor and rose to his knees. Only then was he able to release the clips at his neck, yank off the helmet, and gasp for breath. In the next moment the armor vanished, teleporting away in the usual manner, except that this time it hadn't been through his will. Apparently the Overlord retained control over his armor. Thelvyn tried to return to his draconic form, only to find that even that power was denied to him. His enemy could control him as easily as his armor, preventing him from regaining his true form.

"That didn't go at all well, did it?" the Overlord asked in mocking tones. "Your previous enemies worked so hard to fight the power of your armor. Why did they never think to simply take it from you?"

Thelvyn didn't have the breath to reply even if he had wanted to. He knew the answer well enough; no one had ever tried to take the armor from him by will alone because only the Overlord had the strength of will to accomplish that. He felt vulnerable, even rather frightened, to find himself isolated from the protection of his armor and weapons. He realized now that the Overlord's intention was to humiliate him. He tried not to give in to such a simple tactic, but he couldn't help feeling the deep humiliation that was being forced upon him.

"Would you feel better if you could be a dragon again?" the Overlord asked. "Do you think the Dragonking would have a better chance of fighting me? That was what you were born to do, was it not?"

Thelvyn shifted abruptly to his true form, although he had not willed it. He immediately gathered himself to spring, then launched himself at his enemy. The ill-considered move was by no design of his own; obviously his actions were planned for him. Clearly the Overlord intended to demonstrate the utter futility of any attempt to fight, whether Thelvyn wanted to play along or not. If he couldn't even control his own mind and body, then he could not hope to take on the Overlord. All he could do now was wait and hope he didn't suffer too greatly.

Needless to say, the Overlord anticipated his charge and responded quickly, lifting his neck up and out of the way and stepping aside so that he could easily swat his much smaller opponent out of the air with the back of his claw. Thelvyn was caught by the blow in midleap and knocked backward. Kharendaen moved to try to break his fall, but once again she was pushed aside by some unseen force. The force of the impact was great enough that Thelvyn was thrown all the way across the wide pit, crashing his back heavily against the top of the low wall of the pit.

Thelvyn slumped to the floor of the pit and sprawled limply. Waves of pain exploded from the middle of his back, and he could only lie with his back and neck arched stiffly as he waited, trying to endure the first few moments of agony. Kharendaen couldn't help him even if she had been free to go to him. Isolated from the Great One in this strange world, she didn't even have her healing powers as a cleric to call upon.

"Now see what you've done. You've gone and hurt yourself," the Overlord said, moving to the edge of the pit to stare down at him in mock pity. "You should not have undertaken tasks that were beyond your limited abilities. But that was decided for you, wasn't it?"

Thelvyn could barely turn his head slightly to look up. The gray mists were gathering close again, and the darkness seemed all the heavier and more oppressive through the haze of his pain. The Overlord's nightmare face was hovering just above him, and now the Masters had also gathered about the edge of the pit to witness his defeat and humiliation. They did not laugh or ridicule him in any way, nor did they offer any compassion. They only watched him closely, with expressions he could only describe as patient hunger, like a dragon awaiting in pleasant anticipation of a roasted haunch of elk. He believed that they looked upon his defeat as the last remaining obstacle to their conquest of the world they had once tried to claim as their own, and the punishment of those who had once denied their ambitions.

There was nothing he could do to stop them, Thelvyn realized bitterly, not now and perhaps never again. He was too weak to stand up to the power of the Overlord. At that moment, he wondered if he would ever fight again. Pain burned like a raging fire in the middle of his back, and he couldn't move his hind legs or his tail.

"Are you beginning to learn what it means to be a dragon?" the Overlord asked as the faces began to draw back into the enclosing mists. "Perhaps you did not know that even you possessed the tremendous pride of a dragon until your pride was turned to bitterness. What would the dragons think of their king if they knew you had always believed you did not share the faults of their draconic nature, their pride, their temper, their greed, their capacity for cruelty, because you were not born a dragon? You thought you were better than they because you were the chosen of the Immortals."

Thelvyn closed his eyes so that he didn't have to see those faces fading away into the mists, but he couldn't stop himself from hearing those terrible words. He could only weep quietly for all the pain he was being made to endure.

"You thought that you were a king. Now you are nothing more than a slave, a weak and crippled thing. Contemplate that well until I return, and then we will have another lesson in humility prepared for you. I will visit you each day until your dragon's pride wills you to die rather than face me once again."

The voice was gone, but the pain did not begin to release him for a long time. He had been a fool, indeed a far bigger fool than he would have ever thought. Above all, he had been a fool for continuing this quest when he had known he should turn back. He had not yet discovered just how powerful his true enemy was, and yet he had been aware that he was overmatched. He had told himself he needed to know more before he could face the Overlord in battle, and all he had learned was that this was an enemy he could never hope to match. And he was twice a fool for bringing Kharendaen here.

He had no idea how long he lay lost in his torment. Clearly the Overlord and the Masters had long since left him, satisfied in knowing there was no peace or rest for him, even alone with his thoughts. The intolerable pain in his back began to ease slightly after a time, so that he no longer had to pant with the mere effort to draw a breath. He knew he had been badly hurt in the collision with the wall. His terrible injuries would seem to limit the time that he would be tortured and allowed to live. The Overlord had other, greater conquests at hand.

The irony was that he had come to learn the secrets of an enemy he had hardly known, yet the Overlord had known secrets of his own that he had never guessed he kept hidden. Secrets, it seemed, that he would have been better off if he had never known, but which he could not deny. He had thought the fact that he hadn't grown up as a dragon had isolated him from their common faults. And he had always assumed that the fact that he was the chosen of the Immortals, indeed the son of an Immortal, implied that he must somehow be perfectly suited for the task that had been assigned to him. He had assumed a great many things that had seemed simple and obvious and really not all that important, which he now recognized as an expression of his draconic pride.

The Overlord was very right about one other thing. In nothing else had Thelvyn so proven that he was a dragon at heart than in his dragon's pride. He was surprised that he didn't find it quite the insult it had been intended to be.

When he opened his eyes, he saw that he and Kharendaen were no longer in the pit in the immense, mist-filled chamber but had somehow been moved to a smaller chamber or cell of some type, still more than large enough for the two dragons. There was no sign of any window or even a door. He saw Kharendaen sitting back on her haunches with her tail curled around her legs, looking down at him.

"How do you feel?" she asked when she saw him open his eyes.

He started to lift his head, but it hurt too much. "How . . . how long does it take a dragon to die?"

She looked startled and concerned. "A dragon can take a very long time to die, depending upon the nature of his injuries."

"I think my back is broken," he told her plainly. "I cannot move."

"Then do not try to move," she told him firmly. "You might also be surprised by what a dragon can survive, and how quickly you recover."

"I doubt that I will be allowed the time," Thelvyn complained, then lifted his head slightly to look around in spite of the pain. "When did they move us here?"

"We have not been moved anywhere," Kharendaen explained to Thelvyn's surprise. "After you lost consciousness, the darkness closed in all around us, and then these walls formed at what had been the edge of the pit. The Overlord has come to look at us from time to time, somehow removing the walls and then restoring them when he left."

"How long was I unconscious?" Thelvyn asked.

"You have slept these last two days, at least insofar as I can judge time," she told him. "I began to wonder if you would ever be coming back to me."

Thelvyn laid his head down on the cold stone floor and closed his eyes for a long moment. He had been hurt worse than he had thought; he had thought that only a few long minutes of pain had passed, and that he had not slept at all. He wondered what was happening in his own world. Were his allies beginning to think he would not be returning to defend them? He also wondered if there was some way that he could get Kharendaen out of this place, and he wondered what would become of her when he was gone. He had made a hopeless mess of everything. Bitterly he thought the Immortals had been foolish to insist upon sending him to this place.

"Perhaps there was never any hope," Kharendaen said softly, guessing his thoughts. "Perhaps the risk of this journey was simply too great. We took the chance, the only chance we had. You have done the best you can, and you must not blame yourself. You were given the responsibility to try your best, and you have done that."

"There was never any room for failure, not in this matter," Thelvyn said bitterly. "The price of my failure will be our world. I have lost everything."

"You have not lost me."

Thelvyn turned his head away. "You could not leave if you wanted to."

Kharendaen laid back her ears, perplexed. Then she rose and moved slowly around to sit down again directly in front of him, where he could not so easily ignore her. "You have been stung by words that were meant to deceive you. I would not leave you now even if I could. Why do you suddenly seem to think I want to shun your company?"

"I haven't exactly made a good showing as Dragonking, have I?" he asked, then closed his eyes. "I've been playing the part of the hero who boldly saves the world. What a disappointment I've been."

"Do you think that I am disappointed in you?" Kharendaen lifted her head in astonishment, suddenly realizing what was bothering him. She laid back her ears, looking very sad. "What a life you have been asked to lead. Never allowed to know who or what you are, never allowed to know your own place in the world or find your own sense of worth. Having been raised among the Flaem, always having to prove yourself to them, you might come to think that the only measure of worth in the world is by what you have done or what you should be able to do. All that you have ever known is what was expected of you."

"So?" he looked up at her, confused and annoyed. "What else is there?"

"Our deeds and abilities count for a great deal, but they are by no means the only measure of a person's value. I know you do not judge others by such shallow standards, so why do you expect yourself to be judged in that way? Did you think you must earn my companionship by the honor that I received from the dragons from being your mate?"

"No," Thelvyn muttered, not quite certain what he wanted to say. "But I feel that I've let you down."

"There are some things that dragons are . . . especially poor at saying," Kharendaen explained haltingly, rising and walking in a tight circle before she returned to sit beside him. "We always leave certain things left unsaid, things that should have been said, so perhaps I can't blame you for coming to your own conclusions. You've always been able to make it clear to me how much I mean to you. I've taken it for granted that you understood how much you mean to me as well."

In spite of himself, Thelvyn had to hide his smile. There were indeed some things that dragons had a hard time saying, and Kharendaen seemed to be doing anything she could to avoid saying what she really meant.

"I wish we could have had more time to get to know each other better," he said. "All the hundreds of years of a dragon's lifetime."

"If our time together is indeed coming to an end, then there are certain things that should be said," she said, lowering her head to rub the side of her cheek against his own. "You see, I am going to lay an egg."

"What?" In spite of the pain, Thelvyn lifted his head sharply to stare at her. "How . . . how do you know?"

"Because I've developed a craving for nonvirgins," Kharendaen declared, amused by his reaction. "Oh, honestly. Female dragons know such things."

"But how long have you known? When will it come?"

"I've suspected it since before we left Shadowmere," she answered, rubbing her cheek against his again. "That's why, when you decided that it was important for you to remain in dragon form, I welcomed your decision. It is no longer wise for me to change from my true form. But don't get overly excited just yet. A dragon does not lay her egg until shortly before it hatches. I don't expect it to come for almost another year yet."

"Merciful heavens," Thelvyn said softly to himself. "I can't imagine how this happened."

"Didn't Sir George have a little talk with you when we first arrived at Shadowmere?" she asked with tolerant amusement.

He quickly searched his memory. "Yes . . . yes, he did say something about eggs. But what you taught me was much more interesting."

"Then you prefer a practical education over a theoretical one?"

Thelvyn lowered his head, his expression becoming one of determination. "We have to get away from here."

"That simply is not possible," Kharendaen told him. "Even if there were a way to escape, you cannot move. If you tried to move, even if you changed form so that I could carry you away, you would almost certainly not survive. And my clerical powers are gone. I cannot help you."

Thelvyn didn't seem to hear her. He stared aimlessly while he desperately searched for some means that would allow

them to escape. Perhaps it was foolish for him to return to his
old trust, considering how much the Immortals had underestimated the powers of the Overlord, but he had to believe that
the Great One had intended him to be able to defeat his enemies. Surely the Great One had made certain he would be
powerful enough to at least have a chance to defeat the Masters and the Overlord. He was convinced he must have far
greater powers that he had not yet discovered.

All the same, this was the worst time and place for him to
try to discover powers that he had not yet mastered. He would
need the guidance of the Great One, something that was not
available to him now. Then he realized that he might be looking for bigger answers than he needed when simpler answers
were at hand. The free clans of the Veydran had escaped domination for centuries. If he could only recall their secret. . . .

"They know his name," he said at last.

"Who knows what name?" Kharendaen asked, cocking her
head in mystification. "The Overlord?"

"The Veydran know his name, and therefore he cannot
control their will," Thelvyn said as he lifted his head. "If I
could remember the name they used, that would give us a
strong tool in planning our escape."

"I don't recall that they ever spoke his name," she said, still
perplexed. "All I ever heard was 'the Overlord.' "

"That was the word we heard in our minds," he explained.
"But I tried to pay attention to the language of the Veydran as
they spoke. I was curious to know if there was any relationship
between their language and that of the dragons. I was especially interested in learning their name for the Overlord, but
I'm not certain now what I heard."

Thelvyn laid his head on the cold stone floor, trying very hard
to think back over their brief encounter with the Veydran, but
he found that he was growing incredibly weary, and the pain in
his back assaulted him anew. The true seriousness of his injuries
was making itself known to him, so that it was difficult to direct
his thoughts toward anything but his struggle to hold to the fading edges of consciousness. His efforts to remember just what
the Veydran leader had said were already forgotten.

He wasn't even aware he had slept again until he was startled back to awareness, and even then he found himself in a night-mare of fear and pain. The walls of the cell were gone, and once again he lay in the shallow pit in the center of the large chamber where the Masters had gathered to witness his humiliation. The gemstone dragons were gone, or else they remained hidden within the dark mists that had closed almost to the very edge of the pit. The Overlord was glaring down at him, his immense, hideous face half hidden in the mist. Kharendaen stood over him protectively, but the posture of challenge she presented seemed halfhearted and desperate.

Thelvyn lifted his head painfully. It seemed to him that his back and shoulders hurt more than ever. He recognized one important difference from the first visit of the Overlord, how-ever. The first time, he had not even been aware that the Overlord had taken control of his will. This time, however, his will remained entirely his own, at least for the moment.

"Then you are back, Little One?" the Overlord asked con-descendingly. "You dragons are very slow to die."

"I have no plans of dying any time soon," Thelvyn responded. "And I won't allow you to make a fool of me again."

He realized that he had to act quickly, while he still could. If the Overlord were to look within his thoughts, his secret would be betrayed. He would never have a second chance. Looking up, he caught the gaze of the Overlord, staring into those large, malevolent eyes. That seemed to catch the Over-lord by surprise, giving Thelvyn a momentary advantage over his opponent. Then Thelvyn spoke a single word, his voice loud, deep, and clear, the sound of it echoing through the hid-den depths of the mist-filled chamber.

The Overlord drew back suddenly in alarm. The sound of his name apparently did him no physical harm, but it obvi-ously alarmed him. He hadn't been challenged directly in cen-turies, and it shook his confidence. Kharendaen stared at her mate for a moment, then turned back to the Overlord and repeated his name, protecting herself from his control. The Overlord hesitated in apprehension and then drew back into the concealing darkness of the mists to consider his next move. His captives had proven stronger than he had expected, and he wanted to avoid confronting them until he felt certain that they would not surprise him again.

Thelvyn knew he had to act quickly. The Overlord had withdrawn, but Thelvyn had no way of knowing how far he had gone. He closed his eyes and concentrated, reaching deep within his own powers, and for a moment his entire form began to glow with a soft golden light. When the light faded, he rose stiffly, moving slowly and with great uncertainty at first but gaining strength quickly. Kharendaen hurried to his side, fearful that he might harm himself, until she realized that he was calling upon his own powers to repair his injuries.

"We don't have a moment to waste," he told her quietly. "If we don't get out of here right now, we never will. The Overlord might not be able to control us now, but he can still fight us."

"But can you move?" she asked anxiously.

"I have no choice but to try."

At least he was spared the need to try to fly just yet; the spells that were healing his damaged back were still working, and he was in considerable pain even yet. Nor did he dare to attempt to fly through the walls of dark mist that filled the chamber, with no idea of its size or where he could find an exit. He climbed stiffly over the edge of the pit, waiting a moment for Kharendaen to join him before they began to hurry through the darkness, heading in the opposite direction from where they had last seen the Overlord. The mists parted slowly about them as they hurried across the stone floor at a half-run, unable to see more than a few yards ahead of them. They had to be careful not to lose sight of each other.

The two dragons ran for what seemed like several hundred yards, and they were beginning to wonder just how vast this chamber was when they suddenly encountered the wall looming suddenly out of the mist. Thelvyn paused for an instant, staring up as far as he could see along the featureless expanse of smooth, gray stone before he turned to run along the wall to his right. He had to find a way out of this chamber before it was sealed against them, just as the walls had materialized around the central pit to form their prison. When he did not find what he was seeking, he had to wonder if it was already too late. Only a few seconds had passed since they had escaped from the pit, but in that oppressive darkness, each second seemed to possess the weight of a hour.

When he came abruptly to a corner, he had to pause a second time, trying to decide whether he should go back or search along the new wall. Taking a chance, he turned again to his right and began to race along the length of the new wall, running almost blindly in the darkness, certain that the next corner must be hundreds of yards ahead. Just as they approached what he thought should be about halfway along the wall, he began to slow somewhat in anticipation of finding a doorway. Instead, they came suddenly into an open pocket in the mists, as if the gray fog had been blown away from that portion of the wall.

Thelvyn stopped short and sat back on his tail so that he could lift his long neck to look up. Suddenly he realized that there might not be any floor-level entrances to this chamber. The only way in or out could be through passages set high in the wall; the gemstone dragons had the ability to fly, and the Overlord could probably come and go by will alone. Perhaps by chance, there was enough air moving through the passages of the stronghold to clear the air in this one small area as it poured through the unseen opening somewhere above.

Thelvyn stepped away from the wall and spread his wings. He was reassured to find that the pain and stiffness in his back had nearly disappeared. Then he leapt upward and began to climb in a tight spiral, with Kharendaen close behind him. He wondered how the Masters found their way through the mist, unless they possessed some magical instinct for direction. Moments later, he suddenly emerged into open air. The ceiling of the large chamber was more than a hundred yards high, and the misty clouds settled into only the lower portion, filling it like the bottom of a bowl. Now he could see several wide rectangular passageways opening into the chamber, one of them just before him.

He landed on the ledge at the front of the opening, still feeling a bit unsteady. The roof of the passage looked too low for him to try to fly through it. A short distance beyond the opening, the passageway began to climb upward at a steep angle. He folded away his wings and moved quickly out of the way, giving Kharendaen room to land beside him. Then, moving side by side, they began the difficult climb up the steep passage, their claws scratching against the smooth stone of the ramp as they struggled upward. The passage itself was dark, but there was a pale light in the opening above.

The passage was a long, difficult climb. It was less than fifty yards in actual length, but it was so steep that they were constantly in danger of slipping and falling. They were nearly at the top when the form of a gemstone dragon moved suddenly into the opening above, standing dark and menacing against the light. Although it appeared to be alone, it would be difficult to get by it because of the positional advantage it commanded at the top of the steep ramp. The two dragons continued their climb, acutely aware that they couldn't afford to be delayed.

Kharendaen decided it was her turn to get them to safety. Suddenly she darted forward up the ramp. On the steep ramp, she was the quicker of the two, being smaller and lighter, and Thelvyn was still slowed somewhat by his injuries. It was a brave choice, but it was more ill-considered than she had thought. When she came to the top of the ramp, she employed one of her favorite tricks, darting beneath the gemstone dragon and then thrusting herself upward sharply, throwing the gemstone dragon's greater bulk over her back and against the wall at the top of the opening. The maneuver stunned the alien dragon for a moment, long enough for Kharendaen to kick out with her hind legs and send the creature sliding down the ramp.

Unfortunately, Thelvyn was still on the ramp just below the opening. He pulled himself as far as he could to one side of the passage, trying to keep out of the way as the gemstone dragon slid by. For a moment it seemed that he had escaped, but in the last instant, the gemstone dragon caught the end of Thelvyn's tail and held on desperately. There wasn't much that Thelvyn could do about it, since he was barely able to keep his hold on the smooth stones to keep himself from sliding down the ramp with his enemy.

Then Kharendaen hurtled down the ramp, crashing into the gemstone dragon. At the same time, she caught the base of his neck in her jaws in a death hold. The Master released its hold on Thelvyn's tail immediately, and the two of them slid away into the darkness below. Alarmed, Thelvyn braced himself as best as he could and bent his head back to peer down the dark passage. He decided he should hurry to his mate's assistance, but a moment later he saw her swarming up the ramp to join him, looking none the worse for wear.

"Are you through playing?" he called down to her.

"I thought I was being helpful," she insisted. "Why? Are you in a hurry?"

"I was thinking about that big worldgate in the center of the stronghold," he told her. "If we hurry, we might just be lucky enough to get home the easy way."

They climbed out of the ramp into a large passage, pausing briefly to look around. They had emerged into a wide corridor, large enough to easily fly side by side along its length. Other doorways and passages entered this one at intervals, but they were set fairly far apart. The walls and floor of massive gray stone blocks were smooth and featureless. The Masters were obviously not much concerned with beauty or ornamentation. The two dragons spread their wings to fly as fast as they dared along the passage, hoping to escape the stronghold before they had to fight yet again.

Thelvyn had no idea how to find his way out of this place. The only thing he could think of was to keep heading as directly as he could away from the center. He recalled that most of the fortresses that he had seen in the city of the Masters had only one main entrance, and his dragon's sense of direction told him that the gate probably would face the south, to his left. Perhaps he would have done better to have looked for a way out somewhere above, but he was afraid it might take too much time to find a ledge or window. After a short distance, they came to the intersection of another wide corridor leading to the left.

Fortunately the passages of the fortress were straight and regular, laid out with a singular attention to efficiency. Soon the corridor turned once again, back the way they had first come, then opened suddenly upon a large chamber. The dragons found themselves on a high balcony that looked out over one end of a wide hall, the vast gateroom of the fortress. From where they stood, the massive doors of dark metal were set in the center of the opposite wall. The doors were shut and barred, and six gemstone dragons waited below, guarding the gate. More than a score of Veydran warriors, these doubtlessly subject to the will of the Overlord, also waited on the floor below or along the stairs at either end of the balcony. They stood with their wings spread, holding long spears in their hands. They looked small to the dragons but also lean and swift, decidedly dangerous adversaries.

"We can't afford the time to find another way out," Thelvyn said as he stood beside Kharendaen at the center of the balcony.

"What can we do other than fight them?" she asked softly.

"We're going to have to fight," he replied. "I plan to make it a brief one. Be ready to follow me."

Kharendaen did not doubt him, but she wondered how long his strength would hold out after the terrible injuries he had recently endured. She recalled that few clerical spells were particularly useful in a battle of magic, but Thelvyn had always had a few tricks entirely his own. He rose to stand with his forelegs braced on the sturdy rail along the edge of the balcony, as if challenging his enemies, but she could see his eyes glaze as he concentrated on commanding a spell. She wished he would hurry; the Veydran warriors spotted him, shook their spears over their heads, and rushed up the stairs to attack.

Suddenly the floor of the fortress began to shake violently. The tremor was no more than three seconds in duration but very strong; blocks of the fortress walls began to shift and separate slightly, and long cracks split the floor of the gateroom. A large section of the balcony crumbled and fell away, and the gemstone dragons were forced to spread their wings and leap aside. The brief tremor was enough to shatter the outer wall of the fortress. The massive blocks of stone were too large and solid to collapse easily, but they were split by deep cracks, and the doors of the main gate shifted on bent hinges.

But the dragons had not escaped yet. Although the crossbars were broken, the doors remained shut and were now jammed together. Their enemies were disoriented, but Thelvyn knew he wouldn't have the time to try to force the damaged gate open before he was attacked. Looking quickly over his shoulder to see that Kharendaen was safe, he drew a deep breath and released the full fury of his breath weapon. A jet of blue flames that materialized into crackling bolts of lighting leapt and danced over the floor, ripping apart the stones as if they were dried mud. The Veydran warriors were chased down by the branching spears of lighting, their broken and smoking bodies hurled across the chamber. The gemstone dragons who were not immediately slain fled from the merciless destruction.

Kharendaen was alarmed by the ferocity of the attack, and as they flew, she kept herself slightly behind and above Thelvyn so that her mate was free to release his terrible destruction without fear for her safety. At last he turned and headed toward the gate, directing a full blast of lightning against the jammed doors until they exploded outward. Free at last, the dragons darted forward through the gate just as the stones began to collapse in a cloud of dust and rubble.

Thelvyn continued to lead the way, staying low as he followed the streets between the maze of fortresses. The sky above was filled with the winged forms of the Masters and the smaller Veydran warriors, and soldiers of many other races hurried through the streets, but they seemed uncertain of what they were expected to fight. The confusion gave the two dragons enough time to search through the streets for the route to escape.

Following the larger streets, Thelvyn quickly found what he was looking for. Emerging between the long rows of strongholds, the dragons suddenly found themselves in the milling confusion of the central square. Companies of soldiers scattered and heavy freight wagons careened out of their path, but the dragons were too late. The immense worldgate had already been closed.

Seeing that he had no choice, Thelvyn turned and led the way out of the central square, staying low in the streets between the buildings to remain hidden as long as possible. The Masters and whole companies of Veydran had already seen them and were now in hot pursuit. Their only hope now was to avoid having to fight until they were away from the stronghold and able to disappear into the dusty twilight wilderness of that cold, dry world.

CHAPTER SIXTEEN

If Thelvyn had still wanted to learn more about the strength
of the Masters and their armies, this was certainly the time. He
could see at least two hundred gemstone dragons darting back
and forth over the stronghold, although in their alarm and
confusion, they didn't seem to know what they were looking
for. He hoped to take advantage of their uncertainty, remaining half hidden in the streets between the imposing, massive
forms of the fortresses until he and Kharendaen were able to
escape into the wild.

But he had never dared to hope that they would be able to
get away entirely unobserved. Even as the two dragons weaved
an elusive path through the streets, still more gemstone dragons began to fall in behind them, taking up the pursuit. That
was no immediate concern in itself; Thelvyn knew that gold
dragons were faster than the Masters, but when he glanced
back, he saw that Veydran warriors were taking up the chase
as well. That was a matter of some concern, since he had no
idea of their speed and endurance.

Suddenly the street they were following ended, and the

dragons came out from among the great hulks of the fortresses. Now they had to make a desperate dash across the open ground and into the southwestern pass through the mountains that surrounded the stronghold. They entered the pass as quickly as they could fly, passing right over the heads of countless companies of soldiers waiting to be moved forward through the worldgate. Thelvyn waited for the rattle of arrows against his armor and hoped that nothing worse would be brought to bear against them, but it seemed that their enemy was still taken by surprise, unprepared to fight back. Moments later, the dragons were beyond the pass, turning sharply to head west across the fields toward the seclusion of distant mountains.

Thelvyn glanced back after a moment to check on their pursuers. The gemstone dragons were already beginning to fall well behind them, unable to match the furious pace of the gold dragons. But he saw at least twoscore Veydran warriors in pursuit, strung out over more than a quarter of a mile, the nearest only a few dozen yards behind Kharendaen. And as he watched, he saw that they were neither gaining on them nor losing distance. He had no desire to fight so many of the small, powerful warriors, but he realized that if they didn't begin to tire or fall behind soon, he would have to do something.

"How are you holding up?" Kharendaen asked.

"I'm not at my best," he said, surprised at how much he was forced to pant when he tried to talk. "I can't keep up this pace for long."

She bent her head to look at him. "If you want to avoid a fight, would you mind a suggestion?"

"Of course not."

"Then let's begin to climb, as high and as fast as we can," she said. "If my guess is correct, the Veydran are not equipped to fly in high, thin air."

Thelvyn didn't have the breath to reply, but he was grateful for the idea. Because his own experience with flight was limited, he would never have thought of such a thing. The two dragons began to climb at once, rising as steeply as they could with long, powerful sweeps of their wings, even though climbing sacrificed some speed. Thelvyn knew he couldn't endure

much more of this, but he was encouraged to see that the Veydran were steadily falling farther behind. Obviously the Veydran were tiring even more quickly than the dragons, and that
might put an end to the chase.

Every advantage now seemed to belong to the dragons.
There was a high but solid blanket of pale, light clouds above
them, and the brisk wind felt cold and curiously wet for such
an arid place. If they could only climb into those high clouds,
their escape was certain. More than that, the sun was already
setting, and night came quickly to this desolate land. Thelvyn
desperately needed a chance to rest and recover from his
injuries, and he realized that he hadn't eaten or drank in at
least three days. He didn't expect to find food or water in this
place, but he had to have some rest before he could find a way
to escape the world of their enemies.

The miles and miles of neatly laid fields and pastures were
falling away below them steadily, but Thelvyn thought the
ceiling of clouds overhead remained as remote and unreach-
able as ever. He began to fear that the clouds were too high,
beyond the reach of even dragons. He desperately needed to
reach those clouds, which would conceal their escape into the
wild, losing their pursuers and giving him some time to rest.
The shoulders of his wings were weak and numb, and the
damaged muscles all along his back were burning in pain. He
had to constantly remind himself to hold his tail erect so his
rear sails wouldn't drop down to catch the air and slow him.

The Veydran were no longer falling behind, expending
every last bit of their strength to catch the dragons before they
disappeared into the clouds. Thelvyn was beginning to doubt
that he would make it to safety, but then he noticed that, by
some trick of the fading light of day, the clouds had looked farther away than they were. A thousand yards or more remained,
but he was beginning to hope that he could last that long.
Even so, the last few minutes became a desperate race. The
Veydran began to close once again as Thelvyn's strength
began to fail and the dragons were forced to slow their steep
climb.

Kharendaen dropped back behind her mate. If necessary,
she intended to hold off the pursuing Veydrans with her

flames long enough for them to escape, but then they moved up into the clouds, and the mists and the gathering night closed about them. They turned immediately to the south, not daring to level off until they were well inside the clouds. Then they turned once again, back toward the west, locking their wings to rest briefly while they rode the winds.

"Can you keep going for a while?" Kharendaen asked, flying close at his side so that they would not become separated in the clouds.

"I guess I'll have to," he answered, still panting heavily. "There's no place for us to hide until we get well beyond the cultivated lands. That will be another hour, at least. I can ride the wind that long."

"Do you know where we're going?" she asked.

"Back to the ruined town, I think. Perhaps we'll run into the free Veydran again. There are things that I need to know."

Tired and in pain, Thelvyn wondered with each long minute whether he would be able to keep going till the next. He began to fear there would be no point to all his efforts. Their failure to reach the large worldgate at the main stronghold before it was closed against them may have been their last chance to escape this world. Long hours would pass before they could reach any of the lesser gates, more than enough time for the gates to be closed or placed under heavy guard. Then the dragons would be trapped, condemned to wander this desolate world in a never-ending race against their pursuers.

They remained within the cover of the clouds to avoid being seen, trusting their instinct for direction. The clouds began to break up somewhat after the first half hour or so as the winds became stronger and more fitful. Their pursuers seemed to have long since given up the chase, frustrated by the speed of the gold dragons and their tremendous height. The air was cold and thin, making it difficult for Thelvyn to catch his breath, adding to his fatigue.

In time they spotted the wild, rugged land where they had found the ancient town, and they began to descend in a wide, steep spiral. It was difficult even for the sharp eyes of dragons to see much. The crumbling buildings of the ancient village were hidden by the darkness and by the fact that their appearance was so much like the color and rugged texture of the surrounding lands. Finally they spotted the remains of the ruined settlement sheltered in a deep valley, and they searched for a safe place to land, a place where they could observe the sky and the surrounding lands but still remain at least partly hidden. Kharendaen led the way now, landing in what had been the town square.

"I think it's safe to stay here for a time," she said, watching with concern as Thelvyn slowly folded away his wings, obviously in pain.

"Were you able to rest any of the time that we were held captive?" he asked.

"I had time to sleep while I was waiting for you," she assured him, though her answer seemed vague. "I was also given food and drink, but the Overlord wouldn't leave any for you. You haven't had food or drink since before we came into this world, have you?"

"No, but I'll be all right," Thelvyn said as he lowered himself painfully to the ground, stretching out his full length. "I wouldn't know where to look for water, and I haven't seen anything alive in the wild to hunt."

"The free Veydran must exist on something," she observed. "If we must, we could always return to raid the farmlands."

"I don't plan on being here that long."

Kharendaen walked over to look at him closely. Then she sat up on her haunches, bracing herself with her tail so that she could reach out and begin to rub his back gently. Thelvyn lifted his head to protest, then thought better of it. He laid down his head and closed his eyes, and after a moment he gave a deep, rumbling sigh of pleasure. Kharendaen smiled, thinking that he sounded like a gruff old dragon enjoying the hidden contentment of his lair.

"Are you fully recovered from your injuries now?" she asked.

"For the most part," he answered. "I'm in no danger of hurting myself again, but I need a little time to get back to normal."

"At least you have retained your clerical powers."

"I didn't realize at first just how much the Overlord was controlling me," Thelvyn said. "The Masters seem to be unaware that their will is subject to his control, apparently regarding themselves as willing servants, allies rather than slaves. Later I realized that something had been very wrong about that first confrontation, when he made it seem that his powers were vast compared to my own. He was controlling my responses. He wouldn't allow me to defend myself, which gave the appearance that I wasn't strong enough to stand up to him."

"You seemed more evenly matched later," Kharendaen observed.

"I'm still certain that he is very powerful," Thelvyn said. "He commands the powers that you would associate with one of the lesser Immortals. But for whatever reason, it seemed to frighten him unduly when we were able to prevent him from controlling us. He could have put an end to our escape at any time, but instead he chose to withdraw, as if he feared for his safety. Perhaps it has been too long since he has had to confront his enemies directly."

Kharendaen rose up higher on her haunches so that she could push down harder on his back; his dragon's armor made it difficult to give him a good back rub. Then she bent her neck around to bring her face close to his. "Don't you think the Overlord also might have deceived you about your standing among your own kind?"

Thelvyn sighed heavily. "No, I don't think so. Deceit isn't his only weapon, not when he has the power to look inside your own thoughts and use the truth against you. He knows that the truth can wound far deeper and more sharply than any of his tricks. He merely put into words some ideas and impressions that I have always held, that I thought that I was above the common faults of dragons."

"Well, if that is a failing, then it is one I share," Kharendaen told him. "I have often been driven nearly to distraction by the foolishness, the suspicion, the selfishness, and the narrowminded beliefs of the dragons. And, yes, I, too, like to think I am above such faults. But I also prefer to think that most dragons could rise above such things, if they could only be made to

believe that they belong to a wise and noble breed. Perhaps
am an optimist, but I chose to become a cleric not only t
serve the Great One but also the dragons themselves. Are yo
and I really so different, then? I've known you to argue wit
the dragons about changing their ways."

"That may be so," Thelvyn agreed, sitting up slowly. "A
least I've learned an important lesson about myself. But ju
now I find myself desperate to return home. I worry what ma
be happening in our absence."

"I suspect my brother has kept things from falling apart."

"Yes, your brother," Thelvyn said, lowering his head an
laying back his ears. "Marthaen is going to slay me."

Kharendaen looked perplexed. "Slay you?"

"For getting you pregnant." He lifted his head, staring int
the night. "I think our friends have returned."

At least he hoped they were their friends. A small group o
Veydran were approaching the square cautiously from one o
the side streets. Although they were moving furtively, trying t
stay hidden between the ruined buildings, they were not tryin
to hide themselves from the two dragons. Enemy Veydra
warriors would have been more stealthful in their approach
their movements conveying a greater sense of hostile purpose
He waited patiently for them to approach, sitting up with h
tail wrapped around his legs and his neck arched proudly
careful not to move.

A large group of Veydran were approaching this time, nin
in all, and he saw that all but their leader were bearing larg
bundles of some type. As they came nearer, he could see tha
four of the dragon-folk were carrying large skins filled wit
water or some other drink, and the other four carried roaste
meat wrapped in what appeared to be large, dry leaves of som
strange type. He was pleasantly surprised, since he had neve
expected that they would offer him the food or drink h
needed so badly, partly because he had not expected them t
have such things to share.

The leader of the Veydran stopped a few yards away. Th
others remained behind him. After staring at the two dragon
briefly, he bent his neck in an odd gesture of respect. "Yo
have returned."

As before, the dragons did not understand the words that he spoke, but nevertheless they were aware of most of what he said in their minds. Thelvyn bowed his head in return. "We were made the Overlord's prisoners, and I suffered serious injuries from him. But we got the better of him in the end and managed to escape."

"Then you are able to fight him?"

"I would not choose to fight him again, not in this world," Thelvyn said. "I will wait until he comes into my own world, where my strength is enhanced. Then we will defeat him, and our people will be free."

"That is good." The Veydran leader paused, glancing back at his companions. "We have brought food and drink for you. If you need anything else, we will try to get it for you."

"We thank you for your gifts. We need food and drink badly," Thelvyn replied. "I ask only one more thing. Do you know of any other worldgates we could try to use to return home, and, if so, could you lead us to them?"

"We will lead you wherever you want to go, but the journey would do you no good. The Masters seal all the worldgates they do not use, and those they do use are under heavy guard. They fear that their enemies might use their own gates against them."

"Are there no secret gates, perhaps ancient ones that the Masters have closed but forgotten to destroy?"

"It is not possible to forget a worldgate. You can hear them as you come near, even if they are sealed."

Thelvyn lowered his head. "I had suspected as much, but the question was still worth asking. We must try to find our own way home."

"We will do what we can. If you need us again, circle the village once in the air, then land again. We will come to you."

The Veydran brought forth their gifts, then made a gesture of respect and withdrew quickly, disappearing into the night. When Thelvyn and Kharendaen unwrapped the leaves, they found what appeared to be roasted carcasses of some kind of deer, although the taste was more like game fowl. Kharendaen was unable to force her mate to accept more than half of the food in spite of her arguments. She insisted that he needed to regain his strength during his recovery. Thelvyn resisted reminding her that she was now eating for two.

"What do you think?" Kharendaen asked as they ate. "Do we dare try to find the gate where we came in, even with that new stronghold so close by?"

Thelvyn frowned. "Finding that gate should be easy enough. If the winds are still stirring up the dust and sand, the Masters would never see us. They might not even be aware of that gate. Most likely they're watching the old gate near Braastar."

"Marthaen said he would open gate at regular intervals to see if we might be waiting to return home. We might have to wait some time for the gate to open again."

Thelvyn shook his head helplessly. "We can only try."

The dragons rested through most of the night, although they made a point of departing before daybreak in an effort to avoid being seen. The wind had increased somewhat during the night. They remained whenever possible under the cover of clouds, which were heavy but somewhat broken. The clouds offered the best cover the dragons could have, since they were far more likely to be discovered if they tried to fly in and out among the valleys and ravines. From this height, only the sharp eyes of another dragon could have seen them during the brief times when they passed between clouds.

Thelvyn had regained much of his strength with the night's rest, and he was now in relatively little pain. He was becoming impressed with just had badly he had been injured, and how easily that damage could have been fatal. For the first time, he was beginning to appreciate how close he might have been to death. He found himself a bit shaken by that realization. What he could not guess was whether his survival had been a matter of chance, or if the Overlord had deliberately kept him alive to torment him.

Flying at such height, enduring the thin air, was not the ordeal that it had been for him the day before. Traveling six miles or more above the ground also made him feel somewhat insecure, knowing he couldn't land quickly if something happened to him and he could no longer fly. The cold, thin air dried his throat, and he wished they could find water for the empty skins they carried. He wished he had thought to ask the

eydran about how to find food and water in this inhospitable
nd, in case they were unable to return to their own world.

At first they flew above the especially rugged, barren lands
orthwest of the sea of sand, where they had previously
odged in and out through the valleys and along the ridges to
emain hidden. The land did not look nearly so rugged from
uch a great height, and Thelvyn was interested to see that
aere were more definite patterns in the landforms than could
een seen from low altitudes. The ridges and lines of moun-
ains ran in strangely orderly systems, and great valleys looked
ke streambeds cut by recent rains. At least he had the answer
o one of his questions; his sharp eyes occasionally caught
ale, almost hazy hints of white in the deepest crags of the
aountaintops, suggesting snow. At least the dragons would
ot need to suffer from thirst, although he suspected any drifts
f snow would include a generous mixture of dust.

Not long after they entered the sea of sand, the high cloud
over began to break apart, as if the clouds could not endure
ae dry air over the open desert. The clouds didn't disappear
ntirely, but now they offered minimum cover for the dragons.
'helvyn spoke with Kharendaen about whether it would be
etter to fly low, returning to the protection of the fog of gray
ust near the ground. In the end, they decided they would
ontinue to fly at their present height, at least for now, so they
'ouldn't have to endure the dust in their throats or the sting
f sand in their large eyes.

In time, they came within sight of the fortress that stood
ust north of the location of their gate, and they were forced to
y low to avoid being spotted. The hours of flight had pro-
ided Thelvyn with time to assemble something of a plan.
Fuided by their unerring instinct for direction, the two drag-
ns circled around to approach the gateway from the south,
nally landing amid the great boulders of the island of rock
hat rose out of the sands. The worldgate now stood only a
ouple hundred yards north of them, and the fortress was sev-
ral hundred yards more beyond that. Whether or not the
ortress had been abandoned when they had arrived, he felt
ertain that guards would be on hand now to watch for the
scaped dragons. Thelvyn planned to wait in hiding until they

sensed the opening of the gate, then dash through before the Masters could stop them.

"I only hope Marthaen is continuing to open the gate from time to time as he promised," Kharendaen said, shielding her face from the blowing sand with her mate's chest as they huddled together in the shelter of a group of large boulders. "We've been gone for a long time, and Marthaen may have given up hope."

"This isn't our only hope," Thelvyn said, bringing his own head around to escape the sting of the windblown sand, "but it may be our best opportunity."

They hadn't waited long when they suddenly sensed a flare of power, followed by the distinctive presence of an open worldgate. Thelvyn lifted his head sharply, startled that the gate should open only a short time after they had arrived. Then he realized that Marthaen might be opening the passage often, fearful because of their delayed return and aware that they might need to escape hastily. Even so, Marthaen would open the gate only briefly, perhaps no more than a few seconds at a time. The dragons had to reach it in a hurry.

They emerged from their shelter and leapt down through the boulders at a run until they came to a relatively flat shelf where they could jump into the air. They were flying blind in the thick dust, but they had no problem finding their way, drawn by the unmistakable source of magic. But almost at once Thelvyn began to sense that something was wrong. Suddenly he knew they were not alone.

The magic shifted form, and abruptly the fierce wind died and the air around them became as still as death. The windborn sand fell to the ground, leaving only the gray dust hanging in the air like thick fog. He became aware of several vast, dark shapes moving through the dust, and a moment later three massive steel warriors emerged out of the grey darkness, towering shapes moving slowly and deliberately amid an escort of the smaller forms of the Masters. Thelvyn was forced to turn sharply, passing almost directly beneath the head of one of the metal warriors.

A dark shape hurtled down from above as one of the Masters darted in, striking Kharendaen in the middle of her back and driving her downward. The large amber dragon already had her neck in a death lock, but in the next moment she crashed heavily into the side of a low dune. The impact broke her opponent's hold, sending both of them tumbling. Kharendaen was shaken by the blow. The amber dragon rose unsteadily and shook its head, then snarled fiercely as it turned toward Kharendaen, moving in to finish the kill. She lifted her head and blinked, finding herself staring into his fangs, her eyes round with fear.

Thelvyn had circled back tightly, and now he dived to the attack, dropping down with braced legs to strike the gemstone dragon's back with crushing force. His head darted in for a death grip, but at the last moment, he suddenly leapt over the Master's sprawled form and dragged his mate out of the way. In the next instant, the massive head of one of the steel warriors thrust down out of the dense grey dust, striking the side of the dune with a tremendous explosion of sand that nearly buried the two dragons, crushing the amber dragon and driving his broken body deep into the sand.

Thelvyn shook the sand from his back and wings before he grabbed Kharendaen by her shoulders and pulled her free, half carrying her quickly to one side. The warrior pushed its head on through the side of the dune as easily as if it had been a drift of snow, and the two dragons were lifted up and sent tumbling by an avalanche of sand. This time Kharendaen was able to regain her wits, recovering from the impact that had forced her from the air. But the sky was no safe place for them, crowded with the circling forms of the Masters waiting for their own turn to attack. Tucking away their wings tightly, the dragons dropped their heads low and ran as fast as they could, struggling for purchase in the loose sand.

Even on foot, they could move along with surprising speed, their long, leaping gait carrying them across the dunes back toward the questionable safety of the islands of boulders that rose in clusters out of the sand. They ran in an evasive path that the Masters could not easily follow on the wing. When the dragons reached the boulders, the warriors could not easily maneuver their way through the maze of large stones where the visibility was severely limited, and they were left behind.

Then the dragons spread their wings and leapt into the air. In moments, they disappeared into the cloud of swirling dust, escaping the pursuit of the Masters.

"Are you all right?" Thelvyn asked, flying close at his mate's side.

"I wasn't harmed," she insisted, trying not to pant.

Thelvyn paused, having seen the shadowy form of one of the Masters following less than a hundred yards behind them, nearly hidden in the blowing dust. He could not allow any pursuit, since he had always suspected that what one of the Masters knew was known to them all. Without warning, he lifted his head and dropped his tail, using his wings and sails to catch the wind and slow him abruptly. It was a daring move on his part, even more daring than he was aware, and the results were much more drastic than he had expected. Caught completely unprepared, the gemstone dragon crashed heavily into the middle of his back, knocking them both from the sky. With the dunes only a few yards below, they had no time to recover.

Thelvyn's luck turned at that point. The gemstone dragon crashed heavily onto the middle of his back on the long slope of a high dune, and a moment later Thelvyn fell tail first right on top of his enemy. The impact sent them both sliding on their backs down the side of the dune. Thelvyn was somewhat shaken by the fall and struggled to catch himself, while the gemstone dragon was stunned and apparently more seriously injured. Kharendaen appeared out of the clouds of dust a moment later, having circled back. She dived sharply to the attack, taking the large amber dragon by the neck before it was even aware of its danger.

"Leave him be," Thelvyn said, seeing that their enemy was already helpless. "We have to get away from here while we still have the chance."

Kharendaen seemed unwilling at first to release her victim, possessed momentarily by battle fury. All the fear and desperation of the last few days were taking a toll on her, leaving her at the mercy of her draconic instincts, and for the moment, she wanted only to lash out at her enemies. Thelvyn was startled, but he also learned something about dragons at that moment.

If even the proud, self-possessed cleric could be overcome by her instincts, was it any wonder that most dragons had a problem remembering to act civilized when they became enraged?

The moment passed swiftly. As if startled by her own fury, Kharendaen released her hold and stepped back from the body of the gemstone dragon. Then the dragons turned and scurried up the side of the dune, spreading their wings as they vaulted out over the crest. Moments later, they disappeared into the wind-driven clouds of dust and sand, taking care to make certain that they were not being followed. Thelvyn set an evasive course at first, in an effort to prevent the Masters from guessing his next destination. Of course, he could hardly leave clues about something that he had not yet decided. For the moment, he had no idea of what he should try to do next or where they should go.

The brief but furious battle had once more aggravated his back, not enough to be a serious problem, but he was in some pain. That and the need to pay attention to his course as they flew low over the dunes, nearly blind in the clouds of dust, left him unable to give much serious thought to his options for the moment. Within a few miles, they came entirely by chance upon another of the tumbled outcrops of stone that emerged like islands in the sand. He circled around quickly to find a sheltered place where they could rest while he gave some serious thought to the problem of finding another way home.

He found a place where they could climb in among a group of massive boulders and could at least have some relief from the driven sand and the worst of the dust. He was distressed to see that Kharendaen looked very tired and moved slowly and stiffly, having suffered her own injuries during their battle. Nevertheless, Thelvyn seemed to have taken the worst, discovering a yard-long tear in the sail of his right wing from his collision with the amber dragon. At least such damage would repair itself in a few days, even without magical healing.

"They knew about our gate," Kharendaen said, nestling close against his chest. "All they had to do was to wait for us to come to them."

"Fortunately they seemed to have underestimated us once again," Thelvyn remarked. "Now we have to find another way home."

"What choices do we have?" Kharendaen asked, turning her head to look up at him.

"We have a number of options, some better than others," he said, having already considered that question. "We could wait for a while and make another try at our own temporary gate, but I expect the Masters will guard it very closely as long as they know we are still in their world. I expect the old gate near Braastar is being watched at least as closely."

"If nothing else, we could simply fight our way through to one of their other gates," she suggested.

"That's something we could try as a last resort," he agreed. "The problem is that if we have to fight for access to a gate, they'll probably have time to close it first. We could return to their main stronghold and try to dart through that big gate before they can defend it, but I'm concerned that the Overlord will be aware of us if we come that close to his stronghold. That leaves us with the possibility of trying to open a completely new gate at a place of our own choosing."

Kharendaen laid back her ears. "Do you command the power necessary to accomplish such a thing?"

"I think I know how we could try," he said. "Remember the reason why you were told to accompany me. As his cleric, you might still provide some vague link to the Great One. If he could be made aware of our need, he might be able to reach out from his side to help us complete a worldgate."

"But I've been isolated from my clerical powers ever since we first came into this world," she protested. "How can I possibly contact the Great One?"

"In the usual manner, I would suppose. Try to commune with the Great One, reaching out to him across the void."

Kharendaen sat upright with her long tail looped tightly around her legs, closing her eyes so that she could concentrate. A moment later she was disturbed from her thoughts by a distant sound of something large moving through the fog of wind-blown dust, the slow, ponderous steps of some massive creature. She opened her eyes, and both of the dragons listened carefully for a moment.

"The metal warriors are coming," Thelvyn said softly. "The

Masters must have some idea of where to look for us."

"Do we flee now and try again later?" Kharendaen asked.

"No. We should have time for at least one try," Thelvyn decided quickly. "They won't find us quickly in this place. The Great One may have to direct the dragon sorcerers to open a gate for us. We should be as close to the place that corresponds to the source of the Radiance in our own world as we can be."

Kharendaen still looked concerned, and it took her a moment to regain the composure of a cleric. Once again she closed her eyes, and after a moment, her entire form began to glow with a soft blue light. Thelvyn waited patiently, certain that she must be having some success. Then he saw the form of a dragon slowly beginning to appear atop a large stone only a few yards from their hiding place. The image remained indistinct, pulsing into moments of clarity and then fading almost completely away. It was the image of his mother, Arbendael, not the Great One.

"The Great One hears you," she said, although her voice was very distant and blurred. "He cannot leave his own realms of influence to cross the void to this place, but I was able to come near enough that I may at least speak with you. What is your need?"

"We have to open a gateway back to our own world," Thelvyn explained. "All other gates are closed to us, and our enemies are at hand. But I doubt that I have the power to open a worldgate myself."

"I think you have that power," Arbendael told him. "What you lack is the means to find your way home across the void. Open your portal and pass within it. Just as Kharendaen has reached out to guide me to you, I will draw you back home again."

Now it was Thelvyn's turn to work his strongest magic. Standing at the opening leading into the cluster of great stones where the dragons had been hiding, he closed his eyes and opened himself to his own powers, seeking the means to open a worldgate. The spell revealed itself to him, but from the first, his greatest struggle was against himself, for he was in pain and his strength was failing. With great effort, he was able to command his full powers. Then he released the magic, tearing an opening in the continuum. But the substance of space and time resisted his efforts to force the tear to open into an actual passageway large enough for the dragons to use, and he needed great will and effort to slowly force his way in.

He succeeded just in time. Glancing to his right, he suddenly saw the dark form of one of the warriors approaching through the clouds of gray dust, slowing as it came within sight of the island of stone where the dragons were hiding. Thelvyn turned to Kharendaen and shook her back to awareness, and then they leapt one after the other into the tunnel of darkness that now stood open before them.

The dragons knew from the moment they entered the passage that something was very different about this gate, something that was not at all right. They realized they weren't moving through the passage but instead hung suspended between worlds, for there was nowhere for them to go. They could see no distant end to the tunnel, since the far end of the passage had not yet opened. In growing alarm, Thelvyn began to wonder if he had failed. He wondered what would happen if the passage collapsed, whether he and Kharendaen would be thrown back into the cold, desert world of the Overlord or if they would be forever stranded between worlds.

Then, just as he was preparing to reinforce his spell, the dragons began to feel themselves drawn forward along the length of the passage. Thelvyn could only hope that they were being drawn to their own world. Then the light opened before them at last to show them a distant, distorted view of fields of deep grass standing under a bright sun.

Thelvyn emerged from the worldgate moments later, moving quickly to one side to make room for Kharendaen. They were standing in the middle of a pasture bordered by stone walls, with more fields or small stands of woods beyond. A river flowed only a few hundred yards behind them, not the Aalban but the Areste, and the city of Braejr stood only a few miles to the southeast. A small group of farmers were rushing across the field, bearing axes and pitchforks, still too far away to see that the trespassers in their fields were gold dragons and not the Masters.

For the moment, Thelvyn had a more immediate concern. He moved well to one side of the worldgate, indicating for Kharendaen to follow him, and then quickly invoked the magic that would destroy the passage. The gate seemed almost to snap shut, drawing in upon itself in an instant until it became nothing more than a point of darkness standing in the air. A moment later that, too, vanished with a great flash of flames that leapt outward to singe the grass in a fan-shaped patch several yards long.

"We made it," Kharendaen breathed, looking very weary. She lifted her ears as she watched the approaching farmers, who had slowed to a walk now that they were certain that the visitors that had appeared in their field were in fact gold dragons. She sighed heavily. "I feel the need of a long drink and a good bath."

"Soon," Thelvyn assured her. "First I must find out what the enemy has been up to during our absence."

CHAPTER SEVENTEEN

Thelvyn and Kharendaen returned directly to the lair at
Solveig's house, unheralded and entirely unexpected. Sir
George and Solveig ran out to meet them in the moments after
they landed on the stones of the court. Thelvyn folded away
his wings slowly, feeling more weary and in greater pain now
that the need for action was behind him. The dragons wore no
clothes to become travel-worn, but he could see that Kharendaen looked dusty and exhausted, and he was certain that he
must look much the same. When he saw the way his old
friends stared at them, he knew it must be obvious that he and
Kharendaen had been through the worst.

Marthaen arrived a moment later, approaching not from
the direction of the Academy but flying in swiftly over the city
from the wilderness northwest of Braejr. Thelvyn guessed he
must have been somewhere in the western mountains of the
Wendarian Range, leading the dragons to prepare a line of
defense against their enemies. The First Speaker undoubtedly
came in a hurry in response to the opening of the small
worldgate, so he must not have been too far away if he could

have gotten back to Braejr in only a few short minutes. He circled around to cut his speed before he landed in the court.

"Where have you been?" he demanded.

"What a question," Thelvyn remarked sourly, sitting back on his haunches. "Obviously we had a little more trouble than we expected, but we've made it back. The only important thing now is the question of what has been happening here since we left. I assume that you've moved the dragons to the west."

"I had to," Marthaen answered. "There's an army of incredible size and strength coming out of the northwest. I've sent out a call, in the name of the Dragonking, for all the dragons in the world to gather here to fight this invasion."

Thelvyn nodded. "That's good. We have seen lines of soldiers and supply trains that stretched for miles, waiting to be sent into our world. I'm sorry to have caused you concern by being so late, but I'm glad you took the initiative for commanding our defenses in my absence."

"When you did not return after the first day, the Great One advised me to prepare our defenses at once," the First Speaker explained. "He assured me that he would bring you back as soon as he could."

"Then he was waiting for us," Kharendaen remarked. "No wonder we were able to make contact so quickly. I feel better knowing that."

"I don't," Thelvyn said. "If I had thought, we could have been home last night and avoided that last fight."

"Last fight?" Sir George asked, his eyebrows arched. "How many did you have?"

"The Masters are not presently engaged in any actual attacks anywhere you know about?" Thelvyn persisted, ignoring the old knight.

Marthaen shook his head. "They simply disappeared after their invasion of the Highlands fell apart. As far as we can tell, they've been gathering all their strength for a final battle, and we are doing the same."

Because the two young dragons looked so miserable, their discussion was suspended for a time so that they could fly out to the foothills of the Colossus Mountains and bathe in a small lake that Kharendaen knew about from the years when she had lived in Braejr. By the time they returned to the lair, Solveig had arranged for food and drink to be brought to them. They still looked very worn and abused, even after cleaning up. Marthaen threatened to call the clerics to inspect them. Kharendaen reminded him that she was a cleric.

They gave a quick account of their journey through the world of the Masters. Thelvyn was grateful that Kharendaen was willing to relate the events of their journey, since there were long periods of time he did not recall. He was also grateful she didn't speak of certain things he found painful or embarrassing. The others were clearly concerned by all they heard, especially about the Overlord. Indeed, Marthaen laid back his ears and stared at the floor, looking defeated.

"Then for all our efforts, we face an enemy we cannot defeat," he said. "Do we have any hope?"

"I see many reasons for hope," Thelvyn assured him. "Ever since he first encountered the gemstone dragons, he has planned to gather his strength until he could lead them here and make his home in our world. The Veydran told me he will lose some of his own strength when he leaves his own world. It is my hope he will not be nearly as strong as he was when I faced him in his own stronghold."

"And you said you made him retreat from you in fear once already," Sir George pointed out hopefully.

"Do not attach too much importance to that," Thelvyn warned. "I do not know why he fled. He appeared to have every advantage, yet he himself made no effort to prevent our escape. Perhaps he could no longer estimate my own powers, and he preferred not to take a chance. At any rate, the next time he faces me he will be in our world, where I am stronger and where I will be supported by the powers of the Immortals."

"Of course, he will also have the support of the Masters," Solveig added.

Thelvyn shook his head slowly. "I don't think so. Think of the Masters as clerics of the Overlord. We have seen already that he shares his powers with them. For that reason, their presence does not make him more powerful, because he has to divide his strength among them. Indeed, if he were forced to

ght me directly, he might possibly have to withdraw his sup-
ort from the Masters to strengthen himself."

"That may be an advantage we can use," Marthaen said,
uick to understand matters of strategy. "If you have to face
he Overlord in battle, we might be able to draw away some of
is strength by pressing the battle against the Masters at the
ame time."

"We will see," Thelvyn said. "If the Overlord has any fault,
: would be that he seems to be overly cautious, preferring not
o risk himself when his enemies can still fight back. But I also
elieve that he will fight me himself rather than see his care-
ully laid plans frustrated. There must be some powerful rea-
on for him to leave behind his old, established empire to
ome here, considering that he has gathered his strength for
enturies for that purpose."

Sir George frowned. "Considering how the two of you
ooked when you first got here, he might just be longing for a
ood bath."

Once again Thelvyn ignored the old knight. "I don't expect
hat he will be willing to fight to the death," Thelvyn contin-
ied. "He will flee before it comes to that. But he must not
scape, or yet another Dragonking may be forced to deal with
im centuries from now."

Solveig and Sir George left to prepare for a meeting of the
ouncil of the Grand Alliance. Many of the delegates of the
arger and more powerful nations had returned since the lifting
f the siege of the Highlands, while others would have to be
eturned by dragon couriers. Even though all the delegates of
he council weren't present, Thelvyn decided to assemble
hose who were in the Highlands at once. Arranging the
lefenses of their world could not wait, and there was one
ther matter he wanted to have decided.

Marthaen hesitated when the others left, although he was
eluctant to interrupt now that Thelvyn and Kharendaen were
inally able to eat their dinner in peace. But there were certain
natters that he thought needed to be addressed.

"I am curious about one thing," he began. "I have always
een suspicious of one aspect of the Overlord's plan for con-
uering our world, which seems to suggest that he is doomed

to ultimate failure. Either he believes that he can defeat even the Immortals, or else he has never bothered to consider them in his schemes. We have seen in the past that the Immortals will react once a situation has become serious enough. Certainly this is the greatest crisis our world has faced since the fall of Blackmoor."

"I have wondered about that myself," Thelvyn said thoughtfully. "I've arrived at one possible explanation, one that fills me with dread but seems to explain everything. Perhaps the Overlord isn't concerned with the Immortals because he has long since allied himself with the chaotic elements among them, perhaps even some of the Immortals of neutral alignment who would not oppose his conquest of our world. He can never become an Immortal himself unless they wish it, but he would make an exceptionally powerful lieutenant who could finally bring all the forces of evil under a unified leadership."

"I see your point," Marthaen said softly, turning his head away and glaring in cold fury. "If a large enough faction among the Immortals support the Overlord, the rest of the Immortals could not oppose him directly. That might be why they chose you to be their champion."

Thelvyn nodded. "I am like the Overlord in that respect. We are both very much like the Immortals in the powers that we can command, but we are not Immortals, and therefore we are not bound by their restrictions. It remains to be seen which of us will prevail in our final battle. If nothing else, we did gain one advantage from our journey. I now know how to prevent the Overlord from controlling anyone who is not already under his command. Whatever alien magic he commands has one flaw, for he cannot command the will of someone who knows his name."

The delegates of the Grand Alliance were to gather that afternoon in the garden of the palace, which was the most convenient place for the dragons to speak with them. Thelvyn made a point of arriving early, before any of the delegates had arrived, together with his human companions and Kharendaen and Marthaen. The dragons reclined under the trees while the others sat on the stone benches of the garden. Thelvyn was a bit surprised when Perrantin turned up soon after they had arrived. Thelvyn had almost forgotten until that moment that the wizard was in Braejr.

"Since I was here anyway, I found myself nominated to represent Traladara in the Grand Alliance," Perrantin explained.

"That's good news," Solveig said. "Everyone there respects you enough to listen to you."

"You're still something of a hero in Traladara yourself," Perrantin reminded her. "Having you hosting the Grand Alliance here in Braejr carries a certain influence."

"That's all very well and good," Sir George commented. "But do they like the two of you well enough to send an army?"

"I'm not sure it matters much," Thelvyn commented. "Except for the dragons, I'm not certain we'll be able to move any other forces to the northwest in time to do any good."

He paused when he noticed that Ambassador Serran, the Alphatian delegate, had entered the garden, together with his adjutant and a couple of bodyguards. Thelvyn rose and walked slowly over to meet them, trying hard to appear unthreatening. It was a wasted effort; not many people could remain unconcerned while watching the approach of a dragon, and the Alphatian ambassador was no exception. Since Thelvyn once again wore the Collar of the Dragons, he was sure Serran knew who he was. He sat down, facing the Alphatian.

"Ambassador Serran?" he said.

The Alphatian bowed to him, recovering some of his lost composure. "I understand that you were away for a few days, Dragonking."

"Everything is going well," Thelvyn assured him. "However, there is something that I must discuss with you. A very urgent matter about someone that I met in my recent travels. Perhaps you have heard of him."

Watching the ambassador closely to see how he would react, Thelvyn spoke the secret name of the Overlord. The Alphatian's expression remained blank, as if the name had no meaning to him at all. For a moment, Thelvyn began to wonder if his guess about the identity of their spy had been wrong. But then he noticed that the ambassador continued to stare with that curiously blank look, as if he had been stunned. The other Alphatians noticed that something seemed to be wrong with their leader, and they watched him with concern.

"Ambassador Serran?" Thelvyn said softly. "Wake up, Ambassador. You might feel as if you've been asleep for a long time, but now your mind is once again your own. Are you familiar with the one whose name I spoke?"

The Ambassador shook his head distractedly. "No."

"It is the secret name of the Overlord. Can you say his name?"

The Ambassador blinked. "I don't remember it."

Thelvyn rolled his eyes, then moved his head forward and repeated the name quietly. The Alphatian blinked once more and repeated the name. Everyone watched him closely, but there was no obvious change in his condition.

"Do you have a jewel of some type that the Masters gave to you?" Thelvyn asked. "A red jewel, perhaps? Why don't you show it to me?"

The ambassador reached inside his jacket and brought out a red jewel attached to a light chain, to all appearances just like the jewel that Thelvyn had taken from Alessa Vyledaar some weeks earlier. It looked like nothing more than a piece of cheap glass, glowing with a pale red light that faded as soon as he took it out. Finally showing signs of emerging from his trancelike state, the ambassador removed the chain from his neck and held it up. Thelvyn reached out and took it carefully in one claw.

"How many of your people have one of these?"

Thelvyn had not spoken in a threatening manner, but suddenly the Alphatian turned pale and began to shake in fear. It was obvious that his terror was not directed toward the gold dragon; he was beginning to realize the truth of just how deeply he had been entrapped. "The Masters are careful not to enlist too many people to serve them. There are probably no more than a dozen people under their control in all of Alphatia."

"That's not so many," Thelvyn said, sounding bright and reassuring, as if he were already in control of the situation. "What kind of promises did the Masters make to your people?"

"They promised that we would be their lieutenants," Ambassador Serran explained. "They said that if we helped them conquer this world, they would permit us to rule it for them when the conquest is complete."

"They probably said the same thing to the Fire Wizards," Thelvyn said. "What they didn't tell either of you is that the Overlord wants this world for his own. What were the Alphatians going to do for them in return? They expected more than your services as spies, I should think."

The Ambassador shook his head helplessly. "The Alphatian fleet is already on the way, each ship transporting every soldier it can bear. If your battle with the Masters does not end quickly, then we will move our armies in behind your allies and attack them from behind, taking them by surprise. No one was to know that we were secretly allied with the Masters."

"I figured that out a long time ago," Thelvyn told him. "I knew from the first meeting of the Grand Alliance that you were a spy. From the very first, I fed you false information that led the Masters into a trap. So even though you never suspected it, you've been able to help us considerably."

"Can you save my people?" the Alphatian asked eagerly, almost pleading.

"That should be simple enough." Thelvyn bent his head around to look at Marthaen. "Do you suppose we could find two or three competent young dragon sorcerers who could leave at once for Alphatia? The ambassador can accompany them and point out everyone who might benefit from knowing the Overlord's name. They in turn can convince the Alphatian army to help us rather than attack us."

"Our people will fight alongside you once they hear of this, make no mistake," Ambassador Serran insisted. "Knowing now that he planned to deceive us, we have as much cause as anyone to hate the Overlord."

The arrangements were made at once, although the Alphatian ambassador needed to stay long enough to attend the meeting of the Grand Alliance. He was concerned that the dragons should have as much support in fighting the Masters as the other nations could spare, and he wanted all the other delegates to know of Alphatia's complete devotion to the cause. Thelvyn was satisfied with the way things had turned out, but Alphatia's potential duplicity was one of the least of his concerns. Although he did not speak of it to anyone else, he was afraid the Overlord would order the deaths of the Alphatian spies rather than permit them to regain their free will.

Thelvyn took advantage of the final minutes before the meeting to have a quick word with his companions. They withdrew to one corner of the garden while the delegates continued to arrive.

"That was very reassuring," he told the others. "I've been concerned that our forces might be vulnerable to the will of the Overlord, the same problem we had during the invasion of the Highlands. Now we can be sure that anyone who knows the Overlord's secret name is protected from his influence. Besides that, we can apparently use his name to break his influence over his present slaves."

"That's nice," Solveig commented, obviously uncertain that the tactic would be as useful as it seemed. "We could hire heralds to run up to their army shouting the Overlord's name, and that would be the end of the war."

"I admit it won't be as simple as that," Thelvyn said. "But it will allow us to free any of the gemstone dragons we subdue rather than slay them. The Overlord permits them to believe they are willing servants so that they can help channel his powers, directing his vast armies of slaves far more efficiently than he could do alone. We can weaken him by taking apart his structure of command, whether we free the gemstone dragons or slay them."

"At least now we have the absolute support of Alphatia," Sir George remarked.

"I'll believe that when it happens," Thelvyn said. "The ambassador is making promises that are not his to make or keep, and the Alphatians might simply summon their armies back home. At least we won't have to worry about having them at our backs anymore."

The meeting of the Alliance itself went smoothly. The delegates were not informed of the events of his nearly disastrous journey to the world of the Masters. They did know that a vast, powerful army was approaching from the wilderness of the northwest, and that the only thing standing between their enemies and their own lands was the dragons. The idea that dragons would be willing to fight in their defense was still new and strange to them. It helped to make them even more aware of their gratitude and their own obligations to the battle.

Thelvyn elected to speak to them candidly on the subject of their defense against the invasion. He doubted very much that the dragons would be able to defeat the army of the Masters on their own. At best, he could only hope to slow the advance of the enemy long enough for the armies of the Grand Alliance to be brought into the Highlands, hopefully meeting the Masters in a final battle at the defensive line of the Wendarian Mountains. The dragons would be at their best advantage in the mountains, and it would be easier for the others to hold the passes rather than attempt to fight such an enemy in the open. He also admitted to his suspicions that the Overlord himself would come to complete his conquest of their world, especially if his army began to falter.

The council concluded with unanimous pledges of support. Darokin already had an army on the way to the Highlands—indeed it was nearly there—as did Alfheim. And while there was no delegate from Rockhome present at this session, Korinn Bear Slayer had made arrangements for a force of dwarvish fighters to defend the Highlands during the siege. They should arrive soon. Thelvyn still had no idea of what he could expect of the vast fighting force that was already on the way from Alphatia, but at least he could be certain they wouldn't join the enemy. He knew that the Ethengar were a scattered, defeated people, living in exile in the hills of northern Rockhome; he could expect no help from that quarter. Of the others, he could only wait and see.

With such matters settled for the moment, Thelvyn was now eager to depart for the west and join his army of dragons. Time was now of the essence; he wanted to begin harassing the army of the Masters, making sudden strikes and retreating again at times and places of his own choosing. Somehow he had to slow the invading army and weaken it as much as possible, and a series of quick, relentless strikes would cripple the enemy most while sparing the strength and numbers of his own dragon warriors. His own job would be to seek out and defeat the leaders among the Masters, since he alone could dare to take on their most powerful fighters with little risk to himself.

The final problem that he had to face before leaving Braejr was dealing with his old companions. Solveig looked unhappy, but her place was there in Braejr with the people she had a duty to lead and protect. Perrantin was already on his way back to Traladara, riding in the saddle of a dragon courier. Sir George looked adamant even before the subject of his going along was discussed.

"We don't have a spare dragon you can ride," Thelvyn told him, approaching the matter cautiously. "All of our dragon saddles are being used by the couriers."

"Well, I don't really need a saddle, do I?" the old knight retorted. "Thanks to the Great One, who in his infinite wisdom has foreseen that you need my help, I can now fly anywhere I want on my own."

"You can't be expected to fight with dragons," Thelvyn insisted. "I know you would have rather been born a dragon, but even the Great One could not grant such a gift."

"I may not be a dragon, but I am dragon-kin, and all dragon-kin have been summoned to this battle in the name of the Dragonking," Sir George countered. "Don't argue with me, lad. I was there when all this started, on the night you were born, and by the beard of Barenthesis, I plan to stay with you until the end."

Thelvyn rolled his eyes, then nodded reluctantly. "Very well, then. Who am I to deny a worthy mandrake a chance to fly with dragons at least once? But if you have anything to pack, you must get it ready at once. And remember that anything you decide to take along, you will have to carry yourself."

The last threat wasn't serious. Thelvyn knew full well that Sir George would need one of the dragons to carry his weapons for him. Although he had regained his power of flight, a drake simply didn't have the speed or the endurance of a dragon, and, even unencumbered, it would be all he could do to keep up. Thelvyn returned to the lair to collect his harness and weapons, which he now wore in addition to the Collar of the Dragons.

Although he had spent the day warning his companions and allies that the coming battle could well be the final one, its outcome likely to decide the fate of their world, he hadn't had time to think much about that fact himself until their flight into the west. While he was by necessity a leader, he was not a general. He wanted to enter every battle with a reasonable certainty of winning. He wanted to know beforehand that most of the advantages belonged to him, or that he had done everything he could to turn the odds in his favor. Now that simply was not the case. He would have to probe his way through what seemed to be an insurmountable problem, winning all the small battles he could and running away from the others.

If he worked at it very hard, if he avoided every mistake he could, and if he was very lucky, he might slowly but steadily turn the enemy's advantage to his own. But he remembered all that he had seen and learned in his journey into the world of the Overlord, and he knew that he was not likely to win this war. He was afraid the dragons would have to pay a fearful price even if they did win. He couldn't forget how their race had nearly been destroyed the last time they had fought the Masters. While he had been made Dragonking for the express purpose of defeating the enemies of his world, he still felt that he had a duty to defend the dragons from danger. He must not let them spend their lives recklessly to help him fight his own battles. He wished there was some way he could send them home and fight the war alone.

The first part of their journey was a fairly short flight to the western mountains of the Wendarian Range, just beyond the borders of the Highland Frontier. Marthaen had been gathering all the dragons of the world in this region, scattering them in a line from the Highland Range to the south to the hills and forests of the north. They were spread out just enough to give each dragon adequate range for hunting, but even so they would need to move on soon before they depleted all the local game. The irony to Thelvyn was that these were the same mountains where the renegade dragons had once pursued his mother to her death, fearing prophecies they did not understand.

The leaders of the dragons had made their main camp in the deep, soft grass of a meadow on the western side of the mountains. The afternoon was fading quickly toward evening by the time Thelvyn arrived, in spite of his efforts to conclude his business in Braejr as quickly as possible. Because there was so much to do and so little time to do it, he was planning to make a brief stop and continue on to the west at once.

"Do the dragons know what has happened these last few days?" he asked Marthaen as they descended toward the meadow, preparing to land.

"They don't know the specific events of your journey," Marthaen told him. "I sent word only that you had returned safely. So far they know only where you went and why."

As they landed in the meadow, Thelvyn was rather surprised to see all the dragons hurry to gather around him. He supposed they were pleased to see that he had not abandoned them to fight their enemies alone. He did look very much the part of the Dragonking, now that he was once again wearing the collar as well as his harness and weapons. He couldn't help feeling gratified to be the object of their appreciation, especially when he recalled how strenuously they had rejected him when he had appeared before the parliament only a few weeks earlier.

"I knew you'd be back!" Jherdar declared, twice as pleased as anyone. "You're too sly to let yourself get trapped."

Thelvyn smiled, realizing that being called sly was undoubtedly a compliment from a red dragon.

"You do look a bit beaten up, if you don't mind my saying so," Jherdar added, watching them with concern.

"I'm afraid I let myself get trapped after all," Thelvyn said, speaking loud enough for all of his lieutenants and advisors to hear. He thought they should know the worst. "I met the Overlord, our true enemy, and it nearly proved to be the end of me. But we got the best of him in the end, and we came away with one important advantage. We now know his secret name, and neither the Overlord nor the Masters can control the will of anyone who knows his name. Now we can go into the coming battle with absolute certainty that they cannot take control of our minds."

The dragons lifted their heads, looking hopeful and talking

quietly among themselves. Although no one had ever complained to him about it, he knew that the dragons had been concerned about being dominated by the will of their enemies. Now they could go into battle with much greater confidence.

"I understand that you've summoned every dragon in the world for this battle," Thehvyn continued. "Tell me more about this. What total strength of dragons can we expect, and how many do we have already?"

"The total number will depend upon how many of the renegades show up," Marthaen explained. "Even some of the renegades are responding to the summons, and many of their bands are here already. There are at least six thousand dragons in the world, possibly as many as eight thousand. We have five thousand here now, assembled according to their kingdoms under the leadership of their kings and clerics."

Thelvyn sighed. "All the dragons in the world add up to the population of one medium-sized human town, and we alone stand before this invasion. I wonder how many will live to return home again. Do you have any idea of the strength of the enemy?"

"We've been trying to make some determination of their numbers," Jherdar said, glancing at Sir George. "We have some drakes in our company, small enough to go places we cannot go and act as spies. We cannot expect their reports to be perfectly accurate because of the very size of the invasion force, but they tell us that there are some five hundred gemstone dragons, about forty of the metal warriors, and an additional army of at least a million, consisting of monsters and creatures of various kinds. The columns of their army stretch across the land for miles. That was as of yesterday evening, a full day ago."

Marthaen turned to the Dragonking. "You said their forces are still coming through the gate?"

Thelvyn nodded. "Yesterday evening I was at the stronghold of the Overlord. I saw armies approaching from two directions, lined up to await their turn to pass through the gate. The lines stretched off into the distance for miles. There were thousands more yet to come, possibly hundreds of thousands."

"Then what are we to do?" Jherdar asked. "Our dragons outnumber the Masters, but we have no support to take on such a huge army. All the armies of our world combined cannot hope to defeat an invasion of such size."

Thelvyn considered that quickly. "I don't think we should concern ourselves with their army just yet. As vast as that force may be, it is the least of the problems we have to face. I think the Masters should be our most immediate concern. We must try to trap them or draw them away in small enough numbers that they can be overwhelmed."

Marthaen nodded slowly. "If it weren't for the Overlord, we could win this war easily enough."

"Unfortunately the Overlord is the greatest of our problems, and nothing else we do matters unless I am able to defeat him somehow," Thelvyn said. "If we have any success in fighting the Masters, the Overlord will come to their rescue. And when he comes, I must be ready for him. Our battle alone will decide the fate of our world."

He saw that Kharendaen was watching him, and he knew that she could appreciate just how difficult that battle would be. He wondered if she had also guessed the sacrifice that he might have to make to acquire the strength he would need to defeat the Overlord.

CHAPTER EIGHTEEN

The ranks of the enemy moved slowly through the wilderness; there was no reason for such a vast and unstoppable force to hurry toward the inevitable. Their destruction of the civilized lands to the east seemed a terrible certainty, so it mattered not to them whether their conquest of this new world took weeks or months. Indeed, the Masters reckoned that they might need as long as a year to enslave the western continent before moving step by step across the islands of the sea to Alphatia and finally into the uncharted continents of the far east and the distant south. They would never again make the mistake that they had made before by underestimating the dragons.

They had fought their way across a hundred worlds, enslaving many and utterly destroying a number of them. In all the centuries of conquest since they had come to serve the Overlord, they had never lost a war. Now they were prepared to do whatever they must to insure that they did not lose this battle. There was no question that the dragons would try to stop them before their forces reached the inhabited lands. Either they and their vast army would be defeated, a seemingly impossible turn of events, or the dragons would be destroyed. But they knew they would not lose the coming battle. If things went badly, the Overlord himself would come to fight with them, to make their victory certain and absolute. Indeed, the Overlord would be coming under any circumstances.

Their invasion force moved slowly across the land, five entire armies marching side by side a mile apart, each army advancing in a column two hundred yards across. Swift, stealthy scouts, Veydran and other warriors, advanced well ahead of the columns, seeking out spies and traps. Great beasts gathered from many strange worlds led each army, tearing out trees and stones and tossing them aside like playthings, while other massive animals followed behind to trample the torn ground into a hard-packed road. After that came the soldiers, rank upon rank, drawn from many different races, interspaced with trains of supply wagons, great wains the size of small ships drawn by horselike beasts nearly the size of dragons, supplies enough to keep even this huge force in the field for months.

And above the armies of the Overlord flew the Masters, hundreds of gemstone dragons of every color. Others led the lumbering hulks of the metal warriors, who stood like mountains of iron over the ranks of the armies. The metal monsters had been marching slowly outward from the secret stronghold of the Masters for the last six days, and ranks of soldiers and supply wagons were still coming through the great worldgate, taking their places at the ends of columns that now stretched for nearly a hundred miles. They would reach the mountains bordering the western frontier in another five days, although their intention was to head south of the great spur of the Wendarian Range to enter the Highlands through the wide valley of Areste River. They expected to fight their last battle with the dragons before that happened.

They knew what the Dragonking's plans would be, since circumstances left him little choice. They knew that their own disadvantage was the very size of their army, forcing it to move slowly through open land. And they knew that the dragons would not wait to fight them in one last battle, but would harass them at every opportunity, steadily whittling away at their strength. The Masters were prepared to do anything to prevent themselves from being drawn into a contest that they would lose because of their smaller numbers, even if they had to sacrifice large portions of their armies of slaves to protect themselves.

Even so, the Dragonking managed to surprise them. He had realized that any plan that was obvious and simple to him was also apparent to the Masters. He had changed his tactics accordingly.

The dragons came not in small, swift raiding parties but in full strength, five thousand strong, flying as low and fast as they could. Darting in and out between the tops of the trees, they seemed to appear without warning from all directions at once, their attack runs carefully timed so that they all descended upon their enemies at the same moment. And they attacked not at one place but all along the twenty-mile length of the ranks of the invaders. The Masters were overwhelmed almost as quickly as they realized that they were under attack. They had kept their own numbers spread out along the columns of their armies to offer the best protection, and now they couldn't gather quickly enough to combine their strength against the overpowering numbers of their enemies.

The dragons descended upon the Masters in swarms, often five of six of them overtaking a single gemstone dragon at once. The Masters that were caught were driven sharply to the ground, their armor plowing through the torn earth among the scattered ranks of their soldiers, some crashing through the trees of the surrounding woods. Many of the gemstone dragons were slain immediately, their necks broken in death holds. Others were simply held to the ground for a brief moment while the dragons spoke the Overlord's secret name to them in soft voices before releasing their captives and withdrawing quickly. In the latter instance, the Masters would most often rise slowly, as if they were regaining their wits. Then they would spread their wings and leap into the morning sky, heading swiftly away into the wilderness like trapped animals fleeing a cage when the door has been opened.

As Thelvyn had expected, knowing the name of the Overlord

had the power to free even the Masters from his control. Perhaps
they had never before in their lives commanded their own
thoughts and will, knowing only what the Overlord demanded of
them. Now that they were free, they wanted to stay free.

Of course, not all the Masters were slain or freed. Some
found openings between the attacking dragons and fled,
although the swifter gold and red dragons were able to chase
down many who managed to escape the initial attack. But
enough of the Masters were gone that the advance of the
invading army was brought to a stop for the remainder of the
day until the Masters who had managed to escape returned
cautiously from the wild and began to restore order to their
disoriented fighters. As Thelvyn had predicted, it was obvious
that the Overlord depended upon the Masters to convey his
orders and redirect the force of his will among his many slaves.

The dragons continued to attack throughout the day, alter-
ing their tactics to raid quickly in small bands. They could
come and go with relative impunity, although they still had to
be swift and cautious during their attacks now that the enemy
forces had stopped moving to take up a defensive position.
The invaders had brought hundreds of mobile catapults that
launched bolts large enough to do considerable harm to a
dragon. Nevertheless, in one quick and simple move, the
Dragonking had left his enemy at a serious disadvantage.

Thelvyn knew he had taken a chance in releasing some of
the gemstone dragons rather than slaying them. If the plan
hadn't worked as he hoped, many of the Masters would have
been free to fight a second time. Jherdar and several other
leaders among the red and black dragons had been uncomfortable with the plan, but their respect for the Dragonking had
kept them from questioning his judgment. Now, as reports
from their scouts came in during the day, Thelvyn's choice
had been vindicated. Of the five hundred gemstone dragons
that had accompanied the invasion force, more than a hundred were dead and approximately another three hundred had
fled into the wilds.

Early that afternoon, Thelvyn received a message that the
leader of the freed gemstone dragons wished to speak with the
Dragonking. Thelvyn had been expecting something like this.

His hope was that they would be willing to help fight the remaining invaders, or at least provide him with some valuable information. He had been watching the enemy from a temporary camp only ten miles or so from the vanguard of the invading army, together with his chief advisors and his bodyguard.

Three of the freed Masters approached a short time later. Thelvyn hadn't forgotten that the gemstone dragons were larger than all but a few of the mature gold and red dragons, but he was still momentarily startled by their immense size. Their strange armor, like plates that appeared to have been carved from precious stones, made them look more like fanciful statues than living creatures. But there was a change in their bearing; their cold confidence was gone, replaced by uncertainty and fear. Their schemes, their will, even their courage had always come from the Overlord, and they clearly needed some time to learn how to decide matters for themselves.

"Do your people understand what has happened to you?" Thelvyn asked.

The leader of the gemstone dragons glanced quickly to either side before daring to look at the Dragonking. "We understand. We have never been permitted to question our service to the Overlord, and therefore everything he made us believe had seemed right to us. Now we understand what it means to be free."

"Will you fight with us to remain free?" Thelvyn asked.

"We would like to fight, but we dare not," the crystal dragon said, looking very fearful. "We are like the Flaem in that regard. We have been under the will of the Overlord for many generations, and his power remains in us even yet. When he comes into this world, he will be able to draw us back under his control once again. The name that protects you is not enough to keep us safe from him. We must stay far away from here when he comes, or he will enslave us again and make us fight you."

"How far must you go before you escape his influence?"

"We can never really escape him," the crystal dragon explained. "There is no place in this world far enough distant that his will cannot reach us once he comes. But if we are not here, he will not know we are still alive. If he sees us fighting in your ranks, he will turn us against you. That is why we must not be here."

Thelvyn nodded. "I understand. Gather your people and lead them into the east. We will find you when the fighting is done."

"You must be very careful," the gemstone dragon said, becoming fearful again. "The Overlord has changed the gemstone dragons in incredible ways so that we may better serve him. He can share his strength with us, making us stronger and our magic far more powerful."

"Yes, I am aware of that," Thelvyn told him.

"But you have not yet seen the worst. When the Overlord comes, he can command the Masters who remain under his will to transform into terrible creatures of fire and destruction. When this happens, you will not be able to fight them at all. Their touch will bring pain and death. Their breath will rend the sky and crack the earth. However, they will not be able to fly any faster than before, so at least you will be able to flee from them."

Thelvyn stared at the ground while he listened to those words. He looked up after a long moment. "Is there anything else I should know?"

"I can say nothing more," the crystal dragon said. "If the time should come that you must fight the Overlord himself, I am not sure what he will do. I can tell you this, however. What you see is only his magic, layer upon layer of powerful magic. To slay him, you must destroy the ancient spells he has woven about himself. I know not what you will discover hidden deep beneath the magic. No one has ever seen his true form."

"I see." Thelvyn straightened and sat upright. "I do not know whether anything you have said will help me defeat the Overlord, but at least I have a better understanding of what I face. I thank you for that. Now gather your people and go."

The three gemstone dragons bowed their heads in a gesture of respect, then turned and hurried away. Thelvyn continued to sit for a long moment, staring out across the miles of wilderness toward the distant armies of the invaders. The dragons remained silent, watching him closely. They could only wonder if he saw more hope in their situation than they did.

"Ah, well," he sighed at last. "Just when we seemed to be getting ahead, we find out just how far behind we really are."

"If you can believe the words of the gemstone dragons," Jherdar muttered darkly.

"I'm sure they were telling the truth," Thelvyn said, glancing over his shoulder at his companions. "I can't really say that things are worse than I hoped. I was expecting the worst, and this was confirmation of my fears."

He rose and walked slowly a short distance into the deep shadows of the woods. The others followed him, gathering around him when he sat down beneath a large tree. They were frightened to see him look so troubled. He still appeared somewhat weary from his trials in the world of the Overlord, but now he looked sad as well. He glanced up at them.

"There's no point in making any small gestures of defiance," he said. "Jherdar, gather the dragons as quickly as you can."

The red dragon nodded grimly. "I will have the dragons ready for your orders as quickly as I can."

"I have only one last command to give the dragons," Thelvyn said. "I realize now that this is my appointed time. I must face the task that I alone was created to accomplish, or else fail in the attempt. The dragons cannot help me. I can no longer in good conscience ask them to risk themselves in battles that will not matter in the end. I dismiss the dragons from my service, and I beg you to lead them to safety. Do whatever you must to take them to a safe place, even if you must open gates of your own and flee this world."

"You speak as if the battle were already lost," Marthaen declared.

Thelvyn shook his head firmly. "I do not believe that, but I must admit the possibility and be prepared. It is my duty to protect the dragons from their enemies. If I can defeat the Overlord, then the dragons will be safe. If I cannot, then they can't hope to defeat him by themselves. There comes a time when it is better to save what we can than risk losing everything."

The others protested, but Thelvyn refused to argue the matter and he would not listen to their pleas. As much as they hated to admit it, there was some truth in Thelvyn's contention that he alone must fight the battle that would decide the outcome of the entire war. At last Jherdar withdrew reluctantly, still grumbling his dissatisfaction even as he began to gather the dragons to lead eastward. In spite of Thelvyn's assurances, they couldn't help but feel that his dismissal of the dragons was meant that the worst was now inevitable.

Thelvyn realized that some dragons would refuse to leave until the final battle was at hand. He needed Marthaen for a while yet, and he knew neither Kharendaen nor Sir George would leave him until there was no choice. Indeed, he wondered how he could possibly convince Kharendaen to leave short of ordering Marthaen to have the dragons carry her to safety. So many hopes seemed to be coming to an end.

Later that afternoon, the dragons who had remained behind with Thelvyn became aware that something was happening to the west. One by one, they paused and lifted their heads to stare into the distance, sensing something. Even as they watched, great banks of clouds began to gather quickly in the west, spreading quickly across the sky in all directions. Within moments a vast, towering storm loomed dark and threatening above the western wilderness. Even as they watched, the clouds continued to expand, as if reaching out for them.

"What is it?" Sir George asked. The first breath of a cold, damp wind suddenly rushed over them, stirring the branches of the trees.

"The Overlord has come," Thelvyn said. "With things going badly for his army, it was inevitable."

"Does he always wrap himself in storms?" Marthaen asked.

"I'm not sure what purpose the storm serves," he replied as he watched the first sheets of lightning ripple across the dark, seething mass of clouds. "Perhaps he needs to hide himself from light and warmth. Perhaps he's lived in darkness so long that he fears to leave it."

Thelvyn had to make some important decisions in a hurry. Now that the Overlord had entered their world, the time was at hand for him to complete the task that he had been created for. He had to find some way to destroy the Overlord, and failure was not an option. The price of defeat was too great. Whatever choice he made had to be the right choice, because he would not have a second chance.

He couldn't escape the feeling that the Great One must have provided him with some means to fight such a powerful enemy. And yet he found himself reluctant to make the final commitment to the fulfillment of his destiny because he knew the price that he would have to pay. There was an inescapable sacrifice to be made in attaining the full powers that had been ordained for the Dragonking, a sacrifice he must pay even in victory. He realized now that he had been trying to work his way around his fate, hoping that cleverness or luck would show him a way to defeat his enemies. Now he knew that he was only delaying the inevitable.

What else was there for him? He had reached the end of his hope, and he had found no other answer. He would not sacrifice the dragons in an attempt to escape his own duty, knowing that they would fail and he would still be left with the same choice. If his concern had been only for himself, for his danger of losing his new life as a dragon, he might have been filled with the same fear and regret, but he would not be hesitating. His deepest regret, he realized, was that Kharendaen would feel he had betrayed her.

As the dragons watched the gathering clouds, their sharp eyes eventually caught sight of the distant forms of gemstone dragons approaching swiftly. There were eight alien dragons in all, more than a match for the small group that remained with the Dragonking. And as the long moments passed, they were alarmed to see that the Masters were heading directly toward them.

"We'd better leave," Thelvyn said. "Now that we know the extent of the powers the Overlord can bestow upon the Masters, I'm sure there aren't enough of us to fight them."

The dragons spread their wings and lifted into the sky, flying low to avoid being seen. They turned immediately to the east, toward the distant line of the Wendarian Mountains. For a moment, it seemed that the Masters would be satisfied simply to chase them from the area. But suddenly there was a brilliant flash of light, and the dark forms of the gemstone dragons were enveloped in flames, transformed into great winged creatures made of fire like an ascending phoenix, trailing long, flickering trails of flame in their wakes.

Now the dragons settled in for a long run, having no way of knowing when, or if, the Masters would abandon the chase. Thelvyn recalled the words of the freed gemstone dragon, that even in this fiery form the Masters could not outfly a true dragon. But as the first minutes of the chase passed, he was alarmed to see that the Masters were not only keeping pace with the dragons but slowly gaining on them. The gold dragons increased their speed, stretching their broad wings in long, quick sweeps. Marthaen circled around behind Sir George, who was struggling to keep up. Drakes did not possess the speed or endurance of true dragons. Marthaen closed his claws around the drake's haunches to push him from behind, so that Sir George needed only to brace his wings to support his weight.

"What are we going to do?" Marthaen asked as Thelvyn moved in close beside him.

"We can't fight them in the open like this," Thelvyn replied as he looked back over his shoulder. While he thought he himself could probably hold his own against one of the fiery Masters, his companions did not possess his enhanced powers. Only he, Marthaen, Kharendaen, Sir George, and two gold dragon bodyguards remained to fight against eight Masters. And the true dragons had no clear idea of the extent of the powers commanded by their enemy.

"I think we could make it to the mountains," Kharendaen offered. "It's about an hour's flight at this pace, but we can hide or turn to defend ourselves better there. The Masters are still a couple of miles behind us."

"We might make it," Thelvyn said, although he sounded uncertain. "I don't know if we'll be too fatigued to fight effectively, but I see no choice."

He had already decided that if the Masters came too close, he would drop back to buy some time for the others. However, he worried that the dragons would not leave him to fight alone. The dragons would be growing more weary with each long mile of the chase, but the Masters were drawing their power from the Overlord. They would not be tiring, and so they would gradually gain on their prey as the chase continued.

The chase continued for mile after desperate mile. The sun had set soon after the beginning of their flight, and day was slowly fading into dusk. The unbroken stretches of woods and meadows became increasingly rugged and began to rise as they approached the foothills below the mountains of the western spur of the Wendarian Range. After a time, Kharendaen took over the task of carrying Sir George from her older brother, since she could use her abilities as a cleric to renew her own strength. Marthaen seemed to be holding up in the seemingly endless chase, but the two young gold bodyguards were beginning to lag behind.

Thelvyn had never expected he would be the first to begin to struggle, but the damage that he had endured at the hands of the Overlord wasn't completely healed yet, and his back and shoulders ached more with each passing mile. By the time they finally began their long, steady climb into the mountains, he was laboring under a torment of burning pain such as he had not endured since those dark, hopeless days in the stronghold of the Overlord. He knew he was hardly fit to turn and fight their pursuers as he had planned.

Indeed, he no longer saw much hope for escape. As the western sky began to darken with the fading of the last light of day, he saw perhaps a dozen more flickering points of light in the distance, following the first group of pursuers. A second, larger force of gemstone dragons was some five miles behind the first group. The first company of Masters was now barely a quarter of a mile behind the dragons. Thelvyn knew it was inevitable that he and his companions would slow even more as the climb into the heights became steeper, and he doubted they would be able to make it to the high peaks.

Suddenly the night itself seemed to shake beneath a great, echoing roar. It was the battle cry of thousands of dragons as they rose swiftly from their hiding places in the woods below. They launched themselves fearlessly at the gemstone dragons, making the most of the element of surprise and their overwhelming numbers. The Masters responded almost too late, calling forth their enhanced powers. They opened their fiery jaws and arched their backs, releasing great, branching sheets of lightning that danced over the mountainside, exploding stone and earth. The land itself was shaken violently, rent and splintered by gaping cracks, so that entire cliffs and hillsides collapsed in great avalanches of stone and dust. Floods of intense flames washed over the lands, so that great stands of trees flashed into fire and exploded in the fierce heat.

But the dragons were already upon them, darting between the lightning and the fire. They attacked quickly but cautiously, guessing that their usual weapons of flame and claw with be useless against the fiery shapes of the Masters. The gemstone dragons suddenly found themselves caught in a deadly hail of large stones that their attackers had carried aloft. Battered relentlessly by stones, the gemstone dragons were stunned and their concentration was shaken. One by one, the magic that sustained their flames was broken, and they reverted back to their usual form. Then dozens of dragons descended immediately upon each of them, forcing them to the ground, where they were slain.

Thelvyn had circled back sharply the moment he saw what was happening. By that chance alone, he suddenly found himself hurtling headlong toward the leader of the Masters, the only member of his company that had been flying far enough ahead of the others to escape the ambush. They came together so quickly that it was almost too late for either of them to react. Thelvyn stood almost on his tail for an instant, breaking his speed furiously with his wings and sails, then dipped his left wing sharply, as if he intended to dart away and escape.

At the last instant, he reached out and caught the gemstone dragon's wing in his claws, holding tightly while he pulled back as hard as he could with long, quick sweeps of his wings. He knew that he was taking another chance, trusting his armor to protect him from the flames that flickered and danced over his opponent's entire form. The fiery dragon was whipped around sharply, scattering a great flash of flames that filled the air all around them as it struggled to catch itself. Each flailing stroke of its wings and whip of its tail raised a storm of swirling, leaping fire.

While Thelvyn didn't feel the heat of the flames, the gemstone dragon was thrown completely off-balance, and the tremendous drag of his weight made Thelvyn's back and neck explode in searing pain. He struggled to maintain his hold, closing his eyes and holding his breath as much against his own pain as to protect himself from the firestorm that engulfed him. In the next moment, the tough sail of the gemstone dragon's wing ripped away, tearing loose from Thelvyn's claws. Still struggling desperately to catch himself, the stricken Master plummeted downward in a flash of fire like a falling star. A moment later he crashed through the stands of tall pines on the steep hillside two hundred yards below, exploding in a great burst of flames.

Stricken with pain, struggling to keep himself in the air long enough to reach shelter, Thelvyn looked about quickly and then circled around to land in a small clearing atop a stony cliff. The battle was over by that time. The Masters were all dead, and the dragons appeared to have fared very well. They all watched for a long moment, staring westward at the flickering forms of the second wave of gemstone dragons, still several miles away. After a moment, their fires went out, and they circled around to retreat back to the west. The dragons let loose with a mighty cheer that filled the night and echoed and reechoed through the mountains.

In spite of his terrible pain, Thelvyn felt encouraged by the swift victory. All the same, he was dismayed by the amount of destruction the Masters had been able to unleash in the few brief moments before they were overwhelmed. Large portions of the surrounding hills had been raked by the lightning and flames of the gemstone dragons, and much of the land was ripped apart, as if it had been cut by random strokes of some immense blade, plowing aside great stones and shattering trees. Dragon sorcerers raced about the hillside, casting spells of dampening to put out a series of fires that threatened to spread through the forest.

Thelvyn's companions hurried toward him, aware that he was injured. Unsure of the extent of his injuries, Kharendaen and her brother moved in close to his side to support him, while Sir George returned to his more familiar human form the moment he was on the ground. For a long moment, Thelvyn could not even bend his back to lie down in the soft grass. He was surprised to notice that he had not been burned.

"What have you done to yourself?" Kharendaen asked as she called upon her clerical powers to begin easing his pain.

"I doubt that it's anything but my previous injuries," he assured her. "The muscles in my back are killing me."

"You cannot be spared the time you need to rest and recover from your injuries," she said bitterly. "Your pain is so great that you can hardly even fly, and yet you must fight again and again."

Thelvyn did not answer, since there was nothing he could say. A moment later he saw Jherdar approaching the edge of the cliff swiftly. He landed lightly and folded away his wings in a quick snap, then lowered his head respectfully as he approached, looking very anxious.

"Dragonking, are you hurt?" he asked.

"Nothing serious," Thelvyn replied. "I'll probably have to go through life as a sway-backed dragon, but the pain isn't too bad. I am far more concerned at finding all of you here, as grateful as I am for your unexpected and timely assistance. You were supposed to lead the dragons to safety."

"The dragons had other plans," Jherdar said, his usual loud, gruff self returning now that he knew the Dragonking wasn't injured seriously. "If you can speak to them, I'm sure they would very much like to see you. They saw that you were in trouble, and they've gathered to await word of your condition."

Thelvyn rose, moving stiffly forward until he stood at the edge of the cliff. Thousands of dragons had gathered in the meadow below him and all along the wooded slopes of the surrounding hills. Although the night was dark and moonless, he was certain they could see him as clearly as he saw them. They sat in deep, peaceful silence, their heads lifted high as they looked up toward their king with large eyes that glittered in the flickering light of the last remaining brush fires.

"It's all very simple, you understand," Jherdar continued after a long moment, his voice alone breaking the utter silence. "I wasn't about to leave you, and the dragons that look to me as their leader were determined to stay as well. When I told the others they were free to go, none would leave."

"None of them left?" Thelvyn asked.

"No, of course not," Jherdar said. Then he glanced away,

looking a bit embarrassed. When he spoke again, it was in a softer voice. "When it came down to it, we found that we just couldn't leave you. We might not have wanted you as our king at first, but you've turned out to be much more than we could have ever hoped. We know you would do anything to protect us, but you've also taught us that there are many things in this world worth protecting. So if you don't mind, we're going stay right here and fight with you, no matter what happens."

Thelvyn closed his eyes for a moment to hold back the tears. "It seems that the Overlord was wrong on all accounts. Just now, I couldn't be more proud to be a dragon."

"Then we fight?" Marthaen asked. Jherdar lifted his head, ready and eager for battle.

Thelvyn shook his head slowly. "No, not yet. So far we've managed to catch the Masters by surprise, but they've never made the same mistake twice. Given time and careful planning, we could wear them down, but now that the Overlord is here, he won't allow us that time. Yet I cannot face him with any hope of defeating him, not until I have the powers the Immortals have prepared for me."

He rose and turned to walk away from the cliff, moving slowly through the dark forest up the long slope toward the mountains. The pain and stiffness in his back had eased somewhat, but he knew it would be a long time before he would be as swift and limber as he had been before his back had been injured in the stronghold of the Overlord. The wounds of his many battles and the great weariness from his many long journeys would not leave him for long. Perhaps soon such things would no longer matter to him. He had made his final decision. The dragons had shown him the courage and nobility he had always believed they possessed, and that had helped him to face his final choice.

The others followed him closely, confused and anxious. He did not dare to look at his mate, fearful of what Kharendaen would think of his choice. He wondered if she realized what his destiny must be.

A little way farther on, they came to a small clearing. Thelvyn paused at the edge of the clearing, saying nothing as he lifted his head to stare up into the night sky. Jherdar and

Marthaen moved to join him, staying just at the edge of the deepest shadows under the trees, and Kharendaen remained at his side. The great storm in the west had continued to grow over the last hour. It was now a dark mass that stretched from the north to the south horizons, flashing constantly with lightning. A cool wind stirred the trees, but above, the sky was clear and the stars were shining brightly.

Thelvyn stepped forward until he was just within the clearing, still staring up into the night. "Father!"

His companions looked up, startled. Marthaen and Jherdar had never known the identity of his father, while the others were surprised that he chose to acknowledge that tie. As far as Thelvyn as concerned, the time for secrets was past. The time of the Dragonking was almost at an end.

"Father!" he called again. "It is my time."

The air in the center of the clearing shimmered as if illuminated by a shaft of silver moonlight, although the moon was hidden behind the mountains to the east. Then the Great One appeared, standing before them. He did not wear his guise of the great three-headed dragon, but rather appeared as what he had been in life long ago, an old, wise dragon of some ancient breed, more gray than gold.

"Your time is indeed at hand," the Great One said resolutely. "The time of evasions and well-laid plans is behind you. Speak your thoughts, and I will answer you plainly."

"I suspect that the reason you have not been able to act directly is that the Immortals are split into factions," Thelvyn said. "Some would defend our world, while others support the invaders."

"That is so," the Great One said. "The Overlord does not know he has supporters among the Immortals, those who champion the cause of evil or seek the oblivion of entropy. He thinks himself above the Immortals, when he is really just another piece in the game. But he is a powerful piece, powerful enough to influence the course of the game, as are you."

"Now is the time for me to become an active player, for I cannot remain simply a piece and hope to win the game," Thelvyn said. "Can you grant me the power to defeat the Overlord?"

"I cannot grant you such power," the Great One explained. "What you are to become depends entirely upon you. There is indeed hope, much hope, but you are still young, and what you are to become will be the work of many long years."

"What of Kharendaen and our child?"

The Great One seemed to share his sadness. "The life you might have had is no longer possible, for you must move on to the place where you belong. You have taught the dragons much in your short time. Not the least the two of you have taught them is just how deeply dragons can love."

Thelvyn turned his head to look at Kharendaen. At first she looked frightened and uncertain, but then she smiled at him and brought her head around to rub her cheek against his breast and along the side of his neck, assuring him that she understood. She understood that only their duty to the dragons and the Great One could come before their own happiness, but that was the price they were now required to pay.

"What must I do?" Thelvyn asked.

"Go to the Citadel of the Ancients, where you first became the Dragonlord years ago," the Great One said. "Wait in the valley below the peak of Dragonwatch Keep. Your companions may accompany you that far, but no farther. When all is ready, I will tell you what you must do next."

Then his form faded, leaving the dragons alone in the night. Thelvyn sat back on his haunches, balancing on his tail, so that he could reach out and draw Kharendaen close to him. For the moment, he was content to hold her tightly.

"I will go with you," Marthaen offered. "You are my king, and it has been my honor to serve you. And when you go on ahead, I will be there with my sister."

"I'm going, too, of course," Sir George declared.

Thelvyn looked at the old knight, smiling. "I wouldn't dream of trying to leave you behind."

"He can ride in a dragon saddle that one of the couriers brought in this afternoon," Jherdar said, then looked up when he realized that the others were watching him. "If you don't mind, I also would like to go with my king."

"I would be pleased to have you," Thelvyn said. "But our company must be limited in numbers. And arrangements must be made for the dragons to keep themselves safely hidden while I am not here to defend them. They must not try to fight the Masters while I am gone under any circumstances."

"I'll see that it is taken care of," Marthaen said. "When do we leave?"

"There is no time to spare," Thelvyn said. "We must leave for the west as soon as possible to guarantee that we reach the Citadel of the Ancients by tomorrow night."

CHAPTER NINETEEN

The dragons lifted over the final ridge and descended into the deep, narrow valley below the peak of Dragonwatch Keep just as the sun was sinking behind the mountains of the Endline Range to the west. The towering bulk of the citadel stood on a ledge high on the side of the peak, nearly level with the dragons when they first came into the valley, although they were careful to keep their distance. For most dragons, the citadel was a place of evil legend, the place where the Dragonlord had slept for more than thirty centuries waiting for his return to the world. They knew now that history had proven very different from the legends, but the tales of death and fear they had heard since the time of their hatching remained to haunt their imaginations.

But for Thelvyn, this was almost like coming home. His life seemed almost to have begun in this place, on the day when he first put on the armor of the Dragonlord. This was where he first began to learn of the prophecies that surrounded him and the duty he was required to fulfill. It was also the place where he had first met Kharendaen. They were events that now seemed like a very long time ago, a part of a life he would soon be leaving behind.

Kharendaen led the way, since she was the only member of their party who had been to this place before. Of course, both Thelvyn and Sir George had been here once as well, but they had approached by the trails from the south, while only Kharendaen knew the way on the wing. She selected the place where they would wait, descending into the evening shadows deep within the valley, gliding low over the towering trees until she found a meadow beside a swift mountain stream. When Thelvyn landed beside her, he glanced back over his shoulder to see that there was a clear view of the Citadel. Now he knew why she had chosen this place.

Marthaen circled around to land closer to the woods, while Jherdar came down near the edge of the stream. Sir George quickly dropped down from the saddle worn by the red dragon. The old knight immediately turned to stare up at the Citadel of the Ancients, over a mile distant.

"I never thought I'd be coming back to this place," he said. "At least not so soon. Perrantin will burst with jealousy when he learns that he missed this trip. My word, it seems like only yesterday."

Thelvyn glanced at the old knight, smiling fondly. Apparently they had very different views regarding the passage of time in the last few years. His life had changed tremendously in those six years. Sir George was still very much his old self, although somewhat wealthier for his troubles and with his left hand restored, a gift from the Great One. He had had the adventure of his life and more than enough dragons to satisfy him.

"I suppose that we should hunt up something to eat before it gets completely dark," Marthaen remarked, looking around at the rapidly darkening sky. "Jherdar, we should be able to catch a couple of elk in, say, an hour or so."

"Yes, an hour sounds sufficient," the red dragon agreed. "Back in your saddle, worthy knight."

Sir George looked confused. "You don't need me to hunt."

"We need your company more than they do," Jherdar told him as discreetly as possible.

Sir George finally got the hint. He climbed back into the saddle as Jherdar lowered himself to the ground. Then the two older dragons leapt into the sky, following the valley southward before they began to rise and move away to the west. With the deep forests of the Sylvan realm only a few miles to the southwest, between the mountains and the coast, they would be able to find good hunting as well as keep themselves away for the promised time. Thelvyn and Kharendaen both had been trying very hard to hide their amusement, but now they sat back and smiled.

"I didn't know your brother was so considerate in such matters," Thelvyn said as he lowered himself slowly to lie down in the soft grass. The long journey from the east had left him weary and in considerable pain, and he had never quite recovered from his fight with the gemstone dragons the evening before.

"Marthaen is finally beginning to recognize that some things are inevitable," Kharendaen said, moving slowly to lie down close beside him. "Although it seems a little late now."

Thelvyn stared at the ground. "Everyone, including myself, has been assuming that this is a time for farewells. But that seems a little premature. There would be no point in my undertaking this quest if I weren't going to return to fight the Overlord."

"But you cannot stay with me," she complained.

"I cannot stay," he said, "but there might be some other place where we can be together. I don't know where, but there seem to be many possibilities. You loved the person I used to be, before I assumed the shape of a dragon. Will you love whatever person I become?"

Kharendaen did not answer in words. Instead, she rubbed her cheek gently along the side of his neck. "I do not know what is going to happen, but I cannot help but be very anxious all this is over with and we have discovered just what our futures hold. Perhaps we were fools to love so much when we have always known our futures were so uncertain."

"Do you have any regrets?" Thelvyn asked.

"I have no regrets," she said. "But now that the moment is at hand, I find that I do not want our time together to end."

Thelvyn shook his head slowly. "I never expected this parting to be an easy one. Even having these last few weeks to prepare myself has not made it any easier."

She looked at him. "You knew that this was going to happen?"

"I suspected it," he admitted. "Ever since the night when we spoke with the Great One at Silvermist. I realized then that there was only one reason why an Immortal should take such trouble to have a child."

"I should have guessed," Kharendaen said, sitting up on her haunches. "Are you going to take your harness and weapons when you go?"

"I don't think so," he answered uncertainly.

Responding to her gentle prompting, he rolled over on his side so that she could release the buckles of his harness. Then he sat up for a moment so she could pull away the heavy leather straps, tossing the harness and the massive sword to one side. After that, she carefully removed the Collar of the Dragons from his neck and laid it aside, returning to press herself closely against his breast. For a time, he sat upright so that he could hold her against him in his arms, and the two dragons gently rubbed their cheeks and muzzles together.

"How is your back?" Kharendaen asked as they lay very close against one another.

"Not too bad," he admitted. "In fact, it might even help to give it some exercise."

For their last hour together, they were able to forget their concerns as they made love in the fading light of evening. They were still lying together, stroking each other's necks, when their companions finally returned. Day had long since given way to a cool, star-filled night. Marthaen and Jherdar circled discreetly for a time, waiting until they were seen before landing. Each carried the carcass of an elk, already dressed out and ready to be cooked. Jherdar collected firewood from the forest while Sir George hurried to prepare a fire, and in a short time, dinner was cooking.

Thelvyn thought that they should hurry, since he had no idea how long it would be before he was called. He had already put on the Collar of the Dragons once more, waiting patiently while Kharendaen fastened it about his neck. In the absence of other instructions on the matter, he had decided he should wear the collar. It had been made for the Dragonking, and as such, it seemed to be tied to his fate. He also considered again whether or not he should wear his harness and weapons, electing to leave them behind with Kharendaen.

Before they knew it, the meat was cooked, but no one had much appetite. It might be only minutes before Thelvyn was summoned. Kharendaen was bearing the wait with the calm patience of a cleric, but Marthaen couldn't hide his unrest. Sir George was also obviously quite worried, although he had always felt he was something of a father to Thelvyn, and he tried to seem good-natured and unconcerned. Curiously, Jherdar was having the hardest time of all. He was both sad and also rather sullen that the Dragonking was having to make some sacrifice that he did not entirely understand.

"I am reminded of a story told to me by my friend Alendhae, a sorcerer among the Eldar," Marthaen said as they sat staring into the fire. "The Eldar once believed in a concept they called the Burden of Time. On the first day after the world was created, the elemental Immortals brought into being the Eldar, the first and oldest of all the races, who were granted the power to remember, to measure, and to mark the passage of time. They believed that time began only when there was someone in the world who was aware of its passage, and that time would end when no one was left to mark its passage. Of course, Alendhae thought the story only proved the egocentricity of his ancestors."

"That somehow sounds like a very draconic concept," Sir George remarked.

"Remember, they were also our ancestors."

Jherdar sighed loudly, almost a low growl. "Do you know what is going to happen?"

Thelvyn shook his head. "I know nothing of what to expect. Those who have taken this path before me have not said much about what they saw. Cheer up. A few weeks ago, you would have done anything to be rid of me."

"It's not something to laugh about," the red dragon complained, looking off into the night. "You turned out to be a better king than I expected you would. I don't want you to do this, but I love you all the more because you are willing to do it to protect our people. You've never lost your capacity for surprising me."

Thelvyn glanced away. "I should have come alone. This wait is a torment to us all."

"Perhaps it is," Sir George agreed, "but I would still rather be right here with you."

The others paused, suddenly aware that Thelvyn and Kharendaen had both lifted their heads and were staring across the fire into the night. Turning quickly, they saw the image of the Great One standing at the edge of the woods behind them, just as he had appeared to them in the mountains far to the east the night before. Marthaen and Jherdar both rose and moved quickly to the other side of the fire, standing almost behind the Dragonking. Sir George retreated as well, nearly hiding behind Kharendaen.

"I am ready," Thelvyn said, trying to sound brave.

"The time is at hand," the Great One told him. "Now you must go alone into the Citadel of the Ancients, where you will surrender the armor of the Dragonlord. Tonight your time of service as the second Dragonlord will come to an end. Wait there. When all is ready, I will come for you."

"I understand."

"Dismiss your companions to return to the east, where the other dragons need them," the Great One continued. "You will join them soon."

Thelvyn bowed his head, and the Great One was gone when he looked up again. He sat again for a moment, feeling very uncertain now that the moment had come. Then he saw that Kharendaen was watching him, and he leaned forward quickly to rub his cheek against hers. The best parting, he thought, would be a quick one, sparing no time for painful farewells.

"I will be back as soon as I can," he assured them. "Keep the dragons out of danger until I return."

"Remember me," Kharendaen called after him as he moved farther out into the clearing.

Thelvyn looked back at her, surprised by her words. "How could I ever forget you?"

Spreading his wings, he crouched low and then sprang upward, launching himself into the air. He circled once to gather speed, then climbed quickly toward the dark form of the Citadel of the Ancients standing on the side of the peak high above. The others watched him for as long as they could, but after a few moments, he disappeared into night.

Kharendaen lowered her head, looking alone and frightened as she stared at the ground. After a moment, Marthaen moved close to her side and placed his arms around her shoulders, holding her tight. Sir George sighed softly and put his hands in his pockets as he walked away to gather his things for travel. Jherdar pulled what was left of their dinner from the spits and the meat to the edge of the woods for the wild animals. Then he sat down and turned his long neck to stare up at the ancient fortress on the mountainside, as if hoping for a last glimpse of the Dragonking. All the world was silent, waiting. Brooding.

"What a night," he sighed sadly. "I feel almost as if the world is waiting for one of the ancient gods to die, and nothing will ever be the same."

"The world waits for a new god to be born," Marthaen corrected him. "If we did not fear for our friend, this would be a time of hope and joy."

* * * * *

Thelvyn landed just below the steps of the citadel, surprised to see that the double doors were opening slowly at his approach. The doorway was small for a dragon, and he had to crouch and crawl through almost on his belly. A soft light came from portions of the smooth, blue-gray stone, just enough so his sharp eyes could see the inside of the citadel clearly. He paused for a moment, looking up through the eight-sided central chamber, where ring after ring of narrow balconies rose into the darkness far above. The inner wall of each level had heavy wooden doors leading into plain, windowless cells like strong rooms. These chambers once held many of the greatest treasures of ancient Blackmoor.

For a moment, he paused to recall his first visit to this

place. He was rather surprised to notice how familiar this place seemed to him, even after all that had happened to him in the last six years. But his errand this night would not lead him into the levels above. He moved out onto the floor of the central chamber, which was sunken slightly, like a shallow pit surrounded by many steps. Once again he paused in the center of the chamber, this time sitting back on his haunches so that he could remove the Collar of the Dragons and carefully lay it aside for a brief time while he completed his first task.

Once the collar was removed, he shifted to his Eldar form and teleported himself into the armor of the Dragonlord, feeling the protective embrace of its deceptively light weight for the last time. No longer used to two legs, he crossed the floor awkwardly to a short passageway in the back wall of the main chamber. The inner door of ancient wood opened easily at his touch, leading him into a larger version of the cells or store-rooms in the rest of the fortress. The remains of ancient tapestries and other furnishings lay in dusty fragments on the floor.

In the center of the chamber was the place where the armor of the Dragonlord had waited through the centuries, or at least the shell of that place. All that remained was a circular stone rail, like those that might encircle a fountain or pool, with a matching circle of stone on the ceiling, once the frame of the pillar of protective crystal that had encased the armor. In the center of the circle stood the empty frame that had supported the armor itself.

Now that the moment had come, he found himself strangely reluctant to part with the armor. He had not actually physically removed the armor in the six years since he had become the Dragonlord. Each time he had needed to remove it, he had simply teleported it by will into its unknown place of waiting until he had need of it again. The armor had always been a source of tremendous security to him, never failing him even during some very difficult tests of its powers, saving him again and again. One of the first things he had to learn when he became a dragon was having to deal with being vulnerable once again, dependent upon his own strength and magic.

But he dared not delay too long, knowing that he was expected. He removed the armor piece by piece, laying it out

on the floor until he had removed it all. Then he fastened all
the pieces back together on the stand in the center of the stone
ring. Finally he removed the old clothes that he had worn
beneath the armor, folding them carefully and laying them on
the floor just below the stand. When all was ready, he stepped
out of the stone circle and turned back to face it, willing it to
seal itself again. The air within the circle shimmered with a
pale silver light, and the pillar of crystal returned, encasing the
armor once more until some distant day when a third Dragonlord might be called to serve.

At last he left the inner cell, closing the door behind him.
When he was back in the open central chamber, he returned
to his dragon form. As he was fastening the Collar of the
Dragons around his neck, the fact that he was no longer the
Dragonlord was finally beginning to seem very real to him.
Parting with his former life was sadder than he had expected.
He had done many good deeds during his time as the Dragon-
lord. For the first time in a life of great uncertainty, he had
finally found some cause to feel proud.

Once the collar was fastened, he lowered himself slowly to
lay his full length on the cool stone floor while he waited. He
was glad to rest; the pain in his back had followed him even
during the brief time that he had changed form, although he
had no idea why that should have been. The relentless pain of
the last few days was almost enough to make him satisfied to
be leaving his former life behind. He was still very young for a
dragon, but in the last few days, he had begun to feel old and
weary. He knew that, given time, a dragon would recover
completely even from terrible wounds, an aspect of their dual
nature as creatures both magic and mortal. Nevertheless, he
realized he had given too much of himself lately; there would
be no going back to the boundless joy and energy of youth.

Had he succeeded? Had he performed his duty completely
enough to feel that he had done well? He hoped that he had.
Certainly he had been a hero worthy of being called the
Dragonlord, not only in his deeds but also in the spirit of his
duty, knowing the joy of giving to others without concern of
honor or reward. He had been a king of men, and a king
among dragons. And the dragons that had once feared and

cursed him had come to respect and even to love him. And of all the events of his life, that was the one thing he cherished most, that the dragons seemed to be the better for his example.

If anything was lacking at that time, it was Kharendaen. She had been with him from the moment he had first become the Dragonlord, the moment he had begun to fulfill his destiny. And she had been at his side constantly since he had become a dragon, absolute and uncomplaining in her devotion to him, quick and capable in her service. She had become so much a part of his duty that it had been almost as if they were two equal parts of the same destiny. Because he had no choice in his service to the dragons, he had come to overlook the fact that all she had done and all she had suffered had been by her own choice, out of her love and devotion to her people, to the Great One, and to himself.

"There is a time for duty, and a time for reward."

Thelvyn looked up and saw that the Great One stood before him. "Father?"

The Great One looked surprised and troubled. "I cannot expect you to acknowledge something that exists only as a matter of convenience to serve a greater end."

"I have not been unaware of your concern and regret about what you have had to ask of me," Thelvyn said as he rose. "And I think I am not wrong in suspecting there may have been love behind that concern."

"And more pride than you may ever know," The Great One agreed.

Thelvyn placed one claw to his breast and bowed his head. "I have come, and I have done as you asked. As I understand such matters, I must now present myself for the final test."

"It seems that you do indeed understand," the Great One said. "You understand that you were prepared by the events of your life, even by the circumstances of your conception, to become the second dragon Immortal. What you may not understand is that there are four common paths to becoming an Immortal. The one element they share is that each requires a lifetime of absolute devotion and unflagging effort. But there is also a Hidden Path, open only to dragons and other creatures of strong magic, by which one is chosen by the Immortals who sponsor him because of his special qualities of worthiness.

"As you have already guessed, I renounced my own Immortality for a time in order to become your father. By that means, you were predisposed to the Hidden Path. The way has always been open to you, as long as you remained constant in your worthiness. Still, the final decision must remain your own. That too is ordained. Because you did not choose to take this path, you alone have the right to choose whether you want to take the final steps at the end of your path. Do you wish to take the final test?"

"I do," Thelvyn agreed. "My being here testifies to that."

The darkness closed about them, so that Thelvyn could no longer see the walls of the citadel. Glancing up, he could see stars shining in the night sky, and he knew they were no longer within the ancient fortress. Now the forest surrounded them, the edges of tall pines barely visible in the deep, moonless darkness. As he watched, others stepped out of the forest to join the dragons, but they remained quiet on the edge of the clearing. The Immortal Terra stood behind the Great One, and he also saw the bearded Kagyar, lord of the dwarves, and the elf-king Ilsundal. They had come to witness the ascendancy of their chosen champion. He realized now the chance they had taken in trusting in the compassion and devotion of a dragon, a trust they must be anxious to see vindicated.

"You must answer these questions," the Great One said. "First, by what great deeds are you worthy to become an Immortal and an advocate of the dragons?"

"I have served as the Dragonlord," Thelvyn answered, although he was certain the events of his life must be well known to those gathered here. "I have been a king among men and among dragons. Twice I have helped the dragons to avoid a war that would have only served the purposes of their enemies, and I have united the dragons in battle against their true enemy."

"You have served well and wisely," the Great One told him. "Now, what gift have you brought in honor of your service?"

Thelvyn was startled and confused. He recalled now those things that he had learned from the dragon clerics of

Shadowmere during the previous winter. One who wished
to present himself for ascendancy as an Immortal must
prove his worth by his deeds, and he must bring to the
meeting a treasure of immeasurable wealth that he has made
or acquired as a gift for his sponsor. Thelvyn had never considered himself a candidate for Immortality, and so he had
not prepared for this meeting. Suddenly he was afraid that
he would fail.

"I have brought with me only the Collar of the Dragons,"
he said at last, still uncertain. "But the collar belongs to the
dragons, and it is not mine to give. All that I can offer as a gift
is my own life, all that I have been and might have been, all
that I have done and might have done, all the love and companionship that I have known and might have known."

The Great One nodded. "You could offer no greater or
more beautiful gift, for dragons value their lives above all treasure, and thus the offer of their lives is the greatest treasure
they can give."

The Great One paused a moment, glancing briefly at his
companions, as if to see if anyone wished to challenge his
judgment. Thelvyn suspected it was not enough for the
Immortals to simply choose for him to become one of them.
Perhaps it was a part of the magic itself, or perhaps just to cir-
cumvent any challenge from hostile Immortals, but he had to
satisfy all points of the tests or he could not proceed. The fact
was that he had not brought an actual gift, but the others
seemed to think the offer he had made was acceptable.

"There remains only the question of the Seven Tests, each
of which must have been satisfied by the deeds of your life,"
the Great One continued. "You have proven your honesty and
trustworthiness. Certainly you have proven your dedication to
your service, and no one could have been more persistent in
the face of adversity. You have proven your bravery, and also
your mercy. You have proven your wisdom. And above all,
you have shared these noble gifts with your people, teaching
the dragons that they, too, can be wise and even great. You
have changed the lives of your people for the better for all time
to come, and that above all else is the most important deed
required of one who would complete the path to Immortality."

Thelvyn became aware of some subtle change within himself. The pain and weariness of recent days was gone. He felt young again, stronger than he had ever been, so full of life and energy that he felt as if he could leap halfway to the stars before he even spread his wings. His mind was clear and alert, his heart was overflowing with delight. He knew he had begun his final great journey, leaving behind his mortality to become a creature of magic.

The others vanished into the darkness, leaving the two dragons alone in the clearing. Thelvyn's right to ascend to the status of an Immortal had been established, and now the time had come for him to complete his journey. The Great One's form began to glow, becoming transparent as he, too, prepared to depart.

"To complete the process of becoming Immortal, you must continue now into the outer planes" the Great One told him. "Spread your wings and fly, and the proper way will be opened before you. As you travel through the places I will show you, I will explain things you must know."

The image of the Great One faded away into the darkness, and he was gone. Unhesitatingly Thelvyn spread his wings and leapt into the night sky. He climbed rapidly, ascending almost straight up toward the stars in a way that no living dragon ever could, as if he had become almost as light as the wind itself. He found that he was rising swiftly above the dark forest of a mountainous land far different from the place where he had been, for there was no sign of the Citadel of the Ancients or the peak where it stood, or of the valley where he had left his companions. This was the place of dreams, that strange land of illusions where the Great One brought his clerics to speak with him, the place where Kharendaen had taken him on the night he confronted the dragon that became himself.

"There are many planes of existence," the voice of the Great One said, speaking to him out of the darkness. "Many are natural in their origin, as old as time itself, entire universes like our own that exist side by side like the pages of a book, each bearing its own story. There are also lesser planes created by magic, many that we Immortals have opened by ourselves and made our own."

As Thelvyn flew, a shaft of pure silver light, like a beam of intense moonlight, although no moon had yet risen in this world, reached down from the stars to intercept him. He continued to climb into the light, which became brighter with each passing moment.

"A place of your own has already been prepared for you," the Great One continued. "Your home plane is created from your memories, from your desires and your hopes. And so it will always seem to you like a perfect place, your own personal world that is a reflection of what you wish the real world could be. It is as large as you require it to be, as small as a stand of woods or a quiet valley, or as immense as an entire world. It is shaped by your own will, so you can adapt it to suit your needs."

The light had grown steadily to a blinding intensity until Thelvyn could see nothing but the light itself. Suddenly he realized he was passing through a swirling white mist like the inside of a cloud. A moment later the mist parted before him, and he found himself gliding gently on the wind above a land very much like the one he had just left. But this appeared to be a more northerly land than the Great One's place of dreams, a place where forests of towering pines carpeted the deep valleys between high, stark ranges of stone and vast peaks crowned with white snow. He felt a slight bite of cold in the wind, just enough to be brisk and refreshing.

He became aware of the shapes of dragons riding the winds of the distant heights, chasing and playing through the forests, or sitting on high ledges to watch the night. Then he became aware that they were only the images of dragons, nothing more than ghosts. They became more clear and distinct as he watched them, until he could see gold dragons or dragons of great and noble breeds that did not yet exist in his former world.

"This is the home of your heart, a world of dragons you wish in your heart could exist, where good and noble dragons can live in peace and contentment. Through your influence, some portions of the true world may someday resemble your vision. Later, when your present task is done, you will return to this place and adapt it to your will. You will make yourself a great castle, where you will live with four gold dragons who will attend you, earning their titles by proving their worth."

"Any four dragons?" Thelvyn asked.

"As long as they are worthy to serve you," the Great One answered. "Do not forget that you are an Immortal. While your service remains to me and to the cause of all dragons, the golds and the other noble breeds will look to you as their champion, and certain clerics of my own order will elect to devote their special interests to you."

The shaft of silver light reached down to envelop him once again, and he moved into the light as it grew in intensity. Then the mists parted, and he found himself in a very different world, a place of still, deep, magical forests. He knew this was the home world of the Great One, although he did not have to be told that, remembering the sacred place of the Great One in the forest of Alfheim. He recalled now that Kharendaen had once told him the Great One had been a cleric loyal to the Immortal Terra, who had sponsored him. This was the place where the Great One was most at home, in the ancient, mysterious forests whose existence predated the coming of men.

A great palace stood on a hill that rose out of the dark woods, waiting vast and silent just beyond the place where the mist had parted. Thelvyn didn't change direction, settling into a slow glide that led him directly toward the main gate, which opened to receive him as he approached. For a moment, he sailed along a wide, dark passage that led in time to an immense chamber. This was the Hall of the Great One, although it felt more like a place of woodland magic than a castle of cold stone. The walls and ceiling were lost in darkness; great stone pillars were carved in the likeness of the towering trunks of forest giants, and light curtains of green hung like leafy branches.

He paused, seeing that the Great One waited for him.

"There is much yet to explain, and I must speak quickly," the Great One began at once. "The Overlord is on the move, and the time of your final confrontation is at hand. But there are words I wish to impart to you before you return to your world."

The Great One joined him, sitting down on the stone floor

and then lowering himself to recline his full length with his neck raised. "As you know already, until now I have now been the only dragon who ever attained the status of an Immortal. There has always been much that I have wanted to do for our people, but I have only very recently become powerful enough to begin acting upon policies of my own. There are two situations that I have desired to act upon, by two different but related means.

"First, I have always been distressed that dragons have been relegated such minor roles in the events of the world. On the whole, they are the most intelligent, the most magically gifted, the strongest, and among the longest-lived of all creatures. In them are combined elements of monsters, mortals, and Immortals. They should be counted among the major races, equal to men, elves and dwarves, and yet they have been little more than animals, the pawns of both mortals and Immortals. Dragons are routinely slain by the designs of mortals and the Immortals guiding them, for their treasures, for the magic artifacts in their keeping, or simply to magnify the reputation of the slayer.

"In part, the problem is due to the fact that dragons have so few advocates and little representation among the Immortals. This is doubly odd, since dragons may become Immortal comparatively easily by the Hidden Path, a path to Immortality that is almost unique to dragons because of their dual nature as both mortal and magical beings. By the Hidden Path, a dragon can be selected in advance—predestined as it were—to be a candidate for Immortality, since he should not even be aware that he is following the Hidden Path until the time of his final quest. So your purpose is not merely to fight the Overlord. I have long needed you to help me unite the dragons and to stand with me as their advocate and to prevent the other Immortals from using them as pawns in their policies.

"The problem is also in large part with the dragons themselves, for even the lawful dragons can be solitary and fierce, even violent, creatures, and few have been motivated to seek the world outside of their own narrow lives. My presence unified to a limited degree, but I have always sought to change the character of the dragons to make them more sociable, much as Kagyar altered the nature of the dwarves. You have already done much to continue the process of unifying and civilizing the dragons."

"I, too, have seen that need," Thelvyn admitted. "I could ask for no more honorable task than to help the dragons to realize the nobility that I see in them."

The Great One nodded. "To that end, you are now to become Diamond, the first dragon ruler, lord of all lawful dragons. Since until this time the only lawful dragons have been the golds, your subjects will be joined by new races of lawful gemstone dragons, the crystal, sapphire, and ruby, once they are freed from the will of the Overlord. In time, I will also create two new dragon rulers: Opal, ruler of the neutral dragons; and Pearl, ruler of the chaotic dragons. Their presence will help to guide the races of dragons into the future that has been planned for them, for while the primary need of the dragons is for law and guidance, they must also maintain the greater balance, with chaos tempered by neutrality. But of the three, Diamond will always be wisest and most powerful."

"But what about the Overlord?" Thelvyn asked. "Can I defeat him?"

The Great One hesitated, considering the question carefully. "You can defeat him if you are very careful. Since he has come into our world, we can see him now, and we understand his secrets better than previously. The huge, terrible creature you see is not his true self, only a manifestation of his will and magic. That is why you can break his will by knowing his true name, since knowing it disrupts the spells that allow him to function through his manifestation. Knowledge of his true name tells you how to stop him, but you must not only stop him but also destroy him. I do not yet see how that knowledge will help you to accomplish his destruction."

Thelvyn sat for a moment, trying desperately to make sense of the problem. "Perhaps what you have said does tell me what to do . . . or at least how to begin. When will I be ready?"

"You are ready now," the Great One told him. "Look at yourself."

Only then did Thelvyn realize how he had changed. He had assumed his new form as a lesser Immortal so slowly and subtly that he hadn't even been aware of the transformation. Now he understood why his new name was Diamond. His appearance now was that of a great dragon very much like the gold he had been, but with scales that glittered like cut diamonds. He had become the very thing the gemstone dragons had tried to make of themselves, so that they were only pale and incomplete copies of himself.

"Go now, but be careful," the Great One said. "Do not try to rely only upon your new powers to defeat your enemy, for the Overlord is very powerful. You must be patient and clever."

CHAPTER TWENTY

As soon as the Overlord began to suspect the dragons were in retreat, he ordered his forces to press forward. He had been trapped by the cleverness of the Dragonking once before, and therefore he proceeded cautiously, sending out the Masters to search out the dragons. He learned that the dragons were attempting to hold a defensive line along the western spur of the Wendarian Mountains, but they were evasive and seemed reluctant to fight. Now he could use the Masters to keep the dragons occupied farther to the east, giving the rest of his vast army the opportunity to advance quickly.

Of course, the one thing that the Overlord could not know was that the Dragonking was gone, having already departed for the distant west. Without the Dragonking, and with his lieutenants, Marthaen of the golds and Jherdar of the reds, away as well, the dragons had scattered into many small bands to hold out as best as they could. They would attack the gemstone dragons that hunted the mountains any time they had the element of surprise and a clear advantage in numbers, but otherwise they were content to flee or hide from their enemies.

And so they passed that first day and into the restless night, while the Overlord became increasingly bold. Yet even now he did not become reckless. He couldn't forget that the Dragon-king was still out there somewhere, and that nothing would be certain until the Dragonlord was defeated. He was totally unaware that, on that same night, Thelvyn had been transformed into the dragon ruler Diamond.

Marthaen and his companions returned to the mountains the next morning. They had flown all night and looked rather the worse for wear after such a long journey, but there was no time now for rest. The main camp was still in the same place, on a remote, wooded plateau in the eastern edge of the mountains. Dragon couriers began seeking him out at once, and he soon had a fairly clear report of all that had happened in his absence. With no better idea of what to expect, Marthaen knew only that he had to maintain the best defense that he could for an uncertain amount of time, possibly several days.

Once he had heard the reports, he called together his chief advisors, Jherdar of the red dragons, Thalbar of the blacks, the cleric Kharendaen, plus many lesser kings and queens among the dragons who had gathered as quickly as they could. His younger sister had proven herself to be one of the most capable and clever fighters they had, although he was concerned that she might be reaching the limit of her strength. Sir George had invited himself to attend the council, and Marthaen was desperate enough that he was not about to deny the devious but resourceful mandrake.

"The Overlord obviously knows something is up," Marthaen said as he sat back on his tail. "I would like to know if he is just pressing the advantage while it seems to be his, or if he thinks that we have been forced to retreat."

"The Masters have grown very bold," one of the dragons offered. "They seem to think we no longer dare to oppose them."

Marthaen sighed, frowning. "We must convince them that we can hold our own, or they will force us into a retreat. I don't know how long we'll have to hold out before the Dragonking returns."

"I told you I'd hurry back," someone said.

Marthaen turned quickly to see Thelvyn sitting patiently only a few yards behind him, although no one had seen the Dragonking arrive. For a moment, Marthaen simply stared, wondering if Thelvyn's journey had been unsuccessful. He looked much the same as always. Then Marthaen had to duck aside as Kharendaen rushed past to join her mate. Thelvyn sat up on his haunches to take her in his arms.

"How did you get back so quickly?" Marthaen asked, confused.

"I knew a shortcut," Thelvyn said evasively.

"Then your journey was successful?" Marthaen asked.

Thelvyn nodded. "I thought it best to continue for the time being to appear in the form that you have always known me. I am now Diamond, the first new dragon Immortal since the time of the first Dragonlord. In my actual new form, I am what the gemstone dragons were trying to make themselves into long ago, when they tried unsuccessfully to raise themselves to the status of Immortals by their own magic."

For a moment, he assumed his true form. His armor shone like cut diamonds in the morning sun, glittering with such brilliance that the eyes of the mortal dragons could hardly bear to look upon him. The dragons turned their heads aside and drew back fearfully. After a moment, they bowed to him with their necks bent low and one claw pressed to their chests. Only Kharendaen dared to look upon the manifestation of his true form.

After a moment, the overwhelming light faded as he returned to his more familiar form. "I have shown you this so that you will not mistake me for any of the Masters, especially the crystal dragons. Today I will lead you into our final battle. Although this fight is my own, I will need the dragons as a decoy to draw the Masters and the Overlord out into the open."

"We wait to serve you," Marthaen assured.

"Gather all the dragons and bring them here as quickly as you can," he instructed them. "The time has come for me to do battle with the enemy I was brought into the world to fight."

* * * * *

Later that same morning, the dragons came down out of
the mountains in a single massive company, now more than
seven thousand strong. They had been gathering quickly
over the last couple of hours, and their numbers had grown
so great that the Masters did not dare confront them. Now
they flew swiftly to the west, rank upon rank of dragons of
every breed. They seemed to fill half the sky. To all appearances, they were making a bold rush directly at their enemy,
as if they hoped to overwhelm the army of the Overlord by
their very numbers. If the Overlord was hidden somewhere
within his fortress of storms miles to the west, watching them
through the eyes of his slaves, he was not greatly impressed
by their brave show of force.

Thelvyn flew near the head of the army of the dragons, but
he left it to Marthaen and Jherdar to lead the mighty phalanx.
He kept himself hidden among the ranks of the golds, hoping
to remain unobserved for the moment. He meant to reveal
himself when he was ready, but he hoped to keep the Overlord
guessing until it was too late. He watched as the Masters
moved out to intercept the dragons, drawing upon the power
of the Overlord to assume their fiery forms. But when they saw
the numbers of dragons approaching, their fires went out and
they retreated swiftly to the east. Thelvyn expected that they
planned to regroup their limited numbers into a single force to
strike the force of dragons quick and hard, scattering their
determined assault.

That suited Thelvyn perfectly. He could deal with the Masters more quickly and easily if they were all together in one
place.

The great bank of storms, a wall of darkness a hundred
miles across that rippled and flashed with lightning, grew
quickly as the dragons raced swiftly westward. They began to
slow as they came around in a wide circle, aligning themselves
in a path that would lead them directly over the columns of
the invading army, heading into the very heart of the fortress
of storms. The invaders had advanced farther into the east
during the previous day, so that they were now within hours of
the mountains. The dragons forced themselves to their most
rapid pace, the larger, quicker golds and reds in the lead, while

the small white dragons trailed behind, their efforts strained by the warmth of these southern lands.

Before long they saw the invading army far ahead, five massive columns forcing their way through the wilderness. The dragons did not lessen their pace but now dropped lower until they were hurtling only yards above the tallest trees. The armies of the Overlord had already halted to prepare themselves for battle. When the leading edge of the force of dragons was less than five miles away, the Masters moved swiftly forward to defend their army, some three hundred gemstone dragons rising suddenly out of the surrounding forest to intercept the dragons. Their numbers represented nearly all that remained of the Overlord's most trusted servants.

The dragons responded to the challenge unexpectedly, at least considering the determination with which they had descended upon their enemy. Their ranks divided and then began to circle around to either side, almost as if they had lost heart for battle and sought to escape while they could. Encouraged, the Masters pressed forward quickly to descend upon the slower ranks of the dragons in the rear, many of them taking on their fiery form.

Unnoticed in the confusion of the moment, a single gold dragon dropped down almost into the tops of the trees as he continued his attack run directly into the heart of the enemy. Thelvyn knew he would not remain undetected for long, but he hoped to take the Masters by surprise. He was just about to pass beneath their forward ranks when they saw him at last. Many of the nearest gemstone dragons turned sharply and darted down to intercept him.

To the attacking Masters, the lone gold dragon seemed to be caught unprepared during those first moments. The gemstone dragons dived at him swiftly, their strange, fiery shapes striking him with glancing blows, hitting him sharply in the wings and back. Any other dragon would have died under the ferocious assault, blasted by any one of the explosive impacts.

Caught off-balance and disoriented, Thelvyn suddenly found himself falling. He struggled to catch himself, but it was too late. He had been too close to the ground when the attack had started. A moment later he crashed heavily to the ground near the edge of a half-cleared track left by the passage of the invading army. He slid through the loose dirt and brush while soldiers ran to get out of his way.

Thelvyn realized his mistake at once. The Overlord had sacrificed control of his army to retain his command over the remaining gemstone dragons. He was only just struggling to pick himself up when the Masters struck again with the deadly weapons of their fiery forms, focusing their attack against him in a fierce barrage. Great bolts of lighting raked over the ground, ripping the earth asunder. Thelvyn arched his neck and roared with pain as one of the bolts flashed over his back. Then he was thrown violently aside as the ground beneath him was blasted by searing lances of lightning. He was thrown heavily onto his back, half buried in mounds of rock and dirt.

For a brief moment he lay without moving, quickly considering his options while the gemstone dragons continued to bombard him with their deadly barrage of lightning. He was reluctant to reveal his true form so soon, before he had even found the Overlord, but his mortal manifestation as a gold dragon was more vulnerable than his new incarnation as Diamond. Shaking himself free of the dirt and debris, he spread his wings and leapt effortlessly straight up into the sky. At the same moment, he vanished in a blinding radiance as he became the Immortal Diamond, a great dragon made of pure silver light.

The Masters could not endure the sight of him, and they turned their faces away. For a long moment, Diamond hung in midair like a shaft of brilliant sunlight in dragon form. Then he arched his neck and breathed out a shaft of intense light, trapping the Masters one by one for a brief instant within the brilliant light. Their flames immediately flickered and went out as they fluttered helplessly to the ground, stunned.

Diamond immediately returned to his mortal manifestation as a gold dragon, although he could no longer try to hide his true powers now that he had been forced to reveal himself. Once again he turned his magic to the task of fighting back the powerful influence of the Overlord. The remaining gemstone dragons hesitated, dropping their fiery forms as their ties to the powers of the Overlord were broken. As they came to realize that they were free, they paused a moment in their uncertainty before they turned to flee into the wild.

It was not only the gemstone dragons that were being freed. In the forward ranks of the invaders, the great enslaved beasts that had been tearing and tramping roads through the wilderness suddenly turned and broke free from their drivers, crying and rampaging in their fury as they escaped into the wild. Rank after rank of soldiers lowered their weapons as the Dragonking passed over their heads. The towering metal warriors suddenly paused in midstride, then collapsed heavily to the ground with the force of an earthquake, like great puppets whose strings had been cut by a gigantic scissors.

Thelvyn flew low over the columns of the invaders as if he were following a road, mile after mile of soldiers, siege weapons, and supply wagons passing below him. His very presence spread confusion among his enemies as he drove steadily deeper into the Overlord's region of influence, shattering the will that had held an army of over a million strong in absolute control. The great fortress of storms continued to rise before him until he passed into its outer limits into its deep, protective darkness. The cold, damp winds grew fitful, and the constant flashes of lightning cast deep shadows through the forest.

Suddenly the will of the Overlord grew sharply stronger, opposing his attempt to seize control of the invading army. He was able to maintain his own will with increasing effort, but soon he was only holding his own, unwilling to expend the power he would need to force back the influence of the Overlord. It seemed wise to keep some of his secrets in reserve.

He found the Overlord where he had expected, at the rear of his army, surrounded by a score of Masters still subject to his control and five of the remaining metal warriors. The Overlord himself crouched in the center of the protective ring. In size and shape, he was very much like the warriors. Although his actions seemed to suggest cowardice, as they had in his own fortress when his prisoners had turned on him and he had allowed them to escape rather than face them himself, Thelvyn knew that he was actually trying to guard his own secrets. However, Thelvyn already knew this great, monstrous being was only a manifestation of the Overlord's magic and intellect, not his true self.

Thelvyn landed a short distance away and faced the Overlord and his bodyguards. Even though he was as small as a child in comparison to his enemy, he had to hope that his new powers were sufficient to keep him safe.

"This must be our last battle," he declared. "You cannot begin your conquest of this world until you have dealt with me."

The Overlord cocked his massive, nightmarish head as he stared down at the gold dragon. "Your powers have increased, Dragonking. Does your Immortal dare to support you?"

"I am his chosen champion. I was created specifically for the task of fighting and defeating you," Thelvyn answered evasively.

"We shall see about that."

Apparently the Overlord still wasn't ready to fight his own battles. Two of the nearby warriors dropped their massive heads, and the red jewels of their glittering eyes blazed with a surge of power, sending forth bolts of intense ruby light that struck Thelvyn in the chest. The force of the deadly beams hurled him violently backward, and he crashed heavily onto his back. The magic of the ruby light somehow seemed to rob him of his powers, leaving him weak and dazed.

The Overlord began to retreat slowly, removing himself even more from the actual battle. At the same time, his warriors began to move forward as quickly as their eight legs could move, placing themselves protectively between the Overlord and the fallen Dragonking. Apparently none of the nearby Masters were directing the warriors; the Overlord seemed to control their massive draconic forms himself. Thelvyn knew that the full power of the Dragonlord had been ineffective against the warriors, and the Overlord was confident that his small opponent could never be sufficient to break his commanding will.

Thelvyn was struggling to rise when the metal warriors attacked again, the beams of ruby light from their jewel eyes raking over the ground, advancing toward him. The very earth was rent asunder, shaken violently by the devastating blasts, which caused the ground to split open in great, gaping fissures before collapsing slowly into unseen depths.

Thelvyn was struggling to retreat from the fury of the assault when he was struck once more by the beams of ruby light. This time he was held trapped as several of the beams ripped over the ground to focus upon him. He was thrust down against the torn earth and held there, as if by some crushing weight. His neck arched in intense pain. His jaws were wide as if to roar out in his agony, but he had no breath to cry out. It was as if the power of the ruby light was ripping apart his very being. Then the ground beneath him tilted and began to slide away, hurtling him into the depths of the ragged fissure that had opened behind him.

He seemed to fall for a very long time, crashing against first one side of the gaping chasm and then the other as he plummeted into the darkness. Unable to catch himself, he finally landed heavily atop the loose debris of dirt and stone at the bottom of the fissure, snapping his chin violently against the ground. So weak that he could hardly move, he began to lift himself slowly and painfully in an attempt to escape that place before the warriors could trap him there.

Then the darkness at the bottom of the chasm grew even deeper, and he looked up apprehensively to see that one of the warriors was leaning out over the opening of the fissure more than three wingspans above him, as if it intended to climb down after him. It tottered on the edge for a moment before it fell, its incredible weight crashing downward in a shower of dirt and boulders.

Thelvyn instinctively dropped to the ground and lowered his head, preparing himself for the crushing impact of hundreds of tons of metal. Massive stones rained down upon him, and he was nearly buried in masses of damp earth, but the warrior itself slammed to a halt a couple of yards above him, its eight legs pinned against the sides of the chasm. Shaking his head free from the debris, Thelvyn glanced up fearfully. He had not been in danger of death—as an Immortal, he knew he could not easily be killed—but the destruction of his mortal manifestation would have forced him to retreat to his own plane to recover his powers, leaving the Overlord unopposed in his conquest of the world.

Nor was the fallen warrior so easily destroyed. Although it hung upside down near the bottom of the chasm, it continued to struggle. Thelvyn pulled himself free of the dirt and stone covering him and began to work his way through the darkness until he finally crawled out from beneath the trapped warrior. He still felt weak and his powers remained uncertain, but his magic was slowly beginning to return. He ran a short distance along the bottom of the long chasm, intending to climb out in a place where his enemies might not be expecting him. The fissure continued to collapse slowly in a constant rain of dirt and stone, making the task of clawing his way out even more difficult. The effort required to pull himself from the chasm was tremendous, but using magic to free himself would have alerted the Overlord to his escape.

He climbed out at last into a scene of tremendous destruction. The attack of the warriors had devastated the landscape for hundreds of yards around the area of the battle. The ground had been ripped open by several gaping fissures, and boulders and great mounds of earth had been heaved aside. The remaining four warriors stood motionless some distance away, hesitant to enter the region of destruction because of the threat of becoming trapped. Thelvyn couldn't see the Overlord, but that meant the Overlord couldn't see him, giving him a moment more to recover his strength.

What he had forgotten in his desperation was that the Overlord could see through the eyes of his warriors. One of the metal beasts turned its head abruptly toward him, its jewel eyes glowing fiery red. One after another, the immense fighting machines turned and began to move ponderously in his direction, the smoldering lights in their eyes growing steadily brighter. Thelvyn knew they would begin attacking again at any moment, and he also knew he had not yet fully recovered his full strength. Desperate to protect himself, he employed the only defense he could think of, reaching out with his will to attempt to seize control of the crystal eyes of the warriors.

The Overlord was already sending vast amounts of his own power into the jewels, turning them into deadly weapons, but nevertheless Thelvyn's will was enough to prevent the discharge of that power. He had expected the Overlord to back off once the power had nowhere to go, but it seemed that his opponent was more stubborn than he thought, considering how cautious the Overlord had been in the past. The eyes of the warriors continued to grow brighter and brighter until they blazed like small red suns, and then, one after the other, the massive iron heads of the warriors exploded in rapid succession. The enchantments that controlled them destroyed, their lifeless forms collapsed heavily to the ground.

Thelvyn immediately seized the moment to launch his own attack, leaping up and bounding across the ruins of the battlefield. In the next moment, a crushing force like a vast, invisible fist struck him in the chest, knocking him completely off his feet and sending him hurtling backward. Circumstances now demanded that the Overlord fight for himself, setting aside his usual caution to act directly, and he was obviously no coward. But Thelvyn was no longer so easily harmed; after a moment, he was able to spread his wings and catch himself in midair, returning quickly to the circle of combat.

He drove directly at the Overlord, rushing forward at tremendous speed. Although he was hesitant to reveal his true powers so soon, he knew that this was only the prelude to their true battle. He ducked down almost to the ground and then thrust himself back up again, striking the Overlord hard just under his chest, lifting his great bulk completely off the ground and flipping him over to crash heavily onto his back. The Overlord's remaining bodyguards, some twenty gemstone dragons, attacked at the same moment, having assumed their fiery forms. They began to dive at Thelvyn in a series of swift, relentless attacks, pummeling him over and over with bolts of lightning.

He dropped quickly to the ground, trying desperately to think. Already he understood something important about his enemy: The Overlord's powers were most effective when directed through his servants like the Masters and the warriors, but he wasn't very good at defending himself. That might have been due to the nature of his magic or perhaps a reflection of his inexperience; the reason hardly mattered now. Thelvyn decided the time for caution was past; he would reveal his true powers as an Immortal and press the contest to its conclusion.

Again he leapt into the air, and his mortal manifestation melted away in the glare of silver light as he revealed himself to be the Immortal Diamond. This time he made no effort to contain his powers but allowed the radiance of his true being to shine forth, many times brighter than the sun itself. The pure, intense light drove away the fires of the Masters like a wind blowing out a candle flame. The Overlord's command of their minds and will was broken, and they fled.

Even the Overlord had been forced to turn his monstrous face from the radiance, shielding himself with the grotesque armor of his back as he began to slink away. The pure light of the Immortal seemed to be causing him great pain, burning into his very being. Diamond continued to press his attack relentlessly. Suspended in the air above the scene of battle, he arched his long neck and opened his mouth to release a shaft of silver light that washed over his enemy's long back. The Overlord crouched with his head down in an effort to protect himself while smoke and flames spread across his back, eating into his armor.

And then he vanished, retreating from a fight that he had already lost. But Thelvyn was too cautious to believe that he had achieved ultimate victory, knowing he had only forced the Overlord to retreat to a place where he would be stronger. Thelvyn turned to fly swiftly toward the west, following the wide path trampled by the invading army. He was still half of an hour's flight from where he expected to find the stronghold, time that he could not afford to spare if he was to catch his true enemy off guard. He held his wings steady, as if soaring on the winds, but his speed began to increase rapidly until his form began to blur into a shaft of silver light, crossing a hundred miles in as many seconds.

In a region scattered with low, steep hills, he came upon the hidden stronghold abruptly. Like the main stronghold in the world of the Overlord, it consisted of a group of massive fortresses, imposing in size but simple and nearly featureless in design, arranged not in a grid but in two concentric rings. In the center of the stronghold stood the stone arch of the immense worldgate. The land for miles around had been stripped of trees, perhaps during those final days while the invading army had gathered there before marching to the east. The stronghold was nearly deserted now, defended only by a score of gemstone dragons that had already risen into the sky in defense.

Thelvyn slowed quickly from his tremendous speed, although he remained in immaterial form for the moment, rising upward a short distance as he cast about with his mind for the presence of the Overlord hidden somewhere deep within the stronghold. Then he gathered speed again, streaking down like a bolt of lighting as he crashed directly into the roof of the largest of the fortresses. Massive stones shattered before him as he blasted his way deep into the center of the fortress. Then the fortress itself exploded outward in a blinding flash of clear light.

The central chamber of the fortress lay exposed to the sky. The middle part of the ceiling had been rent asunder, and a gaping hole reached up through all the levels of the fortress to the air above. Dark clouds above rolled and flashed with lightning. The dust cleared slowly, and the vast, threatening form of the Overlord stepped slowly out of the darkness to confront Diamond a second time. There was no sign of the damage that the dragonfire had done to the armor of his back; he had renewed his form, and he appeared to be stronger than ever.

"Clever little dragon," he said contemptuously. "You have grown more than you let on."

Thelvyn did not respond, knowing he had to proceed cautiously. He could fight and defeat the Overlord time and again and never win the real war. It was crucial for him to discover his opponent's secret, to find the source of his hidden power.

He moved slowly to one side, circling around his enemy and watching the Overlord closely for any clue to his secret. The source of his power was somewhere very near, he was certain, but he could not sense what it was. Nor could he see through the manifestation of the Overlord to his true self. The retreat of the Overlord from his first battle and his appearance here unharmed proved that this was not his true being. The source of his magic and his consciousness had always prevented him from going into any of the worlds he had conquered. Apparently he had brought it with him into this world, but with great difficulty.

Was it something large? Something difficult or dangerous to try to move? Or perhaps, Thelvyn wondered, it was something too delicate to risk. Somehow it managed to avoid betraying its presence as a tremendous source of magic even as it sent its full power directly to its manifestation.

Thelvyn was caught off guard, having given too much of his attention to his thoughts. The Overlord opened his massive jaws and let forth what at first appeared to be a flash of misty white light, except the light turned solid almost immediately. It struck Thelvyn in the shoulder with crushing force, smashing him backward across the floor of the dark chamber until he was hurled against the stone wall. The shaft of white shattered with the impact, fragments exploding in all directions. Shaken by the attack, Thelvyn was picking himself up when he saw that the object that had hit him had been a column of ice, which now lay scattered in shards across the floor.

Then another massive shaft of ice struck him, blasting him backward against the wall even harder than before. A third column of ice struck him, then another. Spears of ice continued to crash against him and the surrounding wall, like a hail of heavy stones from an army of ballistae, until the stones of the wall itself began to crumble and collapse about him. Thelvyn clawed his way desperately out of the rubble, pushing aside broken stones and emerging moments later from the top of the dusty wreckage.

He had been rather shaken by that last assault. He moved slowly at first as he climbed out of the debris and paced back out into the vast chamber to confront his enemy, his back and neck arched in challenge. The Overlord was watching him in growing rage, but Thelvyn also noticed a hint of fear.

"What are you?" he demanded. "What manner of creature have you become?"

Thelvyn had no intention of answering, but he would not have had the chance in any event. In the next moment, bolts of lightning streaked down from the dark clouds through the gaping hole in the ceiling to strike him. For a time, he could only crouch low, his face turned down toward the floor to protect his eyes, enduring the deadly touch as fingers of lightning played across his back. Even as powerful as he had become, the unrelenting blast of such tremendous energy was unbearably painful. He knew that if he tried to run, the lightning would pursue him. And so he crouched, waiting for it to end. The flash of brilliant light was blinding, and the stones shook with the blast of thunder.

He was not even aware that the attack had ended until he realized that the darkness had returned and the last echoes of thunder were dying away. He lifted his head slowly and beheld a remarkable scene. The hail of raw lightning into the depths of the chamber had filled even the vast space with a tremendous amount of power, burning away the air so that no mortal creature could have lived in that place. Wisps and streams of ghostly lights hung in the air like fog or crawled across the seared floor like mist, glowing in shades of red, yellow, and orange, filling the great chamber with an eerie radiance.

The Overlord stood in the midst of the thin clouds of fiery mists, his head raised high. The crests and spines of his grotesque armor shone with ghostly lights of their own, and he seemed to pulse from the power that he was drinking in, as if he thrived in the deadly environment. Now Thelvyn understood. The Overlord was so distracted with pleasure that he had just inadvertently betrayed his own deepest secret. It was the outer world that was alien to him, robbing him of his powers—warm sunlight and fresh, cool winds and green, growing things. He had nearly destroyed one world to protect himself from the lifegiving things that were like poison to him. Hiding himself in dark storms and deep, remote places like his strongholds renewed his strength.

The revelation told Thelvyn which of his weapons would be most deadly to such a creature. Lifting his head high, he summoned his powers as the Immortal Diamond. The pure, jeweled facets of his armor shone with blinding light, a pure, brilliant white that chased away the ghostly lights that played in the darkness of the chamber. Then, standing tall on his hind legs, he seemed almost to explode in the radiant pure crystal light.

The Overlord flinched and drew back, desperate to shield

his eyes from the light. With nowhere to retreat, he tried t
turn the heavy armor of his back toward the blinding bri
liance, as if the light itself caused him tremendous pain. Th
white radiance began to cut into him with each passin
moment, shredding his substance and tearing it away lik
scraps of paper. Diamond released a final sustained flash o
intense light, and the massive, grotesque body of the Overlor
dissolved in the glare.

But even that was not yet the end of the Overlord. Floatin
in the air where his body had been was the source of his wi
and power, the true self he had kept hidden inside the shell o
the Overlord. It didn't even seem alive. What Diamond sa
was a strange, utterly alien entity of crystal, bristling wit
quartzlike spikes of rose and gold and blue and green. Th
was a creature of the most remote of the outer planes, wher
all things were utterly different from the familiar life of th
mortal realms. Long ago it had wandered through the plane
whether by chance or by misfortune or by deliberate choic
coming at last to a world where its unearthly powers had mad
it seem like a god. But mortal life was deadly to it, so it ha
been forced to create the protective form of the Overlord i
which it could hide.

The pure light of Diamond's very being was destructive t
it. The crystal structures of its being began to grow cloud
and pale, cracking and crazing. Then the dying she
exploded, and thousands of small lengths of crystal fle
apart and scattered across the floor of the chamber, wher
they evaporated like mist.

Diamond subdued his brilliant light, transforming himse
once more to the manifestation of his mortal form, th
Dragonking. The battle was done, and he realized now tha
the Immortals had chosen their champion wisely, for the pu
diamond light of his very being had proven to be his mo
deadly weapon. Spreading his wings, he leapt into the air an
flew up through the great hole that had been blasted throug
the fortress. As he emerged into the sky above, he employe
his powers a final time to seal the chamber and transform
into the tomb of the Overlord. The vast stronghold shook an
began to collapse. In moments, the chamber that had been th

place of his final battle with the Overlord was buried deep in a mound of crushed and broken stone.

Thelvyn turned and flew back toward the mountains of the east. There was no longer any need for haste. All the creatures and objects sustained by the will of the Overlord were now falling apart. The great worldgate sealed itself in a sudden flash of flame, while the last of the gemstone dragons fled into the wild. The Overlord's armies were now without direction, lost and frightened, and the strange beasts that had been enslaved to his will ran wild in an unfamiliar world.

For the moment, Thelvyn felt as lost and bewildered as any of the Overlord's former slaves. The purpose of his very existence had been fulfilled. For the first time in recent memory, there were no immediate challenges to face, no dire enemies to be fought, no sense of desperation driving him from one moment to the next. For the first time, his life was now his own. He hardly knew what to do with it.

Of course, there was still a large part of his world needing to be set right after the devastation of war. But that was a task he would leave to others, for his time was drawing to an end.

* * * * *

The dragons sensed that Thelvyn had defeated the Overlord when they saw the fortress of storms begin to disperse, the lightning grow still, and the dark clouds blow off in the wind. But they had not truly dared to believe in their victory until the Dragonking himself returned out of the wilderness to assure them that their enemy was destroyed. That night they celebrated the triumph of their king in the mountains of the Wendarian Range. They hunted that afternoon and roasted the meat they caught in great, cheerful blazes, drinking from barrels of wine and ale their messengers had brought back from the Highlands and Darokin and other lands when they spread the news of the Dragonking's victory. It was the first time in their long history that the entire race of dragons had been brought together in celebration.

The dragons had more than enough to keep them busy over the next few days. The most immediate problem was what to

do with an invading army of vast proportions that no long
wished to fight. The Masters had ceased to exist with the pa
ing of the Overlord; they were now only gemstone dragon
not so terribly different from their estranged brethren. T
moment they felt the death of the Overlord, they had becon
free of him forever. And so they had begun to timidly seek o
the dragons even that first night, drawn by the lights of t
fires of celebration. The Dragonking had pardoned them a
called upon them to gather together their scattered numbe
so that they could help to set right many of the troubles l
from the invasion.

The Overlord's countless other slaves presented a mu
larger problem, and one that proved more difficult to solv
With the help of the gemstone dragons, the dragon sorcere
reopened the great worldgate to the main stronghold of t
Overlord in his old world, and from there they were able
locate many of the lesser gateways into other worlds that h
been invaded. In this way, many of the slave races of the Ove
lord had returned to their own worlds, homes that most
them had not seen in generations. There were some who cou
not be sent home, either because their worlds had be
destroyed or the gates were lost. After some negotiation, ma
of the nations of the Grand Alliance agreed to take in the
wanderers, so that they came to settle in the Highlands,
nearby Darokin and Traladara, and even in distant Alphatia

The beasts were also a problem, not only in the mountai
ous west but also in places like the Highlands and Rockhon
where large numbers of them had escaped during previo
battles. Most were of exotic breeds, too dangerous to
allowed to run free in this new world, and there was nothi
else to be done but have the dragons hunt them down and s
them. Those that could be captured were returned to t
worlds of their origin whenever it could be determine
Inevitably, some escaped into the wild despite the best effo
of the dragons.

At last the day came when the dragons had done all th
could, and it was time for them to go home. Some departe
for Windreach in the distant east, but most of the drago
would be returning to their own territories throughout t

world. Thelvyn would soon be going to Windreach himself, but first he had to go to Braejr with his companions for a final meeting of the Grand Alliance. Marthaen and Jherdar had to leave for the east immediately to attend to responsibilities of their own, but Kharendaen would not be parted from her mate. Once again Sir George rode in the saddle she wore.

The Highlands had been greatly unsettled during the war, and Braastar stood partly in ruins, but the Flaem were joined by many of their kinsmen who had been held in slavery by the Overlord. Some other captive races settled there as well, and the newcomers worked very hard to rebuild their new homeland. Thelvyn met with the delegates of the Grand Alliance for the last time, thanking them for their assistance before dismissing them to return to their own lands.

Of course, no one but the dragons knew that Thelvyn was now the Immortal called Diamond; that was a secret they would keep to themselves forever. After his battle with the Overlord, he didn't resume his Immortal form but returned to his manifestation as a gold dragon. He was now a lesser Immortal and bound by the laws that governed the actions of the Immortals; soon he would be required to distance himself from the affairs of the world. He met that night for the last time with his companions in the lair at Solveig's house. Darius Glantri was there, as well as Korinn Bear Slayer and Perrantin, who had arrived by dragon that same morning to represent Traladara in the Grand Alliance. As much as Thelvyn regretted it, he couldn't allow even his old friends to know his secret, and so he didn't know what to tell them when they asked what he would do now and when he might return.

"Are you well?" Solveig asked Thelvyn as he reclined in the large bed, a barrel of sweet Flaemish ale beside him.

Thelvyn was surprised by the question. "Don't I look well?"

Solveig shrugged. "Actually, you do. That's the part I'm worried about, considering all you've been through these last few weeks. When you came here a few days ago after your adventures in the world of the Overlord, you looked nearly dead."

"Be assured that I am feeling very well indeed," he insisted. "For the first time, my life now belongs to no one but me. And

I have places to go."

"But first to Windreach," Sir George declared as he stared
at a glass of his favorite cherry liqueur.

"Are you going along as well?" Korinn asked the old knight

"I have asked Sir George to come with me," Thelvyn said
"Perhaps this will be our last journey together. We will see."

"Well, I've been keeping you out of trouble this long," Sir
George said, a remark that caused the dragons to twitch their
ears.

"Just don't forget your other friends," Korinn declared. "At
least now, for the first time in all the years I've known you, I
won't have to be worrying about you."

"We've all spent enough time worrying about Thelvyn to
last a lifetime," Solveig said. "For such a strange, awkward
kid, you've turned out to be quite a handsome dragon."

Early the next morning, the two dragons collected Sir
George and departed for the east. They wandered a bit on
their way, checking to see that all the damage from the invasion of Rockhome was in the process of being repaired. The
rains of late spring had done much to restore the blackened
steppes of the Ethengar to their familiar green. The herds
were gradually returning, and the clans of the Ethengar
would soon return from their exile in the mountains of
northern Rockhome.

The return of the Dragonking to Windreach the next day
was a matter of great celebration. The dragons feasted him
and his companions all through the night. The next morning
he presented himself to the Parliament of the Dragons, for he
knew his time to leave was at hand. He formally introduced
himself as Diamond, the new dragon Immortal, who had
been sent back into the world to guide and to protect the
dragons, and he briefly assumed his Immortal form to prove
his statement. He explained that finally the prophecy of the
dragons had been fulfilled, not as they had feared but with
the hope of lasting peace for the future for dragonkind. He
added that he would no longer be their king; the Parliament
of Dragons would govern their affairs, and he would only be
an advisor.

He tried to give the Collar of the Dragons back to them, but the parliament refused to accept it and asked him to continue to hold it in trust. Marthaen explained that the dragons had already discussed the matter, and it was their wish that Thelvyn should always hold the title of Dragonking in honor of the great battle that he had fought for them.

That night the dragons feasted the Dragonking a second time, after which they went out into the mountains of Norwold to sing. In the past, the dragons had sung their ancient songs on special nights of the year, such as midwinter night and midsummer night, but they had lost heart for the old festivals when the Great One had left them some three decades earlier. Now they felt like singing once more.

This was something very new for Thelvyn, who didn't know any of the ancient songs. He listened with delight as the dragons sat back on their haunches, looped their tails about their legs, lifted their long necks high, and sang to the stars. The song of the dragons was legendary, even among other folk, for dragons had very strong, clear voices, and their great chorus would ring through the mountains on a clear night, carried on the wind for great distances. Elves would walk hundreds of miles to hear them, and weep with joy at the sound.

They built great bonfires on the remote plateau where they gathered, and they brought out barrels of wine and large, deep drums to keep time while they sang their livelier songs. To the surprise of all, it was Kharendaen herself who was the first to dance. Everyone was even more impressed to see how well she danced, for she was young and strong, and very lean and graceful. She rose up on her long hind legs with her wings half furled, bending and swaying between quick, prancing steps in time with the rhythm of the drums. The gold and tan patterns of her armor seemed to shimmer in the dancing firelight, and her large eyes glittered. Watching her, Thelvyn was proud that her love was given to him.

"There has never been another like her," Jherdar said in admiration. "Cleric and warrior. Wise and fierce, brave and beautiful. Only an Immortal could be worthy of her."

Sitting close to his own mate, Daresha, Marthaen smiled in wry amusement. "My little sister has grown up."

Sir George had brought out a bottle of cherry liqueur from

his pack, which he now lifted in salute. "To the best dragons that ever lived!"

"Who is that?" Jherdar asked, staring down at him.

"Why, the whole damned lot of you, of course," the old knight declared. "I hope you're all proud of yourselves, because you've earned it."

"You make us sound like heroes," Jherdar laughed, but then he paused and looked more serious. "I regret that many of our actions from the start were nothing to be proud of. We look at things quite differently now."

"That's what the Great One wanted most of all," Thelvyn said. "He would tell you not to regret your mistakes if you have learned from them."

"Then you forgive us for the grief we caused you?" the red dragon asked.

"I forgave you long ago," Thelvyn said. "Actually, getting to knock you around when I first became Dragonlord made me feel a lot better."

Jherdar laughed. "The only fight I ever had that I'm happy to have lost. But since this night seems to be for handing out praise, there is another who should not be overlooked. First Speaker, what honor do we have for the prince of drakes?"

Marthaen turned his head to look at the old knight. "I hereby proclaim Sir George Kirbey a Fellow of the Parliament of Dragons. At special times, he will be brought to Windreach to speak before parliament on behalf of the dragon-kin. And if Sir George Two-Hands would be gracious enough to give us the hook that he wore for so long, it will be given a place of honor among the treasures of the dragons in the Hall of the Great One."

"That's a bit much praise for me," Sir George remarked. "But I think I will accept it all the same, since it's high time for the dragons to stop overlooking the dragon-kin."

"We promise," Marthaen assured him. "We will never forget that you were there to protect the Dragonking when the dragons refused to."

They sat in silence for some time as they watched Kharendaen dance. She seemed tireless, and she gave the dragons a dance they would not soon forget. Finally she left the firelight, and others took her place as she walked over to sit down close beside her mate. They rubbed their muzzles together softly.

"When are you going to lay that egg?" her brother asked her.

Kharendaen lifted her ears in alarm. "You know about that?"

"You smell pregnant," Marthaen said in jest. "Actually, Thelvyn spoke of it to the Great One that last night in the west. I am pleased the Dragonking will leave an heir among us."

"I appreciate your offer to raise our child in Windreach where she belongs," Thelvyn said. "Kharendaen and I have much to do."

Kharendaen turned her head to look at him, and there were tears in her large eyes. "I thought you had to leave us."

Thelvyn placed his hand gently on her neck, just below her ear. "You've been at my side almost every moment since I first became the Dragonlord, sharing every danger and hardship. I could not leave you behind now."

She settled close against him, and he held her tightly. After a moment, he looked up at his companions. "I must leave now. As you know, the Immortals are not permitted to act directly in the mortal world. An exception was made in my case in order that I could defend you against great danger. But now the old balance must be restored."

"But you will be back," Jherdar said, looking sad.

"I will return to you often," Thelvyn promised. "But from now on, my part will be only to observe and advise, for I still have my mandate from the Great One to help the dragons discover their destiny. But the Great One has allowed me to select four companions among the gold dragons to serve and assist me, once they have proven themselves worthy of such a duty. You must admit that no one has proven herself more worthy than Kharendaen."

"That leaves three more companions," Sir George remarked, looking rather pointedly at Marthaen. "Perhaps there are likely candidates who wish to volunteer."

"My place is here," Marthaen insisted, frankly alarmed at the suggestion.

"I agree," Thelvyn said. "And since you believe in the dragons the way I do, you will best serve me here. Still, there is no hurry to decide anything."

They sat in silence for a time, watching the lively dancing of the young dragons. The conclusion of their labors was at hand and difficult times were behind them, but the end had turned out not as sad as they had anticipated. They were content.

"What about you?" Thelvyn asked Sir George. "If you plan to return to your former life of adventure, then I'm going to have to spend every free moment I have worrying about you."

"Adventure?" Sir George asked. "I'm merely an old dealer in antiquities, mind you. But I think the time has come for me to go home. I've been living among dragons quite long enough. It leaves me dizzy and confused, and I need to be comfortable for a while. I am only a dragon-kin, and I feel rather out of place among true dragons."

EPILOGUE

Three years had passed since the Dragonking had defeated the Overlord and brought a sudden end to a devastating war. After the evening of singing on the plateau, the Dragonking had departed for the east, and he had never been seen again. No one seemed to know what had become of the hero to whom they all owed so much. Sometimes people saw a solitary dragon riding the winds over the distant mountains, and they would think fondly of the brave dragons who had, against all expectations, fought so fiercely to protect them from an enemy they could never have faced alone.

Now most of the signs of war had been erased from the Highlands, except for Braastar, which had suffered much during the invasion. It was a generally prosperous time throughout that part of the world. Most folk were grateful for being saved from certain death or enslavement, and they remembered how everyone had set aside his differences to stand together against a common enemy. And so most lands were still at peace, because people had acquired a new respect for how valuable it was.

On a spring morning, when the sun was bright and everyone hurried about his business, two strangers appeared in the
streets of Braejr. They were an odd sort, obviously foreigners—one man and one woman, each of them tall and thin but
strongly built, with black hair and large eyes. No one had ever
seen them before, but they were well dressed if not conspicu-
ously so and obviously of refined manners, and so no one took
much notice of them. The Flaem were getting used to not only
seeing foreigners but also having them live among them, so a
pair of innocent-looking strangers was not a matter of particular concern. Times had changed indeed.

The strangers presented themselves at the home of Sir
George Kirbey, a comfortable townhouse in a well-to-do area of
the city that was just down the street and around the corner
from where he had lived for several years with Thelvyn Fox-
Eyes. The old knight had apparently stepped out for a while,
and so they let themselves in to wait. Although the door had
been locked, the strange magic commanded by the tall, dark
man made quick work of that. There was no one at home
except for a rather noisy bird, a large green parrot with a long
red tail and a beak that might have done credit to a griffon. The
parrot sat in its cage in the den, alternately ringing a bell that
hung from a chain and then laughing hysterically. It was so
unlike Sir George to keep such a thing in his house that they
were fascinated by it. But the parrot refused to speak, continuing to ring its bell and then laugh its deep, hearty laugh.

Sir George himself returned only a few minutes later. At
first he did not recognize his two visitors, since he had never
before seen them in the form they now wore. Then he realized
that their features resembled the Eldar of Windreach, and he
knew that they were Thelvyn and Kharendaen. He could not
have been more delighted, insisting that they sit down in comfortable chairs in the den with glasses of his best cherry
liqueur. He prepared himself for a long chat.

Unfortunately, it was immediately obvious that they would
have no peace from the bell-ringing bird. Sir George cursed it
in some strange language, threw a heavy cloth over the cage,
and then removed it to a back room and locked the door. He
had only just returned when they heard the distant sound of a

ringing bell followed by an evil laugh.

"You were never one for pets," Thelvyn observed. "Except, perhaps, for an orphan dragon you once raised."

"Oh, that bird is no pet," Sir George declared. "It's the bane of my existence, the punishment for my every sin, the very scourge of my patience. But it was also my inheritance, so what could I do?"

"Inheritance?" Kharendaen asked. "I hesitate to ask what you may have done to deserve it."

"The key to my inheritance, I should say," Sir George explained. He sniffed his glass and sighed, his contentment restored by the sickly sweet scent of the vile cherry concoction. "That red-tailed moron came to me with the compliments of Mage Artacious of Ierendi, a long-time acquaintance of mine and fellow expert and collector of rare antiquities. He passed away earlier this year, and he wanted me to have a cache of ancient treasures he had recently located. Artacious was very fond of puzzles, and also of his little jokes. Only the bird knew where to find the treasure."

"But the bird doesn't talk," Thelvyn observed.

"The bird doesn't *like* to talk," Sir George corrected him sullenly. "The only sadistic joy in its miserable life is ringing that bell and laughing. It can ring that stinking bell day after day, night after night, for weeks on end and never tire of it. I did everything I could to try to get it to talk. Finally I called in Perrantin, hoping he could suggest something."

"Did Perrantin know what to do?" Thelvyn asked. Both he and Kharendaen were having difficulty hiding their amusement.

"Oh, yes. He took away that damned bell, and inside of two hours, the bird was talking its head off. The only trouble was that we had no idea what it was saying. It took us two more weeks to figure out that it speaks only in an old dialect of the Heldannic clans, a rather uncouth language suitable only for disgruntled Heldannic wizards and obnoxious parrots."

Thelvyn finally gave in and laughed out loud. "Now I know why I've missed you so these last few years."

Sir George frowned. "You sound as if any cause for missing me had escaped you until now. That's not my fault. You had to go away, even though things were finally beginning to settle down enough for us to enjoy ourselves."

"You said you needed to go home and be comfortable for a while," Thelvyn reminded him. "You seem to have found yourself a comfortable home, but I can't tell whether or not you've cut back on your adventures."

"Actually I have," Sir George insisted. "Once the threat of invasion was past, Solveig had a lot of work getting the Highlands back in order, especially with all those people freed from the will of the Overlord who were settling here. Once you were gone, Solveig was the only wayward child I had left in my care. I came back here so she could tend to her business."

He spent some time telling his visitors about Solveig and all that she had done in the last three years. The Highlands had continued to prosper, enjoying an increasingly important place in that part of the world. There was a good deal of trade to the south with Darokin and east with Rockhome, and the Flaem were now on reasonably good terms with all their neighbors except for a vague but growing unease with the Ethengar. The clans had become more aggressive and more hostile to travelers since the war. They had lost a great deal in the burning of the steppes. Even though the land itself had long since recovered, the herds had been decimated, and the Ethengar often turned to raiding as a means for making a living.

Solveig remained the head of the council, keeping the Fire Wizards firmly in line while she encouraged them to make positive contributions. Alessa Vyledaar was still a close friend and supporter of Solveig's, and that did much to maintain unity between the Fire Wizards and the government. Solveig had also been successful at beginning to defuse the hatred the Flaem held for the Alphatians, which in the past had consumed a great deal of their time and resources. Unfortunately, there were signs that the Alphatians were beginning to devote some thought to their old interest in expanding their empire, but that was a matter of more immediate concern for their closest neighbors, such as the Thyatians. Curiously, the Alphatians were also trying to sneak back into their holdings in the Norwold, which just proved that some people never learned their lesson no matter how much it cost them.

Things remained much the same in Rockhome. The

rebuilding of the damage from the invasion had long since been completed. The greatest concern now was that King Daroban's health was slowly beginning to fail, and it seemed increasingly likely that Korinn would be the next king. Whether or not his brother recovered enough to be king, Korinn was now quite famous and respected by all, and his brother seemed comfortable in the role of his chief supporter and advisor.

Solveig had settled down and had recently married Darius Glantri, who came to live with her in Braejr in the house that had once belonged to Thelvyn. Kharendaen's lair was still kept ready to serve the needs of dragons visiting Braejr. Sir George believed that the newlyweds were likely to return to Thyatis sooner or later. Solveig had often spoken of returning to her family home in Thyatis.

"What about the dragons?" Sir George asked at last.

"Time passes slowly for the dragons," Thelvyn answered. "To them, it is as if the war has just ended, and their lives are only now beginning to get back to normal."

"Do you think they'll remember the lessons that the Great One wanted them to learn?"

"Oh, they'll remember," Thelvyn said emphatically. "It just might take some time to notice anything. Changes that would take years in some lands might take centuries with the dragons. But some things will never be the same. They've discovered their hidden nobility, and they're finding it harder to act like beasts than they once did. It should be interesting to see what becomes of the Nation of Dragons a thousand years from now."

"If we weren't talking about dragons, I'd be tempted to say that sounds like an awfully long time," Sir George remarked philosophically. "What about the two of you? Have you hatched any eggs yet?"

"Two years ago," Kharendaen said, obviously proud. "Thelvyn always knew that it was a female, but he kept that news to himself. Her name is Therandael. Marthaen and Daresha are watching her now that Thelvyn and I have more to do here in the mortal world."

"I think I'd like to see a little dragon," Sir George mused. "Are you likely to have any more?"

Thelvyn shook his head. "I would have to surrender r
Immortality to sire any more children, and that's not practica

"Then what have the two of you been doing lately?"

Thelvyn glanced briefly at Kharendaen before he conti
ued. "We have been very busy, and we expect to stay busy f
a long time to come. That's the real reason why we cam
Would you care to make a short journey with us into the wil
tonight? It's been a long time since you've flown on the ba
of a dragon."

"It has indeed," Sir George said, obviously intrigued. "
look forward to it."

They had a small dinner that night at Sir George's tow
house, then returned to the den to talk of old times while th
waited for night to fall. Sir George spoke more about his tra
els and adventures since the end of the war, and Thelvyn l
tened in quiet satisfaction. While the old knight had made tl
choice to leave Windreach to return to his old life in the ou
side world, he had gotten used to the company of dragons an
obviously missed them. Once night had fallen, they walk
together through the streets of Braejr until they came to tl
city park. They quickly found a quiet place where Thelvyn an
Kharendaen could revert to their forms as gold dragons. S
George noticed that Thelvyn was already wearing a drag
saddle when he changed form.

The old knight climbed into the saddle, and the two dra
ons ascended into the night sky as silently as they could, risi
unseen out of the city. They turned east toward the Coloss
Mountains, flying swiftly over the deeply wooded foothills an
then climbing into the heights. At last the dragons found tl
place they seemed to have been looking for and circled dov
to land in a small meadow surrounded by the tall pine fore
that covered the lower slopes of the mountain.

"You asked what we've been doing," Thelvyn said as soc
as Sir George dismounted from the saddle. "Aside from guie
ing the dragons, I have found a great deal to do. Lately we'
spent much of our time traveling secretly around the wor
watching the growth of civilization and doing what we can 1
make certain that the future has a place for dragons."

"That's a fairly tall order," Sir George remarked. "I adm

that the war against the Overlord taught the world something about trusting dragons, just as it taught the dragons something important about trusting each other. But they still have a lot to learn about acting in a civilized manner. Even if they do, the rest of the world is going to need a long time to learn to accept dragons."

"I expect the task of finding a place in the world for dragons will occupy me for centuries," Thelvyn admitted. "I'm going to need all the help I can get. That's why we're here. I was wondering if you've possibly had enough of being comfortable and are ready for a little adventure."

"Me?" Sir George protested, surprised at the suggestion. "I'm not a gold dragon, remember? I'm just a wayward drake, and therefore not a suitable companion for the Immortal Diamond."

"There are some things only you can do for me," Thelvyn assured him. "And if you still think that only a dragon is worthy of serving me, then keep one thing in mind. Even that is something within my power to grant."

Sir George jumped in sudden alarm, realizing that something had happened to him. Looking down at himself, he saw that he was now a gold dragon. His first reaction seemed to be one of profound confusion. The change had happened so suddenly and unexpectedly that he didn't know what to make of it. At least a dragon form was vaguely familiar to him, after his many years as a drake. He bent his head around, trying to get a better look at himself, and ended up going around in a complete circle like a dog chasing its tail.

"Do I have your interest?" Thelvyn asked, careful to hide his amusement.

Sir George looked up. "Well, yes. I don't want to seem overly critical, but I think you've set a worthy task for us, if a rather difficult one."

Thelvyn did not answer. He did not want to admit that the task that lay ahead for him and his companions would be far more important and more difficult than Sir George could ever guess. Even the Immortals could not clearly see what the future would bring, but some events were inevitable. He could not guess why or when, but he knew that someday in the centuries to come, the dragons would be forced to go war once again.

If you enjoyed reading The Dragonlord Chronicles trilogy you may be interested in reading more books that deal with those fearsome creatures of legend, dragons.

Dragons play a prominent role in the history of the epic fantasy world depicted in the DRAGONLANCE® Saga. In *The Dragons of Krynn* and its sequel, *The Dragons at War*, editors Margaret Weis and Tracy Hickman have compiled collections of stories that deal with all manner and hue of dragons, good, evil, and just plain mischievous. In Mary Kirchoff's *The Black Wing*, we read about the rise and fall of an evil dragon, Khisanth, who awakens from a centuries-long sleep to discover that the world she knew as a young dragon has been irrevocably changed by the Cataclysm. And finally best-selling writer-editors Weis and Hickman don their authorial caps to pen the thrilling conclusion, and a new beginning, to the Dragonlance Saga in *Dragons of Summer Flame*.

The FORGOTTEN REALMS® fantasy setting offers *The Veiled Dragon*, by Troy Denning, which features the evil dracolich Cypress, worshipped by the sinister Cult of the Dragon.

Finally, Chrys Cymri features a star-crossed dragon accompanied by an android medtech, in two TSR Books™. Join Gonard the dragon as he searches for his soul in *Dragon Can Only Rust* and its sequel, *Dragon Reforged*, which put a science fictional slant on dragon lore.

If you are interested in reading more books set in the exciting MYSTARA® fantasy world setting, Timothy Brown's *Dark Knight of Karameikos* features a heroic knight who must confront a powerful black-armored villain who is ravaging his homeland. In Dixie McKeone's *Son of Dawn*, an orphan leaves his island home to embark on a perilous trek across the continent of Brun to return two kidnapped Shadow Elf children to their royal parents.

Look for these and other exciting TSR titles at your favorite book and hobby stores everywhere.